The Coyote Kid

MARY, HAPPY READING! DC Anderson 12-25-2014

D C Anderson

ISBN: 150257408X
ISBN 13: 9781502574084

ADDITIONAL BOOKS BY
D C ANDERSON

The Wicked Stallion

ALL HISTORICAL REFERNCES IN THIS NOVEL
WERE TAKEN FROM www.wikipedia.org.

Dedicated to ALL THE HORSES
I HAVE KNOWN AND MOST
ESPCIALLY TO MY LAST HORSE
BANDA CHALLENGER
"CODY"
May 22, 1983 to August 24, 2013

Acknowledgement

First and foremost a very special thanks to Rich and Linda, who not only proofread my books not just once but rewrites, correcting grammar and spelling, but also have kept me on track with horse training terminology that I take for granted everyone knows.

Big thanks also to Bonnie and Joanne who jump in and find research on the internet or their phones that I, who am electronically-challenged, don't seem to be able to find.

And a special thanks to all my friends and family who have encouraged, supported and pushed me into publishing my books and keep asking for more.

The Coyote

A very savvy, clever and adaptive member of the canine family,
its scientific name being "Canis Latrans".

The name "coyote" is borrowed from Mexican Spanish coyote,
ultimately derived from the Nahuatl word coyotl, meaning "trickster".

Coyotes flourish over much of North America, in part
because of their keen hunting and foraging skills.

During pursuit, a coyote may reach speeds
up to 43 mph making it one of the fastest terrestrial mammals
in North America, and can jump a distance of over 13 feet.

---Wikipedia.org

Table of Contents

Author Bio

DC Anderson is a retired paralegal with a life that has been filled with training horses and dogs. Her other passion has always been writing and she has always wanted to write books. She has written term papers, poetry and short stories for school and college and many teachers and professors have encouraged her to continue writing. After completing her first book, <u>The Wicked Stallion,</u> it seemed that she just had to go on.

Even though she was born and raised and still lives in Northwest Ohio, she has always had a passion for the American West and her favorite books, movies and television shows have always been Westerns.

<u>The Coyote Kid</u> is the first of a series of three books she has written portraying life in the American West.

I

The Ballin Family

The State of Kansas is named for the Kansa Native American tribe which inhabited the area and means "people of the wind" or "people of the south wind". Kansas was first settled in the 1830s and officially opened to settlement by the U.S. government in 1854. When it was opened to settlement, abolitionist Free-Stators from New England and pro-slavery settlers from neighboring Missouri rushed to the territory to determine whether Kansas would become a free state or a slave state. Thus the area was a hotbed of violence in the early days as these forces collided and Kansas became known as "Bleeding Kansas".

It became a state on January 29, 1861, when it entered the union as a free state making it the thirty-fourth state to enter the union. After the Civil War, the population of Kansas grew rapidly when waves of immigrants turned the prairie into farmland. It was still rich in pastureland and open grazing land, however, and cattle ranchers were prominent in the State.

The town of Winchester was located in the middle of the State of Kansas on the south side of the Arkansas River, west and south of the City of Kansas (which name was changed to Kansas City in 1889). Like many small towns which cropped up all over the West, it was founded in order to attract the ranchers to a stopping off place as they headed their herds of cattle from the western and southwestern states to the City of Kansas' stockyards for shipment to Chicago and points east. These towns, called "cow towns", catered to the cowhands and ranchers who brought herds through the area. A skeleton crew would be left with the herd and the remaining cowboys would head to town to drink beer, whiskey and be entertained by the saloon gals. Besides revenue from the cowboys, the crew cook would also come to town and replenish the supplies needed to continue on the drive. The area around Winchester was predominantly flat grazing prairie with plenty of access to water and supported great herds of buffalo, which made it perfect for cattle.

Winchester was a rural town. The men were ranchers, farmers and business men with small businesses in town. They worked the fields, tended the cattle and horses on the ranches and worked in their stores, the bank and various businesses. The women took care of the family and home. They cooked, cleaned, made clothes for the family, tended gardens and the smaller farm animals - chickens, ducks, the milk cow and other fowl. Anyone deviating from this so-called normal way of life was considered strange.

To say that the town of Winchester was a sleepy little town most of the time was a gross understatement. It had one of everything. There was one general store, one bank, one doctor, one town marshal with one part time deputy to relieve the marshal enough for him to sleep, one livery stable, one saloon that doubled as a restaurant, one school with one school teacher, and oh yes, one gunfighter. Its leading citizen was . . . well, Winchester really didn't have a leading citizen.

Mike Ballin was the gunfighter and he was a good one if there is any good in a gunfighter. He had decided, however, after his first contract in Winchester that that would be the last time he would do a gun fighting job in Winchester. For the sake of his family, he wanted to keep his "occupation" low-keyed in his home town. He didn't even wear his pearl-handled Colt 45 when he was in town lest anyone came to town for a duel with him.

Sam Barton was the owner of the Bittersweet Saloon and would hire Mike for a bouncer on the busy nights in the saloon that is, when Mike was in town and not on one of his "jobs". Sam didn't much like Mike. He was too unreliable. His motto being, "Here today; gone tomorrow". However, Sam also knew that Mike was fast stopping trouble before it got started and consequently he would always rehire him when he came back to town. Just Mike's appearance in the saloon kept the fights to a minimum; people were afraid of Mike Ballin even when he wasn't wearing his Colt 45. Mess around with Mike and a man could get his head handed to him. The local patrons who knew Mike did not want to tangle with him. The visiting cowhands soon learned that also, sometimes the hard way.

When Mike worked for Sam, he carried a rifle – a Henry repeating rifle, the rifle of choice for the time. The rifle did more hitting men than it did shooting them. Sometimes he brought the gun barrel down on top of a man's head when he would start a fight usually over a card game or one of the dance-hall girls. Sometimes he would shoot one of the patrons but only when absolutely necessary as when a man drew a gun to shoot him and he had no other choice. Sam didn't like him to shoot patrons – it was bad for business. Mostly if possible, Mike brought the gun barrel down on someone's arm if they were trying to draw a gun or on their head if the gun had already been drawn and he was close enough to do it. However, no matter what Sam said, he wasn't going to risk his life – he had no problem shooting someone if he was forced.

The saloon was always a rowdy place when the cowhands came to town to blow off some steam. Besides the drinking and possession of the saloon girls, the men fought about card games and actually anything else that happened to be on their minds. This would sometimes escalate into gun duels. Two men would have a face-off, drawing and shooting at each other and many times one of the men would kill the other one. These battles never took place when Mike was on duty. He stopped them before they could get started and that was what Sam liked best about having Mike work the saloon.

Mike wasn't a real tall man, right around six foot tall. He wasn't what you would call stocky but he wasn't real slim either. He kept himself in good physical condition, didn't overeat and never drank too much. He could not afford to get drunk and not be able to react to someone wanting to "call him out". He was a handsome man with dark brown hair very straight and close cut. He had dark eyes that turned black when he was getting ready to confront someone. Those eyes stared many a man into hesitating just long enough when drawing a gun before firing that Mike shot first and Mike had a fast draw and was deadly accurate with a revolver.

Lila Ballin, Mike's wife, worked in the Bittersweet Saloon also. She tended bar and did the bookkeeping for Sam. It was unheard of in the mid-eighteen hundreds for a wife and mother to work and earn a living outside of the home and especially working in a saloon. Ladies that worked in saloons were considered . . . well not ladies exactly.

Every time Mike came home after one of his trips, he would have money and would try and convince Lila to quit working. He didn't want his wife working and especially after they had the baby. He had no answer for her, however, when she pointed out that somehow she and their son, Brett, had to live when he was out shooting people and she had no idea when he would be back home. Sometimes he would wire money home – five hundred dollars here and there and that was the only way she knew he was still alive when he was on one of his sojourns; sometimes she heard nothing at all from him until he came home as much as three or four months later.

As part of the Ballins' salary, Sam let them live in an apartment above the Bittersweet. The apartment was small consisting of a small sitting area with a couple chairs, small settee and where Brett had his bed which was simply a straw-filled pallet in one corner of the room. There was one bedroom for Mike and Lila and a kitchen-dining area. Lila had tried to decorate the apartment and make it feel homey. She had made café style lace curtains for the two windows, purchased some prints, framed and hung them and even had a few knick knacks setting around. But all in all it was a small apartment and that was that.

The Ballins' son, Brett, was a very smart ten-year-old boy probably close to genius level if there were those tests back in the 1860s. Amos Carr, the school teacher, recognized the boy's capabilities and loaned Brett books way beyond his years. Brett was a voracious reader and soon had read every book Carr had and was starting over. Amos Carr couldn't keep up with the boy in mathematics, history, geography, language or any of the extra subjects he threw at Brett that he was not required to teach any of his other students. Brett even taught himself Spanish with the help of some of Amos's books.

The problem was Brett being Mike Ballin's son, the family's unusual lifestyle and the fact that he was also very smart, made him very unpopular with the other children. Their parents would tell them to stay away from the Ballin boy as if he might be as deadly as his father. Maybe he had a little pistol under his belt and would fast draw the kids and shoot them. Consequently, Brett really had no friends - he was a loner.

Brett was small for his age with dark black-brown straight hair and coal black eyes, a miniature of his father. He had his father's eyes; eyes that could drill right through a person and look down into their soul. He was a skinny little kid, slightly built, wiry and as quick as a jackrabbit. Some of the bigger kids bullied him or tried that is. They would try and trap him outside at recess and lunch hour but he could duck under an arm and run away faster than they could hold him. Once he got away, there was no catching him. Brett was not a fighter. He was too smart. He knew he didn't stand a chance of beating these bigger kids and the best thing to do was to avoid them.

For all these reasons, Brett kept to himself reading books and playing around with some games his father taught him. When his father was gone which was a lot of the time, he would play checkers by pretending there was another person on the other side of the board. He would make a move and then jump up and run to the other side and make that "person's" move. He played poker the same way and knew a couple solitaire card games. Sometimes he invented games with the cards or the checker board.

Brett's first love was horses. Horses didn't care how you lived. They didn't care who your parents were or what occupations they had to survive. They didn't care if you were dumb or smart. Horses only cared about how they were treated.

Brett didn't have a horse to call his own. As a matter of fact Brett's family had only one horse – his father's horse, a big bay gelding Brett had named Arthur after King Arthur of the Knights of the Round Table. When his father was gone, Brett and his mother had no way to leave town and Brett had no horse to care for, ride and talk to. Brett constantly talked to horses and they responded to this quiet gentle boy. Animals can tell by a person's aura how they will be treated. They seem to know if a person is kind and gentle but firm and have certain expectations of the animal or if a person is angry, mean-spirited and forceful.

The livery stable was walking distance from the apartment and Brett haunted the place. Pete Mathews, the stable's owner, was constantly telling Brett to stay off the fence of the corral least wise he might fall in the pen and get hurt, to leave the horses alone and basically to "get lost". Brett always snuck back in and tried to stay out of Pete's sight. He would ask the cook at the saloon to give him scraps from the carrots and apples and would take these along with sugar cubes and use them for treats to make friends with the horses especially some of the skittish horses that were unsure about people.

—ⅧⅧⅧ—

Mike and Lila came from entirely different backgrounds. Mike's father was a farmer. Mike watched his father toil in the fields from sun-up to sundown day in and day out in northwestern Ohio. He watched him do all this hard work just to have it not rain and crops fail. He watched his mother do all her tasks: cooking, sewing, making soap, making candles, tending to the vegetable garden, the chickens and other farm animals until her hands would crack and bleed. Mike never knew a gentle touch from his mother her hands were so rough.

Besides Mike there was another brother and a sister. Mike was the oldest and probably the most stubborn. He had made up his mind at an early age he would not be a farmer. Mike had a sure-fire love of guns. He started hunting with his father's rifle when he was only ten years old. His father encouraged this, however, because Mike's hunting did supplement the family with meat which helped immensely to feed the family.

One day when Mike was in town with his father to buy provisions for the farm, he was sitting in the wagon waiting for his father to pay for the supplies and saw two men have a gun duel in the street. He watched in fascination and felt the excitement. He went back into the general store and asked the clerk what kind of used pistols he had for sale cheap. The clerk found one for three dollars and Mike made arrangements with the storekeeper to work off the price of the gun. From that day on every spare moment Mike found was spent practicing drawing and firing that gun. He didn't have a holster to start with so he just tucked it into the waist of his pants. He went back to the shopkeeper and asked if he could work off the price of a holster. The man couldn't pay for help but he could use a good worker and Mike was a farm kid and very strong. He worked off the price of the holster and periodically worked long enough to also be paid in ammunition. After that he practiced constantly drawing and firing the gun.

Lila Ballin, formerly Lila Simmons, was the exact opposite of her husband. She was not very tall – five feet four inches with a slim shapely body and honey brown hair, a fair complexion and big brown intelligent eyes. She was soft-spoken and gentle and very beautiful. She could melt any man's heart.

Her family was from Boston, Massachusetts. Her father was Elijah Simmons, President and owner of Simmons & Son, an expert in the field of manufacturing cannons and ammunition. Her mother, Gladys Simmons, was Elijah's wife and that was the only thing she was. Whatever her husband said was exactly what Gladys did, she had no opinion, no outside interests, no friends of her own. She was the wife of Elijah Simmons!

Elijah was grooming Lila to be the bride of Jeffrey Caldwell, whose family owned Caldwell Munitions. Elijah had it all planned. With this marriage and the merger of the two companies, Caldwell's gun and ammunition plant and Simmons & Son, there would be a monopoly on their products which would make both families even wealthier.

Elijah's son, Joshua, was four years younger than Lila. Elijah was grooming him to take over his business although it wasn't clear if Elijah was ever going to be willing to let that happen. Elijah had his children's lives planned just like he had planned his wife's life. They were being trained for their respective positions and no one had better cross him.

Lila and Joshua had a very close relationship with each other; after all they had no one else. They had no support from their parents. Their mother was just there, had no opinion, and had no say in their upbringing. She was simply a caretaker even though she loved her children very much. Their father told them everything to do and how to think. Neither child had any lasting friends. Elijah did not want strangers in his house and never allowed his children to visit with other families. It was as if he felt they might find out how other people live and he would lose control. So the few friends they had, they had at school and usually the friendships didn't last very long.

When Lila was seventeen years old she went through a rebellious stage. She was tired of her father pushing her to marry Jeffrey Caldwell. Elijah decided that he would show Lila how she would be living if she were not so entitled. Gladys had a brother, who was a store keeper in Winchester, Kansas. This brother was far from wealthy. Elijah sent Lila to Gladys's brother to show her just how good she had it in Boston. His plan backfired.

Lila met and fell madly in love with Michael Ballin, the gunfighter. Mike met and fell madly in love with Lila. She was everything he was not. She was soft and gentle and pure. She always smelled like lilac water. Lila fell in love with Mike because he was everything she was not. He was strong and dominant, tough and virile. They were married within weeks of meeting each other.

When Elijah found out, he declared his daughter dead and forbid anyone including Gladys to ever mention her name in his house again. He told Joshua that his sister died in a freak accident. She fell from a horse and broke her neck.

After the couple was married, Mike got a job keeping control of the patrons in the Bittersweet and they lived in the apartment above the saloon.

For the first year everything was great between the young couple. When Lila announced to Mike that she was pregnant, Mike was ecstatic.

—〽—

One day a business man in the saloon commissioned Mike to goad a man he had a grudge against into a duel. He would pay Mike a handsome sum and Mike could plead self-defense as long as he got the man to draw first. Mike of course won the duel and killed the man. Witnesses stated that the other man drew first and Mike was only defending himself. After that, however, he vowed that would be the last time he would have a duel in Winchester.

A couple more "jobs" came along in nearby towns and Mike found that he could make a lot more money doing this kind of work than working in Sam's saloon. Word spread just how fast and how accurate Mike Ballin was with a gun and he was commissioned for more and more contracts all of which were far from the town of Winchester. Once he went on one of his jobs, it many times led to a rancher or businessman knowing of another job. Consequently, he would leave Winchester and not return for sometimes several months.

That was how it came about that Mike was not with Lila when their son was born. Lila was very upset. She had a midwife but could not believe that her husband, the baby's father, was not there for the event. They had originally agreed that if the baby was a boy, his name would be Brett Michael Ballin. Since Mike was not there for the birth, Lila eliminated him from their son's name all together and she named the baby in the public records: Brett Ballin.

It was soon normal that Mike would come and go as he pleased into and out of the lives of Lila and Baby Brett. Lila was very upset about Mike's leaving his family and she worried constantly about him. They always fought when he would tell her that he was going to leave for another job but when he returned she was so grateful that he was still alive, she would hug, kiss and fuss over him.

After Brett was born and Mike went on more and more of his "jobs", Lila decided that she had to find a way to support herself and the baby. She was never sure how long he would be gone or if he would be coming back. One day, she thought, he will lose one of these battles he took on, he would die and she would never know. There is always someone faster and more accurate. She started talking to Sam about what she could do in the saloon. She definitely did not want to be one of the saloon girls, who not only danced and encouraged patrons to drink, but many times were expected to take men up to their rooms. Lila refused to do that. Mike was her man and she never would forsake him.

Lila convinced Sam that she could help him behind the bar. As she worked the bar, Sam noticed that men were buying more drinks from the pretty bartender than from himself. As Lila gained Sam's trust she even helped him with his books. She found several errors in Sam's bookkeeping and pointed out some ways for Sam to save money. Sam really liked Lila's work. It meant that sometimes he could take a day off which made his wife extremely happy.

Lila would put baby Brett in a basket and set it behind the counter of the bar. She would then take Brett into the back room where the bar supplies were kept and nurse the baby and change his diaper on her breaks. Brett became used to the bar life right from Day One of his baby life. He could sleep right through the noise in the bar and only startled awake if there was a gunshot.

When he cried, Lila would pick him up and bounce him on her hip while she waited on customers until he quieted. Then she would put him back in the basket with a biscuit or sugar teat (a cloth sewn with sugar in it in the shape of a mother's breast, thus the name "sugar teat").

Lila fell into a routine and all went well until Mike came home. She was always grateful that he lived through his last odyssey, always happy to see him and she would kiss and fawn all over him. She was always filled with dread, however, as to how long he would stay until he would get that telegram asking his fee to battle with someone and he would be off again.

When he came home, he came with a bundle of money and of course the first thing he wanted was for Lila to quit her job. They would have the usual argument and she would again point out to him if she didn't have the job, how was she going to support herself and Brett? Finally Lila won the battle but usually not the war. Mike was not happy about her working but he ran out of arguments against it and there was harmony in the household until he was getting ready to ride off again, then it was always the same routine. Mike was home only a short time and true to Lila's expectations, he would receive a telegram from a rancher or businessman who wanted a job done, they would quarrel and Mike would leave. He started getting more and more jobs and staying away longer and longer.

Brett was growing up with only a mother for a parent. When Mike was home, the baby stayed in the apartment with him when Lila worked and he didn't. Sam only had Mike work on the busy nights usually Thursday through Saturday. Mike hated caring for the baby and wasn't comfortable with him but would bow to Lila on this issue and do his best. Lila would rush upstairs on her break and feed Baby Brett.

While he was a small toddler, Lila could entertain him with blocks and other toys as he sat on a blanket in the back room at the bar. However, children don't stay small toddlers and as they grow, they become harder and harder to quietly entertain. Lila finally had to find a sitter to come into the apartment and stay with Brett while she worked. Sometimes one of the saloon girls, Suzi, would volunteer to care for Brett if she had the night off. She loved children, could not have any of her own and became very fond of the little boy and brought him gifts and candy.

When he turned seven years old and since he was a very bright and mature kid and knew what to do and what not to do in the apartment, Lila started leaving him alone and checking on him on her breaks. Brett had by that time learned to read and write, was going to school and would entertain himself with books and games.

It wasn't until a few years later after he turned ten years old that he started getting interested in what was happening in the bar and watching patrons behind his railing in the upstairs hallway. It started one day when he finished all his homework and he heard a gunshot in the bar. It never took him long to complete his homework and the extra work Amos Carr gave him and even the studying he took on himself. He crept out of the apartment and down to the corner where he would kneel down and press his face between the slats in the railing and watch. His mother would have been really angry with him had she known. He knew she always had some clean-up to do after the bar closed so he was careful to go back to the apartment as soon as it closed, quickly undress, get on his pallet and pretend to be asleep before his mother came upstairs to the apartment after her shift.

Brett watched his father work also. He was scary but he did keep the men under control with the rifle. Every time Mike hit one of the patrons, Brett would flinch. He hated seeing people hurt. It seemed to him that there should be a better way of managing these men. He knew why people were afraid of

Mike. He was terribly afraid of his father, also. Mike expected too much from a child and punished him many times unfairly; most of the time Brett had no idea why he was being punished.

From his hiding place outside the apartment, Brett saw several shootings in the saloon. When someone got shot, Dr. Raymond Mowery would be called in. If it wasn't too serious, a shot in the arm or leg, Dr. Mowery would remove the bullet right there in the saloon and the man would be sent on his way. Brett was fascinated by this. He would peer as close as he dared to watch Dr. Mowery open the wound, probe for the bullet and then pull it out. Then he would close the wound, bandage it and give the man instructions on how to care for it.

The thing Brett hated the most about the saloon and also about his father were the guns. If Brett got bored watching the patrons especially on a slow night and he would go into the apartment and lie on his pallet, it seemed that he would just get to sleep comfortably and a gun would go off and he would awaken with a start.

Brett also thought the gun battles that the men got into were idiocy. If they started losing at poker, they accused someone of cheating whether they were or not and that would cause a fight. If someone moved in on one of "their girls", even though the saloon girls were really nobody's girls, there would be a fight. It seemed to Brett that grown men could find another way to settle their differences without shooting each other. Living above a saloon was hard on a kid.

II

The Black Gelding

By the time Brett was twelve years old and Pete decided he was never going to get rid of the kid, he started giving Brett jobs to do in the stable. Brett cleaned stalls, swept floors, fed, watered and groomed horses. Pete would send him to the blacksmith with a horse and he held the horse for the blacksmith while he trimmed its feet and shod or reshod it. Then he would take the horse back to Pete. He would also ride a horse back to a rancher who might leave one with the blacksmith for shoeing, pick up another horse and bring it back for the blacksmith. Sometimes if Pete was busy, he allowed Brett to accept money from customers to groom or care for their horse. Pete soon saw that Brett was a willing and hard worker and accomplished more than some men Pete had hired.

Since Pete's business was renting horses to anyone who needed one, the horses had a lot of different types of riders. The horses Pete rented to customers had to be gentle. Many riders can really mess up a horse's training and they pick up bad habits. When one of the horses got into some bad habits usually from mishandling, someone had to re-train the animal so he would be useful again. If a horse needed some refreshing after having been used so many times, Pete would tell Brett to take him out for a ride. This meant that Brett would take the horse out onto the prairie and ride him for about an hour and work out all the kinks. Brett had a real knack with horses and usually had the animal back to his original training after riding him a time or two. This was how Brett started training horses which actually was re-training. Brett loved his job and he was hardly home after starting to work with Pete and working with the horses.

Pete also bought horses that were not completely trained for riding or driving. He would work with the horses, finish their training and either use them to rent if they turned out gentle enough or resell them at a substantial profit. If the horse was too much for Pete to finish training, he hired a local rancher's son, Dave Hinman, to train it for him.

One of the most beautiful and correctly structured horses Pete ever bought was a big black gelding he had bought extremely cheap and was soon to learn why. When Pete bought the horse, the former owner said he had been ridden but had become cantankerous. The Black, as Pete called him, was high-strung, a borderline outlaw. Pete soon figured out that the Black was too much horse for him and he hired Dave to break him.

Dave only knew one way to train a horse, the cowboy way. Throw a saddle on the horse and buck it out until it stopped bucking, gave in and complied with the rider's wishes. This obviously worked with most horses thus the term "broke to ride". There were a few horses, however, that rebelled against this type of treatment. These horses many times turned into outlaws and were either sold for rodeo horses or shot as incorrigible.

On the first day Dave was to train this horse, he had taken the black gelding to the corral with a bridle on over his halter and a rope on the halter. Dave tied the horse to a post, slapped the saddle on him and jerked the cinch up hard, fast and tight. Suddenly the horse went berserk and lunged forward knocking him down and nearly stepping on him. The horse leaped backward and the rope tying him to the post snapped. Dave was trying to get away but The Black was rearing and striking out, spinning and bucking. The horse was not aggressive and not trying to hurt Dave, but the man was vulnerable as he was on the ground, trying to roll away and dangerously close to the Black's deadly hooves.

Brett heard the commotion and went to the corral to see what had happened. He saw Dave on the ground and the gelding rearing, bucking and screaming in rage. The reins on the bridle were flying as the big horse reared.

Brett ducked under the fence and grabbed a rein. He lunged to the side pulling the horse off balance so that he had to land on his feet and away from Dave. As the horse started to rear again, Brett again lunged to the side throwing the horse off balance which took him away from the man and he was able to crawl under the fence.

As soon as Dave got out of the corral, he ran and got a rifle. He was going to put an end to this outlaw's bad behavior. Pete stopped him telling him he had no right to shoot his horse. Pete was watching Brett and even though he was afraid for the boy, it looked like he could handle himself with this rebellious horse. This didn't set well with Dave. A twelve-year-old boy, a small boy at that, handling a horse he couldn't. Every time the horse lunged and reared, Brett deftly stepped sideways away from the horse and pulled on the rein which put him off balance and back on the ground. Brett was quick and light on his feet and by using the laws of gravity and physics, he was able to throw the horse off balance enough so that it didn't take a lot of physical strength to put the horse back on the ground. He had to put all four feet on the ground or fall over.

After several times of doing this, the horse froze. He was snorting and snuffling, clearly trying to understand what was happening. He was getting tired, very sweaty and out of breath. He had been handled by many men who like Dave tried to force him into submission and he was not a horse which would yield to brutality. Brett was not frightening, however, not at all like the big men who had treated him brutally, yelling and many times striking him. The horse suddenly realized that this handler was not yelling and striking at him and had not done anything to hurt him. Brett was still holding one of the reins and he started talking in a quiet voice and approached the horse slowly but confidently. When he was able to get close enough, he quickly undid the cinch and dropped the saddle to the ground. The horse jumped sideways away from Brett and the saddle.

Brett hung onto the rein and talked to the horse softly, walking toward the horse as he lunged to the side, "Whoa-a-a, easy boy. I won't hurt you."

Once the saddle fell to the ground, the horse seemed to be more at ease. More than likely Brett thought, Dave had drawn the cinch on the saddle up so fast and tight that it had pinched the horse's flesh and was hurting him and that was why he had exploded. The Black stood quivering and making low nickering sounds. Brett continued talking in a soft tone to the horse. He knew better than to reach for the Black's face – a good way to get bit. Instead he started scratching him low on his neck. He would then work his way up his neck toward his head talking the whole time. If the Black started prancing and getting anxious, Brett backed off. If the Black tolerated Brett scratching his neck, Brett continued further up towards his head.

"That kid's going to get killed," said Dave.

"SHHH," said Pete.

After a long time of Brett petting and talking to the horse, he started leading him around the corral. The Black accepted this and Brett then led him over to the fence. Brett climbed up on the fence and talking gently and low to the horse, he eased his leg over the horse's back and sat on him. The horse jumped sideways, landed stiff-legged and froze. Brett did nothing but ride it out. He didn't try and make the horse do anything. He didn't punish the horse by yanking on the reins which is what some riders would have done, when the horse jumped away. He simply held onto his mane so he wouldn't jerk on his mouth and gently gripped with his legs, going with the horse.

He let the horse stand frozen in place until he felt him relax rubbing his neck all the time. Pete was watching all this with interest while Dave kept muttering what did this kid know about training a horse? As soon as Brett felt the horse relax, he urged him forward gently keeping connection to the horse through the reins to the bit in his mouth. He pushed his hands forward slightly on the sides of the animal's neck squeezing the calves of his legs on his sides.

The big black gelding started in a relaxed walk around the corral. He walked all the way around the corral. When he had done that, Brett stopped him gently pulling back on the reins and slid onto the fence. He didn't want to drop right to the ground because he didn't want to startle the nervous horse.

He then stroked the horse's neck and turned to Pete, "That's enough for today," he said with the confidence of one who had been training Pete's horses forever. He led the horse back into the barn and gave him a good rub down talking to him all the time. He then put him in a stall and gave him a measure of hay.

Dave looked at Pete and said, "Are you going to let that kid tell you what to do with your own horse?" Dave was steaming over the fact that Brett had done something he was unable to accomplish with a horse he was ready to shoot.

Pete looked at Dave and said, "Yes".

After that first day, Brett started working with the Black every day. He rode him bareback at first and worked with the horse until he responded well to Brett's gentle hands and easy urging with his legs. It took several days before Brett started him under saddle. Brett was so gentle and soft spoken that the gelding started responding to his cues from both his hands and his legs. Brett watched the horse's head and paid attention to the position of his ears. A horse telegraphs his every move with his head, and his ears tell a rider about his mood. If the gelding startled and froze, Brett let him look over whatever it was that had scared him. When he felt the horse relax, he urged him on and the gelding would walk on. Brett had good balance and when he saddled a horse he didn't "screw the saddle down tight" but he would tighten it just enough to keep it in place. This way there was never a danger of pinching the horse and making the saddle uncomfortable for the horse.

One day when Brett was riding the gelding in the corral, he said to Pete, "Open the gate." Pete looked at him quizzically but Brett had been right in how he handled the horse to this point and who was Pete to question what he wanted to do now? The livery stable was on the edge of town so Brett could ride the horse out onto the prairie. The day was warm with a bright sun and Brett was enjoying a canter on the Black across the wide open prairie. He wouldn't let him run all out but made him maintain a pleasant rollicking canter. Brett had found that when training a horse to never let them race full speed. It accomplished nothing and taught the horse that he could be in control. He never ran a horse at top speed until he was fully trained and Brett knew he was in control and not the horse.

After riding the horse on the prairie and teaching him he had to listen to Brett's cues no matter where he was, Brett started riding him into town getting him used to all the sights and smells horses encountered in the strange situations in town. If the horse startled, Brett rode it out not jerking or hanging on the horse's bit but merely keeping gentle contact with his mouth via the reins and holding onto the mane if he felt unbalanced until the horse stopped. He had an uncanny sense of how a horse would jump and he was hardly ever thrown from a horse's back. As the Black got used to more and more sights, he shied from things less and less. With Brett's soft hands and gentle leg pressure, the horse gained more confidence and found that this rider would not jerk him and hurt him, never yelled or punished him. Brett wouldn't even wear spurs with him. The Black was sensitive and really didn't need spurs. Perhaps if Brett was to continue his training, he might need them for more advanced training but at this point, he felt that spurs would be counter-productive.

The Black was in training with Brett for six weeks when a rancher came in the barn looking for a beautiful horse for his daughter. He would pay a lot of money for the right horse. Pete showed him the black gelding. The rancher looked him over and liked him immediately. He wanted to take him right then and surprise his daughter.

Brett overheard the conversation and said to Pete, "No, he can't do that." Pete looked surprised. Who was this kid to tell him what to do with his horse? If he spoiled this sale, it would be the last horse he rode for Pete. Brett looked at both the rancher and Pete and said, "This horse has to be handled in a special way especially right now until he gets more confidence. Your daughter needs to come here and ride him and let me show her some things about him."

Pete wanted the sale. This was why he bought these horses but Brett had worked hard with the horse and had asked for nothing in exchange. Pete had been paying Dave quite a bit of money to break these horses and he had miserably failed with this horse.

Pete removed his hat, "The kid's prob'ly right," said Pete. "Bring ya' daughter here and let Brett tell her how ta' ride the horse. He does need mo' trainin' 'nd I'd hate ta' see yor kid git hurt."

The rancher nodded. In the afternoon, he came back with his daughter and introduced her to Pete and Brett. "This is Annie," he said. He showed her the black gelding and she was instantly in love with the horse. She stroked his face and whispered in his ear. The horse seemed to take to her as well. He needed a gentle rider but one who was also firm and knew exactly how to handle him when he became excited and nervous in some situations.

Brett saddled him and took him to the corral. He mounted him and showed her what he had taught the horse. How to rein the horse and how he cued him with his legs. He then told Annie to mount her horse and they would go for a ride. Pete opened the gate and Annie and Brett rode out of town and out onto the surrounding prairie.

It was a beautiful autumn day, the sun peeking over the big trees and shining off some of the small water holes in golden hues reflecting from the trees brilliant fall colors. As they rode across the deep grass cantering easily along, they saw some mule deer standing at the edge of the woods and scared up a few small animals. No matter how often Brett observed this countryside, he never tired of it.

They cantered the horses in big lazy circles. Brett showed her all the horse could do and told her as well what the horse was not really ready to do. He told her that this horse could make someone an excellent mount if they were gentle with him; but that he was a very strong animal and if abuse or force was used they would have their hands full and could possibly get seriously hurt. Trying to do too much too soon would be a real setback in his training and could possibly ruin the horse.

After riding for some time, Brett stopped the animal and dismounted. He asked the girl if she would like to try him out. She jumped at the chance. She mounted the Black and Brett mounted her horse. They rode into the meadow and Annie cantered the gelding. Brett gave her instructions as they went.

"Keep a lighter touch on the reins. Keep soft hands," he said. "Use just soft leg aids and don't push too hard. If he startles, stop him and let him look at what he has shied at and then when he relaxes, urge him on gently by simply squeezing the calves of your legs. It's not necessary to kick him in the ribs, he responds to soft squeezes with your calves."

They rode through the meadow and after a good canter, Annie stopped the horse and started stroking him on the neck. He certainly was a beauty, she thought but she was getting a little tired of Brett's instructions. He reminded her of her little brother and she would never take orders from her little brother. Annie was still petting the horse on the neck when she decided she would like to know how fast he was and she would show this little upstart how she could handle this horse, after all, he didn't know everything.

She suddenly kicked the horse as hard as she could in the ribs much to Brett's surprise and chagrin. The gelding lunged straight up in the air as if he was jumping a six-foot fence leaving Annie on the ground.

Brett was angry. "WHAT DO YOU THINK YOU ARE DOING?" he yelled. He fully expected the horse to take off for the barn and as far as he was concerned the girl could walk home. After the first lunge that the Black made and as soon as he rid himself of his rider, he stopped dead planting all four feet and looked around behind him as if to say, "Don't do that to me."

Brett laughed. He had taught the horse to ground tie but he wasn't sure if the horse really knew it well enough that he would stop. No cowboy wants to be stranded miles from anywhere. The one thing that cowboys teach their horses and teach them well is that if the reins touch the ground, the horse is to stop and stand as if tied there – thus the term "ground tied".

Annie looked up at Brett from the ground and she laughed. "I'm sorry," she said, "I should not have done that. Will you let me ride him again?"

Brett nodded and said, "But now you know how strong he is. If you handle him correctly you will have a wonderful companion. If you are too rough, you will ruin him. This horse's spirit will not be broken. He will just turn into an outlaw."

Annie knew he was right. He really knew his horses. When Annie and Brett reached the barn, Pete and the rancher were sitting outside on a bench smoking hand-rolled cigarettes. Annie begged her father for the horse. The man settled up with Pete and he made a large profit on a horse that his original trainer was going to shoot.

After they left, Pete turned to Brett and handed him ten dollars. "Havta' admit ya' did a good job," he said.

After that Brett became his trainer and every horse he sold that Brett had worked with he gave Brett an additional ten dollars besides the hourly pay that he gave him for the other work he did. Brett had found an outlet for all his loneliness, working with horses.

III

The Gunfighter and the Doctor

The next time Mike came home from one of his trips, he carried in a brown paper-wrapped package. He called to Brett that he had a surprise for him.

Brett answered him, "What is it Mike?"

Brett had been taught to always call Mike by his first name and never to call him "Pa", "Dad" or any name meaning father.

—⁓—

Once when Brett was only four years old he called his father, "Pa". He had heard a little boy call his father, "Pa" when they were in the general store and he thought he would show his father how much he loved him by calling him, "Pa".

Mike turned on him sharply, "What did you say?" Brett whispered, "Pa" with his head down and his eyes staring at the floor realizing that he had made a mistake and his father was very angry.

Mike slapped him across the face, "Don't ever call me that again. Do you hear me? You call me 'Mike'. Got it?"

Tears streamed down the little boy's face as he began to cry. Lila jumped up pulling her son into her waist and ran her hand down the boy's cheek where the red mark was from Mike's slap, "Mike, he's just a little boy."

"I told you. Teach him to call me Mike. I don't want anyone to know I have a kid, and for that matter a wife either."

"He just forgot."

"Well maybe now he won't forget," and Mike went downstairs to get a drink in the bar which was his usual routine when he became angry or upset. Brett never forgot after that.

—⚬⚬—

"Here," Mike said, "Open it," handing the package to Brett.

Brett couldn't remember his father bringing him anything and ripped off the paper. It was a used gun, a Colt 45 and leather belt and holster. It had a wooden handle not the fancy mother-of-pearl handles like his father's guns. There were notches in the handle indicating that the former owner had killed at least four men with the gun. The holster probably also belonged to the same man. Brett stared at the gun. What was he going to do with this? He didn't like guns and knew nothing about them.

"What's that?" said Lila looking on in horror. "Why would you bring him that and where did you get it? Take it off your last victim?"

Mike frowned at her remark, "Lila, please." Although it was obvious to everyone what Mike was doing as a gun fighter, he didn't exactly like it addressed in this way especially in front of his son. "It's time the boy learns how to handle himself," Mike answered.

"He's only eleven years old."

"I started hunting when I was ten. He needs to start. It takes a few years of practice to get good at it."

"Oh, and you have decided what he's going to do with his life?"

"It doesn't matter what he decides to do with his life, he needs to know how to defend himself. Come on Boy," and he grabbed Brett by the arm and hustled him out the door before Lila could continue with the argument.

He mounted his horse and pulled Brett up behind him. They rode out of town to an old vacant farmhouse outside of town. Mike showed Brett how to load the gun and how to aim and fire. He told him about being both fast on the draw and accurate. He said the man who has both is going to be the winner. Sometimes it is better to take a little more time to shoot and be accurate than to rush into shooting and miss. "Rushing can destroy accuracy and the other man's bullet can then tear into you," Mike said.

While Mike was home he took Brett every day to the farmhouse much to Lila's chagrin. He made the boy learn to shoot and worked with him until he started to get more accurate shooting the bottles and cans he placed on the fence. Mike showed Brett just how good he was. He pushed matches into the spaces in the fence railing. He then fired right down the line lighting every match and then whipped out his other gun and shot off the heads of the matches.

Mike only had one holster and only used one gun. However, when he had the guns custom made, he had two made in case one would break when needed. When he practiced, he practiced with both guns. The balance could be just a tad different between even the same looking guns made by the same gunsmith. A good gunman practiced with two guns so that one did not feel strange if he needed to use it.

Lila seeing him take Brett out every day for shooting was still upset with him. The last thing she wanted her son to be was a gun fighter like his father. Mike always backed off from her when she was in one of her moods and for the whole first week he was home, he slept in the big chair in the living room letting her have the bed. She mellowed after the first week and he moved back into the bedroom although Brett still heard her chastise him about insisting that Brett learn to handle a gun.

Mike stayed several weeks before he got the telegram that always sent him off on another job. When he was ready to leave, they again had an argument and no matter how hard Mike tried to make amends with her she was still upset with him. Even Brett could tell that Lila was getting more and more distressed about Mike leaving, how long he was gone and what he did. As the word got out about how accurate and fast Mike was with his shooting skills, he got more and more requests from ranchers and businessmen and was home less and less.

Mike said to Brett before he left, "Keep practicing Boy. You'll get it," and then he walked out the door. Brett was now at the age where he also wondered each time Mike left if he would ever see him again. As soon as Mike left, Brett put the gun and holster away and didn't touch them again. Brett still hated guns and hated the violence he saw in the bar.

A couple months went by and one night late after the bar closed, Brett heard someone at the door and Mike drifted in. Brett still pretended to be asleep on his pallet and Mike kicked off his boots and went into the couple's bedroom. Brett heard Lila squeal with delight, laughing as she greeted her husband. As angry as Lila would get when Mike left, she was that much more exhilarated when he came home. She was so thrilled that he made it back home, she catered to his every whim, hugging and kissing him and all the animosity between them had been forgotten.

The next morning after breakfast, Mike asked Brett how he was doing with the pistol. When Mike found out that Brett had not been practicing with the gun he had brought him, he was furious. "GO GET YOUR GUN," he yelled at Brett.

Lila tried to interfere, "Mike he's still a boy. I don't want him . . ."

"You are not the only one raising him," Mike turned on her.

"I'm the only one here," she retaliated.

Mike's eyes got real dark and for a moment Brett was afraid for his mother. Mike was a lot of things, however, he had never hit a woman and he would never hit Lila. Instead he turned on Brett, "GET YOUR GUN, BOY," he shouted.

Brett went to the closet and took out the gun and holster. Mike grabbed the gun and holster out of his hand and he grabbed Brett by the arm with his other hand and angrily dragged him out of the apartment. He shoved Brett's gun in his saddlebags, mounted Arthur and pulled Brett up behind him speeding off so fast to the vacant farmhouse that it was all Brett could do to hang on and not fall off the back of the horse.

This time he was all over Brett, yelling at him. He quickly set up some cans and handed Brett the gun. "Let's see what you got, Boy."

Brett recognizing his father's anger was very nervous. He couldn't hit one can.

His father slapped him across the face hard. Brett put his hand to his cheek where his father had hit him rubbing his cheek. "SEE," said Mike, "THIS IS WHY YOU HAVE TO PRACTICE. You are not even as good now as you were when I left. If you don't keep practicing, you lose what you have gained up to that point. At this rate you will never progress."

He grabbed Brett by the arm and pulled him closer to the cans, "NOW DO IT AGAIN AND DON'T MISS."

By now Brett was shaking but he did hit a couple cans. His father had him so nervous he again started missing easy shots.

Mike said, "We will stay here until you hit every can I put up on the fence even if it takes until the moon comes up. If you can't do it at this distance, move a little closer BUT HIT THOSE CANS – ALL OF THEM."

It took three more tries until Brett got all the cans his father placed on the fence and when he had done it instead of giving him any kind of praise, he simply said, "Now you can walk home and while you are walking think about how you will practice with your gun." Mike turned to mount his horse and Brett started taking off the holster.

Mike turned on him, "NO, YOU LEAVE THAT GUN ON AND YOU WALK WITH IT ON. YOU GET USED TO THAT GUN UNTIL IT IS A PART OF YOUR RIGHT ARM. DO YOU HEAR ME BOY?"

Brett nodded and Mike mounted Arthur and rode off.

It was a good two miles back to town and it took Brett over an hour to get back home. He was near tears with frustration and at one point he stopped and sat on a rock staring at a lake that was on the way back to town until he could settle down and get his composure back. He wasn't sure what he was going to meet up with when he got home so wasn't real anxious to get there.

Brett hated the gun practices but as much as he hated the guns, he was again that much afraid of his father. Many times in practice his father would slap him if he missed the target he set up for him. Brett thought to himself, what did that prove? Even at his age he knew that making Brett nervous by slapping him just decreased his chances of success.

Brett noticed, however, that once his father got away from the practice house, he wasn't as demanding. He actually could be fun and Brett enjoyed his company. Brett was no longer a small child and Mike found that he enjoyed being with Brett also. In the evenings that Mike didn't work and Lila did and Mike and Brett were alone, Mike taught Brett card games including poker and they played checkers. Being the bright kid he was, he caught on fast to checkers and his father was almost not able to beat him in the game after he had played several times. They talked about a lot of different things and Brett learned things about his father he never knew. Mike told him about his boyhood and his parents and that he had a brother and a sister. Everything changed back to the love-hate relationship, however, when they went out to shoot.

Soon, Mike left again but this time Brett felt a little different. He was maturing and his boy hormones were kicking him toward manhood. He found he started liking to shoot the gun and started practicing more especially when his father wasn't around to make him nervous. Brett would ride one of the horses he was training to the shooting house and practice with the gun his father gave him. He didn't dare get out the gun when his mother was around but he did practice his draw in the evenings in front of a mirror in the apartment when she was working. During the day when he took the gun to the shooting range, he usually put it in a duffle bag and pretended it was equipment he needed to work with the horses.

The next time Mike came home and wanted to go shooting, Brett was anxious to show his father how good he had become. He sorely wanted Mike's approval for anything he did. He went to the livery and bridled one of the training horses. He rode the horse bareback. He didn't really have a saddle although he could always borrow one from Pete. He liked to ride bareback; he liked to feel the horse under him. He could feel what the horse was going to do and these young high-energy horses that Pete had been buying were skittish.

As he came out of the barn riding the horse, Mike frowned. "Why don't you put a saddle on that animal?" Mike said.

"I like to ride bareback."

"Indians ride bareback. White men ride with saddles. Where are you getting this stuff you are doing with these horses? Just strap a saddle on them, get on them and break them. Get it over with. What are you trying to prove?"

Brett said no more. He didn't want to start a shooting session off with his father angry at him. There was no sense arguing about how he trained the horses anyway. Mike had decided that there was only one way to train a horse and wasn't going to listen to what a kid, any kid but especially his own kid, had to say about it.

Again, Brett realized that he could not ever get approval from his father. However, Brett was getting older now and he could be as stubborn as his father. Every day when they went to the shooting house, Brett rode a horse bareback. Mike would just shake his head.

At the shooting range Mike watched his son shoot. Brett thought he was getting good but Mike still didn't say anything. He didn't slap Brett though so Brett thought he might be improving some.

Mike wanted to see his draw and when Brett showed him, Mike twisted his mouth in a half-approval. "Better," he said. Brett was disappointed. Couldn't his father give him more than that? He had worked many hours. One time Mike smiled; Brett was ecstatic. He took this to mean that Mike finally approved even if just a little.

One day after a couple weeks of working hard at the shooting house, Mike waited until he thought Brett had emptied his gun shooting cans and bottles. Mike was standing about twenty feet behind Brett. After Brett emptied the gun, Mike called his name. Brett turned toward him. "Put your gun in the holster," said Mike. He was standing with feet apart, his right hand slightly above his gun still in the holster. Brett recognized the gunfighter stance. His stomach did a flip. What was this?

"Draw," said Mike and he drew his gun so fast Brett could hardly see the movement. As Mike said "Draw", Brett drew his gun. Brett was nervous and as the gun came out of the holster, the tip of the barrel caught on the edge of his holster and he accidently pulled the trigger. There was still a live round in the gun and the shot went into the ground right in front of Mike's feet.

Brett turned snow white. He was convinced that Mike would kill him. No one fired at Mike Ballin and lived to tell about it. Brett opened his mouth to apologize but nothing came out. He looked at Mike and Mike started laughing. He laughed and laughed and finally said, "A little different facing a man with a gun, huh?"

"Come here," Mike said, and Brett walked slowly over to his father wondering what he was going to do to him now. He closed his eyes waiting to get slapped but instead Mike undid the rawhide lace that tied the gun to Brett's leg. Then he loosened the belt and brought the holster down lower on his hips, pulled the belt tight and said, "Now tie down the holster. You had your belt too high. In order to clear leather you have to have it low enough to bring it out smooth and be ready to shoot. When you are riding, you pull it up but when you are going to duel with another gunfighter you need to drop it some. Now, try a couple fast draws and DON'T SHOOT ME!" He wasn't angry however, he was still laughing.

Oh that was just what Brett wanted to know – how to do a gun duel. He sure hoped that never happened.

Again his father left and again Brett worked hard with the gun so that when his father would come home, he would be that much better than the last time they met at the shooting house. He would practice his draw in front of the mirror again and again after his mother left for work. He so wanted his father to just say once how proud he was of some accomplishment that Brett had done.

He also continued his voyeurism at the railing overlooking the Bittersweet. He really liked watching the doctor work when someone got hurt. He peered as far as he could over the rail to see all he could see.

On a busy Saturday night Brett couldn't see where his mother was. Two men got into an argument in a card game and one of the men shot the other man in the shoulder. Dr. Mowery was called. Brett got real brave. He stealthily crept down the stairs and knelt down behind the doctor to get a closer look. He watched the doctor closely and when the doctor reached back and fumbled for an instrument, Brett reached for it and handed it to him.

Brett had watched the doctor remove bullets so many times that he knew which instrument to hand him next and assisted him throughout the procedure. When the operation was done and Dr. Mowery gave the after-care instructions to the wounded man, he turned to see who had assisted him. He was very impressed when he saw it was Brett. "Why, thank you Brett," he said as he gathered his instruments and put them in his bag. Brett quickly went back upstairs before his mother saw him but he felt exhilarated.

It never mattered to Brett how much blood was involved. The blood didn't bother him at all. A man received a severe cut in his arm from a broken bottle, again in a fight. Dr. Mowery came and again Brett snuck down into the bar and helped him. This time however his mother caught him.

He was handing Dr. Mowery some sutures when he heard his mother say, "BRETT?!" in a shocked voice. He looked up at her standing over him. "What are you doing?"

"Helping Doc, Mother," he replied.

"He's a big help if it is all right Mrs. Ballin," said Dr. Mowery.

Lila backed off. She guessed her son was growing up. After that Brett helped Dr. Mowery all the time, until one day Dr. Mowery asked him if he wanted part time work. He then started working regularly for Dr. Mowery. He learned a lot and the doctor was so impressed with the boy that he started letting him assist him in surgeries. Brett gave up working at the stable but kept training the horses. He managed to stay very busy working with Dr. Mowery, training the horses and practicing with the Colt 45.

At this time in the rural western towns, it was usually customary for children to stop their education when they reached their teens. Most of the farmers and ranchers were happy if their children could read and write and do their sums. Advanced education was reserved for the wealthier families. If a family wanted their son to become something different than what the family business was such as a doctor or attorney then they would send the boy to a boy's school that was actually a pre-college school.

Since the Ballins were far from wealthy and Brett worked so hard helping to support his mother, it was out of the question for him to continue his education. He still visited with Amos Carr and Carr shared whatever new books he might have. He actually loved Brett's visits enjoying so much talking to a young man who took such an interest in education. He tried to give Brett all the help and encouragement he could. When Brett told him he was thinking that he would like to be a doctor, Amos was overjoyed. He applauded Brett's decision and said he would help him all he could toward that goal. It seemed that Amos Carr knew more about Brett's intelligence and goals and gave him more approval and support than his own parents.

Consequently, Brett continued to read every book he could, borrowing medical books from Dr. Mowery and devouring them. He knew all the anatomy of the body including names of the bones, muscles, tendons and internal organs. He knew where all the internal organs were located in the body. Brett studied the medical books and then when he assisted Dr. Mowery in the surgeries, he could put what he had learned in the books to practical use. What he didn't understand or wanted more information about, he would ask Dr. Mowery when he went to work with him. Some of his questions, Dr. Mowery couldn't answer and would look at the boy in amazement. The doctor was actually learning some things from Brett because it forced him to look in the books to clarify something Brett had asked.

When Mike returned this time, he found that his son had matured a great deal. He was now over a year older than when he first started handling the gun, had grown, filled out and was a very busy young man. Brett made no excuses for what he was doing. He didn't curtail his activities because his father came home. Mike found that his son had a lot more confidence and Mike was not going to shame him into doing something he didn't want to do. Brett was growing up even before his time for he was hardly thirteen years old.

On a hot sunny day in the summer, Brett was riding one of the horses he was training in a wooded area outside of town. He noticed a loose saddled horse grazing at the side of the road. He rode his horse up to where it was, dismounted and caught up the reins. There was blood on the saddle. He tied up the two horses and walked off the road looking around. There a little ways from where he was he saw a man sitting propped against a tree.

Brett went up to him. The man was barely conscious. There was blood on the left side of his shirt in line with his shoulder, a lot of blood. Brett bent over the man and pulled back the shirt. He palpated around the wound which brought the man into full consciousness from the pain. Brett knew that the bullet was still in there. The man opened his eyes. "This bullet has got to come out. You've lost a lot of blood."

"You're just a kid," said the man.

"I know how to take it out Mister but if you don't want me to, I will tell you, you may not make it back to town the way you are bleeding. As soon as I try to move you, you are going to start bleeding harder."

"Go ahead," the injured man said, "I guess I don't have anything to lose."

Brett went to the man's saddlebags. He found a pint of whiskey, a pen knife and matches. The man was riding a bay gelding. Bay horses have a red body color with black manes and tails. Black tail hair on a horse is the coarsest of any mane or tail hair. Brett pulled a couple hairs from the horse's tail.

He went back to the man, held his head up so he could drink some of the whiskey. Brett poured some of the whiskey on his hands and on the wound to try and sterilize everything as much as was possible under these conditions. The man grimaced and rose up a little in pain when Brett poured the whiskey into the wound. Then Brett poured some of the whiskey on the knife and lit a match. He held that up to the knife to sterilize it. He palpated the wound area again and figured out about where the bullet was. He picked up a stick and told the man to bite down on it and he did. This seemed to be a take-charge kid the man thought and he did exactly as Brett told him to do. The man squeaked and writhed in pain as Brett shoved the knife into the wound next to the bullet. As quickly as possible Brett popped out the bullet and dumped the remaining whiskey into the wound. "Don't pass out on me," Brett said. "We have to get you to town. I'm going to put a couple stitches in this wound to try and stop the bleeding." He was able to work the horse hair through a tiny hole in each side of the wound he had made with the knife and tie it off. It wasn't perfect but it might help hold it together and stop the bleeding. He then tore apart his shirt and made bandages and bandaged the arm.

"Can you ride? You will have to help me get you on your horse. I can't lift you by myself. Then I can get you to Dr. Mowery's."

Brett went and got the horse and the man took hold of the saddle horn with his good hand and put his foot in the stirrup. Between him and Brett they pushed and shoved and got him into the saddle. Brett then mounted his horse and took the reins of the man's horse and led him to town. When he reached Dr. Mowery's office, he asked two men walking on the street to help get the injured man upstairs to the doctor's office. Once the man was in the doctor's office, Brett rode on to the livery stable to take care of both horses.

Dr. Mowery took the make-shift bandage off the man's arm and after pushing on the wound said, "Who took this bullet out?"

The man said, "The kid that brought me in." The doctor was impressed. Brett had the makings of a fine doctor.

—⁓—

After Brett unsaddled and took care of the two horses, he started for home. When he reached the door of the apartment, he heard his parents yelling. He knew immediately that Mike was getting ready to leave again. Their battles always set him on edge. The walls to the apartment were thin and he could hear exactly what they were saying. This sounded like a bad fight. He sank down on the floor by the door in the hallway, brought his knees up to his chin and wrapped his arms around his legs. He wasn't going to go in and get in the middle of that battle.

Mike was telling Lila that he was leaving for a big job. "I can make so much more money doing this than what Sam pays me in the saloon," he said, using the same line he always used on Lila when he was getting ready to leave.

"But your son needs you right now. You and he are finally getting along. He's reaching manhood and he needs a man in his life."

"I have to support us also, Lila. Brett has his own mind. He's doing what he wants to do."

"When are you going to stop this? Every time you leave I have to wonder if you are going to come back. Will you be lying dead somewhere and we won't even know? We can make it with both of us working and living here and we could all be together."

"You have been wanting a house. It's possible that this will give us some money toward buying a real house where Brett can have a real bedroom instead of lying on a pallet in our living room. He's getting too old for that. I'll quit after this job."

"You'll quit after this job. You'll quit after this job. You say that before every job you take. I'm at the end of my rope, Mike. If you leave now, you can stay gone." She turned on her heel and ran into the bedroom and slammed the door.

Brett realized that his father would probably come charging out and go down to the bar for a drink. He got up quickly and ran down the hall and around the corner. Sure enough Mike came out the door of the apartment, slammed the door and went downstairs.

Brett came back and went into the apartment. There was nothing fixed for supper. He found some cold beef in the ice box; he got some bread out of the cupboard and made a sandwich and ate that with a glass of milk. Then he sat on his pallet and read. After a couple hours he fell asleep still with his clothes on. He heard his father come into the apartment and he could smell the whiskey. It was unusual for him to drink that much. He slept in the big chair that night and his mother never came out of the bedroom. The next day his father was gone.

I V

The Sickness

When Mike left on one of his trips, Brett always paid for it with his mother. This time was no different. Lila fell into one of her usual depressed moods. She could never convince Mike not to go and do his "work" and it left her worried about him as well as frustrated and depressed. Usually this mood went on for a few days and then she came out of her slump and got back to her busy life. Brett did notice as of late that each time Mike left her depression lasted longer.

Brett always tiptoed around her during this time, did what he could for her and asked for nothing until she got on with life. This time, however, she didn't seem to come out of it. She started with the depression the day Mike left and she seemed to become more and more depressed, edgy and withdrawn as each day passed by. Brett didn't think she was eating very much and sometimes what she did eat, Brett would hear her awhile later heaving it all back up. Brett also was sure she wasn't sleeping. He heard her get up in the night and sit at the dining room table. No matter how hard he tried Brett couldn't do anything right. He asked her several times if he could do anything for her and what was bothering her.

She finally yelled at him, "NO, THERE IS NOTHING YOU CAN DO AND NOTHING IS BOTHERING ME AND PLEASE STOP ASKING ME THAT."

After that and since nothing was changing with her, he started spending more and more time at the stable and at Dr. Mowery's. When he came home, nothing was ever made for supper and he started eating in the saloon or going to bed and not eating at all.

He talked to Dr. Mowery about depression in people but Dr. Mowery basically knew about physical ailments and said he knew nothing about how to treat mental ailments. He told Brett that there were hospitals that treated those kinds of patients but there weren't any nearby. Brett wished with all his might that his father would come home and maybe they could get his mother to one of those hospitals or after Mike came home, she would be all right again. Where the hell was he anyway?

A couple months went by and it didn't seem like Lila was getting any better and they had not heard anything from Mike – no money – no telegram – no nothing. She went to work and came home and quietly went to bed. One day Brett came home and Lila was very sick. He took her temperature and she had a high fever and complained of stomach cramps. Brett went and got Dr. Mowery. He came and gave her medicine for her stomach and told Brett he could use cold compresses on her forehead to reduce the fever. He saw how thin she was and told Brett that it was possible the stomach cramps were from hunger. Wasn't there anything she could eat?

Brett then tried to get her different food that she could tolerate. He brought her broth, both beef and chicken. He tried porridge. He was even able to get the storekeeper to order them some rice and he found out how to cook that for her. He concocted a milk shake with raw eggs and some other additives he read about in a medical book. She sometimes attempted to eat what he brought her but never enough to do her much good and many times she regurgitated it back up.

Brett took excellent care of his mother while she was sick. He held her shoulders while she vomited in a basin of water which he always had ready. He would wash her face and neck and clean the basin as soon as she was through. He made sure she got her medication. He stayed with her, washing her face, forehead and laying a cloth under her neck wrapping it around her neck to cool her down. He followed Dr. Mowery's instructions explicitly and spoon fed her the chicken or beef broth or whatever else he thought she might tolerate. She would hardly eat it and he had to beg her to try and eat anything.

He bathed her regularly and changed her gowns and bedding and washed everything keeping her, her clothing and bedding clean. All was not enough, however, and she got sicker and sicker. She was getting so thin; she was all bones covered by skin and the worst was that she didn't seem to care. He prayed for his father to come home. He felt like this had something to do with Mike leaving; his mother just couldn't take it anymore.

No matter what he did, she was not getting any better and she kept calling for Mike. She had now dropped into a state of hallucinations and mostly slept. Brett would be wringing out the cloth in the cool water in the basin and as he would place it on her head, her eyes would open, "Is Mike here yet, Brett? Is Mike coming?"

"He's not here yet Mother but he's coming." He didn't know what else to say. He had no way to contact his father and he hadn't heard a word from him. He hadn't even sent them any money. WHERE WAS HE? WAS HE ALIVE EVEN? Brett was getting more and more agitated.

Her delirium continued and she continued to say, "Mike, Mike, please come home, please."

"I'm here, Mom, please get better. I'm here, isn't that enough? I need you Mother; I love you."

Brett kept asking Dr. Mowery what he could do but Dr. Mowery had no answers. He came once a day to see her but all he could do was to treat her symptoms. He also was aware that with all the medical books Brett read and how astute the boy was about medical conditions, Brett could see that his mother was failing and failing fast.

Brett stopped doing anything except take care of his mother. Dr. Mowery praised him for what good care he was taking of her. He felt so bad for the boy and wished there was more he could do. He had done some research but couldn't find anything that helped treat what was wrong with Lila. He could only treat her symptoms and hope that anytime now she would snap out of it not only for her sake but for Brett's. He really liked the boy and Brett had no one with his father out of the picture.

Then in September, Lila died. Brett was devastated. He felt like he should have done something more. Dr. Mowery tried to convince him that there was nothing more he could have done. He told Brett that he couldn't save her, how did Brett expect to save her. He said that he had never seen anyone more devoted to caring for a relative and Brett should be proud of himself but everything he said made no difference, Brett was consumed in grief and placed a lot of blame on himself.

Since Brett had no other relatives or friends and his father had still not returned, Dr. Mowery stayed with him after Lila died. Brett sat next to the bed holding his mother's hand with his head down.

Bruce Russell, the undertaker, and his assistant came. He looked at Dr. Mowery and motioned toward Brett. Dr. Mowery rose and went to Brett. "Come on, Son," he said putting his hand on Brett's shoulder. "They have to take your mother now."

Brett stood up, kissed his mother on the cheek and allowed Dr. Mowery to lead him downstairs while they prepared to take his mother to the funeral home and prepare her for burial. Dr. Mowery led him to a table and told him to sit down and he went and bought two sarsaparillas from Sam. He sat down with Brett and gave him the drink.

Sam Barton, who had always treated Brett like he never existed came over to the table where he sat with Dr. Mowery and told him how sorry he was and how much he would miss Lila. Brett nodded and said "Thanks" to Sam.

After the undertaker had taken Lila away, Brett said good-bye to Dr. Mowery and went back upstairs. He cleaned up the apartment, washed, undressed and fell exhausted onto his pallet. It dawned on him after he lied down that he could now sleep in his parents' bed but it somehow didn't feel right.

The next day was the funeral. Funerals were simple in Winchester, Kansas. Bruce and his assistant brought the body to the cemetery. He had hired men to dig a grave. The men then took the pine box from the funeral wagon and placed it in the hole. There were not many people at Lila Ballin's funeral. Brett, Dr. Mowery, Sam and a couple of the saloon girls were the only ones there.

The minister came and said some words which made no sense to Brett. He had only seen the man around town and really didn't know him at all. He had never even spoken to him and Brett had never been to church. The minister of course knew nothing about Lila but he said something to the effect that she was a good woman and would be sorely missed by her husband, Michael, and son, Brett.

Right, thought Brett — sorely missed by her husband, Michael. Did he ever miss anyone? Yes, as a matter of fact he did miss everything. His mother had told him that Michael missed Brett's birth. He was never there for any of Brett's scholarly achievements and now he missed his own wife's death and her funeral. He sure did sorely miss things.

Then the minister went on reading from the bible. Something about believing and having everlasting life, it made no sense to Brett. She was dead, how
was she going to have everlasting life? The minister continued, "We commit
her body to the ground, earth to earth, ashes to ashes, dust to dust . . ." Brett
was only half listening; none of it made sense to him. He was still dwelling on
what he could have done to save her even though he had no answers.

Suddenly, he heard his name several times and someone touching his
shoulder, it was Dr. Mowery. He pulled himself out of his trance and looked
up. The minister was expressing his sympathy to Brett. Brett thanked him.
Dr. Mowery pulled out a ten dollar bill and handed it to the minister. After
the man walked away he said to Brett that it was customary to give the minister
a fee for his services. Brett nodded but wondered why – he had not invited
him and what he said made no sense.   Brett muttered that he would give Dr.
Mowery the ten dollars back. He had to take some money to Bruce Russell
also for the funeral. Dr. Mowery said to forget it and to consider it a token of
his appreciation for how hard Brett worked for him. Dr. Mowery put his arm
around his shoulders and walked with him back to his office and then Brett
went on to his apartment.

When he came back from the funeral and walked into the saloon, Sam
called him over. He asked Brett when he could be out of the apartment. He
had someone who wanted to move in as soon as possible. Brett never gave it
a thought that he would have to move. But then how could he make enough
money to afford it? He didn't answer Sam but just walked away and went
upstairs to the apartment.

He packed up the stuff he wanted, his personal belongings, clothes, the
Colt 45 and then some mementos. He took all the pictures they had had
done whenever there was a photographer in town, a book written my Charles
Dickens he liked and some other mementos including a small iron horse that
his father had given his mother from one of his trips and put what he wanted
into a duffle bag.

He took all the money they had stashed away in a small music box and then
he walked downstairs. He told Sam he was out of there. Sam said, "Hey, wait
a minute Boy. Your mother hasn't worked here for a month. You owe twenty
dollars for rent for the last month." As if by rote, Brett dug the money out

of his pants pocket and handed Sam the money and left the saloon never to return.

He went to the funeral home and paid for his mother's funeral and thanked Bruce for taking care of the arrangements for him.

After he left the funeral home, he walked to the park and sat down on a park bench by a tree to collect his thoughts. He took his remaining money out of his pocket and counted it – $10.75. Good thing he didn't feel hungry. Sitting there he heard a meadowlark singing his song. He noticed a crust of bread lying off on a trail and watched as a crow flew down and pecked at it. Another crow joined him and they tussled but both flew in and out pecking at the bread but staying out of each other's way. He had to smile at the birds. He sat there a while looking at the various birds, squirrels and chipmunks running around the park area. He wished he could trade places with them – they looked so happy. At least they had each other. He now knew what lonely felt like.

After he sat for a while he got up and walked to the livery. He found Pete and asked if he could sleep in the tack room. He didn't mention that it would be permanent. Pete said yes and he was sorry about his mother. Brett took his few belongings and went into the tack room and arranged things the way he wanted them. There was a cot in there because sometimes some hired man would sleep there. It was getting late, almost dark and Pete had gone home.

Brett came out of the tack room and sat down on a stack of grain bags. He propped his legs up on the bags, wrapped his arms around them and rested his chin on his knees. He sat there a long time listening to the horse noises and dozed off. He awoke with a start and it was dark. He got up and went into the tack room and fell onto the cot and didn't even undress. End of another chapter in the life of Brett Ballin and he was barely thirteen years old he thought as he drifted into sleep.

—⁓—

To relieve his mind with the death of his mother and try and get over the guilt of thinking he should have somehow saved her, Brett filled his days with work. He worked in the stable and with Pete's horses as well as with Dr. Mowery. When he got a chance he would ride out to the shooting house and practice with his gun. He also borrowed Pete's rifle and practiced with it. He thought it would probably be a good idea to learn to shoot a rifle also.

One warm fall day Brett was really having a bad day. He kept thinking about his mother and if there had been something more he could have done to save her. She had been gone about five weeks and it was her birthday. He was bitter about his father leaving them and knew his father was partly to blame for his mother's illness. He was a roundhouse of emotions – helplessness, anger, frustration, depression and rage. He mounted a horse he had been training and rode out to the shooting house galloping the horse the whole two miles. He pulled the horse to a sliding stop outside the old run-down house and tied him to the fence.

He quickly gathered and set up some cans and bottles on the fence. All of a sudden all his feelings took over and he went totally out of control. All right, he thought, his father wanted him to learn to shoot, he would show him when he came home. He would show him how good he had gotten with a gun. His father wanted him to be a gunman well all right he would do it – maybe he would even outdraw and shoot him.

He pulled his gun in a fast draw and started shooting at his targets, his dark eyes on fire, feeling the rage and all the pent-up emotions take over and he shot wildly shooting all the cans and bottles until his gun was empty. He didn't stop shooting however; he stood there firing the empty gun at the targets, his face contorted into an ugly stare at what he had done. His eyes were dark and bloodshot and it scared him to be so out of control, it wasn't him. He kept things orderly – he was the take-charge kid. Suddenly he dropped to his knees on the ground letting the gun fall from his hand and his shoulders started to shake and he started crying and that went into racking sobs and he put his head in his hands and rolled onto his side curled in a ball and lied on the ground shaking, sobbing and sucking in his breath – the first he had really cried since his mother had died and he wasn't sure if he would ever be able to stop.

—⁓—

Fall came and went and winter was knocking on their door. By the end of November it was getting very cold in the tack room especially at night. Pete told Brett he should find a place where there was heat. When Dr. Mowery found out where Brett was living, he told him to move into the doctor's office for the winter. He could sleep in the laid-back chair that Dr. Mowery used to stitch patients or pull teeth. It wasn't the most comfortable chair for sleeping but it was by the heat stove and it was warm and Brett very much appreciated it especially after a few nights shaking in his blanket in the tack room.

Finally one morning after the long Kansas winter with wind and snow so deep that sometimes Brett stayed in the doctor's office all day, Brett walked out to go to the stable and he noticed that it was a little warmer. The sun was out and shining bright. The melting snow was dripping off all the roofs in town. Brett had a lot of work to do at the barn. A lot of their regular work had not been done very thoroughly; everything had been given a lick and a promise due to the deep snow and cold. He worked all day cleaning the barn and grooming the horses.

In March, spring came in rainy and cold and one late afternoon Mike Ballin rode into the livery wet with rain and cold. Brett was grooming a horse in the cross-ties in the aisle of the barn when Mike rode the big bay gelding into the barn. He dismounted and took his hat off batting at the rain-soaked poncho. Brett heard him but did not turn around. He had seen him coming out of the corner of his eye. Brett didn't know if he would ever get any feeling back for anyone again after losing his mother so tragically and he knew at that moment the only feeling he had for his father was hatred.

It was late, almost dark when Mike rode in. He was surprised to see that Brett was still at the barn. He said in a surprised voice, "Brett?!"

Brett didn't turn around but continued brushing the horse even more vigorously. "Brett?" he said again. Still nothing, Brett ignored him. Mike walked up and pulled the boy around, "Look at me Boy when I speak to you," he said irritated that Brett was ignoring him but then he got a shock.

Brett retaliated, "DON'T YOU TOUCH ME!"

"What's the matter with you Brett?"

"MOM'S DEAD BUT I'M SURE YOU DON'T EVEN CARE!"

Mike looked like someone had just shot him. "Your mother is dead! How did it happen?"

"She got sick and died. That's how. Maybe she was tired of living alone."

"She had you."

"Think that was enough for a woman like Lila? She loved you. She wanted you. It didn't matter that I was there. She asked for you constantly. The whole time she was sick. Where do you go for so long Mike? Huh? Where do you go that is so all-fired important that you can leave your family for months at a time? That you can't even be there when your wife dies? When you even miss her funeral? When you don't even attempt to make contact with us?" He leaned against the horse resting his forehead on the horse's neck, the months of pent-up feelings finally released. He stopped brushing the horse but still wouldn't turn around and face his father. He felt worn out – exhausted from his outburst confronting Mike but no way was he going to cry. No way would his father see any weakness in him.

Mike walked up and put his hand on Brett's shoulder.

"I told you," snapped Brett, "don't touch me."

Then he whirled around, went in the tack room and picked up a jacket. He looked at Mike, looked him straight in the eyes – and maybe Mike thought he was looking in the mirror. His son's black eyes were dancing with hatred. "We don't have the apartment anymore. I sleep at Dr. Mowery's until it warms up and then I'll move back in here. You can sleep wherever you want." He unhooked the horse and led it back to its stall. He then turned on his heel and went to walk out but Mike blocked his exit although he didn't touch his son.

"When?" he said quietly. "When did she die?"

"September 8."

"Where is she buried?"

"By the big oak tree. There's a marker. Not much of one but a marker. You'll be able to find it."

"Will you go with me to visit her grave?"

"No." The only time Brett had been back to the grave since the funeral was to place the marker on the grave. He walked out leaving his father standing there holding his hat in his hands.

"Brett, you can come to the hotel. You can sleep in my room or I'll get you one for yourself," he yelled after his son.

"What makes you think I would want to sleep in the same room with you?"

He didn't see his father for a couple days. Then Mike came to the livery and said they were leaving. He told Brett to pick out a horse from Pete and

Mike would buy it for him and a saddle as well. He said that Brett was now old enough to start learning how to make a living and he would teach him.

"And I don't get anything to say about this? What if I don't want to leave? What if I don't want to be with you?" retorted Brett.

"Well you can't stay living in a stable."

"And why not? It beats living with a killer."

Mike flinched at his son's words. He was hoping the boy would cool down after a couple days but he could now see that all the built-up hate and frustration was going to take a little longer to settle things between them. "I guess I deserve that. And I guess I deserve your rage. I see you have had to forage for yourself for several months. That wasn't fair of me but I'm ready to try and make it up to you."

"How? By teaching me how to kill people? What makes you think I want to be like you?"

"Let's not quarrel. I had enough of that with your m-o-t-h . . ." Brett's fist caught him fully on the jaw. His head snapped back and he was stunned that his son would hit him. He was also surprised by the strength in his young son's hand. He looked at the boy and rubbed his chin. When Brett reared back to hit him again he grabbed his arm. "Brett, stop this. I'm sorry. I should not have said that. Come on Boy. You're old enough now that we can do some traveling together and find out things about each other. Please, let's just ride out tomorrow together. Pick out any horse you want that Pete has for sale and I'll buy it for you. I know how much you love horses. This will be a horse of your own."

Mike released his arm and patted him on the shoulder, then turned and walked out of the barn and left Brett standing alone in the aisle. Brett thought he saw some regret and emotion spread over his father's face – for the first time ever. He stared at him walking away, Mike's shoulders slumped.

Pete came out of the hallway where he had been listening but did not want to interfere. "So ya'll are gonna leave with your father?" he asked as he spit a stream of brown tobacco juice on the ground.

"I guess I have no choice."

"Brett, maybe it'll be a good thin'. You and your pa been at odds all your life. Maybe he's right. This will be a good time to get to know each otha'. Some men cen't relate to young'uns. You are now older and he cen talk to ya' and treat you like a partna'."

Brett nodded.

"So what hoss you thinkin' ah buyin'?"

Brett thought for a minute. "The small red gelding, I'll name him Little Red."

"Well he ain't the best hoss in the barn," said Pete.

"I know, but I like him. He has a lot of heart and I'm not finished with his training."

Pete snickered. That would be Brett he thought, take the horse because he hadn't finished training him yet.

Mike came back a couple hours later and asked Brett if he had picked out a horse yet. Brett told him that he wanted the small chestnut gelding. Mike looked at the horse and said, "He's not very big and doesn't look real strong."

"He fits me. I'm not very big and not real strong," said Brett sarcastically.

"All right," he turned to Pete, "How much? And he'll need a saddle and bridle."

"A hundred dollahs," said Pete.

"A hundred dollars? That's outrageous for that horse."

Pete knew when he had a good thing going. "That's what thet thar hoss costs and thet's with the saddle and bridle," he said.

Mike took out his money and counted out a hundred dollars and gave it to Pete. Pete turned and handed Brett ten dollars.

"What's that about? Think I got snookered here," said Mike jovially.

"Brett trains my hosses. When I sells a hoss he trains, I give him ten dollars. Thet's our deal."

Brett turned and reached out to hand the ten dollars to his father.

"Keep it," said Mike and waved it away. "Be ready at eight in the morning. Do you want to spend the night in the hotel? You can sleep in my room. There are two beds."

"No" said Brett. I'll stay at Dr. Mowery's. I need to finish up some things."

V

The Trip

At eight o'clock sharp Mike came into the barn. Brett had both horses saddled and he had his bedroll and saddle bags on Little Red. Mike put his bedroll and saddle bags on Arthur and mounted. Brett turned to Pete and said, "Thanks for everything, Pete."

"I'm goin' ta miss ya' Kid," said Pete. "You're the best hoss traina' I ever had. Good Luck Brett," and he reached out and shook Brett's hand.

Brett mounted Little Red and rode out of the barn but he didn't follow his father, instead he turned toward the cemetery. When Mike saw what the boy was doing, he turned his horse in the same direction and followed Brett.

Brett rode into the cemetery and up to his mother's grave. He dismounted and dropped the reins. He walked over just beyond her grave where some wild flowers were growing. He picked them and went back to her grave. He had made the marker from wood and had burned her name and the date of her death into it with a running iron. He knelt on his heels, pulled a few weeds off her grave, laid the flowers gently down and put his hand on top of the grassy grave. He bowed his head and silently said good-bye. After a few minutes, he mounted his horse and turned to where Mike was sitting atop his horse. They rode a couple hours without talking at all. Mike in the lead and Brett simply following behind.

"This is going to be a very boring ride if neither of us talks," said Mike.

It did not break the ice; Brett rode along refusing to talk. Mike started whistling to break the silence. Actually, Brett was enjoying the ride. After he had thought about it, he was excited about the change. Mike had been right. He couldn't live in the stable the rest of his life. He finally had a horse of his own and a new adventure. Maybe it would work out. He really had not had a lot of time with his father and this might give him a chance to get to know him. He pushed Little Red and rode up beside Mike. "So where are we going?" he asked.

"I thought we could ride into Rimfire. There are a lot of ranchers around there and perhaps I can pick up a job."

Brett cringed. Mike was going to shoot someone again. Where would Brett be when this took place? Was he going to see his father kill someone? "Do you really have to do that? Can't you give that up?"

"You don't have to be around. Besides it isn't always killing. Brett, it's all I know."

"You worked in the saloon in Winchester."

"The pay is so lousy. You can hardly live on what I was making in the Bittersweet. Let's just take it a day at a time."

The conversation ended and Mike started whistling again. Suddenly, Brett felt like racing his horse. He wanted to see what Little Red was made of. He pressed his sides with his heels. The little gelding broke into a canter and Brett urged him on faster and faster. He drew in the reins until he just barely had contact with the horse's mouth, put his head down beside the horse's neck and encouraged him to fly. The chestnut was faster than what Brett had thought. Mike took off after him laughing and calling to Arthur to keep up with the little chestnut. The two raced down the road for at least a mile or more. When Brett saw that his horse was breaking into a sweat, he eased off. He gently made contact with the horse's mouth and brought him down to first a canter and then a walk.

As the sun went down, they started looking for a place to make camp. They found a place surrounded by a few trees and several rocks. It made for good shelter. After taking care of the horses, they started a fire and made some supper. Brett was loosening up. His anger was dissipating. After all, if he had to travel with this man, he might as well make the best of it. After supper in the glow of the fire, Mike brought out a deck of cards and he and Brett played poker. Brett won a few hands but so did Mike and they figured they had both broken even. They laughed at the end of the game and then they rolled up in their blankets and went to sleep.

Brett slept better than he had for a while. It was kind of good to be with someone again; someone who cared about him. Despite all he had gone through with his father, he knew the man loved him and he knew he was trying to make up for his shortcomings. Pete and Dr. Mowery were always good to him but he didn't feel a connection with them. Whatever Mike was, he still felt connected to the man, after all half his genes coursed through Brett's body.

Brett awoke in the night and lie in his bedroll thinking about his life as it existed now. He heard the wolves in the distance calling their pack together for a hunt. He also heard some rustling in the bushes close-by and rolled over to see a raccoon foraging along the edge of the camp. He smiled – brave little bugger wasn't he? He didn't come any closer and rustled his way back into the woods.

The next day the two rode into Rimfire around noon. Brett said he would take care of the horses. Mike told him he would be in the saloon. He gave Brett some money for the horses' care. Brett took them to the livery stable. Normally, the owner or his worker cares for the horses but Brett was in no hurry to go to the saloon. He stripped off their saddles and gave them both a good rubdown. He got each of them a bucket of water, some hay, a good measure of oats and paid the stable owner. When he couldn't think of anything else to do with the horses, he walked slowly down to the saloon.

He stopped once and sat down on a bench and watched people walking down both sides of the street. He stopped at the general store and bought a couple sticks of candy. He put one in his pocket and ate one. He didn't want to walk into a saloon eating a stick of candy so he crossed to the other side of the street and sat on a bench until it was gone.

Finally he figured he had wasted all the time he dared and he went to the saloon. He went inside, looked around and saw Mike playing cards and drinking beer. He walked up to the table, "Mr. Ballin," he said remembering not to call his father by any daddy-name.

"Oh," Mike said, "All right, Kid, I'll be done here shortly. Why don't you go over to the hotel and check us in. I'll meet you there."

One of the men said, "Who's the kid, Mike?"

"I'm teaching him to shoot," lied Mike. "His father's got bucks and he wants the kid to know how to handle himself. He's paying me a pretty good chunk of money to teach his kid how to shoot a gun."

—w—

Mike never wanted anyone to know he had a son. They could easily take the kid and use him to get to Mike. This was the reason he never wanted the boy to call him by a daddy-name. It actually was for Brett's safety. Mike was a hard man. He had grown up in a household where there was no attention paid to the children. They were born to work and work they did. There was never praise, hugging, kissing, and no affection at all. But even though he had a hard time showing it, he really loved Brett. And he had really loved Lila. Strange as it seemed, he didn't feel guilty for all the men he had maimed and killed. But he did feel guilty for not being there for Lila when Brett was born and for not being there for both Lila and Brett when she was ill and died. He would have that hurt until they put him into the ground.

At the hotel, the clerk wanted payment in advance even though Brett told him his companion would be over shortly to pay the clerk. Brett did still have the ten dollars that Pete had given him so he paid the four dollars for two nights. He got a room with two beds. He took his stuff up with him, his saddle bags and bedroll. He sorted out his clothes and other belongings and took out a book to read while he waited for Mike.

After lying down on the bed and reading for about a half hour, Brett fell asleep and didn't wake up until Mike came in. He pretended he was still sleeping and he soon drifted off again. He was exhausted.

Brett awoke in the morning to Mike washing and shaving. "I found a job," Mike told him. "It's not in town. I'm going to ride out to a ranch. Do you want to come along?"

"No," answered Brett. Why would his father think he wanted to see some-one get killed? "I'll hang around town and see what it's like here."

"Well don't get too attached. We won't stay long."

From that point on this was the way it went riding with Mike. Get into a new place, do a job or two and get out of there like the devil rode your tail. If Mike couldn't find a job, they wouldn't stay but then rode on; if he found a job, he did it and it was the same scenario. When a gunslinger shot a man, he always made sure it was self-defense. Always made sure the man drew first. But he didn't hang around to debate the issue. There were always relatives that could come after him and there was always the possibility that some overzealous law-man would think that it wasn't quite a fair fight and arrest the winner. Mike had never stood trial for any of his shootings and he wasn't about to start now.

Their first year together passed, spring came and went and they continued from town to town all summer. The initial excitement had worn off and Brett was getting tired of riding into a town, staying a day or two and moving on. His father kept making him practice and kept pushing him to draw against him. He never was quite as fast as Mike. In his own right though he was fairly fast on the draw and probably just as accurate as his father. He was a good shot and he liked the shooting part. He thought the dueling part however was the stupidest thing two men could do. He made up his mind no one would ever be able to call him out in the street for a duel. He just wouldn't go. It even made him nervous to face his father and play his father's game of "let's see who's faster". He sometimes held back a little and thought he might be a little faster than how he drew because he was drawing against his father. Mike would laugh when he beat the boy on the draw but he could tell that Brett did not like this game. Mike was good at reading faces, he had to be and his young son's face said it all.

It was now over a year that they had left Winchester, having left in the previous spring. Fall was coming, it was late August, and one day they came into a small town in Kansas called Mineral Springs. Mike had said this was a town that he had never been before.

By this time, Mike was starting to realize that he couldn't make Brett into something he was not. He watched the boy as he kept to himself, reading books. He saw that he was about as good as he was going to get with a gun. He knew that the boy's heart was not into handling the guns much less being a gunslinger. Not once had Brett expressed any interest in going with Mike on one of his jobs. Instead Brett completely avoided it and the only time he wore his gun was when they were out on the trail in case they ran into highwaymen. It was not unusual for highwaymen to attack riders for their money.

Brett had studied a medical book that Dr. Mowery had given him as a departing gift until the binding was broken and the pages were falling out. While Mike played poker in the saloons to make contacts in order to get jobs, Brett stayed in their hotel room or at the livery. Sometimes he would talk the livery owner into letting him ride a recalcitrant horse. They never stayed long enough to give Brett a chance to really train the horse but he could show the owner a few things about the horse if the man was willing to listen that might help make him a more biddable animal.

After a couple days in Mineral Springs, Mike quit gambling early one night and went back to their room. It was about 9:30 and Brett was already in bed and asleep. While Mike gambled the evenings away and slept late in the morning, Brett went to bed early and was an early riser and would take care of their horses.

"Brett, wake up," Mike said, shaking the boy, "I want to talk to you."

Sleepily, Brett opened his eyes and rubbed them with his hands. He sat up and swung his legs over the edge of the bed. The room was dimly lit by a lamp. His father never did this and he wondered what was up.

Mike handed him a glass of water. "Here drink this and wake up. I have something important to say."

Brett sat up and took the glass. He put a couple fingers in it and splashed it on his face, rubbed his eyes again with his fists and then finished drinking the water. "I'm awake."

Mike sat on the edge of his bed opposite his son and facing him. "Brett, how old are you now?"

"Fifteen."

"What do you want to do with your life? I mean if you could do any job, what would you like to do?"

He never hesitated, "Be a doctor."

"That's what I figured. You know Son, I've been doing a lot of thinking over the last year we've been together. I've been awfully hard on you. I wanted you to grow up and be me but better. But you have too much of your mother and too many brains to do what I do. I ruined my life. I know that now. It just got to a point where there was no turning back. I ruined your mother's life too, probably killed her. Besides you, the one person in my life I loved and loved me unconditionally. I'm not going to ruin your life.

"Brett, I'm setting you free. You want to be a doctor. Your mother's people live in Boston, Massachusetts. There are great schools there. Her father is a very prominent business man. His name is Elijah Simmons and your grandmother is Gladys Simmons. Here, I've written down everything I know about them. They shouldn't be too hard to find. They are very well-known in Boston. Your grandfather has a big manufacturing company there.

"You can get a very good education in Boston. And after you complete the preliminary stuff you can go to Boston University and go to medical school.

Look up your grandparents. They will take you in and help you. They hate me but they will probably be thrilled to have a grandson with your intelligence who wants to be a doctor. Don't be shy. They are good people. They just didn't want their daughter to marry me and they were probably right."

He turned and opened his saddlebags. "Here is $2,000 to get you started. Use it sparingly but use it for your education. That's what I have been doing the last year, saving up to give you this money. Take it." And he handed it over to Brett.

Brett sat on the edge of the bed stunned. He tentatively reached out and took the money. He thought maybe he really hadn't woken up. Was this the father that used to slap him if he missed a shot when they were shooting at the vacant house?

"Tomorrow," Mike went on, "we'll part company. You head east and north. I'm going to head south. I don't know where I'm going yet just drifting as usual. You can ride until you get into a little too much city. Then sell Little Red and your saddle and take a train or stagecoach the rest of the way to Boston. I know you don't like the idea of selling Little Red but you won't be able to pay for his keep if you try to take him to Boston. Some sacrifices have to be made Son for our ultimate goal. Any questions?"

Brett looked down at all the money in his hand and back to his father. This was such a surprise, he was in shock and not quite sure what to say. Finally he said, "Will I ever see you again?" There was a time when he would not have cared but he had just spent over a year with his father and he realized how much he really did love him and emotion flooded into him.

"Sure. We can keep in touch. There is the United States mail you know. I'll find you at your grandparents' home and then let you know where you can write me. I'm thinking I might try cow punching. It never appealed to me before but I am getting tired of looking over my shoulder all the time."

Tears welled up in Brett's eyes and hard as he tried some trickled down his cheeks. Deep down he didn't really want to leave his father, not to mention that it seemed scary to be all out on his own. Boston sounded like a far-away place and crowded, a big city – lots of people. He suddenly had a fear that his father would take his tears for a sign of weakness and yell at him, but that didn't happen.

"Hey," Mike said gently. "It will be all right. You'll see." Awkwardly, because Mike had never held his son except when he was a little baby and he was forced to take care of him. He moved over to Brett's bed, sat down next to him and took him in his arms. "Come on now. I want you to realize your dreams. We'll get back together and I'll be so proud to say I have a son who is a doctor."

Brett smiled at his father and choked out a "thanks". He felt like his father finally approved of who he was.

In the morning, Brett woke early. He was washed, dressed and ready to go out the door when Mike first woke up. "Where are you going?" asked Mike.

"I thought I would go get the horses ready. I'll bring them to that little café down the street and we can get breakfast."

"Sounds good."

Brett walked out carrying his saddle bags and bedroll. He walked to the livery, brushed and saddled the two horses and put his bedroll and saddle bags on Little Red. He was leading the horses up the street back toward the hotel. As he approached the café where they had agreed to meet, he saw his father walking toward him.

Mike had just walked passed an alley when a man jumped out behind him. Brett saw the gun.

He screamed, "M-I-K-E, LOOK OUT – BEHIND YOU!" but it was too late.

The man shot Mike in the back twice and as the bullets spun him around, the man shot him in the chest. Mike never even got his gun out of his holster. Brett dropped the reins and ran to his father.

The man was jumping up and down and yelling, "I shot Mike Ballin. I shot Mike Ballin."

Brett reached his father who was lying on his back. He knelt down and picked up his father's head and shoulders and pulled him into his chest cradling him in his arms. He pressed his hand against the wound in his chest trying to stop the flow of blood and he screamed, "Someone help him. Get a doctor. Oh Dad, hang on please Dad hang on."

Mike looked up at his son, "Go to Boston, Brett. Be a good doctor. I love you, Son."

Brett let out a sob and choked, "I love you too, Dad," before Mike died. Brett looked down and there in his holster still remained Mike's pearl–handled

Colt. The man was still running back and forth and screaming, "I shot Mike Ballin. I shot him." Brett reached for his father's gun in the holster.

A big hand reached over his shoulder and removed the gun. It was the town marshal. He took the gun from the holster, put his hand on Brett's shoulder and said, "Vengeance is not ours to take, Son."

He stood up letting Brett stay with his father. He yelled at the man, "Evans, shut up or I'll shoot you myself."

Brett buried his head in his father's face. Someone had caught the horses and led them up near-by and tied them to the hitching post. Minutes passed by, Brett holding his father. Why? Why now just when they had resolved so much between them? It took a while before the undertaker got to them and Brett held his father in his arms the whole time as if to comfort him.

The marshal walked up to Brett. He gently put his hand on Brett's shoulder. "Come on Son. The undertaker is here."

He almost literally had to pick Brett up. His knees were so weak. He was covered in his father's blood. The kindly marshal led the stunned boy to his office. He had grabbed Brett's bedroll off his horse. The marshal had a small room off the jail where he slept and ate. He took Brett in there and set down the bedroll. He gave Brett some warm water and towels. "Here," he said, "wash up and change your clothes. You can leave those clothes lay and I'll dispose of them. I'm sorry Boy, for what happened."

Brett just stared at the bundle. Then he did as he was told but didn't remember doing it. Mike's belongings were still in his room. The marshal took Brett back to the hotel and paid for another night's stay for him. He told the boy that the funeral would be tomorrow and they would bury Mike on Boot Hill. Brett just nodded and sat down on the bed, placed his hands on his chin, elbows on his knees and stared at the floor.

The marshal also told Brett that the man who had killed his father was in jail and would remain there until the circuit judge came through and decided if he should stand trial or not. As gently as possible he told the boy that Mike wasn't exactly a very innocent victim. He couldn't say if his killer would be punished or not. He did say, however, that the man would probably be shunned by many people. Even if they feared Mike Ballin, no one would condone someone shooting him in the back.

Brett listened and nodded; what did it matter anymore. The next day they buried Mike. A minister came and said words over him. They were the same words that were said for his mother, something about believing and having everlasting life and ashes to ashes and dust to dust. Brett just listened to the meaningless words. He did remember, however, to give the preacher ten dollars as Dr. Mowery had taught him when his mother died.

The marshal had come to the cemetery and stood next to Brett. He felt bad for the boy. When it was over he told Brett to come back to his office. There he gave Brett his father's gun and holster and five hundred dollars which they found on Mike. He told Brett that he hoped he would ride out of town and not try to use the gun. He had taken all of the bullets but he realized that Brett could buy more. Brett realized that it would be hard to shoot his father's killer with the man in jail and he really didn't think he could ever kill anyone anyway unless it was in self-defense. Even when he reached for his father's gun in the street, he felt almost grateful that the marshal beat him to it. Then he didn't have to make a decision he may later regret.

Brett thanked him for his kindness and left. He put Mike's guns in his duffle bag along with the money Mike had given him, the collection of pictures they had taken through the years and the small iron horse that Mike had brought back from one of his trips and gave to his mother.

He walked to the livery stable, went to where Arthur was stalled and stroked the horse's face and said good-bye. He sold the horse, Mike's saddle and the old revolver Mike had bought for him to the livery owner and strapped on Mike's black holster and pearl-handled Colt, tied it down to his leg and collected Little Red.

As he mounted Little Red to ride out of town, he thought: one more chapter in the life of Brett Ballin *closed.*

VI

Boston and School

After Brett had mounted Little Red, he rode out of Mineral Springs and out onto the Kansas prairie, the wind was blowing a good breeze as is common in Kansas especially on the wide open prairies. Fall was in the air and the wind was carrying a promise of winter. Some tumbleweed blew across their path and Little Red shied and snorted. Brett laughed at the little horse. He came upon a huge buffalo herd and skirted around it. He had never seen a herd that large and wasn't sure if Little Red had either. After all he had been through in the last couple days riding the little chestnut out into the wide open spaces was a perfect solution. Whenever Brett was troubled he always found solace in horses whether it was riding, training, grooming, caring for or he even found peace sleeping in the stable at Pete's listening to horses.

He rode for several days north and east toward St. Louis, Missouri. He didn't push the chestnut because he knew it would be a long time before he got back to this country that he loved so much. When he reached St. Louis, however, as Mike had told him to do and with great regret he sold Little Red and his saddle. He said good-bye to the little horse and made the livery man promise he would be kind to him. Choked up, he walked to the train depot and bought his ticket to Boston.

The train pulled into Boston Station and Brett got off. He had his bedroll, saddlebags and duffle bag; he needed a plan. There were coachmen hanging around the train station to take passengers to their various destinations. Brett hailed one and had him take him to a hotel. He registered for a night and took his stuff to his room. He had taken off his father's gun and holster before he got on the train and had put it in the duffle with the extra gun, the money and other belongings he had. He now laid down his belongings, locked the door and left the hotel room.

He hailed another cab and asked the driver if he knew Elijah and Gladys Simmons who owned a company called Simmons & Son. The coachman's answer was, "Doesn't everyone?" Brett got in the cab and told him to take him to their home. Upon arrival, Brett got out of the cab and paid the driver.

When the driver asked if he wanted him to stay, he said, "Yes," thinking he would have to go back to the hotel to get his belongings and then come back in the morning to stay. He was trying to act confident with the cab driver as a way to muster up his courage to approach the huge mansion and his grandfather. He stepped out of the cab, straightened his shoulders and pulled himself up as tall as possible and started for the door.

Part way to the door, he stopped and looked around. He had never seen such a place – it looked like some of the Southern mansions he had seen pictures of in some of his history books. The Simmons Estate was huge and beautiful. It was no wonder everyone knew where his grandparents lived. It was a plantation style home, with a huge front porch, painted white with big white pillars in front, a fountain stood in the middle of the yard, statuary and lots of flowers and gardens surrounded the house and the property. It was right in the city but the lawn and surrounding estate was easily several acres. There was a coach house and of course a stable. Several horses were out in the pasture and a horse and buggy was tied in front of the stable. Horses, thought Brett, he was going to like it here. The place was so big and had so much room it should be no problem fitting one more person tucked away somewhere.

Brett walked up to the big double front doors and knocked using the door knocker. A Negro man in a white uniform answered the door. Brett removed his hat and said, "Hello. Is Elijah or Gladys Simmons in?"

"May I say whose calling?"

Brett was very nervous. "They don't know me but my name is Brett Ballin."

"Who is it Cyrus?" came a booming voice from the hallway.

"It's a young man, Sir. Says his name is Brett Ballin."

Elijah Simmons entered the foyer. He was a big man with gray hair, a full gray beard and mustache. He had a frown on his face and it looked like it was frozen in place, like if he did try to smile, his face would crack and it would shatter and fall apart. He was robust, dressed in a tailored black suit and he carried a no-nonsense air about him. For a moment the name "Ballin" didn't register with Simmons. "Who are you?" he asked.

"My mother is your daughter, Lila, Sir. I am your grandson. I came to Boston to go to school," Brett said but when he saw the look of incredulity on the man's face, he was starting to lose his nerve. "My father," he stated meekly, "thought maybe I could room with you just until I get out of school," he trailed off, his voice going softer as he spoke the last words. From the expression on his grandfather's face he was starting to feel that this was hopeless. Brett never looked down or away though. Even when he felt scared or intimidated, he held his gaze with his father's dark deep eyes and he did so now looking at his grandfather.

"Preposterous," bellowed Simmons although even he hesitated and was taken aback by those dark eyes especially on a boy. Perhaps, however, he was somewhat looking into a mirror. "My daughter died when she left here, went to Kansas and married that saddle tramp. If she died then, there is no way she could have had a child. I don't have a grandson. GET OUT."

Even though he was somewhat aware when he first met the man that it might not go so well, Brett was still taken aback. He couldn't believe that someone would act this way toward their own grandson. He had not done anything to this man – he was innocent. He had no back-up plan. What would he do now? He had traveled all the way from Mineral Springs, Kansas, by horseback and train and was literally exhausted and had just been told to "get lost". He turned and walked back to the street.

A bedroom door at the top of the stairs was ajar. Gladys Simmons heard the entire conversation. It wasn't too difficult with her husband's booming voice. She closed the door and tears formed in her eyes. Lila had a son, her grandson. Oh no, what to do!

Brett walked to the cab and got in.

"Where to?" asked the driver.

"Take me to the school," said Brett. He might as well see if he could strike out there also.

"What school?"

It didn't dawn on Brett that there would be more than one school. "The school I would go to. We just moved here so I don't know exactly," he answered.

"How old are you?"

"Fifteen."

"That would probably be Jefferson." And the driver clucked to the horse and drove off.

When they got to the school, the driver pulled up and again asked if Brett wanted him to wait. Brett didn't know what he would have to do so he said no and paid the driver.

He then walked up to the front door of the school, went inside and saw the door with a sign stating "Office" above it. He removed his hat and knocked on the door. Someone called to come in. There was a lady sitting behind a desk with a nameplate stating she was "Alice"; she asked what he wanted. He told her he wanted to enroll in school.

"Where are your parents? They'll have to come in. There are forms to fill out and sign."

Brett felt a cold chill run up his spine. He hadn't thought of parents. He was totally striking out today but he decided he wasn't going down without a fight. "They are very busy. We just moved here and they have to find a place to live and get jobs. Can't I fill out the forms?"

"Well then why don't you come back tomorrow? Do you have your transcript?"

Brett was confused. What's a transcript? "Yes," he said nervously, then, "I mean no, my school was very small. I don't know if they did transcripts."

"Well how do we know what grade to put you in if we don't know what you did in your last school?"

"Can't you give me a test or something?"

A fifteen-year-old asking for a test that was a revelation, she thought. She went to the file cabinet, whipped it open and pulled out the hardest test the school had. The school year had barely started and she was already swamped with work and now this, a kid with no parents, no transcript, didn't know where he belonged. She handed him the test and a pencil. "You can sit over there," she said motioning to a desk in the corner of the room.

Brett started reading the test. Was this a joke? Did they think he was an idiot? The test was so easy. Brett had not been in an official school for three years but he studied and read so much and worked with Amos Carr that he had educated himself. He sat down and went through the test answering question after question right down the line. He was done in about ten minutes. He took it back and handed it to the secretary.

Oh great, thought Alice, as fast as this kid was done with the test, he probably couldn't answer half of the questions. What was she going to do with him? He looked like some kind of "country bumpkin" with the cowboy hat and boots. He better shed those or the other kids were going to have a field day with him.

She took out the answer sheet, Number One was right. She started down the line. He had answered every question correctly and in record time. No student had done that. She saw students sit in that hot seat and struggle with question after question writing and then erasing the answer and redoing it. There was one essay question and Brett could write better than some of their teachers. Where did this mystery child come from?

She handed him the application forms to fill out. He went back over to the desk and started filling in the blanks. It was the usual: name; parents' names: Michael and Lila Ballin; date of birth: July 11, 1850; address: Oh Lord, thought Brett what was he going to do about an address? He left it blank and went on. Last school attended: that was easy "School in Winchester". Maybe he shouldn't say that. What if they contacted Mr. Carr? He put down Rimfire. There was no school in Rimfire. Last grade completed: tenth sounded good. He wrote that down. When he had completed the form, he took it back to her and told her that his parents didn't have an address yet but as soon as he had one he would let her know.

"You will still have to have your parents or at least one of them come in and sign the form."

Brett had an idea. "What if I take it to them to sign and bring it back? I don't think they can get in here when the school is open. Just too much to do when you move to a new place you know."

The secretary was tired of spending so much time with this kid. He probably didn't belong in this school anyway. He was so far ahead of any class they had here. She wasn't even sure what class to put him in. She had so much work to do. Well he was only fifteen and the students in the junior class were sixteen. Yes, that should work; she would put him in as a junior. She didn't want to go any higher than that since he would have to get acclimated to Boston. That would still be a grade ahead of where he should be for his age. She told him that would be all right and Brett left feeling proud of himself for outsmarting the school secretary.

Now he had to work on finding a place to live. He mentally checked off the possibilities. He could find a job and that would help him live but he probably would have to establish himself a little before that could happen and could he work enough hours with school to earn enough money to live on. He had his father's money. No, that was going for college. His father had saved that money for him and it was definitely not going to be used for anything but college. He would pretend he didn't have it except that he had to protect it of course. He had some money left from the money he had gotten after his father's death but not enough to pay for a room for any length of time.

He started walking around the school and looking into ways he could live cheap. There was a park behind the school. He went to the park and sat on a bench thinking about his predicament. Then he saw it. A tool shed in the park. He walked over to it and around it. It would give him shelter. He checked out the condition of the shed. It didn't look like it was being used anymore. Some of the boards were loose but if he tore them off, he would lose some of the shelter. He found a window. When he opened the window, he could just barely squeeze through it.

Inside the shed he found what he had expected – tools. He rearranged some things and left to buy some necessities. He bought an oil lamp and oil; a warmer blanket than the one in his bedroll although he would use that one also. He bought another pair of pants and two shirts. A person needed more shirts than pants. It was possible to wear the same pants for several days as long as he changed the shirts no one would know he had on the same pants. He had some money left so he splurged and bought an apple, some beef jerky, bread and cheese and for his special moment in Boston, two stick candies.

Now that he had his living quarters, such as they were, established he hailed a cab and went back to the hotel. He spent the night in the hotel knowing it would be a long time before he could enjoy such luxury again. He slept in as long as allowed and after checking out, he had the coachman take him back to the school where he walked to the shed.

He was feeling better. The heck with his grandfather – he could make it on his own. After all he was a Wild-West Kid.

On Monday he reported to his class a little early. He introduced himself to the teacher and took a seat. He had checked in at the office and received the books he would need for his courses. He turned in the signed application form to Alice and told her his family still did not have an address but as soon as they did, he would give it to her. She smiled at him. He seemed like a polite very nice boy she thought.

In the classroom no one was there yet so he took out one of the books and started reading. When the students came in, a big boy walked up to his desk and said, "You're sitting in my seat."

"Sorry," said Brett and moved to another seat. Another kid also big came up and said he was sitting in his seat. Brett moved again. When the third boy walked up to him, Brett just got up and moved without having the boy say anything. Brett didn't want trouble. He was finally in school – advanced education and he just wanted to be there. As all this took place, in the back of the room sat a tall boy with sandy brown hair and deep blue eyes watching.

The next few days were uneventful until Friday of the first week Brett was in school. It was lunch break and boys and girls were all outside in the yard. Some of the girls were jumping rope; some of the other kids were throwing balls around; some were still eating lunch; and some were just in groups talking. Brett sat under a tree eating an apple and reading a book. Brett had discovered an orchard nearby and he had picked a few apples off the trees. He didn't consider it stealing. He didn't take more than he could eat. It was like they said about hunting wildlife. As long as it wasn't wasteful . . . well anyway that is how Brett justified it.

The three boys who had taunted him on the first day of school walked up to where he was sitting. "Hey, Bookworm," the leader said. Brett looked up. The boys expected him to cringe and sink into himself. Brett was much smaller than the smallest of these boys. He was only fifteen years old and a year ahead of where he was supposed to be. These boys were brilliant; they were seventeen and eighteen years old and three years behind where they were supposed to be. Brett stared and those coal black eyes set the bullies back a notch. There was no fear in those eyes; bullies like fear. If anything, they got darker and he stared right back into the eyes of all three boys, stared right down to their souls if they had one.

Then one of the boys kicked his book and it went flying. Brett still stared at them. Slowly he reached up, took off his cowboy hat and ran his hand through his hair. Then in a flash he made his play. He brought his feet under him and he lunged at the nearest boy head down, he drove his head straight into the boy's stomach. There was a whoosh of air as the wind got knocked out of the boy and he was knocked aside. He grabbed his stomach and folded. Brett dodged another kid, grabbed up his book on the run and raced for the schoolhouse just as the teacher came out and rang the bell for the students to come back in. Brett raced passed the teacher and into the building. The teacher looked at him in astonishment as he passed. He had never seen a student so eager to come in from lunch before.

Back in a corner of the schoolhouse field a ways from where the boys were and the tree that Brett was sitting under, stood the tall sandy-brown-haired boy watching. Something about this wild kid with the dark hair and black eyes who was able to get around three bullies yet read books constantly intrigued Timothy Osterhaus, something indeed.

Weekends were boring for Brett. He was trying to find some kind of part time job but wherever he looked they either had nothing he could do or wanted him to work fulltime and drop out of school. Brett refused to do that. He had come to this town to get an education and an education he would get. Sometimes shop owners would give him a couple dollars to sweep and mop their floors. He started making rounds to the shop owners who let him do these tasks. Soon he had a route and gained some income that way. He had to be very careful about how he spent his money. He was concerned about winter. It was October and he had heard that the winters in Boston could be brutal. He had nailed burlap bags up on the inside wall of his shed to try and keep out the wind but that probably was not going to be enough in the winter.

He was always grateful when Monday came and he could go back to school. He managed to dodge the bullies quite successfully by sitting on a bench which was located closer to the school door where many times one or two teachers would congregate. He felt like a coward but he also knew there was no way he was going to continue getting around them any other way and he sure didn't stand a chance fighting with them.

One day the tall sandy-haired boy, who had been watching him, walked up to where he was sitting on the bench. He was reading one of his favorite novels, <u>Oliver</u> by Charles Dickens. He guessed he could now relate to Oliver.

"That's a great book," said the big kid.

Brett jumped a little startled that anyone would talk to him. All the kids had ignored him probably thinking him strange with his cowboy boots and Stetson hat. He was used to being alone, however, and it didn't bother him that much. He looked up at the big kid.

"Can I sit there?" said the boy pointing to the bench next to where Brett was sitting.

"Oh . . . oh yeah, fine go ahead," Brett answered and he slid over to make room for the boy.

"My name is Tim, Tim Osterhaus," he smiled as he sat down on the bench and he had a comforting smile and a kind voice. Brett didn't fear this kid as he did most strangers. "Don't worry about the last name, it is kind of cumbersome – just call me Tim."

Brett smiled back, "Brett," said Brett. "Brett Ballin." Just then the teacher rang the bell and they rose from the bench to return to the classroom.

Brett didn't notice Tim for a couple days but Tim was watching Brett. One thing he noticed was that he hardly ever had anything substantial to eat for lunch. He ate an apple or a carrot and sometimes a piece of jerky or a small piece of cheese with a cracker. Tim thought that was so strange for a boy. He couldn't subsist on that – didn't his mother ever make him a sandwich?

Again one day at lunch Brett was sitting on the bench. This time he was reading a medical book he had gotten from the library. When Tim noticed him reading that book he thought, really, a medical book? He walked up and again asked Brett if it was all right to sit with him.

Brett nodded.

"Brett," he said, testing him, "my mother packed me two sandwiches." He had asked his mother if she would pack him an extra sandwich. "I don't know what she was thinking. I can't eat two sandwiches. Here I see all you have is an apple, would you like one of them?"

A sandwich, thought Brett. His stomach did a cartwheel. "Are you sure you don't want it?" asked Brett.

"No, really, I can't eat two sandwiches."

Brett started to eat it and it tasted so good he actually started wolfing it down. When he realized that Tim was looking at him a little odd, he slowed down and took smaller bites. It was ham and cheese and he couldn't remember tasting anything that was this good in a long time.

Tim was watching him and couldn't believe how hungry Brett seemed. He did look awful thin. After that Tim brought him a sandwich every day. Brett one day asked him why he didn't just tell his mother that he only wanted one sandwich but Tim just laughed and said as long as Brett wanted the extra sandwich what did it matter.

—⁓—

To cut the boredom and get the feel for his neighborhood, Brett took long walks. He found some things that were helpful. He supplemented his bread and cheese diet with a few vegetables and fruit from orchards, gardens and vendors' stands when they weren't looking.

When his hair got so long he absolutely couldn't stand it hanging on his neck, he would go to the barber shop and pay for a cut but not until then. He never spent money he didn't have to spend and he never even gave it a thought to spend any of the money his father had given him - that was for college. He still had some of the money from selling his father's horse and the money his father had on him when he died but that was just about gone.

The sandwich he got from Tim and sometimes a cookie or piece of fruit that Tim shared with him was his main meal of the day. He didn't know why Tim kept giving him part of his lunch but it tasted so good and Brett was so hungry it was hard to turn down. Tim always insisted he didn't want any more and Brett gave up arguing with him.

He and Tim started making it a habit to eat lunch together or rather for Brett to partake in part of Tim's lunch. To try and even things out Brett would sometimes give Tim an apple he had pinched from the orchard. They started talking about things they liked to do and books they liked to read. Brett saw that Tim was really a bright kid and it was a real change for him to have a friend and someone he could share things with. He had never really had that. He was really getting to like Tim but was still cautious. It seemed that as soon as Brett started liking someone, something always happened and it was Brett that got hurt. Once or twice in Winchester, he would make a friend and then their parents found out who he was and they quickly stopped that friendship.

Tim told Brett a lot about his family but Brett usually just nodded and listened. Whenever Tim pushed Brett to get information about his past or family,

Brett would evade his questions or just give him a little information and quickly change the subject back to something they were doing in school or some book he had read that he thought Tim would like. Tim thought it strange but he liked Brett and figured he would tell him things when he was ready.

—◦◦◦—

It was in the middle of the day on a Saturday and he was walking back to his "home". Suddenly a carriage pulled up just passed where he was walking, stopped and a man got out. He walked up to Brett and asked if he was Brett Ballin. Brett stared at the man but didn't answer. He was trying to figure out what he should do. He wasn't sure he was quick enough to dodge him and he was far too big to mow over the way he had the bully. He'd probably break his neck driving it into this big lug's gut.

They were by the park and there was no one around. He was thinking he was going to try and run for it when the man saw the boy's skepticism, grabbed him by the arm and said, "No one's going to hurt you. There is someone in the carriage who wants to meet you. Come along."

He walked Brett holding onto his arm just strong enough to keep him in tow and keep him walking. The man opened the carriage door and nearly lifted Brett forcing him into the carriage. He slammed the door behind Brett and leaned on it folding his arms. Brett slunk down in the seat in the corner and saw the form of a woman in the carriage sitting across from him all dressed in black with a black veil covering her face. She looked daunting and Brett swallowed hard.

"You're Brett Ballin?"

Brett nodded slowly. Who was this lady and what was she going to do with him?

"Take off your hat. I want to see your face," and with that she pulled back her veil. She was elderly and had a kind look. Her hair was a very light gray almost white. She was thin and looked very frail but had soft brown eyes. There was something familiar about her as if he should know her.

Brett took off his hat. He shrank back a little.

"No one is going to hurt you," said the old lady. "You need not be afraid. I'm your grandmother and I want to help you."

Brett stared at her in disbelief. "My . . . Grandmother? You want to help me?" he asked.

"Yes," she said. "Winter is coming and they are not nice in Boston. You are going to need shelter. Here." She handed him two keys. "These are for a run-down apartment building my husband owns. One key will get you into the building. The other key is a pass key and will get you into any of the apartments in the building. The building is on Pine Way. Do you know where that is?"

On his walks Brett had been on Pine Way. It actually was almost directly behind the park. "Yes," he said.

"You'll have to be careful and watch for anyone coming around that might work for my husband but they aren't being used anymore. They are in very bad condition but they could give you more shelter than that shed you are living in. There are coal stoves in the apartments and I will get you money to buy coal and maybe some food also."

How did she know where he lived? And then it hit him. He had seen a man hanging around the school. The man was out in front when he came out the door and Brett had had a bad feeling about him. He thought the man had started to follow him but he couldn't figure out why anyone would care what he did. At the time Brett thought it was just a coincidence and he was imagining things but now he realized she had him followed.

"Thank you," said Brett.

"Here," she handed him an envelope. "Here's some money to help you. I'm sorry my husband treated you as he did. There is nothing more I can do. I'll try and get you money on a regular basis."

She reached over and put her hand on his chin and turned his head toward her. He didn't pull away. She leaned forward to look at him. "You do look like my Lila. How did she die?" she said softly.

Brett looked down; it was painful for him to talk about his mother. He still blamed himself for not being able to save her. "She just got sick and died, two years ago," he finally said, "I tried to save her but I couldn't."

"I see. Good Luck to you." And with that she dismissed him. She reached over with her cane and struck the door. The man outside leaning on the door opened it and let him out. Brett glanced back at the old lady and ran for his shed.

The next day he moved everything into the apartment house. He picked an apartment in the back so it would be less conspicuous. There was a back door to the building where he could come and go without being seen from the road. The apartment was small, about the size of the one he had shared with his mother and father in Winchester. There was an old mattress in the bedroom and an old chair in what was the living room. He set up the oil lamp on a wooden crate by the chair; hung his three shirts and extra pair of pants on a hook and stored the duffle bag and saddle bags in the kitchen cupboard. He took his two blankets and laid them on the bed. There was a kitchen so he put the little bit of food he had in the cupboard. He was home. It sure did smell bad though. He wished he could somehow clean it but he didn't know how. The well had gone dry a long time ago. He would have to bring water from the school for him to drink.

He opened the envelope. There was a hundred dollars in it. That certainly would help. He couldn't believe his fortune, a new place to live and loads of money. Things were looking up.

VII

The Osterhaus Family

Peter Osterhaus was a tall boy, about six feet two inches and he was only sixteen years old. He had sandy-brown hair and deep liquid blue eyes that could melt a girl's heart. He was always smiling, always cheerful, athletic and one of the most popular boys in his junior class. He was intelligent and a good student. Everyone liked Peter and he seemed to like everyone. He had no problem getting dates.

Marguerite Carter was just the opposite of Peter in many ways. She was a year younger than Peter being a sophomore. She was average height for a girl but a word to describe her might be "ample". She had medium brown hair, fair complexion and she never got a date unless her brother, Richard, "fixed her up". Marguerite, however, was a confident happy girl. She didn't worry about not getting dates or not being popular with the boys. She wanted to marry and wanted most to be a mother but her confidence in herself showed and she decided that if it didn't happen, then she would find a career. Marguerite took life as it came at her.

Peter's family was wealthy, not real wealthy but lived comfortably. His father was a very successful business man. Peter had a brother, Joseph. Joseph was younger than Peter and not quite as outgoing as Peter but well liked in school. Peter's family had dinner parties in their home; went to plays and concerts; supported the Boston theatre and the symphony orchestra; and were invited to many social events.

The Carter family consisted of six children counting Marguerite. There was David, the oldest, then Richard, Marguerite, Charles, Jacob and Amanda, who was the youngest. They were all very close in age however. George Carter worked in a factory, working long hours and taking all the overtime he could get in order to support his large family. The Carter family went on picnics, played ball in the park, went on buggy rides down by the river and swam in the Atlantic Ocean. In general they found ways to entertain themselves without spending very much money. The Carter children, however, were far from neglected. George and Matilda Carter spent all their free time with their children doing all these activities and more. Every Friday evening was family night and they broke out all the games they knew. They played card games, checkers and cribbage Matilda and Marguerite made popcorn and as a special treat, George always brought home some sarsaparilla. The Carter children did not know that they were not rich.

In school one day, Marguerite had been talking to one of her friends and upon saying good-bye turned her head to look back and wave while still walking and around the corner came Peter Osterhaus. Marguerite ran full blown right into Peter, her head hitting him hard in the chest. Her book and papers flew everywhere. She had been working on a term paper and there were many papers.

Peter took hold of her shoulders surprised by her running into him, "Whoa–a–a. Are you all right?" he said.

Marguerite laughed and apologized profusely. Peter helped her pick up her papers and book. Peter liked her smiling face and her laugh almost instantly. He was so tired of phony girls. They giggled at everything he said, flirted with him and if he became interested in them, they immediately started flirting with some other guy to make him jealous. He knew almost instantly that this girl was different. She was deeper, had kind amber eyes, a genuine smile and was self-assured. He said, "Are you new here?"

"Lived in Boston all my life. Been in Jefferson since my freshman year," she said it as a fact not nasty.

"How come I never noticed you before?"

"Don't know I'm certainly hard to miss. Gotta go, late for class," and before he could say more she was gone.

She really peaked his interest and he started watching for her. He would walk a ways with her between classes and talk to her. She was always nice to him but never seemed interested. He was a little hurt by this and wasn't used to a girl putting him off.

One day he waited for her after class outside the school. There was a small café near the school and the kids would go there for snacks, sarsaparilla, lemonade and the like as well as dinner dates. Peter decided that once and for all he was going to get this girl to pay attention to him or give up. Giving up had never been an option for Peter but how long could he try? When she came out of the school, he asked her if she would like to go to Joe's Café for a sarsaparilla. She said yes but couldn't stay long because she would be expected at home.

They walked to Joe's and Peter got them a booth. They ordered their drinks and Peter started talking before he knew it. "I had to finally drag you somewhere to get your attention," he said. "Are you purposely ignoring me?"

"Well, I just thought you were being nice since you knocked my books and papers out of my hands that day," she teased.

"You ran into me; I didn't knock them out of your hands," he said defending himself.

She started laughing, "I was teasing you."

He laughed then. This girl WAS different! No giggling and calling him silly names like "Petey-y-y". She was honest and straight forward. He did like her. He made his decision.

"Well," he said, "I'd like to ask you to the school dance this weekend. I know it's short notice and if you already have a date I understand."

The shock of what he said hit her full on. One of the most popular boys in the school asked her, Marguerite Carter, to the dance. She wasn't going to show her surprise however. This was a part of her confidence. "Let's see," she teased some more, "I guess I could turn down Joe, Bob and Dave who already asked me. Yes, sure I'll go with you."

She wasn't going to give him the satisfaction of seeing how excited she was. It wasn't until she got home that she started jumping around excitedly and screaming for her mother and sister. When she told them the news, they all started screaming until her father came in and asked them what all the racket was about. Amanda said, "Do you believe it, the most popular boy in school asked Marguerite to the school dance."

They only had a few days to get her a dress and the three women went into action. They went to the general store and bought material, thread, buttons and anything else that was needed to make the dress. While the girls went to school, Matilda worked on making the dress. It was a peach color and was very becoming with Marguerite's medium brown hair and skin tone. Matilda did not make the dress real fancy – no lace or bric-a-brac. It was low-cut in the front but tasteful for Marguerite's ample bosom and she had cut it lower in the back with a simple little braid across the back at the top of the dress leaving her back partially bare. It was simple and plain but very becoming.

Richard Carter heard about all the excitement but instead of being happy for his sister, he was filled with dread. He knew what game these uppity high class boys played with girls who were not popular. They had contests to see how many of them they could take out and then dump. The contest included seeing if they could talk the girl into having sex with them, many of the girls still virgins. They then got back together after these dates and compared notes talking trash, laughing and joking about the poor unfortunate girl. They played on the lonely unpopular girls because they were so hungry for a boy's attentions.

He waited for Peter in the hallway between two of the class rooms. When Peter walked by, he called to him, "Hey, Osterhaus."

Peter turned, saw Richard and walked up to him smiling. He knew who he was although they really did not know each other. Peter thought maybe Richard just wanted to meet him since he was taking out his sister.

When Peter reached Richard, Richard said, "I know what you are up to and you better not hurt my sister. I have an older brother and two younger brothers and if you think for one minute you are going to hurt her, you will be tangling with the four of us. You mess with a Carter, you are messing with all the Carters. Understand?"

Peter was taken aback, and then he understood. He too had heard boys bragging about their victories with girls. He thought it was disgusting. He had never had those intentions not with any girl. "Hey," he said in a quiet tone of voice trying to calm Richard and show that he wasn't the least bit aggressive, "I'm not ready to marry your sister but I wouldn't intentionally hurt her either. Sorry if you got that impression." He held out his hand to shake with Richard.

"Believe me Mister. You mess with my sister and you are going to wish you were dead after my brothers and I get through with you." He turned on his heel and walked away without shaking Peter's hand.

While helping her sister get ready for the dance, Amanda had thought about what she had heard about Peter Osterhaus. Several of the girls had talked about him. They said the most forward thing he did was to kiss them good night. Most of the girls wondered if he had a medical condition or something, he never tried anything with them. His kisses were not even passionate. He dated a lot but hardly took the same girl out twice. Well thought Amanda that was all right. If he was not interested, why should he string a girl along? Better to drop her immediately than to keep dating her if he knew he wasn't interested in her.

At first Amanda worried about that. What if he dated Marguerite twice and then dropped her. When she thought about it, however, she thought well, don't people have that right? She decided that no matter what happened just going to the dance with Peter would raise Marguerite's status in the eyes of the students. Maybe Marguerite would decide that he wasn't right for her. Marguerite was sitting on a stool that was in front of her vanity in her bedroom and Amanda was putting the finishing touches on her hair. When their mother left the room, Amanda said, "Marguerite, enjoy tonight for what it is. A fun date and a fun dance."

Marguerite knew what her sister was telling her. She knew what she was. She placed her hand on Amanda's cheek and said, "Oh Amanda, I'm just in this for a good time. Peter seems like a real nice boy and he's a lot of fun. I don't know why he asked me to this dance but I don't expect it to go any further."

At precisely six o'clock Saturday evening Peter knocked on the door of the Carter home. George Carter answered. Peter said, "Hello Sir, I'm Peter Osterhaus," and held out his hand to shake George's hand.

George took his hand and invited him in. He told him he could sit down. "The girls are still upstairs. You know girls and dances."

"Yes Sir."

"So you are going to be a senior next year huh?"

"Yes Sir."

"Do you have plans after school?"

Peter was used to this the standard father interrogation. "Yes, I want to go to college and then medical school."

"Be a doctor huh? Well, that's great. Oh here they come."

Peter rose and so did George. Marguerite came down the stairs first with Matilda and Amanda following. Peter took in a breath. The peach colored dress was the perfect color for Marguerite. The make-up was not gaudy but very light just highlighting her complexion and the lip gloss was pale just a little darker than Marguerite's natural color. The ensemble was set off with Matilda's mother's pearls around her neck.

George Carter too was astonished. His daughter was absolutely radiant. The ugly duckling had turned into a swan.

"I didn't know the color of your dress so I bought a white corsage. I hope that is all right."

"Perfect," she said. It was a wrist corsage so she held out her hand so he could slide it over her hand and onto her wrist.

At that moment Richard came into the room, walked up to his sister and kissed her on the cheek. "You look stunning, My Dear," he said.

She laughed at her brother. He was always her champion. "Oh" she said, "You probably already know Peter. This is my brother, Richard, Peter."

"We have met," said Richard rather coldly.

Peter knew when he had the advantage and said, "Yes, nice to see you again, Richard," and held out his hand to shake Richard's. Richard had to shake his hand this time or be a jerk. He coldly shook Peter's hand, held it a little longer, squeezing it and his look said, "Don't mess with her". Peter smiled his most endearing smile and nodded his head toward Richard. He was enjoying this.

Peter and Marguerite had a great time at the dance. Peter was fascinated with Marguerite. She laughed in the appropriate places, had a wonderful sense of humor and most of all was honest and straight-forward. By the end of the evening he knew he was going to pursue a relationship further with her. He took her home and walked her up to the porch. She turned and looked at Peter and said, "I had a great time, Peter. Thank you for asking me," then she turned to go into the house.

He took her arm and gently turned her back to face him. He then took hold of both her arms just below her shoulders and gazed into her eyes. She looked back and felt herself suck in her breath a little. He was so handsome and had the softest gentlest blue eyes and such a firm but gentle hold on her and it wasn't just his hands that had the hold on her. She smiled at him.

"Would it be all right Marguerite if I gave you a kiss good-night?"

Marguerite was frozen and she nodded unable to speak.

He leaned into her and started to kiss her but felt her soft lips, her sweet breath, the smell of her perfume blended with the natural smell of her and he wrapped his arms around her and drew her into him and he kissed her very deeply turning his head back and forth to reach all of her mouth. She reciprocated thinking that she had never kissed a boy this deeply yet it all seemed so right.

When they broke apart, Peter stroked her hair on the side of her head, brought his hand around to her face and pushed a strand of hair back from her cheek and said, "I had a wonderful time tonight. I hope you will let me ask you out again."

Marguerite couldn't believe her ears. This handsome beautiful gentle young man asked her permission to take her out again. "I had a wonderful time also, Peter. Of course, I would go out with you again."

He reached forward and gave her a gentle peck on the mouth and said, "Good night."

Marguerite opened the door and stepped inside and Peter turned to leave. She stood inside the door with it still open watching him walk down the walk to his buggy. She could still taste his kisses and that night she lie in her bed still giddy over her first date with this handsome boy. She fell asleep thinking of those deep heavenly blue eyes and how they had looked at her. In the morning, she brought herself back to reality. She really liked Peter but because boys didn't always take to her, she was a bit apprehensive. She didn't want to get hurt and Peter was too good to be true. He was a perfect gentleman all night and treated her like she was special. She thought she might be falling in love on her first date with him and although she knew she shouldn't, part of her couldn't help it. He had asked if he could ask her out again and she sure hoped he would – that it wasn't just a thing to say when he dropped her at her door.

That was not the case, however, Peter did ask her out again and again. He and Marguerite dated all through the summer. When they went back to school, Peter was in his senior year and continued dating Marguerite all school year and through the summer after Peter graduated. Richard and his brothers did not have to catch Peter in a dark alley and beat him. He and Richard buried the hatchet and became really good friends. Peter forgave Richard and since they both loved the same girl, Peter understood where Richard was coming from.

The summer after Peter graduated flew by and then it was getting close to the time for Peter to go away to college. The couple liked to drive to the park and there was a special park bench they chose for their own by a small lake with lots of ducks and geese. Peter brought Marguerite stale bread from his house since bread didn't go stale at the Carter home with the large family they had. The couple would tear up pieces of bread and throw it to the ducks and geese and laugh as they raced around scarfing up the bread.

This was their last time together before Peter would leave for college. Marguerite was just going into her senior year in high school. Peter asked Marguerite to marry him. She said, "No".

He was hurt and said, "Why won't you marry me?"

"My Love, how many girls do you know in the senior class that are married? I want to finish high school. I think there is something else you should think about also."

"What's that?"

"Well, you are going away to college. We are going to be separated. I think you should think about dating other girls."

Peter was horrified. "You're breaking up with me?"

"I just think you should have that option."

"Do you want to date other guys?"

"Lord no. And I'm not saying we shouldn't see each other. When you come home for visits, we can date. It's just that you are going to be far from home and if you find someone you might like better . . ." her voice started to crack.

"He-e-e-y," he said softly and took hold of her chin and turned it to his face. He saw the tear run down her cheek and he reached up and wiped it away with his thumb. "I did that, remember? Through the first three years of high school. Then I found this really special lady with feelings and depth and I fell in love. When you love someone, you don't want to even go out with anyone else no matter how far away you are. I won't hold you back though. If you find someone, all I ask is that you tell me right away. Don't keep me on hold."

"That's not going to happen, Peter. There will never be anyone else. If we don't make it, I'll figure out a career and stay single."

"Sealed with a kiss," he said and he took her into his arms and kissed her boldly and deeply running his hands through her hair and pulling her head into his so that she would feel his kiss all the way down to the bottom of her toes and she kissed him back the same way. They held each other close and sat on the bench until they absolutely had to return to their homes.

The couple was married when Peter graduated from college. Peter's parents offered to pay for the entire wedding since they loved to put on parties and had the room at their home for a lot of guests. Prior to the wedding the Osterhaus family and the Carter family met and went out to dinner at a fine restaurant. Then Matilda and George invited the Osterhauses over for dinner and to meet the rest of the Carter family. The two families liked each other instantly and they became great friends and had many gatherings with both families.

After Marguerite graduated from high school, she took a job as a retail clerk in a ladies' dress shop and saved all her money for their future even working after the couple married and while Peter was in medical school.

A few months before Peter was to graduate from medical school, Marguerite had an announcement. She told her husband first and then the couple told the two families. The first Carter-Osterhaus grandchild would be born in approximately six months. Enter Timothy Osterhaus.

VIII

Tim & Brett

When **October came** in so did rain and wind and Brett knew November was going to be even colder and draftier in the old tenement house. He went through the other apartments looking for anything that he could use. He found a hammer, nails and some old blankets and a canvas tarp. He dragged the mattress into the front room and nailed the tarp over the entrance to the bedroom so he was only in the living room-kitchen area. He stuffed pieces of old blanket in the holes around the window. He was trying to have minimal space for the coal stove to heat using less coal.

In the next few weeks his grandmother caught him twice and each time gave him a hundred dollars. He spent a lot of it on coal for the stove and of course food. Sometimes after his grandmother gave him money, he would splurge and eat out in a restaurant. That was a real treat. Because bread and butter were unlimited, he would take some and put it under his shirt for later.

He was getting more and more familiar with his grandmother and answered questions about Lila but said nothing about Mike and she never asked about his father. It was like the subject was taboo. He never volunteered anything however about any other aspect of his life in Winchester.

He was so bored when he wasn't in school and so lonely that he started watching for the carriage. One Saturday she stopped him and brought him into the carriage. After they had talked, she gave him the envelope and they were preparing to say good-bye, she asked if she could hug him. By now Brett had relaxed with her and he really liked her. He let her hug him and she kissed him on the cheek. He turned his head, smiled at her and kissed her on her cheek. This seemed to please her very much. She gave him another hug and patted his back, "Be safe and warm." That was the last he saw of his grandmother for a very long time.

On a Friday after school, Brett took off like he always did around the side of the building and ran full bore into the three bullies. This time they got him good. Tim had ridden the chestnut mare to school that day because his father had something to do and was not able to come by the school and get him. Tim was late getting out of class talking to one of the teachers. He mounted the horse and turned her toward home when he saw the bullies attack Brett. They caught him totally unawares, had him on the ground and were in the process of punching and kicking him.

Tim charged up on the mare and leaped right on top of two of them. Tim was no small boy and very athletic. He threw them off Brett and pulled him to his feet. When a third boy came at Tim, he punched him a good one in the face. Tim grabbed the reins and jumped up on the mare. Then he grabbed Brett's arm and Brett swung up behind him.

Tim yelled, "Ha-a-a" at the horse, kicked her in the sides and they charged out of there. They ran the mare for about a mile before stopping. Tim turned and looked at Brett's face. It was a mess. He had an eye that was rapidly swelling shut, his nose was bleeding and could be broken; blood had splattered all over his shirt and there was a scrape that ran along his cheek. He was holding his side and gasping for breath.

"Hold on," said Tim and he started the horse in a canter.

"Where are we going?" asked Brett.

"My house. My dad is a doctor and you need one. That nose might be broken and you might have broken ribs."

"I don't need any doctor and I want to go home. Just stop and let me off."

"Brett," he said, "If your nose is broken, you need to have it fixed. You don't want to go through life with a crooked nose do you? Broken ribs can puncture a lung. Don't be an idiot. You read more medical books than most doctors. You know these things."

How did Tim know that he read medical books? Oh, yeah, he saw him at lunch hour reading on the bench. He no way wanted to go to anyone's house. "Tim, PLEASE, just drop me off – here is fine. I'll get home."

"Uh huh, my Dad will fix you up. Don't worry, he won't charge you and he's a really nice guy."

Brett was quiet but he was scared. He didn't want to be around strangers especially adults. He didn't trust them. Well-meaning strangers brought in Children's Services. That meant an orphanage, in other words, prison. They arrived at the house and Tim brought Brett into the living room. He was dripping blood on the floor from his nose and Tim quickly got a towel and gave it to Brett so he could hold it on his nose.

"Where have you been? You're late," said his father entering the room and then he saw Brett.

"Oh my goodness, here, come into my office."

Peter put his hand on Brett's shoulder and guided him into his office which he kept in his home. Even though Peter had an office in downtown Boston, he also kept an office at his house for emergencies. The whole neighborhood knew he was a doctor so let a kid get a cut and they rushed him over to the Osterhaus house. Peter never minded helping people. He felt it was a neighborly thing to do and he loved his occupation.

"Dad, this is my friend, Brett. He just moved here."

Peter had a leather reclining chair that most doctors had. It laid the patient down so the doctor could work on them but they weren't flat. It was curved and the patient was in a half sitting position. The same kind of chair Dr. Mowery had in Winchester. He led Brett into the office and put him in the chair. He could see that Brett was very uncomfortable and scared.

Scared wasn't the half of it, Brett was petrified. He sunk into the cool dark chair and tried to keep himself from shaking. He was still holding the towel up to his nose. Would these people turn him in? Would they make him go to a hospital? He had to get out of here. How serious were his injuries? He was in a lot of pain especially in his face but his side hurt like it was on fire where the boys had kicked him. He could breathe though. He had read where if a person's ribs were broken, it was hard to breathe.

"Tell your mother to bring me some warm water and towels will you Tim and a piece of ice in a towel? We'll clean him up and see what we have here." To Brett he said, "Take it easy Son. I'll try to not hurt you as much as possible but some of this is going to hurt. It can't be helped."

Tim brought in the water and towels and Marguerite came to the door to see what was going on. She was carrying the piece of ice wrapped in a towel.

"Heavens," she said when she saw Brett's bloody shirt, the bloody towel and his swollen face. "What did you boys get into?"

"Oh some guy called Brett out. You should see what happened to him." He didn't want to say what his part was. He also didn't want to tell his parents about the bullies. That just caused more problems when the parents got involved. And it usually made matters worse for the kid being bullied.

Peter was working on Brett. He took the bloody towel off his face he had been holding up to his nose. He took the ice-towel from Marguerite and held it up to Brett's eye and placed Brett's hand on it. He took a clean towel, dipped it in the warm water and gently started wiping his face especially around his nose. The boy was flinching every time Peter touched anywhere near his nose.

"I'm sorry Brett. I know it hurts but I have to get this cleaned up so I can see how much damage is done."

After he had it all cleaned up, he said, "This is going to hurt but I have to see if your nose is broken." He placed his index finger and thumb on each side of Brett's nose and as gently as possible worked it back and forth a little. Brett jumped. "I know that hurts and I'm sorry. I don't think it is broken. Let's just leave it alone."

Marguerite came back with more ice and Peter held it on Brett's nose to stop the bleeding, reduce the swelling and relieve the pain. While Peter was trying to clean up his face and help him with the ice packs, he bumped him in the side. Brett jumped and groaned.

Peter caught that and asked, "Do you have pain in your side?"

Brett nodded.

Peter unbuttoned his shirt and saw he was bruised all along one side of his ribs. He felt all along his ribs and Brett winced with the pain of his touch. Then he felt all along his stomach and abdomen.

"Where does it hurt? Just along your ribs? Do you have any pain here or here?" Peter asked as he pressed on his stomach and the rest of his abdomen. Brett shook his head no just the ribs. Peter helped him take off the bloody shirt. He put his stethoscope over his chest and told Brett to take a deep breath. He did this several times. He then told Brett to lean forward and he did the same thing along his back. Peter then took his temperature and his pulse. His pulse was racing but Peter thought that was because he was scared. He seemed fine besides the superficial injuries.

"Well, I don't think you have any broken ribs. I think they are just bruised. Your lungs seem clear and I don't feel anything. You will be sore for a few days. Tim, why don't you get him one of your shirts? It will be too big but he can't put this one back on. Also, get a glass of water from the kitchen."

When Tim brought the shirt and water, Peter helped Brett carefully put on Tim's shirt and rolled up the sleeves. Then he went to his medicine cabinet and took out some pills. He shook one out and handed it to Brett, "Here, take this. It will help with the pain. I'll give you some to take home." He wrote on the envelope how often to take the pills, put some in the envelope and handed it to Brett. Then Peter leaned back against his desk and glared in his fatherly way at the two boys.

"All right Boys. I wasn't born yesterday, all this damage did not come from a fight with one boy. What's going on?"

The two boys looked at each other. "Really Dad," Tim started.

"Tim, you've never lied to me before. Are you going to start now?"

Tim looked at the floor, "Three bullies," said Tim and Brett glared at him. "They've been picking on Brett since he came to school. They're real mean kids. They pick on whoever they think they can. They love to pick on the new kids. Geez Dad, they are seventeen and eighteen years old, Brett didn't stand a chance."

"Should we be going to the school principal about this?"

"No Pa. You can't do that. It just makes it worse. We'll work it out."

Brett thought what is he talking about? *We'll* work it out. They weren't after Tim, they were after Brett. He was grateful that Tim had rescued him but it wasn't Tim's problem. It was Brett's, but he didn't say anything.

Marguerite came in, "How's it going in here? I have supper ready."

"Come on boys," said Peter, "let's eat."

"Oh thanks, but I have to go home," said Brett. He jumped up a little fast and groaned. He hurt all over.

"Brett," said Tim, "it's dark out and you're three miles from the school. Don't you live somewhere around the school."

"Well it's actually closer than the school from here," he lied. "It's all right I can walk."

"Is there some reason you can't stay for supper?" asked Peter, "and then I can take you home."

How was anyone going to take him home? He couldn't let them see how he lived. But whatever was for dinner, it sure smelled good. He couldn't remember the last good meal he had had besides the sandwiches that Tim gave him for lunch. How was he going to get out of this one?

Tim said, "You could spend the night and Dad could take us both to school in the morning."

"Good idea," said Peter. He really didn't want to hitch up a horse and go out this late.

That was a solution thought Brett and he was so hungry and he could smell all the good food smells. "All right," he said reluctantly.

There was beef stew and fresh bread and butter with milk to drink for the boys and coffee for the adults.

"You're in luck," said Marguerite, "we don't usually have dessert but I made an apple cake."

The conversation turned to Brett, and Peter asked who he lived with.

Good question thought Brett. He said, "Oh my aunt but she works a lot. She's working tonight."

"Oh," said Marguerite, "what does she do?"

Brett couldn't think of anything so he said, "She's an accountant." Where did that come from?

"She's an accountant and she works at night?" asked Peter.

How stupid was he? "Well, she has a part time job also. She works a couple nights for extra money—a bookkeeping job."

"Where are you from?" asked Marguerite.

What's with all the questions? Maybe it wasn't worth staying for dinner. "Oh a small town in Kansas, Winchester." Try to keep it as truthful as possible.

"And your parents? Are they still in Winchester?"

PLEASE, stop with the questions. What should he answer? Saying they were still in Winchester might be a good idea but it might be too much of a stretch. "No, they died. Killed in a buggy accident," another lie.

"Oh I'm sorry," said Marguerite. She sensed he was getting upset and she backed off. She really was just trying to make conversation and didn't mean to make him feel uncomfortable but it was probably painful for him to talk about his parents.

The food was sure great. Maybe it was worth it after all. He kept telling himself to stop eating so fast – he was ravished. They offered him a second bowl of stew and he took them up on their offer. After emptying the second bowl, he sopped up all the gravy in the bowl with a piece of bread as his dad had always done. His bowl was so clean it probably didn't need to be washed. Then he had two helpings of apple cake. He couldn't believe that anything could taste so good. The two adults looked at each other. What was with this kid? He acted like he hadn't eaten in weeks. Didn't his aunt cook for him?

After dinner they went into the sitting room and Tim and Brett played checkers. When it was time for bed, Tim took Brett to his room. He had bunk beds, Peter's idea in case Tim wanted a friend to sleep over. Brett was the first friend Tim had invited overnight. He told Brett he could have the top bunk. Brett crawled into the warm bed and snuggled down into the mattress pulling the clean sheet and blanket over him. Everything was so clean and smelled so good. He sure could get used to this. He snapped himself out of it. No way, Ballin, he thought you have to go back to that tenement house.

Peter and Marguerite often talked about whatever events took place during the day at night in bed. This was a private time when they could discuss things between themselves without Tim being around.

After each had washed and changed into bed clothes and crawled into bed, Peter started, "There's something with that boy. I can't put my finger on it but there is something a little scary."

"Yes, I know what you mean. Did you get the feeling that he was doing an awful lot of lying at supper? And the way he ate. When was the last time he has eaten? His aunt must work so much, she doesn't cook?"

"Yes, not sure I like Tim hanging around him. Getting into fights. Tim has never gotten into fights before."

"Yes Dear, but Tim has never really had a close friend before. He brings kids home and we never see them again."

"Well can't he pick a friend that is not quite so mysterious?"

"Peter, we can't pick his friends for him. He needs to make some of his own decisions."

"So are you thinking we should just let this go for a while?"

"Yes, I don't think there is any danger, he's just a boy and let's see how it shakes out."

All through the month of October Tim and Brett became closer and closer. Tim asked Brett to his house on several occasions. Brett didn't take him up on it every time although he really liked Tim and his family. He would have liked to visit more, he had never had a friend like Tim and then there was Marguerite's great cooking; but he felt they would think it strange if he didn't reciprocate and ask Tim to his house and that wasn't going to happen. When he wanted to get out of going to Tim's house, he used excuses like his aunt needed him to do something or he had other plans. Every excuse he could think of whether it made sense or not.

One warm and sunny Saturday at the end of October, Brett was sitting in the park reading a book. He heard hoof beats and when he looked up Tim was riding the mare and coming at him with a bat in his hand. What was this about? Tim got off his horse and took a ball out of his saddlebags. Tim was a very athletic boy.

"Want to play ball?"

Brett didn't know the first thing about ball. "No," he answered.

"Why not?"

"Because I would beat you," said Brett.

"Huh. Just try," and he threw the ball at Brett and Brett fumbled the ball three times in the air before he finally caught it.

Tim was laughing but he could see that Brett knew nothing about playing ball. So Tim started teaching him. Not embarrassing him but showing him some things and pretending like "let me show you a better way" instead of "I know you don't know anything," and embarrassing him.

All of a sudden out of the one side of the park came the three bullies and they were charging at them. They got to Tim first hitting him right in the face. Brett grabbed the bat and used an end to punch one of the boys in the stomach. Then he swung the bat as another boy went on the attack and caught him square in the middle of his body, bending him in two. Meanwhile Tim is whaling on the third boy. The two boys ran for Tim's horse and jumped on. One of the boys ran after them and grabbed Brett's leg. Brett cracked down on his hand with the bat. He screamed and grabbed his hand. The boys raced off.

Tim dropped Brett near his house after Brett got all excited about not asking Tim to come to his house. He said, "My aunt will kill me if I bring someone home on cleaning day," he weakly explained. "The house is a mess and she hadn't finished cleaning it when I left. Just let me off here and I can walk."

After Tim got to his house, he realized he had to do something about his torn shirt. He ran in the house and raced upstairs to his bedroom before anyone saw him. He quickly got the ripped shirt off and hid it. Then he looked in the mirror. Oh no, he had a black eye. What was he going to do? His parents were going to kill him. He went into his father and mother's bedroom and found some of his mother's make-up. He smeared it on the eye. It was tender–ouch! He looked in the mirror–not bad. He went back to his room and got his baseball hat and put that on pulling it down. He didn't think that would fly but he was going to try. He came downstairs just as his mother was calling them to dinner.

After Marguerite brought out all the food and they sat down to eat, Peter looked over at his son. He "smelled a rat" immediately the way his son was acting.

"Why do you have your hat on in the house?"

"Oh forgot," said Tim and removed his hat but kept his head down.

Peter looked at him oddly again, "What did you do today, Tim?" Peter was no dummy.

"Nothing much."

"I noticed the mare looked a little sweaty. Did you ride her?"

"Yeah."

"You didn't rub her down. That's no way to take care of a horse. You know better."

"Oh sorry. I'll do it right after we eat." It would be good to get back outside before anyone noticed the eye. He was bent over his plate and kept his head down.

Peter stood up and walked over to where Tim was sitting. He picked up a napkin and dipped it in a glass of water. He took hold of Tim's chin and raised his head up. He took the wet napkin and started scrubbing the eye and not very gently.

Tim was squirming from the pain. Finally, he said, "Ouch! Dad, take it easy. That hurts!"

Marguerite looked up curiously and then in astonishment. As Peter scrubbed the eye, the make-up was coming off and the boy had a real shiner.

"You've been with that boy again haven't you? And in another fight? Tim, you have never been in a fight in your life and now that makes two within a couple weeks. I'm not sure you should be running with that boy. I think he is trouble."

"Oh Pa, it's not his fault. It's the same three bullies and they keep picking on him. We got them good this time though. I don't think there will be any more trouble."

"That kid is wild. And he's going to get you in big trouble. Tim, it's not worth it. Find another friend."

"He's a nice kid, Dad, and I really like him. You know I haven't had many friends. Please don't make me give up his friendship. He needs a friend. You don't know how it is out there Dad. If a kid is smart and tries to do the right thing, he is ostracized by all the other kids. Why do you think I haven't had many friends? Kids don't like smart kids that get good grades. That's why they are picking on Brett. He's so smart Dad. He aced the entrance test and kids struggle with it. He's only fifteen and he's in my grade. You should see the books he reads. Most adults wouldn't understand them. Please let me work it out with him. He'll settle down once he learns he can trust us."

"He's a stray cat," said Marguerite.

"A what?" said Peter.

"A stray cat," repeated Marguerite. "He wants companionship and love but he doesn't trust anyone. As soon as he starts to like someone, something goes wrong and he gets all scared and runs away. He tries to act tough and arches his back and hisses but he is actually scared to death."

"Well stray cats bite," said Peter.

"Only when cornered," said Marguerite matter of factly, taking another mouthful of potatoes and rolling her eyes at her husband.

The subject was dropped. Peter knew when he was losing. He decided he would be careful and watch what was going on but Tim was right. He had few friends and Peter could see he really liked this boy.

The bullies gave up on Brett after that. They didn't like the odds-two against three.

IX

The Holidays

In November Tim asked Brett his plans for Thanksgiving. He told Brett that since it was just him and his aunt why not bring her to their house for Thanksgiving dinner. He said they always had plenty to eat. He told Brett about his mother's family, the Carters. Everyone brought lots of food and they had a great time. Tim saw the strange look Brett gave him, almost fearful when he talked about family and gatherings. Brett hemmed and hawed around and finally said he thought his aunt had other plans.

A week after Thanksgiving Tim told Brett his parents had purchased tickets for a play on Saturday and told him he could invite Brett. Peter would pick the boys up on Friday after school. They could go to the play on Saturday and Peter would take them to school on Monday morning. It sounded exciting to Brett; he had never been to a play. Besides the apartment was so cold now, he was really grateful to get out of it even for a few days. He hadn't made contact with his grandmother in weeks and had very little money to spend. He still went from store to store sweeping and mopping and with that money he bought food and occasionally coal for the stove in the apartment. He never had enough money and now that there wasn't any more fruit in the orchards due to winter coming on and the vendors had their produce inside their stores, it was harder for him to steal fruit and vegetables. The last thing he wanted to do was get caught and get a record so he didn't even try to take anything without paying for it.

Brett used the last of his grandmother's money to buy a new shirt, get a haircut and go to the bathhouse. He even bought a string tie. He wanted to look his best for the Osterhauses when he went to the play.

Peter picked up the boys at school on Friday. Brett didn't want to leave the duffle bag in the apartment with the money and the guns in it so he put his clothes in there and used it as his suitcase. They went back to the house, had a good supper and then Peter asked Brett if he knew how to play chess. "No," he said, "just checkers and poker." Peter taught Brett how to play and he really liked the game. It was a thinking man's game. He caught on fast and Peter could see he was going to be a worthy opponent.

On Saturday morning, the boys went for a ride on the horses. Brett loved that. It had been so long since he had gone riding. They took the matched pair of bay geldings. The horses were all trained to pull the buggy, the pair of geldings was used as a team to pull the two-seater carriage and they were all broke to ride. Tim and Brett rode out into the country and even though Peter forbid Tim to race his horses because it was too dangerous, the boys did it anyway and had a great time.

Brett asked Tim what the horses' names were. "They don't have names, Brett. They are just transportation."

Brett said disappointedly, "They are more than just transportation Tim. Horses have personalities. They are living creatures not just like a wagon."

When they got home and took care of the horses, Marguerite told them they should start getting ready to go to the play. Brett put on his new shirt, pants and tie and looked quite handsome. Peter and Marguerite complimented him on how nice he looked and he puffed up with pride.

Brett loved the play and he was hooked. At one point he got so engrossed that he yelled, "Look out behind you," when the villain was about to attack the hero.

Tim touched his arm and said, "SHHH It's not real. They are acting." Brett was embarrassed. Peter looked at Marguerite and covered his mouth to hide his snicker. He was glad to see Brett enjoying himself. Peter was starting to like the kid despite his mysterious ways.

After the play, Peter took the family to the Hungry Seagull, a restaurant on the waterfront. It was a beautiful place and they had seats by windows that overlooked the ocean and they could see the clipper ships and the huge ocean liners docked at the marina. Brett was fascinated and stared out at the ocean and the ships. He had never eaten in such a place. He didn't even know how to order so he ordered what Tim ordered, a grilled salmon with roasted potatoes.

He watched what Tim did so he made the correct decisions as to what utensil to use and the proper glassware. He made himself eat slowly and relish the food. He figured it would be a long time before he ever ate like this again.

By the time they got back to the Osterhaus home, it was time for bed. Brett was looking forward to crawling into the warm, clean smelling bed. He climbed the ladder to the upper bunk and settled in. Brett was thinking about how wonderful the Osterhauses were to include him in their weekend plans. He was starting to drift off to sleep when he got hit full blown in the face with a pillow. He took his pillow out from under his head and leaning over the bunk, he smacked Tim with it. Tim came up after him and he dove down on top of Tim. They were rolling around on the floor wrestling, when Peter came in. "What is going on?"

"Oh sorry," they said simultaneously and they both leaped back into their beds. Peter went back to bed smiling. "Our son has really found a friend he likes," he said.

Marguerite smiled. "I don't think you are going to break them up without hurting Tim."

"Let's hope we are not making a mistake letting it go this far."

"Peter, our boy is pretty smart. Don't you think we should let him make his own decisions? Sometimes we are overprotective."

"I suppose," but Peter was still worried. He thought Marguerite was getting too attached to Brett also. He knew what she was thinking. Let's keep him. It's one thing to tame a feral cat with a saucer of milk but quite another to get a child who has been practically on his own all his life to settle down and not have major problems. He had seen it at the orphanage with some of the older kids they had taken in. Some of them ended up in big trouble with the law. Still he had to admit there was something redeemable about this boy. He certainly was an intelligent kid. When he stayed over, Peter had heard him explain some school work to Tim and he had to admit some of it baffled him.

—⁂—

Marguerite had always wanted another child. About a year after Tim was born, she got pregnant again. It ended in a miscarriage and Marguerite was devastated. Then when Tim was four years old, she got pregnant again. This time they were convinced it was going to work. They taught Tim about babies; they told him the baby was in mother's tummy – didn't do the stork thing. Marguerite carried the baby full term but when he was born, Peter was worried. He just didn't seem real healthy. Peter didn't like the sound of his heart. It wasn't a strong heart and his little body seemed so frail and he didn't gain weight like he should. When Riley Timothy Osterhaus was four months old, he died.

The whole family was devastated but Peter was especially worried about Marguerite. She fell into deep depression and no matter what he did, Peter did not seem to be able to pull her out of it. He didn't kid himself, he thought the only thing that brought her back was Timothy. Caring for the child and realizing that she still had a little boy snapped her back to reality. Peter decided at that moment that he would never let her get pregnant again. They would have to be happy with Tim.

It wasn't hard to do. After all he was a doctor. He figured out Marguerite's menstrual cycle and approximately fifteen days later he controlled his urges for a few days. It was hard because he and Marguerite deeply loved each other and had a very active and satisfying intimate life in bed. Sometimes Peter would have to go for a walk. He would grab his pipe and go out the door trying to think of anything but his wife in bed. When they went to bed, he would roll over on his side and face away from her. At first she felt rejection but after a while she finally realized what her husband was doing was an act of love. After all she could count too.

One night when he turned toward the wall and faced away from her, she started massaging his back. She started around his neck went up and down his spine, rubbing his neck, his shoulders, spine and working her way all the way to his buttocks. When she felt him relax, she wrapped her arm around him and pulled her body against his and whispered in his ear how much she loved him. Peter smiled. He never regretted marrying one of the most unpopular girls in his school.

—w—

On Sunday, the family went to church. Not wishing to push his beliefs onto anyone else, Peter told Brett that he did not have to go if he didn't want to.

Brett said that was all right, he would go. Brett had never been to church before. He followed Tim and did whatever Tim did. He actually found it peaceful and people were kind. He liked singing the hymns, didn't understand the scripture but thought the minister had some good points to his sermon and it seemed to make sense when he thought about it.

After church, they returned home and he asked Marguerite if he could help her prepare the Sunday dinner. She was very surprised. Her men never offered to help her and she said, "Sure". He liked working in the kitchen and she taught him a lot about how to cook in that one session. She really enjoyed his company and they laughed and had a good time preparing the meal. Brett felt that they had been so good to him, he wanted to do something to help with some of the work and he found that he liked working with Marguerite preparing food.

Christmas was only two weeks away. To Brett Christmas was just another day. Amos Carr had done special things in the classroom back in Winchester for the kids at Christmas. They put up a tree and a nativity. Brett really never took part. His mother bought him some presents usually something very practical mostly clothes. Sometimes she would buy him a book because she knew he liked them but they were usually children's books and way too young for Brett. She never quite knew what he was about. He knew she loved him but it seemed like Mike was her real focal point.

He didn't really know the Christmas story. He knew it was about a kid born in a barn and he was very special; he had his own star. Brett wondered if the kid enjoyed living in the barn as much as Brett did. When he lived in the livery after his mother died, he would lie in his bunk listening to all the horse sounds, the munching of hay, the occasional stamping of a hoof and snorting sometimes a low nicker. It lulled him to sleep. It sure beat being awakened by gun shots which always happened when they lived in the apartment above the bar. He wondered if living in the barn made him special like the kid at Christmas. He wasn't born there though he was born in the saloon. He supposed that probably negated any specialness.

When Tim asked him several times to come for Christmas, he always had an excuse. His aunt was going to have some time off and they were making some plans together. Tim said to bring his aunt. The family would like to meet her, but Brett would get all nervous and would make up some flimsy story. When Tim persisted and finally said if he couldn't do Christmas how about

New Year's, Brett relented and said he'd come for New Year's. Tim said it was just going to be the family and they were planning on having a nice dinner and then play some games. There would be popcorn by the fire and drinks.

Brett was excited that they had invited him. Again he would be in a warm cozy place and get some real food. Most of all though he loved the happiness and expression of companionship that this family had and how they treated each other and included him.

On the last day of class before Christmas break, Tim asked Brett to walk to the buggy with him. Both Peter and Marguerite were in the buggy. Tim took a wrapped package out of the buggy and handed it to Brett. He had a big smile on his face and when Brett looked up he saw them all smiling at him.

"What's this?" he said.

"Just a little something from the family."

"But I didn't know . . ."

"Don't be silly. It's not that much. Gifts are to show you care not to expect something in return."

Brett stood there stunned, looking down at the gift as if he wasn't sure what to do with it. This was so unexpected.

"Open it," said Tim.

He gingerly unwrapped the package and opened the box. There was a hand-knitted muffler and several cut-out sugar cookies. Brett just stared at the gift. He took out the muffler and wrapped it around his neck. "Did you make this for me?" he asked Marguerite. He had seen her knitting when they were playing chess and checkers at different times in the sitting room so he knew she liked to knit.

"Do you like it?"

"It's beautiful," he said running his hand down the scarf. It had hues of brown, gold and orange intertwined in a beautiful pattern.

"You act like your mother never made you anything," Tim said and immediately regretted it when he saw the look on Brett's face. In his mind Tim couldn't imagine a mother never having made her child anything but it was obvious by Brett's reaction that his mother never had.

"There are enough cookies there for your aunt, too," said Marguerite.

Brett was staring at the end of the muffler that was hanging down after he had wrapped it around his neck. "It's so beautiful," he mumbled picking up the end and staring at it, "Thank you."

"Wish you were coming for Christmas Buddy but hope you have a good one."

"Merry Christmas to all of you also," said Brett and he closed the box still wearing the muffler, tucked the cookie box under his arm and turned and walked away. He was getting choked up, his eyes moist and he didn't want to show his weakness. He was having a real hard time trying to figure out this family and why they treated him like they did. Kindness was something he hadn't yet gotten used to.

On New Year's Eve Brett met Tim at the park. Brett said he would just meet him there. They drove home in the buggy and Brett volunteered to take care of the horse. He loved caring for horses and really missed it. When Tim came into the house, his parents asked where Brett was. "Oh, he's out there communing with the horses," he said.

They all laughed. They already knew how much Brett loved horses and knew how much he missed not having one. When Brett came in, stamping the snow off his feet and taking off his mittens and jacket, Peter asked him what the horses had to say.

"They said they all wanted to move out West with me," said Brett smiling.

Everyone laughed. It was a good sound. They hailed in the New Year with drinks, kisses and hugs. Then all went to bed and slept in in the morning. Brett slept so sound he never heard anyone get up. He was warm and cozy and exhausted. It was hard to sleep in the cold apartment. He had no more money for coal and what little he made at the stores, he used for food.

Everyone was up and at the breakfast table when he got up and came downstairs. Whenever he was at Tim's house, he ate like he hadn't eaten in months. Truth was he hadn't eaten like this since the last time he was there. Marguerite could feel how thin he was when she gave him a hug when she greeted him each time he came to their house and thought he was even losing weight. He seemed thinner every time he came. She questioned in her mind how his aunt was taking care of him. She also knew he ate like a teen-age boy when he was there so she had prepared pancakes, eggs and ham, milk and orange juice and he ate every bite of it.

He stayed through New Year's Day and the next day Tim took him home. It was hard to go home. Tim took him back in the buggy and when they got to the park, Brett thanked him and said he could walk from there. Tim watched his friend walk away and tried to figure out where he lived. Brett was so mysterious. What was up with this kid who would be happy and fun for a time and then just as sudden crawl back into his shell?

X

Pneumonia!

When school started again after the Christmas break a few days after New Year's Day, Brett was glad. He had been so bored during Christmas break. The temperature in Boston was down to around zero degrees and his apartment was absolutely freezing. He went to the library after school, did his homework and then read until it closed to get some heat. He sometimes went without eating in favor of buying coal for the small coal stove in the apartment with his mop money; but the coal didn't last very long and neither did his mop money. He hadn't heard anything from his grandmother in weeks.

About two weeks into the start of school after the holiday break, Brett caught a cold. It started as a typical cold – runny nose, sneezing, coughing and sore throat. He was trying to ride it out but the cold apartment was not helping. The cold was settling in his chest and it was getting hard to breathe. His stomach ached from all the coughing.

At school he was in Mr. Nelson's class and couldn't stop coughing. Mr. Nelson yelled at him, "Ballin, if you can't stop coughing, leave the classroom. We all don't want your cold."

Brett got up, left the classroom and went home; home where the cold was so cold there was frost on the apartment walls. Tim watched him leave; he was worried about him. After Brett reached the apartment, he kept his winter coat and mittens on and Marguerite's muffler wrapped around his neck and mouth. Then he bundled up in his two blankets and did his best to try and get warm but all his symptoms were escalating. He was really getting sick.

Tim went home and Peter noticed he was rather quiet. At dinner he picked at his food.

"What's wrong, Tim?" said Peter.

Tim looked up. He knew his father wasn't real keen on Brett and he wasn't sure just how much his father wanted Brett around so at first he said, "Nothing."

"Well, you seem upset about something. You don't want to tell us?" asked Peter.

Tim looked up from his plate and finally said, "I'm kind of worried about Brett, Dad. He has a bad cold. Mr. Nelson threw him out of class today for coughing too much and I guess he went home. I didn't see him after that."

"Oh Tim," said Marguerite, "I'm sure his aunt can take care of him. He probably went home to her."

"Mother, there is no aunt."

Peter said, "I don't think there is either."

"No aunt," said Marguerite in astonishment, "then who does he live with?"

"He lives by himself," said Tim.

"By himself? He's just a boy. How can he live by himself?"

"If you have no one," said Tim, "you just make do."

"Well Peter, don't you think we should do something about that? You do work with the orphan's home. Is there any room for him there?"

"Mom," Tim was shocked, "the orphan's home! Brett doesn't belong in the orphan's home."

"Well, he can't live by himself. How does he eat and where does he stay? The temperature has been running down to zero some days. Does he have heat where he is? Do you know where he is staying, Tim?"

"It's somewhere around the school and the park. He's in the park all the time and he has me drop him off there."

The next day Brett did not come to school. Tim couldn't concentrate on anything all day he was so worried about his friend. When his father came to pick him up, he ran out to him in the buggy. "Dad, Brett didn't come to school today. Something is wrong. Brett wouldn't miss school. He loves school. Something is wrong Dad," he said frantically.

"Calm down Son," said Peter. "Let me think." Neither of them knew where Brett was living. Peter had an idea. "Come on," he said to Tim.

He went back into the school, Tim following him. He went to the office and up to the desk of the secretary whose nameplate read "Alice". He said, "Hi, Alice. I'm Dr. Osterhaus. I kind of have a dilemma here and I'm hoping you can help me. You have a student, Brett Ballin. His aunt came to my office and told my nurse that she wanted me to see him. I guess he has been sick? However, my nurse thought he was a regular patient and forgot to get his address. Can you give it to me?"

"Oh yes, Doctor. He didn't come to school today. Let me check my records." She leafed through some cards. "Oh here it is. The address is 1932 Pine Way. But it doesn't list an aunt. It says here he lives with his parents, Michael & Lila Ballin."

"Oh well maybe the aunt is staying with them or something. Thanks for your help."

Peter started out of the office, Tim walking behind him. "Pine Way?" he said to Tim. "Isn't that a couple streets in back of the school?"

"I think so," said Tim.

"Not the greatest area."

They drove the horse around and found Pine Way. They had trouble finding the right number since the apartments were so run down, they had long ago lost their street numbers. They thought they found 1932 however through the process of elimination. They drove around the building trying to figure out which apartment was Brett's. There was no chimney smoke at all. When they got around to the back of the building, Tim thought he saw something and he yelled to his father to stop the buggy. He jumped out and ran to a window. He turned back to his father, "There is a light on in here."

Peter stopped the buggy and ran up to the back door, it was locked. He pounded on it but nothing. He looked around and saw an iron bar lying on the ground. He picked it up and pried the door open. The door was so dilapidated that it fell open as soon as he started prying on it with the bar. He went to the first apartment and pounded on that door calling Brett's name. No answer. This door was even flimsier and a good hit with the iron bar and the door flew open. He dropped the bar and looked into the cold dreary room. There sat Brett in the back of the room sitting on the dirtiest mattress Peter thought he had ever seen. The boy was bundled up and sat shaking and coughing. His eyes were red and watery and Peter could read the fear in them.

"Brett, it's Tim and Dad," said Tim, "don't be afraid. We're going to get you out of here and get you help." Tim looked at his father, "Dad, it's so cold in here."

Peter nodded.

Brett muttered, "Tim?"

Peter walked up to the boy and reached out to him. Brett recoiled in fear. The cold had turned into pneumonia. Brett was so disoriented he couldn't comprehend that it was his friend, Tim, and his father. "It's all right, Son," said Peter, "We're here to help you." He turned to Tim, "Tim, go get that heavy throw in the buggy. No, wait a minute take out as much of his stuff as you can carry. He's not coming back here." Tim grabbed up the duffle bag, saddlebags and all the clothes he could carry and ran out to the buggy. Peter then walked up to Brett and said again, "It's Peter, Brett, you know Tim's Dad. We are here to help you, Son. Don't be afraid."

Brett recoiled a little but Peter persisted and put his hand on Brett's forehead. His head was on fire; the boy was burning up but shivering with chills. Tim came back in carrying the throw they used to cover with when they rode in the buggy in the winter. He handed it to Peter. Peter said, "Brett, can you stand up?" He helped him to stand and held him while he wrapped the throw around him. Brett was shaking and his knees buckled and Peter picked him up. Peter noticed how light he was. There was nothing to him. Peter knew instantly that he sure had not been eating very well.

Tim grabbed the rest of Brett's stuff which consisted of a few pieces of clothing and they went out to the buggy. Peter set Brett in the buggy and then climbed up. He picked Brett up and laid him across his lap keeping his face turned away from the wind and into Peter's chest trying to get some of his own body heat into the boy and protect his face from the cold air.

"You drive," he told Tim, "And go as fast as you dare."

—m—

When Brett came home after Mr. Nelson threw him out of class, he put the rest of the coal in the stove and lit it. He kept his winter clothes on even his outer clothes, coat, muffler and mittens, and wrapped up in both blankets. He lied down on his mattress. He tried lying on his side but he couldn't stop coughing, his lungs pounded when he tried to lie on his back. He was feverish and his throat hurt so bad it was difficult to swallow. He finally fell into a fitful sleep.

Morning came and he went from chills to hot. His chest felt like something was sitting on him. He couldn't get comfortable. The coal had run out of the stove and the apartment was getting very cold. He sat up; it hurt too much to lie down. There wasn't a muscle or organ in his body that didn't hurt. His lungs felt like they would blow apart; his stomach ached from coughing.

In the afternoon, he heard the pounding of someone on the outside door and then a large bang and the splintering of wood. Oh God he thought, someone is breaking into the apartment. He had to get his father's gun, but he couldn't move. His mind was in a fog and his legs wouldn't work. He couldn't pull himself up to stand. He heard his name being called.

Now the apartment door banged and again he heard the splintering of wood as the door jamb gave way. Someone was coming to kill him or worse take him to Children's Services. Someone said something about "Tim", his friend, Tim? A cool hand was placed on his forehead. Then someone lifted him to his feet but he was too weak to stand. There was a big warm blanket wrapped around him and strong hands lifted him into a man's arms. The man was talking to him but he couldn't make out what he was saying. His head was spinning, his lungs bursting and he started coughing again. The man pulled his head into his chest and turned his face so the wind wouldn't suck his breath away. Then he carried him outside and put him in a buggy. Who had him and what would they do to him? He tried to struggle but the strong hands were too much for him; he finally succumbed and fell asleep in the man's arms. His last thought was do with him what they will he no longer cared.

—m—

When they got to the house, Tim went ahead and opened the front door, yelled for his mother and held the door for Peter who was carrying Brett. Peter took Brett into his office and placed him on the reclining chair. Marguerite came hustling into the room to see what all the yelling was about. She took one look at Brett and knew he was one very sick boy.

"Get some warm water, Marg, and put on your tea kettle and boil some water please. Tim, would you unload Brett's stuff and take care of the horse, please? Better be sure he is cooled out and blanket him."

"Yes, Pa."

Peter grabbed a log off the stack and placed it on the fire in the fireplace. He wanted it as warm as possible in the room. This fireplace also connected to the guest room and that is where he planned on putting Brett after he treated him.

Marguerite came in carrying a basin of water, soap and towels. Peter was busy taking bottles out of his medicine cabinet and mixing several different medications together. "What can I do?" asked Marguerite.

"Start taking off his clothes and washing him. He's filthy. You should have seen where he was living. Pigs wouldn't stay there."

"Poor Brett," Marguerite said, and started taking off all his clothes. She tossed them one by one on the floor for washing. When she got down to his long johns, she raised him up enough to slide the top half of the long johns down to his waist. He started coughing again. She started washing him. Tim came in and she asked him to help her get his boots and pants off. She told Tim to get one of his sleeping gowns and they put that on him, wrapped a throw around him and covered him with a blanket for warmth until they could get him into bed.

Peter listened to Brett's chest with his stethoscope. It sounded like a battle field there was so much going on in there. He raised the boy forward and had Marguerite hold him while he placed the stethoscope on his back and listened to his lungs. He was wheezing and his chest had a rattle. His heart and pulse were racing. His temperature was way up. This kid was in trouble. He started coughing and couldn't seem to stop. Peter pulled the throw up around him to get him warm and stop the shaking.

Marguerite brought in the tea kettle with the boiling water. Peter took Brett's legs and swung them around on the couch so he was sitting on the side and he pulled a blanket over his legs. Brett was too weak and too disoriented to know what they were doing to him.

Marguerite sat beside Brett and held him while Peter gently took a towel and formed a tent over his head to trap the steam and be sure he got as much of the medicine as possible into his lungs. He then removed the lid to the tea kettle and poured part of his medical concoction in the steaming water. Medicinal smells drifted up in the steam. Peter held Brett's face so he was breathing the medicinal steam but not allowing his head to drop so close to the steam that it would burn him. Brett struggled a little as the smelly steam hit his face but with Marguerite and Peter holding and talking to him, Marguerite rubbing his back to calm him, he gave in and let the medicine rise around and encircle his head. Peter kept him there until the steamy pot cooled and there was no steam. Then he laid the boy back down on the laid-back chair and put a poultice on his chest.

When Brett started coughing again and couldn't stop, Peter turned to Marguerite but she was gone. In a minute she was back and Peter said, "Marg we need some of your. . ." and then he saw she had the honey and whiskey concoction that she used to give both the guys when they had colds and were coughing. Peter held Brett up in a sitting position while Marguerite put small spoonfuls of the honey mixture into his mouth. They had to give it to him a little at a time because he wasn't totally awake and they didn't want him to choke. He did swallow it as they spooned it into his mouth.

They were finally ready to put him in the bed in the guest room. Tim went and pulled back the covers and propped up a lot of pillows on the bed so he wasn't lying flat which would have been hard for him to breathe.

Peter carried the sick boy into the room, laid him in the bed and then looked at his two accomplices. "For now all we can do is pray for him, guess it's up to him and God now."

Tim asked, "Is he going to be all right?"

"It's serious Tim. I just don't know. If he doesn't start to get better soon, we'll have to take him to the hospital. He's so malnourished and that is probably why he is so sick. He has no resistance to fight this off."

That worried Tim. If the authorities found out how he was living, what would happen to him?

—⁘—

Brett had felt Peter and Marguerite's kind hands and the warmth of the fireplace and it felt so good to be warm. Someone was holding his head, he tried to pull away but they just spoke softly and held his head and he was too weak to put up a fight. They placed a towel over his head and he inhaled this steamy medicinal cocktail. It was a form of torture he decided. They must want him to tell them something but what. He didn't know anything.

After these people finished treating him, they carried him into another room and put him in a bed. They put blankets on him and tucked them around him. It felt so warm and smelled so good. He drifted off into the best sleep he had had in days. If these people were going to kill him, he would go willingly.

—⟋⟋⟍—

Marguerite told Peter and Tim that she would sit with Brett for a while. Peter made coffee and brought a cup in to Marguerite. He leaned against the door jamb sipping his coffee and watching her work with Brett. She was busy putting a cool wet cloth on Brett's forehead and taking another cloth and wiping around his face. He was sweating profusely from the fever but some of the time shivering with chills. Then she placed another wet cloth under his neck. He muttered something unintelligible but fell into a deep sleep.

Peter thought what are we going to do with him? He couldn't go back to that tenement. He was too self-reliant to go to the orphanage. Peter knew he wouldn't stay there. He would run away. Could they take him in? Peter wasn't keen on the idea but maybe it was a possibility – maybe the only possibility.

Marguerite told her menfolk to go to bed. Tim had school and Peter had his practice she could care for Brett.

During the night Brett fell into hallucinations. Marguerite found out a lot about Brett's past from what he said in his delirium.

"Mike! Mike look out, he's got a gun. . . .No, please NO! Pa-a-a!" He flinched and twisted, throwing his head back and forth, reliving seeing Mike shot. "Oh Pa, someone help him. Please Dad don't die! Oh Pa, why now? Why are you dying now when we just got to know each other?"

Marguerite was horrified. This boy had seen his father shot down. There was no buggy accident. He tossed and turned, very agitated, calling out his father's name.

Marguerite picked him up to a half sitting position and cradled his head and shoulders against her chest, "SHHH, it's all right. You're safe now." She held him stroking the side of his face and hair until he settled down and then she would lay him back down and pull the covers up around him.

Brett also mumbled about his mother, "I'm here Mom. It's Brett, I'm here. No Mike's not here but I'm here Ma and I need you – you can't die." He rambled on about a saloon and about learning how to shoot a gun. Despite the fever and how weak he was, he was very restless and couldn't seem to settle down.

When the chills got real bad and Brett was shivering severely, Marguerite held him in her arms trying to get him warm from her body heat. She rocked him back and forth, his head resting on her ample bosom. She had the blanket pulled up around him trying to stop the chills. She held his head on her chest and was singing a lullaby she used to sing to Tim when he was little and had the croup:

"Hush little baby, don't say a word. Papa's gonna buy you a mockingbird,
And if that mockingbird won't sing, Papa's gonna buy you a diamond ring,
If that diamond ring turns brass, Papa's gonna buy you a looking glass,
If that looking glass gets broke, Papa's gonna buy you a billy goat,
If that billy goat won't pull, Papa's gonna buy you a cart and bull,
If that cart and bull turn over, Papa's gonna buy you a dog named Rover,
If that dog named Rover won't bark, Papa's gonna buy you a horse and cart
If that horse and cart fall down, you'll still be the sweetest little baby in town.
So hush little baby don't you cry, 'cause Papa loves you and so do I.

—⁓—

Brett felt Marguerite lifting him and comforting him, laying his head on her soft warm breasts. It felt so good to be in the arms of an angel with her body heat and breath pouring into him, her bosom a soft warm pillow. He knew even in his semi-conscious mind that she was trying to help him recover and it gave him the resolve to fight off this sickness and come back to reality.

—⁓—

In the early morning hours, Peter walked into the guest room. Brett was sleeping and had stopped shivering. Marguerite was asleep in the chair. He walked over and gently shook her. "Honey, why don't you go lay down for a couple hours in our bed. I'll sit here with Brett. I want to check his vitals anyway."

She nodded and walked off to their bedroom. Peter checked his lungs and took his vital signs. He was starting to respond to their treatments. He went to the basin of water and soaked a towel and wiped down his head, face and neck, leaving a wet towel on his forehead. Then sat in the chair and dozed off and on.

When he woke up later, he gave Brett another steam treatment and a fresh poultice on his chest. After doing all that was necessary to make him as comfortable as possible, Peter got ready to go to his office. He and Tim left at the same time and he told Tim that Brett was doing better. Peter had decided, however, that if Brett wasn't a lot better by that afternoon, he was taking him to the hospital and damn the consequences. He wasn't going to be blamed for killing the kid.

Marguerite was now alone with Brett. She went in and checked on him. He was sleeping soundly. She did some of her household chores and then heard him talking. She went in and he was hallucinating again. He was muttering about his sick mother and Marguerite got the impression that he blamed himself for her death feeling that he had not done enough to save her.

Once when he started with the chills again, she took him in her arms, wrapped a blanket around him and held him close to her so he would get some of her body heat. She hummed to him to keep him calm and rocked back and forth. He opened his eyes and looked at her, "Are you an angel?"

She smiled, "Afraid not – just a mother, Tim's mother."

When he coughed so hard he doubled over with the pain in his stomach, she helped him sit up and gave him some of the honey-whiskey combination. She then laid him down and lightly massaged his belly and put a hot compress on his abdomen to help with the pain from coughing. She put an ice chip in his mouth holding one end with a towel so he wouldn't choke on it but he would get some moisture and cool him.

She brought in some chicken broth and propped him up until he was sitting straight up. She put small spoonfuls of the broth in his mouth. She noticed when she was washing him how thin and undernourished he was, he was all bones. At first he swallowed the broth but then he drifted off to sleep. She left him sleep. She knew he really needed it to get back his strength and beat this illness ravaging his body.

XI

The Burglary

When Peter came home around three o'clock in the afternoon, he went immediately into the guest room to check on Brett. He put his hand on the boy's forehead, he seemed a little cooler. He checked all his vital signs and listened with his stethoscope to his heart and lungs. The boy was doing better, his temperature was dropping and everything seemed to be returning to normalcy. He told Marguerite he wanted to give him another steam treatment and she started boiling the water in her tea kettle. He went into his office and prepared the medication. She brought the steaming tea kettle into him and held Brett in a sitting position while Peter managed the towel and the steam. The boy was a little more alert and seemed to respond a little more to Marguerite talking to him and telling him that they needed to do this for him to get better.

They ate dinner and then Marguerite brought in more chicken soup for Brett. Tim sat behind him and held him in a sitting position while Marguerite spooned the broth into his mouth a little at a time. This time he was a little more alert but still weak. He was able to eat the entire bowl of soup however. Marguerite brought him glasses of water also and told him he needed to drink a lot of water to keep from becoming dehydrated from the fever and sweating. During the night his fever spiked and then broke and by morning he was responding to their treatment much better.

On the fourth day, Brett's temperature and vital signs were almost normal and he was back to acting more like himself. He was eating solid food and Marguerite fixed him milk with a supplement that Peter brought home which helped patients who were undernourished. He was still very tired and slept a lot which is a symptom of pneumonia. Tim insisted on sleeping in the laid back chair in Peter's office so if Brett woke up and needed something, Tim could be there even though Peter thought it was no longer necessary.

It was night when Brett woke up and it was dark in the guest room except for a glow from a dimly lit lamp. At first he couldn't remember where he was. It was warm and he was very comfortable; he sure knew he wasn't in the tenement apartment. He no longer had the pain in his chest and stomach. He laid there in the dark staring at the ceiling. He was awake enough now that he knew he was at Tim's house. He wondered where the duffle bag was. The money and his father's guns were in it. What if it was back in the apartment! He had to check. He pulled the covers back and slowly swung his legs around and tried to get out of bed. He stood up and tried to walk. Suddenly his legs buckled, he grabbed for the bed and instead got the nightstand. A basin and various medications came crashing down on the floor along with him.

Tim was jarred from his sleep by something crashing in the next room. He jumped up and ran to see if Brett was all right. Brett was on the floor struggling to get up. He started shivering from being out of the bed and in the cool room. Tim ran to him and tried to help him but Brett was desperate to find the duffle bag. He pushed Tim away and started yelling, "Tim, I need to get the duffle bag. Where is it?"

Tim yelled for his father as he struggled to help Brett up, but Brett was dead weight he was so weak and he was fighting against Tim trying to rise on his own. Peter heard his son calling him, heard all the thrashing and he ran downstairs and into the guest room. Peter went to Brett, "Easy Son, take it easy. You shouldn't be out of bed. What are you doing?" He helped Tim pick Brett up and sit him on the edge of the bed. Peter grabbed a blanket and wrapped it around the shaking boy.

"My duffle bag, where is it?" Brett asked in a high-pitched voice almost yelling now.

Tim ran to the closet and got the duffle bag. He held it up for Brett to see. "Here it is," said Tim. "It's right here Brett."

"Don't open it," yelled Brett.

"I won't. See no one is opening it. It's going right back in the closet where it has been all the time."

"Come on Brett," Peter said. "Get back in bed. You are getting chilled." Peter pulled the covers back and picked up Brett's legs and slid him under the covers. He pulled the covers up around him. "Tim, go to bed," said Peter. "I'll stay with him a few minutes."

He put his hand on Brett's chest over the covers to calm him. He was breathing hard from the exertion and started coughing. There was a pitcher of water in the room and Peter poured him a glass. He helped him sit up and said, "Here, drink this slowly. It should help you stop coughing."

Brett sipped the water and he did stop coughing.

Peter pulled some of the pillows together to prop Brett up and he wouldn't be lying flat. That would help with the coughing and help him breathe and then he eased the boy back on the pillows. Brett was panting from the exertion. "Nobody here will violate your privacy Son," Peter said. "Now get some sleep. You need that more than anything right now."

Peter sat in the chair with his hand rubbing Brett's chest to relieve some of the congestion in his chest. When Brett had calmed down, his breathing returned to normal and he drifted off to sleep, Peter went back upstairs. Marguerite was still in bed and awake. "What was that all about?" she asked.

"Oh, that duffle bag. I wonder what is in that thing that he gets so excited if it's out of his sight."

"Do you think it is something we should worry about?" asked Marguerite.

"I really don't know."

"Well," said Marguerite, "it hasn't exploded yet."

"That's comforting," said Peter.

The next morning after her men both left, Marguerite let Brett sleep a good part of the morning before she went in to check on him. When she went into the room, Brett was awake and he seemed restless.

"Want to get up?" she asked.

"Yes, I feel attached to this bed."

"Let me get your clothes," she walked over to the dresser and took out some long johns, a shirt, pants and socks.

She helped him swing his legs around. He was still weak. She held out a leg of the long johns for him to put his leg in. He suddenly was aware that he had nothing on under the gown. He reached for the long johns but felt light-headed and shaky. He probably couldn't do it by himself.

"Come on, put your leg in here," she said. He did and then she held out the other leg of the long johns.

"Maybe I can do it," he said.

She laughed and realized that he was embarrassed. "Brett, I have a husband and I raised a boy, I have helped Peter in his office many times; I have seen men's naked bodies. You are not the first, besides who do you think undressed you and washed you when you first came here? Now come on, I have other things to do today."

He guessed he was being silly but he blushed feeling his face get warm. He put his other leg into the long johns and she said, "Now stand up and put your hands on my shoulders to steady yourself." When he did, she pulled the underwear up over his hips and felt him stiffen when she brushed his buttocks with her hands when she was pulling the pants up. She pulled the gown off and threw it on the floor for washing. Young men are so cute she thought. She brought the long johns up and helped him put in his arms. Then she helped him with his pants and to finish dressing. She told him to wait there for a moment. She went into Tim's room and got a sweater. Came back and held the sweater for Brett to put on. They had to roll up the sleeves because it was too big but it would help keep him warm.

"We aren't going to struggle with those boots," she said, "but here are some warm socks. They should keep your feet warm for now." She lifted each foot and put the socks on him.

He stood, was shaky but could walk slowly. He came into the kitchen and sat at the table. She scrambled him some eggs and gave him a big glass of milk with Peter's supplement in it.

After he ate, Marguerite let him go in Peter's office and get a book. He settled in front of the fireplace in the sitting room and was reading. Marguerite checked on him an hour later and he was asleep in the chair. She got a throw and put it over him.

When Peter and Marguerite went to bed that night, Peter asked Marguerite what she thought they should do about Brett. He knew what she would say, "Let's keep him, Peter. He'll be all right once he learns to trust us."

"Just like a stray cat?" said Peter. "You know Marguerite, sometimes these kids that have been on their own and have taken matters into their own hands are trouble."

"Peter, he's had it rough. Do you know that he saw his father shot to death? He also nursed his mother when she was ill and died. I think he thinks he should have saved her. He's a good kid and just needs a boost."

"Oh boy," said Peter, "so that's what some of this acting out is about. That's awful. I assume you found that out when he was delirious?" He still had misgivings but said he would go along with her for now. "The least little thing, however, that puts you or Tim in some kind of danger or he gets Tim in trouble and he goes," warned Peter.

"Yes, Dear," she said, and he knew she didn't believe him.

After dinner that night and while the family was still sitting at the table, Peter asked Brett if he would like to live with them. Brett dropped his fork, looked up stunned. There would be rules he would have to follow just like they expected from Tim. Brett still looked on in disbelief. His own family had turned him away when all he had asked for was a room to stay in, but these people offered him a place in their home and didn't even know him.

He sat there for a few minutes not saying anything; he looked down at his plate. "You don't know anything about me," he finally said.

"We know all we need to know," said Peter, "the rest we can learn as we go along."

He still did not say anything, he sat for several minutes and then he made a decision. He stood up and walked to the guest room. He took the two thousand dollars out of the duffle bag. He would have to earn more money; he was giving this money to them.

He walked out into the dining room, up to Peter and handed it to him.

Peter looked at the stack of money confused and said jokingly, "What did you do, Brett, rob a bank?"

"My father gave it to me the night before he died."

Peter felt terrible for having said what he did. "I'm sorry, Brett, I didn't know," he said. "I should not have said that. Brett, you had all this money and you didn't use it to support yourself when you were in that stinking tenement?"

"He said it was for college, I was saving it for that, but you have been so kind . . ." he was choking up, "You have asked for nothing, even saved my life. I think you should take it to pay for keeping me. I'll earn more money for college."

"Brett is this what was in the duffle bag?" asked Peter.

"Yes," he said nodding his head.

"Well," said Peter, picking up the money, "I'm going to tell you what we are going to do. I'm going to put this money in my safe tonight. I'll pick you boys up after school tomorrow and we are going to take this money to the bank for you to open an account. This will go in it as your father said to pay for college for you.

"Brett, let's get one thing straight. We are not asking you to live here to be paid back. We are asking you to live here because we think you have a lot of potential and we want to see you complete your education in whatever field you choose just like we want for our son. We enjoy your company. You have been good for all of us and especially Tim and that is all the reward we need."

Brett couldn't speak. He was choking up, the tears that had been collecting in the corner of his eyes started running down his face, despite how hard he was trying not to cry and then a sob escaped from him and he sucked in his breath. All he could picture was his grandfather yelling at him to, "Get out!" and these people who knew nothing about him, asked him to live with them. Marguerite, who had really gotten close to him when she cared for him with the pneumonia, got up and put her arms around his shoulders from behind the chair and pulled him back against her chest.

Tears were now running unabashed down his face, he was trying to sniff them back up embarrassed, his head was down hoping no one would notice. He was trying to wipe them away with the sleeve of his shirt. Peter took out his handkerchief and handed it to Brett.

"Don't be embarrassed, Son," said Peter. "Crying is a good thing. It's a great release but then women know that better than men." He smiled and clamped his hand on Brett's shoulder. Brett wiped his eyes with the handker-chief and blew his nose. This was too good to be true. What did he ever do to deserve such a break? No more freezing in the apartment and not having enough money to eat.

—ᴍ—

A couple weeks went by after the Osterhauses invited Brett to stay with them. They gave him the guest room for his own and said he could decorate it any way he liked. It was fine the way it was. He took out a couple of the pictures of his parents and one family picture of the three of them and placed them along with the small iron horse on his dresser. Otherwise, he did nothing more. The guest room, now Brett's room, was the only bedroom downstairs. It was next to Peter's office.

One night Brett was just drifting off to sleep when he heard glass breaking. He sat up now wide awake. He could hear footsteps crunching in the glass. Brett slept in his underwear – had never owned a sleeping gown and wasn't about to start now. He grabbed his pants off the chair and slipped into them. He got out of bed and crept across the floor to the closet. He found the duffle bag, got out one of his father's guns and loaded it. About this time he heard wood splintering. He stealthily walked out of the bedroom and peeked into Peter's office. There was a man with a metal bar prying open the medicine cabinet.

"FREEZE," said Brett. The man whirled around and raised the bar threateningly at Brett. He was far enough away that the only threat was if he threw it. Brett fired a shot into the floor right in front of the man and repeated, "Freeze or I'll shoot you." The man looked at the kid and saw the gun. He froze. He could see the kid's face in the light of the street lamp and he knew this was no kid to be reckoned with.

"Look Kid, let me go. I'll not cause any trouble."

"No way," said Brett, "you're going to jail."

—m—

"What was that, Peter?" said Marguerite.

"Sounded like a gunshot. Stay here." He slipped into his pants under his sleeping gown and went out his bedroom door as Tim was coming out of his bedroom tying his robe shut.

"Was that a gunshot?" said Tim.

"Sounded like it."

The two men looked down stairs and saw Peter's office door and Brett's bedroom door were open. They heard Brett threaten the man that if he moved he would shoot him.

"Get down on the floor and put your hands out away from your body," Brett ordered. "You make a move and I'll shoot you. Don't be foolish enough to think I can't handle this gun."

Peter and Tim ran down the stairs and into Peter's office. The man was lying on the floor quivering. Peter looked at Brett and he could see why the man was scared. The look in Brett's dark eyes said he knew how to handle the gun he was holding and had no qualms about shooting it. His hand was steady and finger on the trigger.

There was a knock on the front door and Tim went to answer it. It was the neighbor, Frank Tedrow. "Everyone all right over here? I heard a shot."

"There's been a break-in, Frank, would you get the Sheriff please?" yelled Peter from the other room.

"Sure I think he just rode by."

Peter grabbed some sash cord off the drapes and tied the man's hands and feet. He turned to Brett. Brett was stock still, feet planted and gun steady in his hand. Peter noticed he wasn't even nervous and those eyes. Locked a man in place he thought. "Give me the gun, Brett," said Peter softly. Peter had one of those quiet soothing voices that could talk people off of bridges but Brett was in gunfight mode. He glanced at Peter but was focusing on the burglar and he wasn't ready to give up the gun. "Brett," Peter said softly, "the Sheriff is going to be here any minute. He'll take the gun away from you, Son. I don't want to see anyone get hurt. Give me the gun and we'll discuss this later, please," he pleaded.

When she knew things were under control, Marguerite put a robe on and came downstairs to see what had happened. She and Tim were standing in the doorway of the office watching Peter and Brett.

Brett looked again at Peter and deftly twirled the gun around presenting it butt first to him. All three Osterhauses could not believe the ease at how he handled that gun. He was not at all nervous about it and the way he flipped the gun around showed that he knew perfectly what he was doing. Peter took the gun. It sure was a beauty but he wanted it out of sight. He quickly opened his desk drawer and put the gun in there. Brett whirled around, brushed past Tim and Marguerite and walked out of the room and went to his room. All three Osterhauses exchanged looks, one more mystery about the wild kid from Kansas.

Sheriff Fred Tompkins knocked on the door. He had a deputy with him and the deputy handcuffed the man and took him away. It was obvious that he was after drugs and Peter told the Sheriff that he could see the man was already strung out on something.

Marguerite and Tim then went into the office, Marguerite sat in one of the chairs and Tim stood and put his arm around her shoulders. Peter explained to the Sheriff that his foster boy had heard the man and caught him in the act of breaking into the cabinet and trying to get the drugs. The Sheriff asked to speak to Brett. Peter said he would get him.

Peter went to Brett's room and rapped on the door. "Brett, open the door will you? The Sheriff wants to speak with you." For a moment Peter thought Brett had run away but then he opened the door and Peter put his hand on his shoulder. In a low voice, Peter said, "Don't say anything about the gun. Let me handle it."

Sheriff Tompkins was a pleasant man and not confrontational unless he had to be. He asked Brett's name and wrote it down on his report. Then he asked Brett what had happened. Brett told him keeping it brief and not mentioning the gun.

"I understand there was a shot fired," said the Sheriff.

"Oh yes," said Peter. "The boy got my gun out of the desk. The shot only went into the floor though. You can see right here." He pointed to the hole in the floor where the bullet hit.

"Son," said the Sheriff. "You shouldn't try and use a gun if you don't know what you are doing. You could get hurt or hurt someone else."

Brett said, "Yes Sir."

"Well, I guess I have enough for my report. I'll keep you informed as to what will happen to this guy. You may have to testify in court," he said to Brett. "But it's too soon to tell." Peter saw the Sheriff to the door shook his hand and said good night.

Peter walked back into the office, opened the desk drawer and took out the gun. It was a masterpiece. He turned it over in his hands - bright silver barrel and mother of pearl handle. The gun was obviously custom-made and had to cost a fortune. Peter looked at Brett, "Your father's?" he guessed.

Brett nodded.

"Brett, I don't hold with guns. I have never owned one and I have never allowed them in my house. When we asked you to live here, we expected an element of trust. You withheld that information from us."

"Please don't make me get rid of them. It is all I have of my father's," he begged.

"I realize you were brought up differently than my son. It's obvious he has taught you how to use this weapon," Peter was turning the gun around in his hands; it sure was a beautiful gun. He looked at Brett.

Brett was silent. He wouldn't look down, he never did - he couldn't. He was looking straight at Peter with his dark eyes but he wasn't defiant instead his black eyes were now softer and sad. Should he tell him about the other gun? He had come into their home and had now violated a rule of the head of the household, he decided he had to be honest even if it cost him the loss of this wonderful home.

"There are two," he said quietly. He turned and walked into his room. The duffle bag was lying on the bed. He took out the other gun which was still in the holster and went back into the office. He whipped the twin to the gun Peter was holding out of the holster so naturally and flipped it around offering it to Peter butt first. All three stared at him still in disbelief that a boy his age could handle a gun as well as he did and so confidently.

"I would never use them to hurt anyone unless it was in defense of myself or someone else. You have my word on that."

The holster was hand-tooled black leather with silver conchos. The workmanship on both the guns and the holster was exquisite. Peter could not help but admire them. Peter looked at Brett.

"Yes," he said, "my father was a gunfighter. He taught me well. Do you want me to leave?"

Marguerite stiffened and Tim looked stricken. They had been listening to the whole discussion and both were in fear of what Peter would do. Peter looked very serious. He had said, "Any trouble and Brett goes."

"Brett, when we asked you to move in here, we didn't take it lightly. We are not going to ask you to leave every time there is a problem. If something happens, we need to work it out. We need to trust each other. That is what I mean about the element of trust. As I said, I don't like guns but I can see what these guns mean to you, so I suppose I could make an allowance in this case under one condition, the guns stay locked in my desk drawer. If you agree to that, you can keep them. Do we have a deal?"

Brett nodded, "Deal." Brett held out his hand toward Peter, "I need to unload it," he said and when Peter handed it to him, he turned the gun so it wasn't pointed at any of them and deftly removed the bullets and put them in the belt. He spun the barrel to be sure there wasn't a bullet he may have missed. Then he holstered one of the guns and wound the belt around the holster and handed it back to Peter. Tim shook his head. He could have shot those three bullies.

Peter turned and opened a large drawer in the bottom of his desk. He put the guns and the holster in the drawer. Then he opened the top middle drawer. Locking the middle drawer locked the whole desk. He took out a key, shut the drawer and locked it. "There are two keys to this desk. I have one on my key ring. This is the other one." He turned and handed Brett the key. "The element of trust works both ways."

XII

Gladys

Gladys Simmons was not a happy woman. As a matter of fact she was most of the time a very depressed woman. She wasn't sure if she ever loved her husband, Elijah Simmons, a wealthy and very successful business man, but she sure knew in their later years that she didn't love him. For many years she feared him but then a person could only live in fear so long and she reconciled with her feelings and instead of living, she merely existed and seemed to have no feelings at all toward him.

Her two children were the only thing in her life that made her happy at all. Lila, her oldest and her daughter, had been the light of her life when she was born. Then three years later when she became pregnant for Joshua and after he was born, she again became happy being a loving mother, her life complete – a little girl and now a little boy. Once the children grew out of toddler stage and old enough to start school, however, Elijah took over and Gladys had little to say about their upbringing. She hardly even got to see the children except on some weekends. Elijah insisted on sending them off to school.

Gladys was a happy outgoing young girl when Elijah Simmons married her. Her debutante party when she was sixteen years old was filled with handsome suitors. It was at that time that her father and Elijah's father came to an agreement that Gladys would be Elijah's bride as soon as she turned seventeen. When Elijah's father told him that they had picked Gladys for him to be his bride, Elijah agreed that that was fine with him. He didn't much care who he married as long as she was pretty so he had attractive children and she conformed to what he wanted her to do as his wife. After all, he didn't have to stick to one woman for his sexual desires so why should he care. He didn't think he would ever be satisfied with one woman anyway when it came to sex.

Gladys's mother groomed her to be the perfect wife. She went to all the best girls' schools where she learned manners, how to dress, the proper make-up to wear, how to act at parties, social gatherings and up-scale restaurants, how to be the proper wife to a successful man.

Gladys's mother also explained to her what she should do to be a proper wife to her husband's sexual desires. She told her that sex with her husband would hurt the first time but after that it was no big deal. Her advice was to just lie back and allow the man to have his way with her. She lied!

On their wedding night in the hotel room, Elijah seemed thoughtful at first. After they had drunk several glasses of champagne which he told her was so that she would relax, he pulled her dress up over her head and removed the rest of her clothes a garment at a time until she was only in her pantaloons. Then he gently sat her on the bed. He knew she was a virgin and he wanted to savor every moment with her the first time. He undressed to his under shorts taking off his clothes and his undershirt.

She was so scared. Her face was lily white and at times she thought she was going to be sick. He started running his hands over her body. She was young and her skin was soft as milk. She had never allowed any boy to touch her this way. Her mother told her good girls didn't do that and she had to "save herself" for her marriage. Then later when she was betrothed to Elijah, her mother told her that once she was married she had to accept anything her husband wanted to do. She closed her eyes, turned her head away from him and tried not to think about what was happening to her.

He said nothing to her, no words of endearment and no encouragement for her to do anything – nothing to show her that he cared. He kissed her but there was no passion or love in his kisses more for his pleasure. His lips pressed so hard against her lips that her lips bit into her teeth making even his kisses painful. When he was ready, he removed the rest of their under garments and then he laid her down on the bed. She was terrified by now. He bent over her and put his mouth on each of her breasts and this got him more aroused. He crawled on top of her and spread her legs apart with his strong legs and then he got totally carried away. He took her like he was some kind of a mad bull. She whimpered and tears clouded her vision; it was so painful, Gladys had all she could do not to scream. She would have if they had not been in a hotel where other people would hear her; the pain was unbearable.

There was never a time when sex with Elijah was not painful. Elijah's sex drive was strictly for himself because he felt that was the way sex was – only for the man. When he took Gladys it was more like rape than love-making. He never had any consideration for her feelings.

Elijah's idea of sex was so unlike Peter Osterhaus who would never dream of hurting Marguerite. He would make sure that Marguerite was ready for him before he had any kind of intimacy with her. They would lie and discover each other's bodies until they were both excited. He kissed her passionately and always told her how much he loved her. She responded with passionate kisses and words of endearment to him. Peter was a gentle and wonderful lover.

He heard other men talk about their prowess. He felt so sorry for their wives. As a doctor he knew the erotic areas of the body and he stroked and worked with Marg until she really wanted him. He would have liked to have done seminars for husbands with regard to sex but in the mid-1800s he would have probably been branded a pervert.

It was so stupid. If a man took the time to bring his wife to peak, the whole love-making experience lasted longer. Marguerite made advances toward him nearly as much as he made advances toward her. Anytime the man could show the woman that intimacy could be pleasurable, he of course could have more sex.

Even when Gladys was pregnant for Lila, Elijah insisted on his wild sex. After the birth of Joshua, their son, Elijah was in a position to buy the thirty-room mansion they currently lived in in Boston. Gladys had never spoken up to Elijah in her life but when they moved into the mansion, she informed him that she was going to have a separate bedroom. She didn't care where he got his sex but it would no longer be with her. He didn't really care that much. She was a lousy lover, just laid there and acted like she was in pain. The prostitutes he sometimes bedded down were better lovers than her. Gladys told him that she would still be his wife, raise his children, oversee the household duties and servants, would attend parties and social gatherings as his wife, but no more sex. She upheld her part in the arrangement and he went elsewhere for his sexual gratification. This went on for the rest of their life together.

He got his sex wherever he could. Many times it was with employees. After all, he didn't have to pay for it with them. They would do it for favors.

If any of them became pregnant, they were fired. One young lady hired an attorney and sued him for child support. She turned up missing and her body was never found. Her child was raised by her parents.

—m—

Gladys of course knew what had happened in Kansas with her daughter. She knew she wasn't dead and had married some local guy. She saw how angry Elijah was and knew that his anger was more that Lila had gone against his wishes and spoiled his plan to have the largest cannon and munitions operation in the East and possibly the country. It had nothing to do with him caring about Lila; it was that she had the gall to defy him. When Elijah declared her dead and Gladys was never to speak of her again, Gladys was devastated. Furthermore, Gladys was never to contact her brother again since Elijah blamed him for Lila marrying Mike.

—m—

The two children, Lila and Joshua, were very close. They went to different schools but came home nearly every weekend. Joshua adored Lila and Lila loved her younger brother also. When her father wired her that she was dead and don't bother to contact them anymore, her biggest regret was Joshua. She thought many times of trying to contact him but was sure her father could intercept anything she sent.

Joshua was only thirteen years old when he was told that his sister had died in a freak accident when she fell off a horse. At the time he wondered why his father never brought the body home for burial. He never questioned his father however and he knew his mother was probably too afraid to even talk to him about it. He had to accept whatever he was told.

—m—

When Brett came that day to ask for lodging, Gladys was upstairs in her bedroom. Her room was right at the top of the stairs and she could see down to the foyer from there. She heard the knocker and opened her door a little to see who it was. She heard the entire conversation. She nearly collapsed. Her daughter had had a son. She had a grandson. She heard her husband angrily deny the boy and turn him away. She could not see him clearly but she could partially make out his face and saw that he was not a large boy and had black hair. He seemed polite, he held his hat in his hands and when Elijah told him to leave, he did so without an argument and immediately. She heard the boy say he wanted to go to school and all he needed was a room. After she thought about it, she decided she had to help him in some way.

She had an account to handle all the household expenses. Elijah's accountant transferred a sum of money each week into her account. It usually was more than she needed and if it was not, Elijah had told the accountant if she needed more, he could give it to her. This is where the money came from to pay a private investigator to first find out where the boy was living and then the money that she gave to Brett.

As they arrived back at the mansion after her last visit with Brett, her husband and two of his henchmen were waiting for her in the foyer. He told one of the men to go out and take the coach and horses to the stable and send in the coachman. When the man came in with Gladys, Elijah turned to Gladys, "Where have you been?"

"Out for a drive," she said. She was an old woman. What was this brute going to do, beat her? She certainly wouldn't last long and maybe that would be a Godsend, except now she had a reason to live.

He motioned to his henchman. He started beating the driver. After several blows, Gladys yelled, "STOP IT, ALL RIGHT. You probably already know anyway. I was visiting my grandson."

"I TOLD YOU, YOU HAVE NO GRANDSON," he yelled back at her.

"No, I heard you say you have no grandson. I have a grandson!"

He turned to the coachman "You're fired. Get out of here. And don't even think about asking for the balance of your salary."

The poor man did not even know he was doing anything wrong. He was just taking the boss's wife where she had asked to go. Gladys felt terrible.

"Well you won't be seeing him again. You are not going to be allowed to leave this house unless I know where you are going." He also notified the accountant that he would be handling all the household expenses and he closed the account that Gladys had.

—✺—

Now it was January and around zero degrees in Boston. Gladys was so worried about Brett. He couldn't be in those apartments. He would freeze. He had no money. All the child was trying to do was get an education. She never heard of a boy his age so dedicated to trying to become a doctor. Most kids would have quit when her husband threw him out.

She had stewed about the situation. She read the newspaper every day praying there would not be a notice that a child's body had been found frozen in those awful apartments on Pine Way. She tried to think of every way possible to get money to Brett. Then she thought of her last hope, her only hope, her son, Joshua. It might not work, however, because Joshua had been so many times put down by his father. He did whatever his father said and would never go against anything he thought his father would not approve of. He was more submissive and lived in more fear than did Gladys because he had to have more contact with Elijah since he worked for the company. Elijah had mentally castrated the boy. Gladys often wondered how Joshua would ever take over the company as insecure and unconfident as he was. Of course, Elijah probably thought he would never die so he never would have to turn over the reins to Joshua.

When it was getting close to the time Joshua usually got home from the company, she went downstairs to the parlor. He many times would come home from the company and visit with her there. It was right off the foyer. She heard him come in and she called to him.

He stuck his head in the door, "Yes, Mother?"

"I need to talk to you Joshua." Elijah was out of town so it was a good time for them to talk without him interrupting.

"All right Mother, let me go upstairs and change clothes. I'm kind of dirty." He was in charge of freight hauling. He scheduled the wagons and usually drove one since many times they were short-handed. He liked doing the job. It got him out of the company and away from his father.

He was back downstairs and in the parlor in a half hour. He had washed and changed into a clean shirt and pants and a suit jacket. The big house got chilly when it was this cold outside.

He came bouncing into the room. He liked spending time with his mother especially when they weren't spied on by Elijah. He gave his mother a peck on the cheek and went over to the fireplace, "Mother, it's cold in here. Let me put another log on the fire," and he took a log out of the wood box and put it on the fire and stoked it.

"Joshua, please come over here and sit down. I have something to tell you and it will be a shock. After I tell you, you may hate me."

He looked suspiciously at his mother. Was she kidding with him? She never did that, that spark had long ago been vanquished by her husband. He couldn't imagine ever hating his mother and now he was curious. He pulled over a chair and sat near her. After he had gotten older and saw how she was suffering from the treatment from her husband, he tried to do more to make things up to her. He really loved his mother very much.

"It's about your sister, Josh. The only way to tell you is right out." She stopped, looked at her son and then looked down at her hands which were twisting a handkerchief in her lap. "She didn't die seventeen years ago. She only died three years ago. I'm so sorry, Josh, that I never told you but I was afraid what your father would do to both of us if I told you. He still would have never let you see her and so I felt it was better to just let you think she was gone." She continued on and told him the whole story about Lila marrying Michael Ballin.

He sat stunned staring at her. He couldn't speak. How dare they? Had he known his sister was living in Kansas, he would have visited her even if it meant estranging himself from his father. They had denied him the right to make that choice all these years.

Then she said, "There is more. There is a reason I am telling you this now. She has a child, a boy, and he is living in Boston."

Joshua almost tipped the chair over backwards in surprise. "A son mother? My nephew?"

"And my grandson," she said. "He came here wanting a room and your father turned him away." Then she told him how she had met with Brett and helped him by letting him in the tenements and giving him money and what Elijah did to stop her from seeing him again.

"But Josh, it's zero degrees out there. He could freeze to death. I know I'm asking a lot but do you think you could find out what has happened to him?" Tears had now started down her cheeks. She had been so worried about Brett. "I met with him several times, Josh; he is a beautiful, sensitive child and only wants an education. He wants to be a doctor. He's very intelligent. I'm so worried about him in those cold tenement apartments. I thought I could get him money so he could buy coal and food but now I can't think of any way to get it to him unless you help him."

Josh stood up and took his handkerchief from his pocket and wiped his mother's tears. "Don't cry, Mother, of course I'll help him," he said, a nephew - his sister's son. He couldn't get used to the idea but he had to see him. He had loved Lila so much. Something deep down inside him awakened, some bit of courage that he thought had long ago been quashed. "No one watches me that close. I can do about anything as long as I don't take too much time. I can also get some money to him."

The next morning he rode his horse to the tenement house. He rode all around it. In the back he noticed that the outside door had been broken in. He dismounted and went inside. The first apartment had been broken into also. He walked in. It looked like it had been lived in recently. There was a new oil lamp there and a book that didn't look real old. He picked up the book and opened it. It had Jefferson High School on the inside cover. He walked back out and mounted his horse.

At the school, he went into the office and up to the desk marked "Alice". "Hi" he said, "Wonder if you can help me. My name is Joshua Simmons." He was hoping she would make the connection. "I just heard that my nephew is going to this school, could you tell me if that is true? His name is Brett Ballin."

"Yes, he does," she said a little reluctantly, wondering if she should be giving out the information to a stranger.

Joshua turned on the charm. He wasn't a real handsome man but was good looking and with a pleasant personality and smile. "Well see his mother is my sister and she and I got into somewhat of a family tiff. You know how that happens. It escalated and I would really like to reconnect with her and her family. Could you tell me the boy's address?" He thought maybe his story might get him some sympathy.

"Oh isn't that terrible? I know how that is. Let me look. Oh, he has a new address. Oh-h-h," she said sadly, "Well I'm sorry to be the one to tell you this but our information shows that your sister has passed and the boy's father also. I'm so sorry."

"That is horrible news and we could have had visits all this time and now that's not possible." He looked down. "Now, I feel really guilty," he said sadly, trying to invoke more sympathy from the secretary. "Well, maybe I can make it up to the boy if you will only help me," he pleaded.

"Well, looks like he has come up in the world. He is living with Dr. and Mrs. Peter Osterhaus and their son. As a matter of fact, Dr. Osterhaus has produced a document for legal custody of Brett. So he certainly is doing well now. He has been sick however, hasn't been in school for two weeks. Oh but Dr. Osterhaus sent a note with his son, Tim, that Brett will be back on Monday."

"Thank you so much. You certainly have been a big help."

Joshua rushed home to let his mother know that Brett was safe and living with a great family. Of course they had heard of Dr. Osterhaus and all his good works around Boston including all he did for the orphanage. His name and picture was many times in the <u>Boston Herald</u> expounding on some of the charitable work he had done and he was also on City Council.

Joshua couldn't get away on Monday but he was waiting outside the school on Tuesday when school was let out. He wasn't sure how he was going to recognize Brett. He recognized Peter Osterhaus from his pictures in the <u>Herald</u>. He was sitting at curbside with the buggy waiting for the boys. He really wanted to get to Brett before he got to the Osterhaus buggy. Then he saw two boys. They were hitting each other and shoving each other back and forth, laughing and talking.

Joshua couldn't believe it. Brett indeed looked like his mother. His hair was darker and he had real dark eyes but facial features and structure was very much Lila's. He said, "Brett?" Brett heard his name and turned. "Can I talk to you, please? Don't be afraid Brett. I won't hurt you. Your grandmother sent me."

Peter got out of the buggy and started walking toward them. Joshua said to Tim, "Tell your father to please stop where he is. I won't hurt Brett and we'll stay right here so he can see us." Tim nodded and ran to Peter. Peter stopped but he watched.

Joshua turned to Brett, looking into his face close up made him feel emotional. He stared and couldn't talk for a minute. Seventeen years since he had seen his sister. Fourteen years he could have had visits with her and he had been cheated out of that by an evil father. Fifteen years he could have enjoyed companionship with his nephew and he had been cheated out of that also. He would have taken the boy in had he only known. He would have gotten an apartment if need be. He made enough money; it was just that he never thought about moving out of the big house. There was so much room there it never seemed necessary. Well, that was history and this was reality. Brett was probably better off with the Osterhauses than with a bachelor. He had a brother and a mother and a father to take care of him. Joshua looked down and then back at Brett and swallowed hard.

Brett was looking at him curiously and wondered why this man had called him over but wasn't saying anything. "Brett," Joshua started tentatively regaining his composure and he looked him in the face, "I'm Joshua, your mother's brother, your uncle. Gladys is my mother and she sent me here. My father found out about her visits with you and put a stop to them. My father is evil and he can stop about anything. My mother has always been a prisoner. I hope you can understand. She never stopped trying to figure a way to help you. She finally came to me. I wish she would have sooner but it's complicated. Life with my father is . . . well, not pleasant."

Brett was trying to take it all in. "My uncle?! My mother's brother?!"

"Yes, I know it's a shock. I was shocked also when I found out that my sister lived fourteen years longer than what I was told and she had a son. I was told she died seventeen years ago in a freak accident – a fall from a horse. My father disowned her when she married your father. We want to help you, Brett – your grandmother and I. Here." He handed Brett an envelope. "I'll try to get here with more money as much as possible. You can use it any way you want. You can use it for yourself or give it to the Osterhauses. We are so glad you are safe and living with a fine family. I better go, Dr. Osterhaus is getting inpatient. Be safe, Brett."

Brett held out his hand to shake Joshua's. It was obvious that Joshua was starting to get emotional. He took Brett's hand but then emotion took over and he pulled the boy into him in a hug. Peter started to move forward but then he saw that tears were welling up in the man's eyes and decided he wasn't going to hurt Brett.

Joshua pulled away and looked down and away from Brett because he was embarrassed about his tears. He reached forward and put his hand on the boy's shoulder and said, "Be safe," and walked away.

Brett stood for a moment watching him walk away, and then he walked toward Peter and Tim. Halfway to them, Brett stopped, turned and looked back and saw Joshua canter his horse behind the school and down the road.

"Are you all right, Brett?" asked Peter when he reached them. He saw the boy was a little shook up.

Brett nodded.

They walked to the buggy and all got in. Tim said, "What was that about, Brett?"

"None of our business, Tim. That's Brett's business," said Peter.

The dinner table in the Osterhaus home was always family time. Whenever anyone had something to discuss with regard to the family, they brought it to the dinner table. Brett had learned that the first week he lived with the family. He rarely said anything but they included him in there discussions and if there was a family decision about anything, they asked his opinion along with theirs. After they had eaten, Brett quietly slid an envelope over to Peter.

"What's this?" asked Peter.

"It's for you," said Brett. He had opened the envelope and there was a nice note from his grandmother. She had apologized for not keeping up her visits but told him that it wasn't possible. She said how glad she was that he was with such a good family and mind his manners so he could stay. Brett kept his grandmother's letter and then closed the envelope to give the money inside to Peter.

Peter opened the envelope and looked at the money. "Brett, there is $200 in here. Is this the envelope you got from the man we saw you with at school today?"

Brett nodded. He waited a minute before he said anything not sure how much he wanted to share with them. Not sure how much he could open up even to these people who had been so good to him. "You should take it and help pay for keeping me. You deserve at least that much."

"Brett, we are not going to take money for caring for you. This can go in your account toward college."

Suddenly Brett decided they deserved to know more. "The man you saw me with . . ." he paused and then went on swallowing hard, "he's my uncle, my mother's brother. His name is Joshua Simmons . . . of Simmons & Son."

Tim couldn't hold back, "What?" he exclaimed.

Marguerite put her hand to her mouth.

"You see," said Brett, "I have relatives in Boston. That is why my father told me to come here. He said my mother's people would take me in and I could go to school. He was wrong. Elijah Simmons is my grandfather, my mother's father and when I asked him for a room so I could go to school, he threw me out. When my grandfather threw me out," he paused finding it hard to say, "he said his daughter died when . . . she married Mike. He said therefore . . . I couldn't exist. He said he had no grandson." Brett looked down which he rarely did but he felt the rejection all over again. Then his head popped up and he asked, "Do you know who he is?"

"Of course," said Peter, "one of the most well-known cannon and munitions manufacturers in the East. He made a fortune from the Civil War."

They all stared at Brett in disbelief. Brett went on, "My grandmother is Gladys Simmons. She was trying to help me. She is the one who got me the keys to the tenement house and she gave me money. But my grandfather caught her and cut her off from funds as well as won't let her leave the house. That's what Joshua told me today."

"Whew! That's quite a family history," said Peter, "I didn't know we had an aristocrat living with us," he smiled at Brett.

"Well," said Brett smiling back at Peter, "only on my mother's side. My father's side is an entirely different story."

"Brett, I'll put this in your account tomorrow," said Peter. Will the mystery ever end with this little stray of Marguerite's he thought? A lot of things now made sense. This kid was really something. All he had been through and yet he just kept marching on. Peter vowed to be more patient and try and help him all he could. How could a grandfather tell his grandson he doesn't exist?

XIII

The Bullheaded Gray

A month after Brett had recovered from the pneumonia, Peter called him into his medical office. He motioned Brett to the reclining chair, "Take off your shirt," Peter said, "I want to examine you." Peter noticed that Brett had put on much-needed weight – Marg's good cooking. He was filling out and had lost the gaunt look to his face, had good color to his skin and Peter thought he might have even grown a little. He was turning out to be a very handsome boy. "Sit there in the chair and don't look so worried. I just want to be sure your lungs are back where they should be. Should have done it before this but I guess when you have someone living with you and you see them every day, it is the kind of thing you forget about. Having any breathing problems – any weakness anywhere? Shortness of breath?"

Brett shook his head, "No Dad," somehow he had come around to calling Peter and Marguerite "Mom" and "Dad" when both said he could call them that if he was comfortable with it.

Peter moved his stethoscope all over Brett's chest and back and asked him to breathe deep and exhale as well as to cough. He put his hands on both sides of Brett's jaw checking the glands in his neck. After Peter's examination, he pronounced Brett cured, said his lungs were clear and he could do whatever he wanted but added "within reason" and smiled at him and slapped him on the arm. "You don't know how close you were to having a date with the Grim Reaper. I was ready to take you to the hospital. I gave you one night to get better."

"Well thanks for not doing that – that would have landed me in the orphan's home."

"A-h-h-h, your mother would never have allowed that."

Brett looked at him seriously, "But you would have?" He knew Peter was the last hold-out in the family with regard to having him there. He also knew that he didn't blame Peter. He understood even at his young age that a man had to protect his family.

"Probably," Peter said looking for a reaction and then he added, "not," and he laughed. "Go on. Get out of here and go play with your horses."

Peter never thought he would feel fatherly about another child. There had been several children at the orphanage that he could take home but none of them got under his skin the way this kid did. Marg was right – there was something about this boy.

The two boys' junior year of school ended and summer arrived. Brett really wanted to ride some horses or actually to train some horses. He asked if he could take the chestnut mare and see if he could find a stable that could use him.

He walked into a stable about two miles from the house and introduced himself. The owner, John, introduced himself and his friend, Jake. Brett asked if they had any horses that could use training. He didn't say it to John but Brett didn't even care if he got paid for it. He just wanted to ride and he liked the challenge of horses with problems. The two men standing there looked at each other and smiled. Yes, there was this gray gelding. Brett asked to see the horse.

John told his groom to bring out the gray gelding. The groom led a big heavy-boned gray horse out of the stall. The horse pinned back his ears and he tried to bite the man. The groom jerked the chain under the horse's jaw and he backed up. He was a flea-bitten gray which means he was a basic gray color with speckled dark pin-size spots on him. He was big and ugly, had a roman nose, narrow between the eyes and small beady eyes. He had straight pasterns and not a lot of shoulder angulation. For that matter not a lot of rear angulation either. He had some scars here and there. He had either been abused or did it himself, one of those horses that had a high pain threshold and barged ahead no matter what obstacle was in his way.

Brett was no fool, but because he was young, the men thought they were going to put one over on him. He knew that this kind of horse was bullheaded and didn't have any regard for his body and for that matter any regard for the rider either. Whoever bought this horse sure didn't know much about horses. Structure can say a lot about a horse's behavior and temperament and Brett knew this horse was trouble. He had asked for a problem horse and it looked like he was getting it. He asked innocently, "What are the horse's problems?"

"Well, for one thing, he's a little hard mouthed," said John, no surprise to Brett there. Brett walked around the horse placing a hand on his body here and there and watching his ears. He could tell that the horse resented him touching him. Brett thought he had this guy figured out. He wasn't a smart horse and he was very cold-blooded. Then he more than likely had been abused. Generally that is the case with this kind of horse. They can be so stubborn that someone loses his temper and abuses the horse which only makes matters that much worse.

"Do you have a headstall and some rawhide?" he asked John.

John looked at him like for what but he said, "Yes, I do."

"Well, if I can borrow that, I'll be back tomorrow to ride this cayuse." Brett said as he slapped the horse on the rump and noticed the horse pin his ears back and shake his head. Brett knew the horse would like to bite him.

John took Brett into the tack room and showed him what he had. Brett took the supplies he needed and went home.

At dinner, Brett asked, "Why don't your horses have names?"

Peter said, "I don't know. Guess we never thought of it. You want to name them, be my guest."

"I do," said Brett. "Matter of fact, I have names for them."

"All right," said Peter, "let's hear it."

"The bay geldings are Morgan and Virgil. They are named after Wyatt Earp's brothers. And I named the chestnut mare Suzi."

"Sounds fine to me," said Peter, "but why Suzi?"

"Suzi was one of the girls in the saloon where my mother worked. Most of the girls ignored me as just a pesky kid but Suzi was real nice to me. She used to sit with me when I was little when my mother worked and she bought me stick candy all the time. She died of syphilis."

Peter spit his coffee out and grabbed a napkin.

Marguerite couldn't stop laughing.

Tim looked a little stunned.

"What?" said Brett, "she was really nice just like the mare."

In bed that night, Peter said to Marguerite, "I'm so glad our horses are named for two gunfighters and a whore who died of syphilis." Marguerite started laughing again.

"Should have named them yourself," she said.

—m—

Later that night when everyone retired to the sitting room after dinner, Brett was busy braiding some rawhide.

"What are you doing?" asked Tim.

"Making a hackamore."

"What's a hackamore?"

"Instead of putting a bit in a horse's mouth, this works on the nerves in the sides of his mouth."

"You're going to ride a horse without a bit?"

"The horse has a hard mouth; a bit won't work. This is a Mexican bridle."

"You had Mexican friends in Kansas?" asked Tim.

"Yep, Carlos Rodriguez Gonzales and so on and he taught me a lot about riding horses. This hackamore can be used on horses whose mouths are so hard they can't be handled and colts which have a real soft mouth. The reason a horse has a hard mouth is mishandling; someone has been too hard on him and toughened his mouth so a bit is nearly useless. Riding a colt with a real soft mouth with a hackamore keeps his mouth soft. The Mexicans are great riders and trainers. You can learn a lot from them."

"Just be careful with some of these horses. This horse doesn't sound very safe," said Peter.

"I know what I'm doing."

"The last words of an injured cowboy," said Tim.

The next day, Brett got up early and went to the stable. He walked since it really wasn't that far and carried the bridle with him. The same two men were there and just waiting to see him ride this horse. He could tell they were real anxious to see what he was going to do with the gray.

Brett took the horse out of his stall and tied him. While Brett was brushing him, the gray turned to take a bite out of him. Brett turned the metal curry comb toward his nose and bopped him with it on his soft nose. This happened a couple times until the horse was starting to get the idea that biting resulted in punishment. Brett kept the curry comb as he led the horse out to the corral.

He stood the horse and turned his body so that he was facing the horse's rear and wasn't near his rear leg. He pulled up on the outside rein until it pulled the horse's head slightly to the right. This kept him from bringing his head around and biting Brett as he mounted. With his body slightly bent toward Brett, it also worked that if the horse tried to lunge, he would lunge into Brett which would actually pitch him into the saddle instead of lunging away from Brett which would cause him to lose the horse and possibly get hurt. He turned the stirrup around and put a foot into it and swung up swiftly onto the horse's back. Just as he thought the horse tried to kick him from the rear throwing his leg forward called "cow kicking". Had Brett mounted the horse as anyone would mount by facing his front, he would have gotten kicked because he never would have seen it coming.

The problem with this was now his back was to the horse's head but because he had tightened up on the outside rein, when the horse went to turn his head to bite him, Brett jerked the outside rein throwing the horse off balance and right into Brett throwing him into the saddle. Since he couldn't bite Brett in the back on the left as he mounted, when Brett brought his right leg over the saddle and went to put his foot in the stirrup, the horse tried to bite his right leg. Brett was expecting something like this and again he brought the metal curry comb down on the horse's tender nose. Maybe you'll eventually learn thought Brett. He had bitten and/or kicked many a man with his tricks, probably why he had so many scars. Someone had probably beaten him losing their temper with his antics.

The two men looked at each other. They were impressed. The kid was quick and he knew his horses.

Once mounted, Brett squeezed his legs to cue the horse to move forward; the horse stood still. Brett kicked his heels into the horse a little harder. Nothing happened. Brett turned the horse's head almost doubling the horse around until he was forced to move or fall over. Once he moved, Brett again kicked him and he started up. He made a mental note to get some spurs. The horse had really been ruined and had dead sides.

Brett rode the horse letting him get used to the hackamore. At one point the horse tried his leap forward and run for the barn called "barnstorming".

Brett was quick with the hackamore. He brought his hands down low to stop any head tossing knowing that it was possible for the horse to hit him in the face if he threw his head back. The hackamore clamped down on the sides of the horse's mouth. The gray fought back shaking his head, snorting loudly, snuffling and pulling back against Brett's hands. He shook his head violently but he couldn't get rid of the sensation around his nose and he sure didn't like it. Brett didn't jerk or try and punish the horse but simply held his hands firmly in place until he gave into Brett's hands. Once he gave in to Brett, Brett instantly let off with the reins and he learned that he was again able to breathe and the discomfort in his face was gone.

Then Brett asked the horse to walk on. This went on for quite some time – more than an hour. Brett would ask the horse to respond, he would shake his head and pull at the hackamore. When he did that Brett worked with him pulling back and easing up until the horse started to cooperate. Every time the big gray bolted for the barn, Brett again caught him mid-leap with the hackamore and kept his hands firmly in place and turning the horse into himself so it was impossible for him to run and he was forced to give into Brett's hands. When Brett could get the horse to trot and walk on a loose rein around the corral, he quit.

"Hey," said the owner's friend, Jake. "Aren't you going to canter him? I'm waiting to see how you handle that. Come on Kid let's see what you got?"

Brett could not be goaded into doing something he knew would be more than what the horse could handle in his training. If he did, it could be a setback instead of productive. "No, he's done what I asked, time to quit for the day." He dismounted and led the horse into the stable. He pulled off the tack and put the horse back in the crossties. He again groomed the horse. This was something the horse was not used to. Usually, he was "rode hard and put away wet" as the cowboys say.

Each day the horse got a little better. Brett refused to canter the horse until he could walk and trot without fighting against Brett's hands and the hackamore. If he tried his barnstorming act which he tried many times, Brett's hands went down and hard on the hackamore, holding him tight and turning him in place until he quit fighting Brett. The horse found out that if he cooperated with Brett and gave in to his hands, he had no discomfort around his nose and mouth. If he fought with this rider, Brett simply did a give and take on the reins until the horse stopped fighting. Wearing the spurs helped him give the horse better leg cues since this horse was insensitive to Brett's legs.

The gray even started to not mind Brett grooming him before and after being trained. He was one of those horses that wouldn't show it, but Brett thought he even got to the point where he enjoyed being groomed. Once he knew what Brett was about, he started cooperating with him when he rode him, also. Brett was very consistent. If it was wrong, he made the horse understand that it was always wrong and if the horse did it right, Brett rewarded him and let him know he was right. He never lost his temper, never beat the horse into submission or even punished him harshly. The punishments he used correlated with whatever bad behavior Brett was trying to correct so the horse understood what he could and could not do.

He rode the horse almost every day (not on Sundays per Peter's instructions) for about forty-five days. Brett didn't disillusion himself. This horse was not going to be a horse for everyone. He would have to have someone who had a use for a tough horse. He had too many bad habits and a lot of his behavior was heredity related which showed by his structure. Sold to the wrong person and he would go back to exactly the dangerous animal he was when Brett started riding him and would have every potential of getting someone seriously hurt. The gray did have some good qualities though and Brett felt that in the right hands, he could be a useful horse.

When Brett walked into the barn to ride the horse one day, John asked him, "Do you think the gray is ready to sell?"

"To the right buyer and if he is willing to listen to me on how to ride him."

"It's the Sheriff. Can you tell him about the horse?"

"Sure."

John introduced Brett to Sheriff Fred Tompkins and the two shook hands. "Aren't you the kid living with the Osterhaus family?" he asked.

Brett nodded.

He was looking at the big gray that was now in the crossties. Brett walked up to him with John. "Brett here has been riding that gray. He can tell you all about him."

The Sheriff looked at Brett and he said, "He's got a rock-hard mouth, he's bull-headed and if you are not careful he may bite or kick you. The good news is that if you use a hackamore on him and ride him the way I show you,

you don't have to worry about his hard mouth. He's absolutely bullet-proof. You'll never have to worry about him bolting in a dangerous situation. He's so cold-blooded nothing bothers him. He'll also never give up on you. He'll go until he drops and dies. If you show him that you are not going to tolerate his biting and kicking he will stop it. He hasn't tried to bite or kick me in weeks. I'd like to say I broke him of it but I know better. You will have to show him because I'll guarantee you he'll try it with each new person that handles him. I think he'd make a helluva police horse but don't let your kids ride him," and Brett laughed.

John was getting angry when Brett told all the bad things about the horse but Brett wanted people to know what they were getting into. He tried to convince owners that lying did no good. They would just get the horse back probably with more issues and an angry buyer. Be honest up front and the buyer can't say he was not told. Part of selling horses that had had training issues was selling them to the right person.

Brett took the horse out into the corral and rode him for the Sheriff showing Sheriff Tompkins all that the horse could do. He was very honest, however, and told him that he had to be tough with him and not let him get away with anything. This horse would probably test him for a while until he figured out that his rider could handle him. He showed the Sheriff how to stop his biting and kicking behavior. He told him he should wear spurs with the horse and he showed him how he had counteracted all his bad habits.

After Brett demonstrated what all the horse could do, he had the sheriff ride the horse. Brett stood in the middle of the corral giving him instructions on how to handle the hackamore. The sheriff liked the horse. He didn't care that the horse was ugly and he liked the qualities of the horse that Brett had outlined. The gray wasn't a bit skittish and when they tried him with gunfire, he never flinched. Brett laughed – he was about the most cold-blooded horse Brett had ever seen. The Sheriff followed the instructions Brett gave him on how to ride the horse. He asked Brett if he thought it would be possible to ever use a bit on him.

"No," said Brett. "Once that mouth is that tough, it is like it's calloused. You go back to a bit and he'll go back to his old ways and he'll run right through it. He's a very strong horse and you'll find yourself in trouble especially with what you want him for. He could put you in danger. Don't do it."

The City was paying for this horse, consequently John got a very good price for a recalcitrant cantankerous horse that he originally thought was worthless. Sheriff Tompkins bought the horse and had him for many years. As Brett predicted, "he was a helluva police horse and he never let his kids ride him".

John said to Brett, "You put a lot of time in on that animal. What do I owe you?"

"Oh," said Brett, "the last guy I worked for gave me ten dollars every time he sold a horse I had worked with."

John handed him twenty dollars. "You know when you came and asked to ride a horse, I was getting ready to shoot him. Jake and I were going to do it the next day. He was such an outlaw and really dangerous. I was afraid he could even kill somebody. We were mean to throw you up on him. You proved us wrong. You are some horse trainer."

"I find that a lot," said Brett. "A lot of the reward for me is seeing problem horses whether an outlaw or a scared skittish horse that someone is ready to kill saved and put to use. That horse is going to make a really good police horse. He's unflappable."

"No argument here. I have another one waiting in the wings. Ready to tackle him?"

"Sure," said Brett.

His summer between his junior and senior year of high school was spent riding and training horses. Everyone at home noticed how much he had changed doing the horse training. He had always channeled his anxiety and energy into training and riding horses and he was a much happier and more relaxed person when he could do just that. His new family noticed how tan he was by the sun and how he filled out, his youthful body muscling and looking more and more like a young man than an emaciated little orphan boy.

Peter said at lunch one day when he asked where Brett was and both Marguerite and Tim just looked at him, "I don't know if that kid is going to be a doctor or a horse wrangler," and shook his head.

XIV

Carter Ball

Even though Brett rode almost daily at the stable, except for Sunday, he didn't spend the day there. Many times he went and worked the one or two horses he was training and then came home usually in time for lunch. Sometimes Tim went with him. They would ride the two geldings to the stable and then Brett would take one of the horses he was training while Tim continued riding one of their horses. Tim was a big help especially with the colts.

As the word got out what a good trainer Brett was, he rode at other stables as well. None of the stables in the area were as large as John's, however, so he mostly rode for John. If a private owner needed some training on a horse, he would board it with John and Brett would work with it. This worked out to both their advantage as John was paid board while Brett trained the animal and Brett received a training fee.

Virgil and Morgan were both seasoned horses and very calm. They had seen about everything there was to see so nothing really bothered them. For that reason Brett would ask Tim to ride close to the colt he was breaking and let the colt pick up on how the experienced horse reacted to different things. Once out of town, the countryside around Boston was beautiful. Brett loved going out in the rolling hills with the long white fences of the big estates. There were long stretches of good grassland for the horses to canter across and stretch their legs. One of the favorite pastimes for both boys was to ride to the Atlantic Ocean. There was a beach area that they had found to let the horses run along just into the water.

If Brett and Tim were taking the two bay geldings to the ocean just for a fun ride, they usually rode bareback. Then they would race along the beach and one of the boys would throw the other one off their horse and into the water. They would wrestle and throw water at each other rolling around in the huge and beautiful ocean. Brett would look out and see nothing but water and it always astounded him how big it was; that on the other side was a whole other world. They could only do that, however, with Virgil and Morgan because they would stop up on land and wait for their riders to stop the fooling around and come and ride home.

Even though Brett couldn't knock Tim off his horse and they couldn't roll around in the ocean when he rode the colts, he still liked taking the colts there. He would swim them out a ways and let the animal get the feel of the waves coming in. Tim would always stay close in case the colt got scared and panicked. If Brett thought the colt was too skittish, he would leave the colt's halter on under his bridle and put a rope on it. When they reached the ocean, he would give the rope to Tim. He would take a couple wraps around the saddle horn of the horse he was riding and keep the colt's head up close to the gelding. Virgil was more patient about this than Morgan. Morgan sometimes got angry at a stupid colt and felt it necessary to reach over and bite him. He never bit hard, just a "don't-be-stupid" bite and it always made Tim and Brett laugh. They tended to use Morgan more because he was bigger and stronger even though he had to reprimand the youngster and Virgil was actually more patient.

After swimming in the ocean, they went through a pond they knew about on the way home to get the salt deposits off the horses and themselves when they went rolling in the ocean. These were the times that Brett enjoyed the most, being with his best friend and his horses. Then knowing that he had a home to go to where there would be good food, a clean bed and he could feel secure.

One of the rules that Peter and Marguerite enforced and insisted that Brett live by was that Sundays were reserved for the family. Peter told him that he had six other days to be with horses.

The family started the day with church. Brett had actually taken a liking to church and even started reading the bible. In his usual "Brett Study Method" he would read, study and ask Reverend Jerome a million questions about God, Jesus and the Christian ways until the minister's head was spinning. Holidays also had new meaning for him now that he understood what they were about.

Finally, he also knew what the good reverends in Kansas were talking about when both of his parents were buried and they mentioned "everlasting life".

After church, Marguerite and her assistant, Brett, always made a big family dinner. This was one of the highlights of his week. He had learned to love to cook and it gave him some alone time with Marguerite. He liked talking to her and running everyday experiences and questions by her. She was a great listener and a very good adviser. He thought she would have made a good counselor. He was able to open up with her more than either of the men even Tim. She was so gentle and understanding. She was never irritated about anything he asked her and always encouraged him to talk about whatever he liked. The rest of Sunday was spent playing cards, chess or board games or just doing family time in the sitting room or outside in good weather playing some game or sport.

In the evening there was always a real nice dessert usually cake and coffee. Marguerite even taught Brett how to make a cake. His first attempt was disastrous. It was a chocolate cake and looked like a volcano that had erupted. The cake and icing were all blended together and the cake had a hole in the middle. Everyone laughed but they all ate it and it was actually quite good. Brett said he liked making things that could be eaten and disappeared so his failures didn't live on to eternity.

One Saturday, Peter sprang a surprise on Brett after dinner and during family talk-time at the table. He told Brett that he was going to meet Marguerite's family – the Carters the next day. There was going to be a picnic at the Osterhaus house for the entire Carter family. All three of the Osterhauses looked at Brett. As predicted, he wasn't happy. He didn't like strangers; he especially didn't like a lot of strangers. They all noticed a mixture of fear and possibly anger creep into his expressive eyes. He first said he'd go riding but Peter said, "NO" and very firmly. Brett was going to have to start partaking in some family time. The Carters were wonderful people and very much a part of their life and Brett had to meet them. There would be more parties and there would be Christmas and Brett needed to find out what family life was about. Brett said no more. He knew when he was whipped. They had been too good to him to fight it.

The Carter family was like no other. George and Matilda Carter indoctrinated their in-law children into their family just like their own children. The youngest son, Jake, was the only unmarried Carter. When someone asked the Carter parents how many children they had, they didn't say the six natural children instead they would always answer "eleven". When someone married, their spouse became a child and was treated that way.

—⟋⟍—

Peter only had the one brother, Joseph. Peter's father died when he was fairly young of heart disease. His mother died soon after. Then when Joseph was twenty-eight years old, he died in an industrial accident. Peter was devastated. The Carters surrounded him with love. They did everything for him. There was always a Carter or two at the funeral home and they were at his beckon call. He mentioned something he needed, someone made sure he had it. They took over his life to the point where he almost wished they would back off. He realized however that they were only trying to help him get through the worst time of his life by giving him all the love and support they could.

Tim was only ten years old and it was hard on a kid to spend so much time at a funeral home especially for an uncle he had adored. So one of the Carters would take him to their house and he could play with his cousins. They drove Peter and Marguerite to the funeral home for the funeral. They took charge of a wake afterward. Everything was done for Peter and they surrounded him with love. They became his brothers and sisters even more than before.

—⟋⟍—

When the Sunday of the picnic came, Marguerite was up early preparing food. Everyone always brought lots of food but Marguerite always felt she had to prepare the most. Charles was a farmer and he had provided a beef haunch. Peter had dug a pit in the back yard and put the haunch on the spit early so it would be cooked through. Tim and Brett helped him prepare the meat for cooking and took turns turning the meat on the spit.

Everyone started arriving around noon. There was a lot of commotion as they all exchanged greetings and hugs and kisses. There was lots of food - salads, vegetable dishes and cakes and pies lined the counter in the kitchen.

The family went outside and everyone was getting settled. Richard's son, Ricky, said to Tim, "So where's this new kid I've heard about?" Tim knew. Brett was hiding in his room.

"He's in his room," Tim said, "You won't see him."

Ricky had this malicious grin on his face, "Oh yes we will."

"Don't start something," Tim said, "you don't know how tough he can get."

"Oh, he doesn't scare me."

"He's going to be mad-d-d," said Tim, "and he's a cougar when he is mad."

"Yes," said Ricky, "but we have Hughy."

Hughy was Charles' son. He was a big boy and worked on the farm and was very strong. Hughy was the second oldest of six children Charles and Ellen had; Hughy's sister, Michelle, was the oldest. Hughy was a gentle giant. He could hold a baby chick in his big hands and never hurt it. He had birthed animals and never upset the mothers but he could take a horseshoe and bend it with his bare hands. He loved all his younger siblings and many times helped his mother and older sister take care of the younger children. He also was his father's right-hand-man. He was just a big gentle sweet boy and wouldn't hurt anyone but he was strong as an ox.

"Come on," said Ricky. He got Hughy and Andy, Amanda's son, and Tim went along afraid that Brett would be too scared and someone would get hurt. He thought maybe he could keep him from overreacting.

Peter and Charles were scrubbing and cutting up potatoes and saw the gaggle of boys going into the house. "What do you suppose they are up to?" asked Charles pretty sure he knew.

"Looks like a Brett attack," said Peter.

"Think we should put a stop to it."

"No, I think it's about time Brett discovered there are other people in the world."

"Where's his room?" Ricky asked as the boys went into the house.

Tim pointed to the room next to Peter's office. The door was shut. Ricky opened the door just enough to peek around the edge of it. "Are you Brett?" he asked in a sing-song voice.

Brett looked up. He was lying on his bed reading a book. He didn't answer. He thought the answer was obvious.

Ricky continued, "Can you come out to play?" he said in the same irritating sing-song voice.

Disgusted with Ricky's behavior Brett said, "I'm reading."

"We see that but we need another member for the team."

"Go away. I said I'm reading," Brett again said.

Suddenly Ricky came through the door and said, "Get him, Boys."

To Brett's shock four boys, Tim included grabbed him. Tim got up by his head talking to him and trying to calm him but he was having none of it. He was fighting like a tiger, his black eyes dancing. Black eyes meant nothing to the Carters after all they had Hughy. The boys carried him outside.

Charles said to Peter, "Think we better do something. The kid is getting really scared." They set down the last of the potatoes and walked over to where the boys had Brett pinned on the ground.

"All right. That's enough," said Charles and started pulling boys off Brett. He grabbed one of Brett's arms and Peter grabbed the other and they pulled him to his feet. Charles was the farmer and very strong between him and Peter, Brett was going nowhere.

"You're all right," said Peter in a soothing tone to Brett. Brett tried to pull away but both Peter and Charles held onto him.

"Come on," said Charles, "let's get up a game of ball."

"I don't like ball and I don't know how to play ball," said Brett angrily the fire burning in his eyes and about as angry as Peter had ever seen him but the two men still held onto his arms so he couldn't run.

"Oh that's because you have never played CARTER BALL!" and he shouted it. Boys and girls came running and they all ran out to the field behind the house with bats and balls. Brett was swept along and not allowed to get away. He was effectively trapped and found that there was someone in his way every move he made mostly Peter. Peter grabbed his arm at one point and said to him very low so no one else heard, "Brett, settle down. No one here will hurt you."

Brett looked up at Peter and thought he'd go along for now and first chance he got, he would run. Peter had a way about him. No one ever heard him shout and with Brett he even talked softer than usual but he was hard to deny. He reeked of authority that was hard to skirt and Brett respected him and had come to trust Peter.

Carter Ball was not like any ball anyone had ever played. There was no choosing of sides so that someone felt like they were the last and the worst. Instead the men picked out the players and told them whose team they would be on. They picked the players by their capabilities. Tim and Ricky were the best players so they were separated one on each team. Then the rest were divided up so that there were beginners and experienced players in equal numbers on both teams.

Richard had more or less invented Carter Ball so he was the designated pitcher and he pitched for both teams. That is all Richard did was pitch. It went something like this:

If the batter was a good player, Richard pitched hard and fast. If the batter was a beginner, Richard lobbed the ball in almost aiming for the bat. The batter could hardly miss the ball. When the batter got a hit no matter how far it went, he was guaranteed a spot on first base. If the ball just dribbled out onto the infield which was usually the case with beginners, Richard would run to it, pick it up and turn to throw to first base. If the runner wasn't quite there, he would either fumble the ball and pick it up again or throw it over the first baseman's head so he would have to chase it down. Then if the runner still wasn't on first base, the first baseman would fumble the ball. The batter was guaranteed to get to first base. After that, he was on his own but he would get to first base. Even the women and girls played Carter Ball. It usually worked out that the more experienced players made the most outs.

So teams were chosen. Because the men wanted Brett to get to know the family, they put Tim on the other team and Ricky (the hated one) on Brett's team. To keep him comfortable though and from running away, they left Peter on his team. It shook out to be Peter, Brett, Hughy, Ricky, Andy and Michelle (Charles's daughter) on one team. Tim, Charles, Billie (Richard's younger son), Jake (Marguerite's youngest brother), Amanda and Sally (Amanda's daughter) were on the other team. Of course Richard pitched.

Brett struck out his first time at bat. Even with handicaps it happens. The second time he came to bat, he got a hit. He was so fast however, that Richard only had to fumble the ball once and he was on first base. The other teammates brought him around the bases and he came charging into home plate for a run and right into Hughy's big arms. Hughy squealed in delight and lifted Brett up off his feet in a big bear hug and swung him around patting him on the back like he had just won a national event.

This went on until food was ready and everyone gave it up and went to eat. Someone asked the score but most did not even know what it was or who had won. That was "CARTER BALL". Because he was so fast and everyone had been told about how he loved the West and had been raised there, Brett got dubbed the "Coyote Kid" and he never hid in his room again.

In the fall there was a different spin on Carter Ball. It was a form of football but no one was allowed to tackle. It was touch football and the runner had to stop when tagged by a member of the opposite team. Brett was so fast that if he could get the ball and get anywhere in the clear nothing could catch him. There were half-hearted tries but usually someone would just say, "There goes the Coyote Kid." And that was that.

One time though the whole family on both sides decided to ambush him. He got the ball and was making his run which he loved to do, when everyone converged on him from both teams and all sides. The "no tackle" rule went out the window although it was really more of a family hug as they all wrapped their arms around each other and the whole gang of players rolled on the ground. Someone yelled, "We tackled the Coyote Kid and everyone laughed Brett rolling around with the whole gang of Carters laughing also.

Brett no longer feared this bunch. He took it and laughed and rolled with them and felt their love. He bragged about his new name and signed his name "Brett, The Coyote Kid" to everything relating to the family.

There were more Marguerites in the world however it seemed that they were all in the same family. Carter Ball was Carter Love.

XV

Christmas

All summer and into the fall there were several Carter-Osterhaus picnics. When it got too cold for picnics, there were parties at the families' homes. They accepted Brett as if he had been there all his life and Brett learned to love all of them. He became especially close to Hughy and Ricky.

Brett found out that Hughy loved chess. The two boys became avid players. Hughy was not college material but he wasn't dumb either. Brett taught him some plays that he had learned in books. Hughy caught on fast, practiced at home and Brett found him a challenging opponent. Brett had started out letting Hughy win once in a while so he would continue to play with Brett but soon he wasn't letting Hughy win. The adults had to pry the boys off the board when they wanted them to participate in other games or food.

The picnics turned into Thanksgiving and they had dinner at Peter and Marguerite's home with everyone bringing some food. Brett helped Marguerite prepare a turkey with stuffing. After Thanksgiving and a month later everyone was preparing for Christmas.

A few days before Christmas, Peter was at one of his council meetings and Tim was on a date. Tim went out with a lot of girls and never seemed to date anyone on any regular basis. He would date a girl more than once but he might date a couple other girls in between. He was always honest with them and if they started putting any pressure on him about being his one and only, he simply told them he wasn't ready for that. Usually he then stopped asking that girl for a date. He didn't want to lead any girl on. He often joked and said, "He was too young to be tied down." Tim was a very handsome young man and fun to be with and a great dancer. He was always out for a good time and girls liked him but he just hadn't found the girl that could steal his heart.

He and Ricky went out together many times and went to clubs and danced with girls rather than took girls out. Tim actually liked that better because he didn't feel like he was under any obligation to explain himself to a girl who was looking for a steady guy. He tried to get Brett to go with them but Brett was still a loner and shy around girls. He would sometimes go with Tim and Ricky but it never really appealed to him.

Sometimes Tim would practically force him to go out with one of his girlfriend's girlfriends. Then he was so shy with the girl, they really didn't want to date him again and furthermore, he didn't care. He was perfectly content to stay home or be with horses.

Thus on this day, Marguerite and Brett were home alone. In the kitchen Marguerite was making Christmas cookies and Brett was sitting at the table cracking walnuts for her cookies. "Mom, can I ask you something?" asked Brett.

"Sure."

"What kind of love is stronger, the love a wife has for her husband or the love a mother has for her son?"

Marguerite thought she knew where he was going with this. He had done a lot of muttering about his mother's illness when he was sick and delirious. "Well, Brett, that's a hard question to answer. They are different kinds of love. You can't love your spouse the same way you love your children. I guess if I have to give you an answer, I'd say neither is stronger, they are equal, just different. Why do you ask?" She wanted to keep him talking. He had hidden so much from them that if he wanted to talk, she wanted to encourage him. She thought it would be good for him to open up a little.

"Umm," he said, "when my mother was so sick, I took care of her. I saw that she got her medication when she was supposed to have it; I bathed her, changed her bedding and washed it and washed her gowns. I stayed with her the whole time even when she was dying. All she kept saying is, 'Is Mike here yet?' and calling for my father. Mom, I was only thirteen years old, I still needed her. Why wasn't our relationship strong enough to hold her? Why did she not say anything about me?"

Marguerite took a break. She poured two cups of coffee and walked around the table and set one in front of him and sat down next to him. "Brett, how was your relationship with your mother before she was taken sick?"

"It was all right. I mean my mother wasn't the kissing, hugging type but seeing how her parents are I guess I understand that. I had no doubt that she loved me. She always took care of me and bought me things. She was never mean; never even spanked me or hit me."

"Then maybe she called for Mike because he wasn't there," Marguerite said. "You were there and you were her mainstay. She didn't need to call for you. Brett, it sounds like she tried to give you the best home she knew how with the money and skills she had to work with. You should remember the good times you had with her and not her last illness. When a person is sick, all kinds of things go through their mind. You know there are all kinds of diseases we still don't know that much about. It may be that she had one of those. I think you are thinking that you should have cured her and since she died, you failed. You can't put that on yourself. You're going to find if you continue to become a doctor that some people die and sometimes with no explanation as to why and there is nothing anyone can do."

He nodded, "Thanks, Mom."

Christmas Eve was at the Osterhaus home. Brett read about the child born in the barn and now he knew how special he was. After their dinner, the whole family, Carters and Osterhauses, went to the midnight candlelight service at the church. Brett found it very peaceful. He sang the hymns with everyone else and participated in the candlelight ceremony. He went to bed that night thanking God for all his good fortune.

On Christmas morning the family opened gifts and Peter and Tim prepared breakfast. It was a tradition that Marguerite always had Christmas off for cooking and since Brett did so much cooking also, they decided that he too could have it off. Peter and Marguerite had bought Brett a Charles Russell print of the West. Of all things, it was of a bronc rider and the horse was in full bucking mode. They thought that was appropriate because in no way would Brett ever let a horse buck that way. His way was a much gentler method. It was beautiful and Brett did not know what to say. Right after breakfast he insisted that Tim help him hang it in his room.

Marguerite had also knitted him a sweater for the winter. He actually knew about that because she kept having him stand up and she would measure the length of the sleeves and the waist. He thought that is what he was getting for a gift so the painting was a complete surprise. He bought both Peter and Tim Western hand-tooled belts. John knew someone who did exquisite work with leather and Brett ordered two of them for the men. He purchased a beautiful silk scarf for Marguerite. Tim bought him a really nice dress shirt. The family liked to go to plays and concerts and Brett always wore the same shirt. "I'm tired of looking at that beige shirt you wear," Tim said. The one he bought was bright blue and very handsome indeed especially with the new navy blue suit he had bought right before Christmas for a play they had gone to. He was growing and filling out and his old clothes were not fitting him anymore.

The rest of Christmas day was spent at Charles Carter's farm. Brett and Hughy played chess until adults again pried them away. Dinner was served and gifts exchanged. Names had been drawn and each person got a gift.

Afterward, Hughy took Brett out and introduced him to all the animals. Hughy had names for practically every animal on the farm except the ones they planned to slaughter. He said he couldn't name them and then kill them. Although Hughy was kind, he still realized that the animals had a purpose and it didn't bother him to kill and dress them out as long as it was done humanely.

Even though the family exchanged names sometimes special gifts were given. Hughy gave Brett a hand-made chess board and chess set. He had made the board himself in his father's workshop. It was a work of art. The squares on the board were of light and dark wood and had a varnish over it. He had purchased the chess men but had hunted until he found a set that would be perfect for the board. Brett didn't know what to say. He hugged Hughy and said it would be their personal board.

Brett was good with braiding leather. He braided Hughy a leather belt. Hughy thought it was the greatest gift he had gotten. He was such a big boy that it was hard for him to find a belt that fit and it fit just right. Brett had guessed at the size and tried to make it a little bigger so it would be sure to fit. He was pleased when it fit Hughy and the big boy proudly strutted around showing off his belt to everyone's laughter.

After dinner and gift opening, all the younger Carters plus Tim and Brett all went outside and had a big snowball fight. Ricky and Brett went into a wrestling match and ended up rolling around in the snow washing each other's face in it. Ricky was bigger than Brett and probably stronger but Brett was sneaky and so fast. He could wriggle out from under Ricky and then shove his head back into the snow and the two boys would laugh, usually Ricky grabbing Brett's leg and pulling him down into the snow for more wrestling. When the others saw the two boys rolling and wrestling in the snow, they all piled on and everyone was rolling and wrestling, throwing snow in each other's faces, laughing and having the best time. The Carters were instrumental in teaching Brett that he need not be so fearful with other people.

A week later the family celebrated New Year's Eve in the same way they had the year before when Brett first visited them for the holiday. It started with a good meal of roast beef, mashed potatoes and gravy, sweet corn and chocolate cake. After a couple hours, they popped corn, made a sugary treat called fudge and brought out special drinks. Everyone went to bed happy, full of good food and warm, both by the fireplace and by the love that permeated all over the house. Brett snuggled down into his warm clean-smelling bed. He thought back after he lost his mother and how he felt so empty and as if he would never be able to love anyone again. Now here he was with a wonderful family. He felt warm, well-fed, secure and very much loved – he was a part of a family. It was hard for him to believe that just a year ago, he was starving and freezing in that awful tenement apartment.

Because New Year's is such a marker for what is going on in people's lives after the family celebrated New Year's Eve and everyone was in bed, Peter said to Marguerite, "Do you realize we have had Brett for almost a year?"

"It actually seems longer than that," said Marguerite, "hard to think of a time we didn't have him."

"What do you say we adopt him officially?"

Marguerite could not believe he said that. All his misgivings and now he wanted to make Brett a legal part of their family. Marguerite was ecstatic, "Oh Peter," was all she could get out she was so choked up.

"I talked to Mark Wagner about doing it legally for us. I have all the information but I think we really have to talk to Tim and be sure he understands what it means."

"Brett talked about going over to the stable tomorrow. He has a gift for John. That would give us a chance to talk to Tim."

On New Year's Day, Peter, Marguerite and Tim stayed at the lunch table after Brett left to go to the barn. He wasn't riding now, it was just too cold but he wanted to take a Christmas gift to John.

Peter explained to Tim what all Mark Wagner, their attorney, had told him – exactly what it means when you adopt a child. Peter wanted Tim to fully understand that if he agreed, Brett would have all the same rights as Tim in the family. He would split the parents' inheritance, be able to make medical decisions for all three of them, he would be as if he were born to them.

Peter told Tim that he didn't need to make a decision right away, he could think about it. If he decided to keep things as they were, Brett would still stay. Tim needed no time to think about it. He loved Brett and was excited that now Brett would be his real brother. He wanted to tell Brett as soon as he came home.

Peter and Marguerite agreed that Tim could tell him. Brett hardly got in the door and had taken his coat, hat and gloves off when Tim yelled at him to come into the sitting room. Tim sounded excited and Brett wondered what was going on. He went into the room and Tim nearly accosted him. "Guess what?" said Tim, "we have made a decision, all of us, to adopt you and make you an official part of our family. Isn't that great?"

It took Brett totally by surprise. He never even thought they would want him in their family legally. He stopped, standing still in the doorway and stared at them, his eyes wide and mouth fell open. They wanted to adopt him? Was he really worthy to be in this family? Fear suddenly gripped him that he could not live up to their expectations. All he could do was shake his head and say, "No," and turned and ran into his room, shutting the door behind him.

Tim turned and looked at his parents stunned, "Brett, why?" he managed to choke out as Brett went out of the room.

Peter got up. "I'll go get him and let's see what this is about." Peter went to his room and knocked. "It's Dad, Brett, can I come in?"

There was a long silence at first but then he heard Brett say, "Yes" rather weakly.

Peter walked in and Brett was standing in front of the window looking out. His hands planted on the window sill, his head down taking deep breaths almost in a panic attack. Peter stopped halfway across the room, "Do you want to tell us why you don't want to be a part of our family?" Peter said gently in that voice that pried information out of anyone whether they were willing to give it or not. "If you truly don't, it's all right you can still stay here and we will all still love you but we would just like to know why?"

Brett continued facing the window, looking down and wouldn't face Peter. "You don't know anything about me. I would bring you nothing but grief."

"I see," said Peter, "so you are planning on changing? You have brought us nothing but joy so far."

"I'm nothing like Tim. He's perfect. I have . . . these feelings sometimes."

Marguerite and Tim were standing in the doorway.

"Brett," said Marguerite, "I think we know quite a lot about you. You have told us a lot and you can tell us more as you are ready. Your past is of little significance to us, we are only concerned with what you are now and want to see you have a good future."

"My father was a killer. What makes you think I won't be a killer?" he was now practically yelling.

Peter snickered a little, "Last time I checked, being a killer, if that is what your father was, is not hereditary."

"My life has been crude. You live in this beautiful home and have wonderful families and great relationships; you just don't know what it's really like out there in my world."

"Brett, all of that is what we want for you," said Tim.

"Look," said Peter, "Marg and Tim are right, all that is immaterial. What we have always wanted for both you and Tim is a future. You are more worldly than we are that's true but we don't care about that. We see a lot of potential in you Brett. Sometimes everyone needs a helping hand. You've done so much on your own that you have a hard time taking that helping hand. You're still a kid and you don't need to put on a brave front with us. We want to be your family, to love you for the rest of all our lives. We don't expect you to be another Tim. We know you are not like Tim. That's why we love you both. Because both of you bring different qualities, different attitudes, different skills and different ideas into our home and our lives. If you accept our offer to be a true member of our family, we can truly be there to support each other emotionally, physically and legally to make decisions for each other. Do you understand what I'm trying to say?"

"So you want me as I am? What if I get into trouble and bring down the law or something worse into the family? I live on the edge," he said turning around and facing all of them.

"Would you turn one of us away, if we did something to bring down the law or something worse?"

"Of course not," he jumped right on that.

"Then why would we turn you away? That's what families are about. There for each other no matter what."

"This is overwhelming."

"Do you want to think about it? You don't have to give up the name 'Ballin' if that is what is bothering you. I wouldn't expect you to. If you have children, they should carry your name, your heritage. You may take our name if you desire, but you certainly don't have to. It makes no difference to us what your name is."

"I'll let you know at breakfast. Is that all right?"

"Sure. Just know though Brett whatever your decision, we love you the same and we want you to stay here for as long as you want. If you can't decide right now, the offer will remain open as long as you like."

Brett nodded, "Thanks," he said meekly.

Brett put on his coat, muffler and gloves and went for a long walk. When he came back, he went immediately to his room and sat with his head in his hands thinking. After a while he lied back on his bed, his hands behind his head still trying to think. These people were so wonderful. Should he spoil their lives by becoming one of them? Everyone left him alone to think it through.

When he came into the kitchen for breakfast, everyone was already at the table. He sat down and picked up his fork but didn't put it into his eggs. All three stopped eating as he started to talk. "If you are sure, I'd love to be a part of this family. It would be a dream come true."

Everyone raised their orange juice glasses and made a toast – here's to the four of us, a new family, all for one and one for all. And this really was another chapter in the life of Brett Ballin, Brett thought, but not closed – *opened*.

XVI

Graduation

Peter notified Mark Wagner to go ahead with the adoption. It took a couple months to go through all the adoption process, there had to be home visits and other investigations which were standard procedures.

On a Saturday afternoon, Peter called Brett into his office. He was sitting at his desk. There was a stern-faced middle-aged lady dressed in a gray uniform – a straight skirt, jacket and white blouse, her plain brown hair done up in a bun and a flat gray hat perched on top of her head. She was sitting very stiff and upright in one of Peter's chairs across from his desk. She was holding a clipboard with paperwork attached and there was no smile on her face – her gray eyes that matched her uniform glanced at Brett as he walked in. She was the picture of authority. Brett looked for a badge but didn't see one. What was this about? He got very nervous and wanted to bolt. Peter saw how restless he got when he saw the visitor. He introduced her as Miss Olson with the County Children's Services Board. Peter noticed immediately that Brett brought himself upright and for a minute he was afraid Brett would run. Peter, however, had a way of settling Brett and his look now held him in place.

He stood up, walked over and put his hands reassuringly on Brett's shoulders. "Miss Olson just wants to ask you a few questions, Brett." His thin smile tried to relax the boy but Brett was already stiff, his face pale, his dark eyes unreadable. Peter slapped him on his back and walked out shutting the door. Brett stood and watched Peter leave and flinched when the door clicked shut, the sound amplified in his mind - sort of reminded him of how a jail cell door might sound when it shuts.

Miss Olson seemed to soften when she turned to talk to Brett but he still didn't trust her. Like he had done to the bullies, he was preparing himself to butt her in the stomach with his head and run.

"You can sit down, Brett. This won't take long," she said motioning to a chair that had been placed in front of her. Brett sunk into the chair and placed his feet in the charging position. She then smiled at him and the questions she asked were not hard ones and he easily got through the interview. Surprisingly, she stood shortly to leave, she said, "You are very fortunate – Dr. Osterhaus is one of the most prestigious men in Boston. You probably didn't know that did you?"

Brett shook his head slowly gazing up at her. Was that it? Was that all she was going to ask him? She wasn't going to say that he was unworthy to be in this family and had to go to the orphanage?

"Well," she said, "I am happy for you. I wish all my placements were so easy."

Brett just sat there and blinked away his surprise. She wasn't such a bad person.

At dinner that evening, Tim said, "Brett, what did that lady ask you today?"

"Oh," said Brett, "She just wanted to know if this is really where I wanted to live and how I was treated here."

"And did you give us a good report?" asked Peter digging into his mashed potatoes.

"I said it was all right, I guess, except for the beatings."

Peter dropped his fork and looked astonished at Brett – his face a cloud of concern.

Tim ducked his head down, smiling hard and trying not to laugh.

Marguerite covered her mouth with her hand and looked down trying to stifle her laughter.

Then Peter got it – he'd been had. He picked up his fork and shook it at Brett and Tim, "You boys would probably benefit from a couple good beatings," and he laughed.

"What did I do?" yelled Tim and everyone laughed.

There was a little more paperwork to this adoption since Brett was not in any court system in Massachusetts. Mark was astounded at how he had gotten away with all he had done. "There are no records whatsoever showing that he exists here in Suffolk County," Mark told Peter. He contacted the county seat for Winchester and finally got a record of his birth. When he met with Peter after finally getting the record that there was a "Brett Ballin" he said, "This kid is a real talker, Peter. He got into school with nothing but a story."

Peter laughed, "Just another Brett mystery, Mark. I'm at the point where nothing surprises me about him. He sure has brought an element of excitement to my household."

At the final hearing for the adoption, the judge made a statement. "I don't usually get adoptions when a child is sixteen years old. I must commend you Dr. & Mrs. Osterhaus for giving this boy a home and a future. Young man I have read your school transcript and you are an outstanding student. I hope you appreciate all the Osterhauses have done for you and what they can do for you in the future. Do you have a career choice?"

"I really appreciate my family, Your Honor, and yes, I would like to be a doctor."

"Good choice. Your grades reflect that you should have no trouble. I see here you would like to keep the last name of "Ballin". I can understand that; it is your heritage. Is there anything else you would like to request of the Court at this time?"

"Yes, Your Honor. Although I would like to keep my last name, Ballin, I would like my entire name to be Brett Peter Ballin."

Peter was pleased. He put his hand on Brett's hand on the desk where they were all sitting.

"I think that is a fine gesture on your part. It will be in the final order. A new birth certificate will be issued to you in the name of Brett Peter Ballin with Peter Osterhaus and Marguerite Osterhaus listed as your parents. Is that all?"

"Yes Sir."

"It is so ordered. Court is dismissed."

Brett at first felt guilty. He felt like he was betraying Lila and Mike but on second thought he decided that he would always have their memories and he would think of them as his "First Parents" while Peter and Marguerite would be his parents. How many kids get two sets of parents? He couldn't help but feel that Mike and Lila would be grateful to the Osterhauses for all they did for their son. Maybe if there really was a heaven, at least his mother might know what happened to him; he wasn't sure about where Mike was.

—∿—

Periodically, throughout the school year, Joshua would come to school and see Brett. He would always give him money. They talked more each time but Joshua was always nervous and worried that someone his father knew would see him or that his father may have him followed, consequently he never stayed long. He would give his nephew a hug each time they parted and tell him the standard line, "Your grandmother sends her love and be safe."

Brett would always pass the envelope to Peter after removing the note that his grandmother put in for him. Peter would always say, "This is going into your account, right?" Sometimes Brett took out a few dollars for spending money especially in the winter when he wasn't training the horses but the majority of the money went into his account.

Winter started fading and spring was coming on. It was a rainy spring typical of Boston and Brett went back to working the horses as much as possible. He was busy with school so he didn't ride every day but he rode whenever he could. Weekends he and Tim often rode and he trained the young horses while Tim rode either Virgil or Morgan. Tim was really getting into riding. Before Brett, he never rode that much. The horses were just transportation but now he really enjoyed it and it was something he could do with Brett. He liked helping Brett with the colts also. He made no pretense at being a trainer but he did learn a lot and could do whatever Brett needed him to do whenever necessary.

One night at dinner, Tim announced that he had some news. He had been chosen Valedictorian of the senior class. Everyone congratulated him and was excited for him and most excited of all was Brett. Tim had to explain to Brett what it was and after he did with some reserve since he felt Brett was smarter and probably more deserving, Brett nevertheless praised him.

"I'm not sure it should be me," pointed out Tim, "I think it should actually be Brett."

"Tim, look if the school felt you should be it, so be it. I think it is a great honor and I'm proud to say that my brother is Valedictorian. Besides now you have to make the speech."

Peter said, "Well, I'd like to say that we are very proud of you, Tim, and I think Brett is right. The school figured it out to be you and you should accept it. Don't cheapen the honor by thinking that you don't deserve it."

"Well, thanks Mom and Pop and I thank you Brett. You're a gracious loser."

"I'm still the best horse trainer in the family!"

Graduation day came and Tim made a great speech. Brett smiled broadly and clapped hardily for his brother at the end of his speech. He ended up third after some girl. He didn't care. He was graduating that was all that mattered. Brett wasn't into position but he didn't want Tim to think that his award was not special so he made a big fuss about it.

When the boys came into the arena and took their seats, Brett thought he saw Joshua and his grandmother sitting in some of the chairs by the door. Wasn't it dangerous for them to be here?

After the ceremony and as the students were walking out to join their families, Josh gave him a wave and his grandmother smiled. He waved back and was about to go to greet them when he saw Elijah Simmons coming into the building with two burly body guards. Brett looked on in horror. He motioned to Joshua to get his grandmother out of there. He saw Joshua get up and help his mother up and start out the door. They needed some diversion Brett thought.

Peter and Marguerite had stopped to talk to some other parents. Brett used this distraction and left his family because he didn't want them involved and started toward his grandfather. Peter saw him walk away and couldn't figure out what he was doing.

Brett walked up to his grandfather and said in a low voice, "What are you doing here? I'll tell you what you told me 'Get out'." His only purpose was to give Joshua enough time to get his grandmother away. When Peter saw Brett approach the important-looking man, he excused himself, told Tim to stay with Marguerite and he followed Brett.

"Get out of my way, Boy."

"You have no business here," said Brett, "you certainly don't care if I graduate or not." He was trying anything to give Joshua more time to get his grandmother out of the building and into the buggy.

Peter caught up with him. "Brett" he said, "Come on, what are you doing?" He didn't know why Brett had accosted this obvious big shot with two burly body guards. He hadn't seen Josh and didn't know Brett's grandmother.

"I said get out of my way," and Elijah pulled his hand back into his chest to backhand Brett.

Peter grabbed Brett's shoulders and pulled him back against his body to avoid any chance of the boy getting struck but he was now losing his temper. He was no small man and in his own right, was prestigious in Boston also. He suddenly realized who this was and no one not even a big shot with two body guards was going to hit his son. "You hit him and he'll end up owning your company," he said, "I have good attorneys also."

"Then get him out of my way. I'm looking for my wife."

Peter then had an inkling why Brett had done what he did. "Come on, Brett, let's go," and he tried to pull him in the opposite direction away from Simmons and his entourage.

Just then another one of Elijah's flunkies came through the door. "They are out front, Sir, getting into a buggy."

Elijah turned and started out the door and Brett pulled away from Peter and went after him. He didn't know what he was going to do but he had to protect his grandmother somehow. She had risked her life for him and he had to do something. Peter tried to grab him as he charged out the door but he missed so he followed him.

They all streamed out onto the front lawn of the school. To Brett's astonishment, his grandmother sat in the buggy and Joshua was standing in front of her and outside the buggy. He was standing straight up and his arms were folded across his chest. Brett had always thought Joshua was a milk toast, petrified of his father but he sure didn't look like he was scared now. He was standing rock-solid, arms folded and looking his father straight in the eye.

Brett stopped for a minute and Peter caught up with him but then he started again toward the buggy. "Joshua, get her out of here," he yelled, but Joshua never moved and there was no fear written across either his or Gladys's face. She, too, was staring at her husband and his body guards. A person can only beat a hound dog so long before it turns on him.

Elijah and his henchmen walked up to the buggy. Brett and Peter stood back but could still hear what was being said.

"What are you doing here?" Elijah yelled at his wife.

"I came to see my grandson graduate."

"I told you not to have any more contact with him."

"You have told me a lot of things, Eli. I'm done with you telling me things. Joshua and I are moving out. We have a new place."

"What? You can't survive without me."

"I'm going to try. I haven't survived very well with you so maybe it won't be that hard."

"And you," he turned to Joshua, "You are no longer my son. You're through. Don't even bother to come back to the company."

"I'm not," said Josh. "I have another job and I'll keep my Mother quite nicely. It's something FATHER how you keep throwing away your children. Now you can be alone – see how you like it. By the way, Father, I have a gift for my NEPHEW, Brett." He shouted, "nephew" for emphasis.

"For all the years you lied to me about my sister and kept me from her and her son; for the fourteen years they lived in Kansas and I missed visits with them; for all the years you felt my mother and I were nothing but your slaves to do whatever your bidding was for that day. For showing me what a man is . . ."

"You were never a man."

"Well then, I didn't have the best example, did I? When you so generously gave me forty percent of your holdings for Simmons & Son as your heir and let me think that the business would be mine someday. FATHER, I wouldn't know the first thing about running that business. You never let me get involved. Simmons & SON, what a joke. . . ." he put the emphasis on "Son". He took an envelope out of the buggy, "I'm giving half of my holdings, twenty percent of YOUR company to my sister's rightful heir and keeping twenty percent." He walked over and handed the envelope to Brett. He gave Brett a hug. "Here Brett, congratulations on your graduation."

"You didn't, Joshua." Elijah was now red in the face. "You would give that bastard twenty percent of my company?"

Peter felt his anger grow, he stiffened but Brett seemed calm. He was just standing there listening. This man had hurt him deeply when he turned him away; he couldn't hurt him anymore. Brett had washed his hands of him. He moved closer to Joshua as Joshua walked toward him to hand him the envelope and he was staying there, enjoying seeing his uncle confront his grandfather.

After Joshua handed the envelope to Brett, he started back towards the buggy, "Hmmm," said Joshua, "seems like even you said his parents were married so I guess he's not a bastard after all. But then, Father, you should know because you have enough of them running around."

He stopped halfway and turned to Peter, "Dr. Osterhaus, would you take Brett and your family out of here please. Sorry Brett for ruining your day. I didn't plan it this way."

"I'm not leaving until you and Grandmother leave," said Brett, "I have to know she is safe. She helped me when I needed it. She risked her life for me."

"Go Brett," said Joshua, "we'll be all right. We still have some irons in the fire we need to talk about."

Brett walked around the men and up to the buggy where his grandmother was sitting. He stepped up into the buggy and gave her a hug and a kiss on the cheek. She smiled at him, took one of his hands and put her other hand on his cheek. "I'm so proud of you, Son. Go with your new family. They are great people. Don't worry about us. We'll be safe."

Brett stepped down, walked up to his grandfather, stopped in his tracks and looked him straight in the eye. The man noticed that not once did the boy shrink away from him and the look in those dark eyes was like a mountain lion looking at prey, but then it was probably in the bloodline but hard to say which side, probably both.

Brett turned and walked back to Peter. Peter put his hand on his shoulder and they walked up to Marguerite and Tim who were standing farther back and waiting. Tim would have joined his father and brother but didn't want to leave his mother alone and he wanted her to stay back. He was afraid for them all. It was a public place which negated some of the danger but he was still worried.

After they were out of ear-shot, Joshua looked at his father. "You probably don't know my friend at the <u>Boston Herald</u>, Roger Mason. I went to college with him; he was my roommate. Of course I could never bring anyone home so you would never have met him. But he has a very interesting transcript about you and your dealings. It is in his safe at the Herald. If anything happens to any of us - Mother, Brett or myself, it will be released for publication. There is enough information in there to send you away for the rest of your life, Father. If anything, I mean anything happens to one of us, if Brett falls off his horse and breaks his arm, that paper will be released. So you might want to hire henchmen to keep him safe.

"In case you are wondering where I got my backbone, it came from a fifteen-year-old boy who only asked to borrow a room temporarily so he could get an education from a man who had thirty of them." With that, Joshua mounted the buggy and drove off leaving his father to fume and sputter.

Brett and his family continued with their plans and went to the Hungry Seagull for dinner to celebrate Brett and Tim's graduation. This time, Brett ordered dinner by himself and used the correct utensils and drank from the correct glasses and insisted on paying for the meal for his family from money he had earned training horses. He toasted his valedictorian brother with a glass of lemonade and smiled a big and infectious smile which lately more and more people saw on this happy boy.

—꩜—

The next day at dinner Brett asked Peter if he would take him to see Mark Wagner, the family's attorney.

"Yes, but why?"

"Just need an attorney," said Brett turning his head sideways and looking up over his glass of milk, "remember the element of trust?"

Peter made an appointment and took Brett to the law office. Mark came out and shook Peter's hand and greeted him and then took Brett inside his office. Brett showed him the stock and told him he wanted it split amongst the entire family.

Mark said, "That's very nice of you Brett but I have a suggestion. "

"I'll listen."

"Well realistically you and Tim will outlive your parents. You are really watering down the stock dividing it four ways. Why not give Tim ten percent and you keep ten percent. The dividends can be used to help with college and medical school for both of you which in essence helps your parents and when they pass, the stock will already be in your names."

"I like that," said Brett, "go ahead, but I have a favor to ask."

"I'll do it if I can."

"I know my father is still worried I'm in trouble and that is why I came here. We talk about the element of trust but he is still a father I guess. Would you tell him I'm not in trouble?"

Mark laughed, "Sure."

He walked out with Brett. "We'll get that taken care of Brett." He turned to Peter "The kid's got a head on his shoulders," he said. "By the way, Peter, I don't handle criminal matters. Get my drift?"

"All right," Peter said and shook Mark's hand.

A couple weeks later, Mark stopped by the house. Marguerite was the only one home. She answered the door and said, "Oh Mark, come on in. Can I get you a cup of coffee?"

"No thanks Marguerite. I just have to deliver these papers to Brett. Would you see that he gets them?"

"Will do. Thanks."

When Brett came home from riding, Marguerite told him the papers were in his room.

After dinner, Brett said, "I have something to say."

Everyone looked up from their plates. Brett rarely instigated any conversation at the family dinner table and so the entire family looked up with interest.

He got up and went to his room. He had opened the big envelope and taken out the two smaller ones; one addressed to "Timothy Osterhaus" and one to "Brett Ballin". He picked up Tim's and walked back to the table.

"Here," he said and handed it to Tim.

"What's this?" said Tim.

"What do you always tell me? Open it."

Tim opened it and gasped. "Brett, you can't do this. It's not right. You deserve this."

"You are always saying that if you refuse a gift, it hurts the person giving it. If you refuse my gift, I'll be hurt."

"What is it?" asked Peter.

Tim was choked up and handed the certificate to Peter. Peter read aloud, "Ten Per Cent Simmons & Son Stock Timothy Osterhaus."

Marguerite gasped.

"Wow, Brett, are you sure you want to do this? This is your family's company," said Peter.

"Hold on everyone, just wait one minute. I have been here a year and what has happened? You took me in when I was so sick I should have died. You gave me a room that was bigger than the apartment I grew up in. You have paid for my schooling, bought me clothes, fed me and bought me gifts and then brought me into your family. Now when I fall into a little bit of fortune, you are telling me I can't share it with you? Sorry, but that dog won't hunt!"

They all looked at each other and laughed. "Tim, I guess you're stuck," said Peter.

XVII

The University

Between training horses, Carter-Osterhaus picnics and all the other activities the family did, the summer flashed by quickly for the two brothers. Both Brett and Tim were accepted into Boston University. Because transportation could be a problem, it was just easier for them to live on campus. However, they went home each weekend. Marguerite missed her boys too much to let them stay in school all the time. Both Peter and Marguerite would come to get them on Friday afternoons and they always did dinner at a restaurant. They took turns each week picking the restaurant. It was a game they played. They tried to guess what restaurant the person whose turn it was to choose would pick and that person would try and fool them.

Fall came and it was the end of October, and the boys were coming across campus toward the parking lot where their parents were sitting in the two-seater carriage with Morgan and Virgil hitched to it. Both boys were in a good mood since they would be going home and they were jogging along toward the carriage when a shot rang out. Tim went down. Brett dropped his books and grabbed him as he fell. They weren't far from a couple big landscaping rocks. Brett dragged Tim behind the rocks, laid him down and pulled open his jacket and his shirt and looked at the wound. The bullet hit him in his back behind his shoulder on the left side. Tim was groaning and writhing on the ground in a lot of pain.

"Take it easy, Tim, it's not serious," Brett said trying to keep his brother calm.

Peter pushed Marguerite down in the buggy and jumped out. Brett could see Peter running toward them and saw that Tim was not bleeding badly. He pulled off his jacket and tore off the sleeve. He wrapped it around Tim's arm for a tourniquet. When Peter reached them, they both lifted Tim to his feet and half carried him while he walked as best he could to the buggy, all of them keeping low and using trees for cover. Brett and Peter lifted him in and laid him on the floor of the carriage between the two seats so he would be out of firing range. His mother was sitting on the floor and pulled her son into her arms. Brett said, "Stay down," to his mother.

"Take care of him," Brett yelled at his father as Peter jumped up into the carriage and picked up the reins on the horses, "and get Mother and him out of here. I'll get home. Don't worry about me." Brett slapped the nearest horse on the rump and started running.

"BRETT," yelled his father and he shook his head. He had fully expected Brett to jump in the buggy also but he knew he had to get Tim and Marguerite out of there so he drove off.

Brett tore off around some trees, another shot went out but he was running full tilt now and dodging through the trees. A campus security guard came from the parking lot, gun drawn and ran toward where the gunman was. The gunman shot him in the chest. Brett had just ducked behind a tree trying to formulate a plan. When he saw the security guard go down, he raced for his gun. One look told him the man was dead.

A couple more shots rang out but they came nowhere near hitting him. He was on the move. Brett grabbed the guard's gun dropped onto the ground on his belly so he wouldn't be a good target and rising up on his elbows shot the gunman in the right arm and the man dropped the gun. It was a shot his father warned him never to make. Never try and do some fancy shot by only winging them; that was dime novel stuff. Shoot them in the chest where you are sure not to miss and sure to stop them but Brett wanted this guy to live.

He raced up to the fallen gunman and kicked the gun away before he could get it. The man was holding his arm and screaming at Brett not to shoot him again.

"Who hired you?" yelled Brett.

The man said, "Don't shoot me. Please don't shoot me again." He saw the look on Brett's face, those deadly black eyes shining in the sun and he was at his mercy and he was afraid. "Please," he pleaded meekly.

Brett fired the gun hitting the ground right between the man's legs so close to his manhood that the man felt the ground kick up and dirt splattered on his pants. The gunman jumped and a dark spot suddenly appeared on the front of the gunman's pants. "Guess where the next shot is going. NOW YOU TELL ME WHO HIRED YOU," Brett screamed at him.

"No, no. He'll kill me if I tell you."

"Well," said Brett, "would you like to be killed by a friend or an enemy?" and he pulled back the hammer dropping his arm and aiming right at the man's pants where the wet spot was.

"Elijah Simmons."

By now the police were starting to arrive. Brett ducked out of there. There were enough witnesses that could say what happened. He threw the gun near where the security guard had fallen. Brett felt really bad for the guard's family, but he only hesitated for a moment. He ran back to where they had dropped their books and picked up all the books. Then he ran off the campus and down where the main road joined the campus road. He ran for a while and then started walking to get his breath back. When he felt like he didn't look like a fugitive, he hailed a coach and ordered the driver to take him to Hamilton Street. Just in case the man was interviewed by the police, he had him drop him off at the end of the block and paid him.

He walked home and in the door. His parents were in the office working on Tim. Brett went in and put their books down. "How is he?"

Peter had Tim lying on his examination table on his stomach with his shirt off. "I have him sedated so I can get the bullet out," said Peter.

Marguerite was helping, handing him instruments. She looked frazzled.

"Mother," he said taking hold of her by the shoulders, "I can do this. Why don't you go lie down?" He kissed her on the cheek and quickly walked over where a basin of water was setting and he scrubbed his hands and arms with the soap and water.

She seemed grateful not to have to watch her son being operated on. She had assisted Peter at other times but this was her son.

Brett peered over his father's shoulder and looked at the wound. He watched what Peter was about to do. "Dad, your hand is shaking."

"I know Brett. This whole thing has me . . ."

"Let me," Brett said.

Peter gave the scalpel to Brett. How did Brett do it? He had probably chased down the gunman, gotten back here and now was operating on his brother. Talk about someone who was calm under fire.

Peter watched as Brett cut the wound a little more in order to make it easier to get to the bullet.

He saw how sure and steady Brett was with the scalpel. Brett asked Peter for the probe to locate the bullet.

Peter handed it to him and said, "You've done this before? I shouldn't let you do this. You are not licensed."

"SHHH," said Brett, "you're supervising. I lived above a saloon. I've seen this operation hundreds of times. Even did it myself once." He then took the forceps from Peter who was holding them and went in to get the bullet. "Give me that basin of water. I want to save this bullet."

"Brett, when you came here, you were only fifteen years old," Peter said picking up the basin and holding it for Brett.

"Yep," said Brett, "kids out West grow up fast." He went in with the forceps to get the bullet as he talked.

Tim stirred and groaned. "Better give him a little more ether. AHHH got it." He pulled the forceps from the wound and dropped the bullet into the basin.

Peter put the mask back on Tim's face and added a couple more drops of ether.

"Do you have any gut?"

Peter pulled the gut out of a bottle of liquid and threaded a needle and handed it to Brett. "If you put a stitch inside the wound, it heels better. I like gut because it dissolves on its own." Brett put in the stitch and then stitched the outside of the wound.

"Do we have anymore clean warm water?"

Peter went to the kitchen and took the water off the stove and brought it back to Brett. Brett carefully bathed the wound and surrounding area. Then he dried it and bandaged it. "Let's put him in my bed," he said, "then we don't have to carry him upstairs." Peter nodded and they carried him over to Brett's bed. They finished undressing him and Peter went and got a sleeping gown for him. After getting the nightshirt on him, they laid him on his stomach so there wouldn't be pressure on the wound.

"Go to bed, Dad, I'll stay with him. Mom needs you."

"Tell me what happened after we left."

"Nothing much. They got the guy."

"Did he say why he shot Tim?"

Brett looked at his father, "Dad, he wasn't shooting at Tim."

Peter looked at him. He sighed and walked upstairs.

Brett sat by Tim's bedside all night. In the morning when Marguerite tried to spell him, he told her she was welcome to sit there but he wasn't budging and he moved his chair over to make room for his mother. Marguerite brought him coffee and a fried egg sandwich. He checked Tim's vitals periodically and changed the bandage but he never asked for a thing and never said a thing unless he was asked a question. Both Peter and Marguerite were very afraid for him. The wild eyes were back. Her stray cat had turned into a cougar.

In late morning Tim started to rouse. Brett helped him sit up and got him some chicken broth Marguerite had made for him and some water. "You lost some blood so you should drink plenty of water."

"What happened?"

"You were shot. It was an accident. You'll be all right. Here drink the water, easy not too fast." Brett helped him sit up, propped pillows up behind him and then tipped his head up a little and held the glass for him. He handed Tim the bowl with the soup but his hand was shaking and he started to spill it. Brett took it away from him, sat down in the chair and started feeding him.

"You're hungry. That's why you have the shakes. They'll be gone as soon as your body gets some nutrition." He sat and fed his brother all the chicken soup. He went into his father's medical office and got some pills, came back and gave Tim two of them and handed him the glass of water. "For the pain," Brett said. Then he helped Tim slide back down into the bed and he fell asleep.

In the afternoon there was a knock on the door. Peter answered it. It was the Sheriff.

"Dr. Osterhaus, are your sons here? I understand one of them was shot?"

"Yes," said Peter, "he's doing better. They are both in the bedroom here." He led the sheriff into Brett's room where Brett was still sitting with Tim catering to Tim's every need. He would take his vital signs and write them down on a pad of paper and compare them to the last time he had taken them.

When the Sheriff entered the room, Brett stood up and extended his hand, "Oh, Brett," the Sheriff said, shaking his hand, and Peter was surprised he knew Brett by name. Probably shouldn't be, Peter had no idea what Brett got into when he wasn't at the house. "Love that horse you sold me." Peter breathed a sigh of relief. "You sure were right. He's great under fire, nothing bothers him. He is a little bull-headed but no matter what happens I can depend that he won't get skittish on me and bolt."

"Glad you like him. I thought he would be good for you."

The Sheriff looked at Tim. He was awake but he could tell he was groggy so he directed his comments to Brett. "Wonder if you could tell me what happened at the University yesterday."

"Sure," said Brett. He told him how Tim was shot and he had drug him behind the rocks. He said his father took Tim to get him help and Brett was going to try and see if he couldn't help apprehend the gunman.

"I ran through the trees so as not to be a target and then I saw the security guard coming from the parking lot. He fired at the gunman and as the gunman went down, he shot the security guard. I felt really bad. The security guard was badly wounded wasn't he?"

"Actually killed," said the Sheriff.

Peter could see Brett was shaken up but the Sheriff did not know Brett as well as Peter did, so he thought the Sheriff wouldn't notice.

"I thought so," said Brett. "I grabbed up our books and ran to the road. I hailed a cab and came home."

"So you didn't see a third man with a gun?"

"No Sheriff," Brett said innocently.

Peter looked at Brett. He could see Brett was lying but maybe the Sheriff would believe him. Peter didn't want Brett in trouble so he didn't say anything. Besides he really didn't know anything. When he was driving Marguerite and Tim out of the University, he heard the shots and he worried Brett might be involved but as Brett had told him, his first concern at that point was to get help for Tim and get Marguerite and Tim out of danger.

"Witnesses say a man came out of the woods and was yelling something about 'who hired you?' at the gunman. The man shot between the gunman's legs. Didn't hit him but scared him pretty good. He has powder burns on his pants so it had to be close up. The gunman isn't saying anything though."

"That's all I saw."

"From the witnesses' description, the man sounds a little bit like it could have been you. Makes sense you might be upset about your brother. Know anything about that?"

"Me?!" Brett exclaimed, "Sheriff, I hate guns, guns kill people."

"Well," said the Sheriff, looking at Brett coyly, "I'd sure like to find that man from what everyone says I'd like to hire him as a deputy. Guess I'll be moving along."

Peter was taking it all in. So that is what Brett was doing. That kid was going to get himself killed. He saw the Sheriff out. Peter sure hoped Brett would stop this stuff and soon. He went into the sitting room, lit his pipe and picked up a book, opened it and pretended to read. He knew he could only control him so much and why worry Marguerite. She was in her chair knitting but she looked up at her husband and worry lines crossed her face. She knew her men were holding back.

When nightfall came and everyone had gone to bed, Brett took his gun and holster out of the desk and buckled the holster around him and tied it down to his leg. He went out the back way and saddled one of the geldings. He rode toward the Simmons mansion.

Peter was gazing out their bedroom window which faced the barn. Either someone was stealing one of the horses or Brett was going somewhere. Peter ran his hand through his hair and went to bed.

Brett hid outside the mansion and watched for a while. Shortly after midnight and he still had not seen anything to help him do what he wanted to do; he gave up and rode home. He put up the gelding. He didn't want anyone to know he had his gun so he hid the gun and holster in the barn.

The next day was Sunday and Tim was starting to feel better and got out of bed. Brett helped him dress and Peter put a sling on the injured arm. Peter and Marguerite left for church; the two boys decided to stay home. Tim didn't quite feel up to it and Brett didn't feel right about going to church with what he was doing in the evenings. The boys were drinking some root beers and playing checkers in the sitting room.

"What happened after I was shot?" asked Tim still looking at the checker board.

"Your move," said Brett staring at the checker board.

"Brett, I thought we shared things with each other. I'm not totally stupid and I wasn't passed out. I saw you take off through those trees. I read the accountings in the newspaper. There was a third man. That security guard could not have shot the gunman. It doesn't make sense. Come on tell me what happened just between you and me."

Brett, who had been leaning over the board trying to concentrate on the game, looked up, "The security guard," said Brett, "another innocent dead thanks to the infamous Elijah Simmons."

"How do you know he was involved?"

Brett stood up, leaned over Tim and looked down at him, "Because I shot that guard's killer and he told me. OH TIM, I WISH YOU COULD SHARE! Share the look on that guard's face when he went down. I see that guard's face every night before I go to sleep. What were his last thoughts? For his family? How about you? Two more inches to the right and we would be attending your funeral today - my fault again. I pulled that bullet out of you because I saw our father shaking so badly, he couldn't do it and the whole time I knew. I knew I was to blame. I wish to hell you could share all of it but the truth is that if I had stayed out West where I belong, you would not have been shot, that man could go home to his family and you and Mom and Dad would not have loved an outlaw. I TOLD YOU NOT TO ADOPT ME. I'M TROUBLE AND ALWAYS WILL BE!"

He got up, hit the checker board, the checkers went flying and he left. Tim jumped as the checkers flew by him, "BRETT DON'T . . ." the front door slammed, "blame yourself," said Tim.

Brett went for a walk and came in shortly after his parents came home from church. No one said anything to him. They had always found that when he got like this, it was best to let him work it out for himself. He stayed in his room and wouldn't come to dinner. Tim told his parents what had happened with the checkerboard. He said that Brett had gotten upset when Tim wanted more details about the shooting and blamed himself for Tim being shot. He didn't tell them about Brett shooting the gunman. Peter had a pretty good idea anyway since he heard what Brett told the Sheriff and what the Sheriff had said.

Marguerite prepared a tray and took it into him. She knocked on his door. "Brett, will you let me in? I have some dinner for you."

He opened the door, "Come on in Mother. The door's not locked." He was nervously pacing the room wandering back and forth and gazing out the window.

"Do you want to talk about anything?" she asked quietly setting down the tray on a small bedside table.

He stopped pacing, looked down and shook his head. The boy, who would look any man straight in the eye and bring him to his knees, could never stare at his now mother. She was the one person who could make him look away.

She decided not to push it. She walked over and kissed him on the cheek, put her hand on his cheek and then left the room. A little later he brought out the dirty dishes. He had eaten everything. He went to the sink, took the tea kettle off the stove and poured hot water in the basin and washed his dishes. Everyone was in the sitting room. He dried the dishes, put them away and went out to the barn. He ran a quick brush over all the horses, got them fresh water and gave them all a measure of oats and hay.

He went back in the house, poured himself a cup of coffee and walked to the sitting room. "Horses are fed," he said.

"Thank you," said Peter, "Care to join us?"

Brett went into the room and sat on the hearth by the fire. After a while he got up and put a log on and stoked the fire and stoked the fire and stoked the fire!

Marguerite set down her knitting and got up and went over and touched his arm. "Help me serve the cake," she said their traditional Sunday evening dessert.

He was quiet but he did take plates to everyone. He again sat at the hearth and tried to choke down some cake. It just didn't set well with him. He went back to the kitchen and threw it out. The first time in his life he had ever thrown away food. He went back in his room and lie down on top of the covers of his bed.

When night came, Brett left again. He broke all their rules. He didn't ask permission to use a horse; he didn't say where he was going; his gun was strapped on and tied down gunfighter style. This time though Brett struck pay dirt.

Elijah Simmons came home and started up on his porch. One of his body guards was in jail which left only one body guard. As they walked up the walk, they didn't notice the shadow behind a pillar. Once on the porch the body guard suddenly slumped to the floor of the porch from a blow to his head by a pistol. Someone grabbed the old man's arm and a gun was stuck in his ear. "Don't make a sound. I'm pretty fast. I can shoot you and get out of here before anyone comes," the gunman said in a harsh whisper.

"I've come with a message. You touch any one of my family again and you're a dead man. You think you are tough. My father was a gunfighter, remember? He taught me well. Like father; like son. You know, anyone can be killed if the gunman is willing to forfeit his life - ask Abraham Lincoln. You hurt any of my family again and I won't care about my life, I will get you. Do you understand?"

When there was no answer, Brett shoved the gun deeper into the old man's ear and said, "Answer me, Grandfather," he spit out the words.

The old man jumped as the gun was shoved deeper into his ear. There was something really sinister about this kid. He had underestimated him. The blood that coursed through his veins was a combination of "wild west" and "eastern cruelty". "Yes, I've got it."

"Just in case you don't think I know what I'm doing," he fired the gun and shot off part of his grandfather's ear.

The old man clasped his hand to his head, blood trickling down between his fingers, squealing from the pain of the shot along with the pain of the ringing in his ear from the close-range gunshot and Brett was gone.

He went home, put the gelding away. It was close to midnight. His family would be in bed. He crept in the back door not making a sound. There was no light on. He went into the office and didn't light any lamps. He reached down and untied the holster off his leg, unbuckled the gun belt and unlocked the desk drawer.

"Did you kill anyone, Son?"

Brett jumped. His father was sitting in the dark in his chair. "No Father."

He finished taking off his gun belt, wrapped the belt around the holster, and put it in the drawer, shut the drawer and locked it.

Peter rose and walked over to where he stood. He reached up and took hold of Brett's chin and turned his face so they were eye to eye, "Tell me the truth."

"I won't ever lie to you Dad. I didn't kill anyone."

"Hurt anyone?"

Brett took hold of his father's hand, took it off his chin gently and held it for a moment between his two hands. Then he let go of his hand, turned and walked out of the room without answering him. He went into his room where Tim was sleeping. He turned up the lamp on the table by the bed. He put his hand on Tim's forehead. "He feels hot, might have a small fever."

He took out a thermometer, shook it down and put it in Tim's mouth. "Not bad," he said, "just a couple degrees." He picked up his stethoscope and listened to his heart and took his pulse. He turned to go to the kitchen to get some water and bathe Tim's forehead to try and keep the fever down and give him some comfort.

His father was leaning against the door jamb watching Brett. "Some things are best left unsaid," Brett said and brushed past his father.

Peter knew he wasn't going to get anywhere with him so he went up to bed. He laid awake for quite a while thinking about this boy who could go from sweet and loving to a mountain lion hunting prey and then back to his old sweet self with his family all in the turn of a coin or the rise and fall of a gun depending on how a person looked at it.

XVIII

Murder

On Monday the boys went back to the University even though it was much too soon for Tim to return. He and Brett shared a room and so Brett was determined to help him. Tim didn't want to miss any of his classes. He was an intelligent boy but he had to keep up. Brett was at genius level and he could get something once he read it through and hardly had to study. He also had studied so much of his life and read so many textbooks that some of the information at the University he already knew. What he didn't know, he picked up quickly.

Tim went right to classes on Monday but when Brett came back to their room in the afternoon, he found him curled up on his bed in a fetal position, writhing in pain. Brett put his hand on his forehead and he was hot.

Tim looked up at Brett and with great difficulty he said, "Oh Brett, I'm in terrible pain and sick to my stomach."

"I'll go to the social worker and have him get Dad to come get you."

"NO. I'll get too far behind. Please don't do that."

Brett wet down a towel and laid it on Tim's head, "I'll be right back."

Peter had given Brett pain pills in case Tim needed them. Brett got him some food and came back to the room. Tim was no better, he was rolling on his bunk and when Brett approached him he groaned.

"Here," said Brett, "Sit up, eat this and then take three of these pills." Peter had told Brett that he could give Tim as much as three of the pills but it would make him groggy. If he got into a lot of pain, however, three would of course help him better than two.

He helped him sit up but Tim shook his head, "I can't eat, Brett, I'm too nauseous."

"You have to eat something or these pills will make you sick. Come on, eat a little of this." Brett got him to eat part of a sandwich and then he gave him the pills. Brett changed his bandage, checked his pulse and heart rate and took his temperature.

"You have a temperature, not much of one but up a couple degrees. Maybe I should go get the campus doctor and get you something stronger."

"No," said Tim, "give this a chance to work." He lied down on the bed and Brett wet the cloth again and laid it on his head, then he took a second wet cloth and raised his head and wrapped it around his neck to cool him. Tim groaned and soon fell asleep. He slept fitfully for a few hours. Brett made sure he got more pills as directed by Peter waking him up and giving him more pills during the night whenever he could have them.

The next day, Brett convinced Tim to stay in bed and rest. He had bought some crackers at the commissary the night before. He left him the pills, told him how to take them and not to skip any. He also told him to eat some of the crackers so there was something in his stomach and he wouldn't get sick on the pills.

There were two classes that he and Tim did not have together. Brett skipped his classes and went to Tim's. After class, Brett again got them something to eat from the cafeteria and took it back to their room. Tim was much better. He wasn't in near as much pain and his temperature was back to normal. Brett got him to eat some of the soup he brought and take more of the pills. He then showed him what he had missed in all four classes, gave him his notes on the lectures the professors gave and went through anything he needed help with.

Tim looked over the work but he was in no condition to really assimilate the notes and Brett saw that he was fading fast. He could see by his eyes that he was still in pain and needed more rest. He again increased the medication so Tim would get a better rest and Brett woke him one more time during the night, made him sit up and take more of the medication. At this point Brett figured he needed rest more than he needed anything else.

The next morning Brett convinced Tim to stay in bed one more day and when Brett got back to their room, Tim was so much better. He was sitting at his desk and reading some of Brett's notes from the previous day.

By Thursday he was able to go to the classes and when he came back to the room, he was tired but not in as much pain and not exhausted like he had been. Brett changed his bandage every day. The wound looked good, clean, dry not seeping and not angry red or infected. He checked Tim's pulse and heart rate and took his temperature periodically and kept notes to see that he was improving. His fever had broken and he seemed to sleep better. Brett didn't wake him for the pills.

Brett also helped Tim catch up on any studying he needed. Brett easily caught up with his studies once he got back to his two classes on Thursday.

Peter and Marguerite came on Friday as usual to take the boys home for the weekend. They noticed that Tim and Brett were simply walking to the carriage instead of running like they usually did. Brett was carrying all the books. When the boys got into the back of the carriage, Brett said, "I think we should pick up some food and go home. Tim is tired." Tim didn't argue.

Brett insisted that Tim rest on the weekend. If he asked Brett a question about anything Brett had written in notes or covered in class, he sat with him while he studied and helped him until he got it. He knew Tim still wasn't thinking clearly with his exhausting week and the pain medication. Brett didn't go riding, didn't do anything but hang around the house and be available if Tim needed him. He did all of Tim's chores and completely took care of the horses, a chore he liked anyway.

Peter cleaned Tim's shoulder and re-bandaged the wound and said Brett had taken good care of it. Between Peter and Brett they kept Tim on schedule with the pain medication so he wouldn't get into too much pain.

In bed on Sunday night, Peter said to Marguerite, "I'll say one thing, the love between those two boys sure does go both ways. Did you notice Brett even gave up horses this weekend for his brother?"

Marguerite just smiled.

Tim recovered fast after that and didn't miss any more classes or need for Brett to fill in for him. Tim and Brett had always studied together and he still had questions sometimes and Brett was always ready to help him. Tim was always in awe of how intelligent Brett was. One day when they were studying something really complicated and it was taking Tim several times to understand what Brett was telling him, he said, "How do you just pick this stuff up so easy. This is difficult. Dad sometimes can't figure some of this out."

"It just comes easy to me," said Brett. "Everybody has a strong suit and a weak suit. It doesn't mean any one thing is better than another."

—m—

Several weeks later, Peter was at the kitchen table reading the morning paper, drinking his coffee, when he gasped audibly. Marguerite turned and his face was white. "What's wrong?" she said in alarm.

Peter started reading out loud to Marguerite from the <u>Boston Herald</u>, "'Cannon and Munitions Mogul, Elijah Simmons, Found Dead in Buggy' is the headline," he read.

Marguerite threw her hand to her mouth.

Peter read on, "Elijah Simmons, founder and President of Simmons & Son was found dead in his buggy on Sunday, November 25. He was shot in the temple twice. There was no evidence of a robbery. His wallet and money were still on him. There are no suspects at this time.

"Surviving are his wife of forty years, Gladys Simmons, and son, Joshua Simmons.' No mention of Brett, thank God. Funeral arrangements will be blah blah blah."

"Oh, Peter, you aren't thinking Brett are you?"

"I just don't know what that boy is capable of when he gets angry."

"He wouldn't kill someone. I know he wouldn't."

On his way to the office, Peter went to the University with the newspaper. He wanted to catch Brett going to class. He knew that Brett and Tim had different classes first thing in the morning. He sat down on a bench by the sidewalk where Brett would have to pass by to class. Brett didn't see him.

"Brett," he said. Brett turned and was surprised to see his father. "Did you see this in the paper?" he asked holding up the <u>Herald</u>.

"Tim saw it and told me."

Peter rose and walked over to his son, "I'm only going to ask you once and you said you would never lie to me. Did you do this, Son?"

Brett raised his eyebrows and got a shocked look on his face. He would have been insulted if anyone else had asked him, but there was no way he would ever get angry with this man. "No Pa, I promise you I did not do it. I couldn't even kill that evil devil but I won't mourn him either."

Peter went on to his office. He had never known Brett to lie to him. He usually could tell if he was hedging on information he was withholding. He didn't see that in the boy's eyes either. He looked straight at Peter, answered straight out, no hemming and hawing around. He'd have to be an awful good liar to do that and still lie. He prayed Brett did not kill his grandfather. He sure did not want to think of him as a killer.

It was Saturday morning and Brett had put on his Sunday suit, the navy blue one and wore the beige shirt. He thought the bright blue shirt Tim had bought him for Christmas might be a little too bright. He was tying his string tie when Tim came into his room.

"Where are you going?" asked Tim.

"To my Grandfather's funeral and pay my last respects." His tone was more like he was going to a party.

"Brett, are you crazy?"

"Why not, he can't hurt anyone now can he?"

"Brett, you shouldn't be happy that someone is dead."

"Sorry Big Brother, some people deserve to die."

"Brett, did you kill your grandfather?"

Brett stopped instantly, turned and looked his brother in the eye. His whole demeanor changed. He was very serious. "You are the second person that has asked me that. If it wasn't that I love you two so much, I would be insulted. I'll tell you what I told him. No, I couldn't even kill that evil bastard but I won't mourn him either.

"Get your head out of the sand, Tim. When someone is a danger to other people, why shouldn't they be executed? The law does it don't they?"

"That's different. That's legal. Murder is not legal."

"I don't consider the death of my grandfather however it happened as murder and sometimes the law's hands are tied and others have to take over." He finished tying his tie, "Have to go or I'll be late. Taking Suzi, she said she wanted to go for a ride today."

He rushed out to the stable. He had already saddled Suzi. He mounted her and rode off.

"Where's he going?" said Peter coming down the stairs and seeing Brett ride by the window.

"To his grandfather's funeral."

"Oh Lord, is there no end to that boy?"

"Dad, do you think he killed his grandfather?"

"He says not so I guess I have to take him at his word." He still had doubts.

Brett rode up to the funeral home and tied Suzi up to the hitching rack. He went inside. There were lots of people there. He took off his hat respectfully as he entered. His grandmother was sitting off to the side. He walked up to her and gave her a kiss on the cheek and she squeezed his arm. Joshua was talking to some people. He then walked up to the casket and looked in. He could finally look at the old man without feeling the hatred burning in his eyes.

"Looks good doesn't he?" he heard Joshua say as he walked up and put his hand on Brett's shoulder.

"Down right peaceful," said Brett.

"Can't figure out how that piece of ear ended up missing. Fresh wound, too," said Joshua.

"Must have cut himself shaving."

"That must be it."

The two men walked away. Brett went over to where his grandmother was sitting. "Sit down here, Brett, next to me," she said and she took his hand. When people came up to show their respects, she introduced him as her grandson. Only a few people said Josh's son? "No" she said, "Lila's". And made no further explanation and no one asked anything further either. They just smiled at him, shook his hand and went away.

After a couple hours of this boring stuff, they had a short service and took the body to the church cemetery. Gladys and Joshua insisted that he ride in the funeral carriage with them. They went from there to their church for a funeral dinner. Brett almost laughed, Elijah in church. What did God think of that, he thought? Talk about throwing out the money changers.

Joshua drove him back to the funeral home where he got Suzi and rode on home.

Tim asked how the funeral was.

"Oh never had such a good time at a funeral in my life," he said.

"Don't let Mom and Dad hear you say that, that's blaspheme."

"No, blaspheme is burying that evil jerk in a church yard."

About six months later, Peter came into his office and checked with Nancy, his nurse, to see who his patients were for the day.

"You have a new one," she said, "a Joshua Simmons."

"Oh, what time?"

"Ten o'clock right after Mrs. Brown."

"Oh Lord, Mrs. Brown, I suppose she has more stomach problems." Mrs. Brown was a hypochondriac. Peter usually examined her, listened to her and then gave her Bismuth for her stomach. "She is going to get an ulcer worrying about the ulcer she doesn't have. Did Joshua Simmons say what it was about?"

"He said he thought you would know who he was."

"Go ahead and put him in my office when he comes in."

Promptly at ten o'clock Peter was able to hustle Mrs. Brown out and Joshua came in. Nancy took him to Peter's office, "Mr. Simmons is here."

"Send him in." Peter stood up and offered his hand, "Joshua, how's your mother?"

"She has never been better. I think the visits with Brett have really helped her. Thank you for letting him come."

"Oh I think he enjoys it. He comes home happy, talking about you and her and how you are now so much happier living where you are."

"Well, I won't keep you, I know you are busy. I just have a little something for Brett. We sold the house and the company and liquidated all the assets. The company was sold to Caldwell the other munitions expert in the area. Brett will be getting new stock certificates. They will actually pay more dividends. Caldwell with Simmons is a very sound company. I'm working for Jeff Caldwell. Doing freight like always but I love it. I have kept enough money that I think will last mother for the rest of her life. She and I wanted you to have this for Brett."

He handed Peter a bank draft for $10,000 made out to Peter.

Peter looked up at him in astonishment.

"We put it in your name so you could disburse the funds for his schooling. That is what we want it for, for as long as it lasts. You can use it anyway you need to."

"Do you want an accounting?"

"Heavens no, we trust you. After all you have done for him. We would not even have him if it weren't for you. You saved his life. There is no way you can embezzle those funds. It would just be a pay back."

"Well, I really thank you. This will help a lot and don't worry it will all be used for Brett's schooling, two boys in college keeps me hopping."

Joshua stood up to leave and Peter couldn't let him go without asking. "I have to ask you a question, Josh."

"Go ahead."

"Do you think Brett killed your father?"

Joshua started laughing. "I know Brett didn't kill my father. The men who killed my father aren't even in the country now." He gave Peter a hard look. "It's amazing what body guards will do and for so little money."

Peter got a cold chill looking at this man who had grown up under a tyrant's thumb and had broken loose. "I don't understand why he hated Brett so."

Joshua said, "It was probably my fault for giving Brett the stock. I think Brett was a constant reminder of the stupid thing he did when he cut off his daughter and then Brett owned part of his company. After that attack at the University and your other son was injured, I knew it was the only way to protect Brett. I tried a bluff with a newspaper story release at Brett's graduation and he found out I was lying. You know even a squirrel becomes vicious if cornered. See you around." And Josh walked out.

Peter felt guilty for not believing Brett but he felt relieved that he finally knew the truth. He would never doubt him again.

XIX

The Engagement

The two boys graduated from college and were accepted to Boston University into the Medical School program. After the graduation ceremony, the Osterhaus family and Gladys and Joshua Simmons all went out for an up-scale restaurant dinner at the Fox and Hounds Restaurant, one of Boston's finest.

After they were seated and had ordered dinners, Brett was sitting next to Tim and he looked around the table. He heard everyone talking and laughing and he thought how happy and relaxed they all were. He smiled at them, glad for all the happy chatter that was coming from people who had been under such stress. It had been three years now since Elijah's demise and everyone seemed to have recovered at least on the surface. Good does triumph over evil but it sure leaves a lot of damaged souls in the process. One man had effectively changed all of their lives. Of course Gladys and Joshua had the deepest scars but they all had a scar or two. Then there were the people who were no longer on earth because of Elijah Simmons's acts of cruelty. Every time Brett walked to the parking lot of the University where Tim had been shot, he still thought about the security guard, who had been killed by Elijah's body guard, and he knew there were more bodies buried out there thanks to Elijah and his greed for power. Good may triumph over Evil but at what cost?

Suddenly someone was jabbing him hard and saying, "BRETT." It was Tim, "Where you been Buddy?"

"Oh sorry, just thinking."

"Your Grandmother wants to know about your plans."

"Yes, Grandmother, Tim and I have been accepted to Boston University Medical School."

"Oh that's wonderful; there are no doctors in the family."

Big surprise, thought Brett, only killers of people not savers of people.

"Brett won't tell you but I will," said Tim.

"Tim, be quiet," said Brett.

"Brett graduated first in our class. There's nothing this kid can't do." Tim said proudly and grabbed him by the back of his neck and shook him.

"Well I'm still second string in Carter Ball," said Brett.

Everyone laughed and it was such a good sound.

—m—

Anxious to get started in Medical School, both boys decided not to wait until fall but to take summer courses. Brett already had a good start on his education. He had been studying medical books since he was thirteen years old but he still had to prove it to the University.

The first year of medical school flew by and Tim and Brett were soon in their second year. Soon they were getting close to graduation. Tim had been accepted to the Boston Medical School Laboratory for his residency since his interest lay in research, while Brett was accepted into Boston General Hospital. Brett was only twenty-one years old.

—m—

In the fall on a Saturday afternoon, Tim came into Brett's room. "Hey, Little Brother, why don't you go with me to the party over at the Holdens'? About time we got out of here and have a little fun. We've been hitting those books big time or maybe I should say I've been hitting the books big time – my genius little brother here acing everything without even trying."

Tim was the party-guy. He loved going out and he loved parties since he didn't have to take a date and could drift around dancing with several girls all evening without a girl getting jealous. He was always out for a good time.

Brett still hardly ever dated. He was shy with girls and didn't find anyone he felt like asking for a date. He ignored Tim's genius comment. "Nah," he said, "I've got some stuff I want to do here."

"If you don't get dressed and go with me, I'm going to knock you out and drag you to the party."

"Tim, you know I don't like parties and you never know when to come home."

"Make you a deal. Go with me and when you say to let's go home, we'll go as long as it is at least a couple hours."

He looked at Tim. He could tell he really wanted him to go for whatever reason, "All right, Tim, you win."

At the party, Brett hung out and watched the other guests. He was drinking some punch and leaning against the food table, when a pretty little blonde came up to him.

"Hi," she said. "My name is Emily, what's yours?"

"Brett."

"Well Brett, how about a dance?"

"I'm not really very good at dancing." He had never danced in his life.

She took the drink out of his hand and set it on the table. Then she took his hand and led him out onto the dance floor. She placed one of his hands on her waist and then took his other hand in hers.

"Now," she said, "just move with me."

He was awkward but trying. She was smiling and telling him what to do. "See," she said, "you can dance. You don't have to stay so far away. Hold me closer."

He was very nervous but he brought her closer. She brought her body into his. She was soft and smelled good. She put her face close to his and he could smell her perfume and then she kissed him on the neck. It surprised him and he jumped a little. "Relax, Honey, I don't bite."

After the dance, she said, "Now you can dance," and walked away.

He was fascinated. He got another drink and watched where she was. When he saw she was free, he poured a glass of punch and took it to her.

"Thought you might like a drink." He handed her the glass.

She was a little shorter than he was. He was not big for a man; he had grown to about five feet nine inches. She was about five feet six. She was slim with blonde hair and bright blue eyes with big eye lashes which she batted at him and he was smitten with her. They stood and talked for a while then did two dances in a row. He started relaxing and enjoying himself, laughing and talking more freely with her. People were leaving and still he was talking to her as if he stopped talking she might disappear. He asked her how he could see her again. She said she worked in the dress shop on Main Street.

Tim walked up to him when just about everyone had left, the music had stopped, and the band was packing up to go. "Hey Tiger, you ready to go home?" He was laughing. He had never had Brett stay to the end of a party and he still acted like he didn't want to leave.

"Oh Emily, this is my brother, Tim. Tim, this is Emily."

"Hi," she said very flirty and tilting her head at Tim.

Tim never had a problem getting girls to like him. He had grown into a tall very handsome young man who was very confident with women. His bright blue eyes always sparkled when he met a girl and most girls quickly took to him. However, he knew Brett liked this girl and he would never infringe on his brother so he just nodded and said, "Hi". Then he turned to Brett, "The party's over Little Brother, we need to leave," and laughed again. He was glad his brother had finally talked to a girl and was having a good time. He had been watching Brett all night and noticed how much time he had spent with this girl and even was dancing with her.

On the way home he said, "Well, looks like you had a good time."

Brett was quiet when they got in the buggy. He was thinking about Emily. "Yeah," he said, "a real good time."

"Pretty girl," said Tim but he was thinking there was something there he felt unsure about – maybe the way she flirted with him when Brett introduced him. Well, guess that wasn't bad after all they weren't a couple but her behavior made him uneasy and Brett's interest in her made him even more uneasy.

A couple days later Brett decided he wanted to see if Emily would go out with him. He found her in the ladies' wear store and asked her to go to dinner with him on Saturday. After a couple dates, Brett decided he was in love and he started dating Emily on a regular basis.

—⚹—

Emily had heard that Timothy Osterhaus had a brother with a different last name. She assumed he must be a half-brother or maybe a relative that they took in. His background didn't matter to Emily. She really wanted to get married so she could get out of her house. Her father was an alcoholic and her mother wasn't much better.

Her mother did nothing – nothing in the house or anywhere else and her father only worked sporadically. She had never found out what her older brother, Johnny, was doing for work either but she thought it probably was not legal. He seemed to always have money and he didn't seem to be holding down an honest job.

The family mostly lived off other people, hand-outs from the rest of the family and charitable agencies that helped people. She and Johnny had always had hand-me-down clothes and a church came and gave them used shoes all their childhood. Emily could never remember having a new dress.

The house was filthy; her mother never bothered to clean it. The two children had always been left on their own to find anything to eat. Her parents bought only a few groceries and church ladies brought them home-canned vegetables and jams and sometimes other baskets of food. Emily had long ago lost any feelings she had for her parents. She was pretty much stone-cold toward most people. She had learned at a fairly early age that she could get gifts and money from boys by letting them take her to bed. Consequently, she played their games; used them the way they used her.

Most of the boys she knew only wanted one thing from her. None of them wanted to marry her. She had to find someone who didn't know about her sordid reputation. She did a little investigation and found out about Brett. He sounded like a good find in his own right. He had graduated from medical school and was now in the residency program. He would soon be a doctor. Doctors did all right financially. His family sure had a nice house.

Luckily he had come to that party at the Holdens'. No one had invited her, they never did, but the Holdens were too polite to ask her to leave. It was her chance. She asked someone who the dark-haired stranger was by the food table and when they told her Tim's brother, Brett, she knew this was it. One thing led to another and she was able to string him along and she knew he was getting more and more serious with each date.

—m—

Brett brought Emily to every family event from church and dinner on Sunday to the Osterhaus-Carter parties. The first party he brought her to was a late fall picnic at the Osterhaus home. It was a cook-out in the backyard. He introduced her to everyone. When he asked her to go to the picnic, he was all excited about introducing her to the Carters.

"You are going to love the Carter family," Brett said, and he told her all about everyone including his chess partner, Hughy, the Carter family's farm and all of the Carter children.

After Brett had introduced Emily at the picnic, Ricky caught hold of Tim and pulled him aside. "That's Emily Jackson isn't it?" Brett had only introduced her as "Emily".

"Yes", said Tim.

"Tim, she's no good for Brett. She went to my school; she was in my grade. She's nothing but a tramp. Every guy in school had her. We've got to tell Brett."

"We can't tell him. He's not going to believe us – he's in love with the girl."

"How serious is he?"

"Serious. He even mentioned to me that he wanted to marry her."

"I'm telling you, he needs to dump her. She will ruin his life."

At Christmas, there was the typical party at the Osterhaus home with the Carter families on Christmas Eve. Emily was acting all honey and sweetness to Brett in her little whiny voice. Tim couldn't take it anymore. He went outside and was standing on the front porch drinking a glass of wine and leaning on the railing, looking out over the landscape at the occasional buggy that went by and enjoying the coolness and quiet of the night air. Emily came outside and stood next to him.

"Hi Tim," she said cocking her head and trying to get him to look at her. "What are you doing out here?"

"I had to take a break," Tim said.

"I know what you mean. All that chatter in there gets to you," she said running her hand up and down his arm.

He stiffened. Many times he thought she was flirting with him, batting her eyes and smiling a seductive smile but this was the first time she had actually made a pass at him.

"I always thought you were a very attractive man," she said, turning toward him and pushing a little on his arm to try and get him to face her. He refused to let her push him and he continued facing forward leaning even harder on the railing of the porch.

"Really?" he said. "More attractive than my brother?" he continued very sarcastically.

"In some respects yes."

"Look Emily, you or no one else can make me hurt Brett so you can take your sexy little body elsewhere. I think I am on to you and don't try Ricky either. He had your number a long time ago."

"Well, you don't have to get nasty."

Just then Brett walked out on the porch. "Oh here you are, both of you. I was looking all over for you."

Tim turned around and faced him. "I needed some fresh air," he said.

"Well Mom wants us inside. We are about to open gifts."

"Oh gifts," said Emily, "I just love gifts," and she went running back inside.

Brett followed her like the dutiful little puppy, Tim thought. Why did he have to marry her? Marry one of the Carter girls; they weren't related to Brett. They were real women not flirting with everyone with that whiny little voice of hers. He had to talk to Ricky and maybe between the two of them, they could convince Brett not to marry her. Well he hadn't announced it yet; maybe he would realize what she was and break up with her.

He went inside as gifts were being passed out. Brett had bought Emily a beautiful gold bracelet he could ill afford for Christmas. There were no gifts from Emily!

—〰—

Brett dated Emily regularly when he wasn't at the hospital working. They spent every day off he had together. On Sundays they went to church although sometimes she would beg off church, it was too boring and have him pick her up on the way home from church. She liked going to dinner better. Mrs. Osterhaus was a fantastic cook. Her mother never cooked. Emily didn't know how to cook either and certainly had no desire to learn.

One day she decided to bring Brett home to meet her family. She just did it to get sympathy from him. She made no attempt to clean the place up before she brought him home. She didn't want to. She wanted him to feel bad for the way she had to live. She had him pretty well figured out; one of these guys who wanted to save everyone. Well he could start with her.

He was so pathetic. He never even made a move on her. He did kiss her and hug her and tell her how much he loved her and of course she said the same thing back to him even though she never meant it. Once in a while when he brought her home in the buggy, they would sit for a while and talk.

One night after Brett had taken her out to dinner and dancing, he stopped the buggy in front of Emily's house and turned to her. He started kissing her and it led to him getting more and more aroused. He put his hand on her breast over her blouse. She could tell he wanted her; she could feel the bulge in his pants as he drew her close. All of a sudden he stopped. He tenderly kissed her and said, "I don't want anything to spoil our wedding night. We have to wait."

How corny she thought. Boy won't he be surprised. The idiot was probably still a virgin. Christmas at his house was such a joke, that stupid Tim! She had to be careful with him. He could cause trouble if he told Brett how she had made a play for him. He was handsome, too but the word was that he played the field and never got attached to a girl. Brett was more gullible.

—⁂—

Shortly after the first of the year, both Brett and Tim had graduated from medical school and were in their residency programs, Tim at the laboratory and Brett at the hospital.

Approximately four months after the Holdens' party where they first met, Brett announced he had asked Emily to marry him and she had accepted his proposal. The Osterhaus family was shocked. Peter talked to Brett and said didn't he think he ought to wait a little longer until they knew each other better but Brett was in love and couldn't wait. On Valentine's Day, he gave Emily an engagement ring.

Tim remembered what Ricky had told him and he didn't know what to do. He didn't like Emily. He thought she was a phony. He had seen her flirting with other guys when Brett wasn't looking although after she had made the pass at him at Christmas, she no longer flirted with him. He didn't think his parents thought too much of her either. She was pleasant toward them and they were toward her but it seemed that both Peter and Marguerite did not warm up to her. He kept hoping Brett would see the light and break up with her but Brett was just too inexperienced with women. He couldn't see what she was doing.

The Saturday after Valentine's Day when Tim and Ricky had gone out to a bar, Tim told Ricky that Brett had given Emily an engagement ring. He and Ricky talked about it over the pool table and decided they would have a talk with Brett.

Ricky came over the following Saturday afternoon. Peter was in his office going over some statements. Marguerite was in the kitchen. Brett was in his room. Tim and Ricky went into Brett's room and Tim said, "Hey Brett, can we talk to you?"

"Sure. What about?"

"Brett, I don't know how to tell you this," Ricky started out, "but Emily went to my school. She was in my grade."

"Really?" said Brett.

"Brett," Ricky went on. He was trying to be as tactful as possible. He didn't want Brett to get angry but he felt he had to tell him how it was with Emily. "Emily has a reputation if you know what I mean."

Brett turned quickly and looked at Ricky, his dark eyes starting to darken even more, "No, I don't know what you mean, suppose you tell me, Ricky?" he now was raising his voice.

"She's just not right for you, Buddy. She's nothing but a flirt. Every boy in my school has had her."

Tim chimed in, "You can't marry her, Brett. I'm telling you she'll ruin your life. At the Christmas party she made a pass at me."

A black cloud swept over Brett's face and he was beyond angry. "LIARS! YOU ARE BOTH LIARS. HOW CAN YOU SAY THAT TIM? SHE LOVES ME; SHE WOULDN'T MAKE A PASS AT YOU. SHE WAS PROBABLY JUST TRYING TO BE NICE AND THAT'S THE WAY YOU TOOK IT. STOP IT – DON'T SAY ANYMORE EITHER OF YOU." Brett pushed passed them and charged out of his room, through the kitchen and out the back door, letting it slam behind him.

D C Anderson

"TIM, RICKY," Peter interrupted coming out of his office, "IN MY OFFICE, NOW."

Peter rarely shouted. Tim couldn't remember the last time his father had gotten angry at either him or Brett but he was shouting now. Marguerite came out of the kitchen to see what was going on. Peter motioned to her to go back.

"WHAT DO YOU TWO THINK YOU ARE DOING? YOU SHOULD BOTH KNOW BETTER. WHO BRETT MARRIES IS NONE OF YOUR BUSINESS."

"But Uncle Peter, she's no good and definitely not good for Brett."

"Yeah Dad, she's the first girl Brett has gotten serious with. You don't ever marry the first girl you date. Brett has no experience with women. He needs to date more before he gets married."

"Look, Brett is in love with this girl. He's not going to listen to you talking trash about her. Besides, just because she was a flirt in school doesn't mean she hasn't changed. Maybe she has grown up and looking for a second chance. All you are going to do with this talk is drive him right out of the family. Don't you get that? He's going to defend his fiancé not listen to you two trying to tell him how bad she is. We have to give her a chance to show what she has become.

"If she hasn't changed and it doesn't work out, where do you think Brett will go when you have cut him off. He won't come back to us because he won't want to hear 'I told you so!' You should support him not drive him away."

Both boys looked at the floor. They supposed that made sense. They never thought of that.

"Now go tell him you are sorry."

"SORRY?!" Tim shouted. "Dad she made a pass at me at the Christmas party. How am I going to live with a sister-in-law like that? Be on my guard all the time and hope that Brett doesn't see something that's not there?"

"You are going to do it for Brett just like your mother and I will. So go mend the fences with him."

"I can't do it. I can't say I'm sorry when I'm not."

"Me neither," said Ricky.

Peter now quieted down and went into his talking-people-off-bridges voice, "How much do you love him? If you love him, you'll show that you support him in whatever he does so that if he and Emily break up, he'll come to us for support and comfort not take the high road. Tim, you know better than anyone how sensitive he is and how he can be. If he knows he will always be able to come to us, he won't be as likely to fly apart."

"I guess you are right," said Tim giving in to what his father was saying. "Come on Ricky, we need to apologize."

"Where did he go?" said Ricky.

Simultaneously both Peter and Tim said, "He's communing with the horses."

Tim and Ricky walked out to the barn and went in. Brett was vigorously brushing Morgan.

"That horse is not going to have any hair left if you don't slow down," said Tim, "Look Brett I guess we weren't thinking. We were wrong. We don't' have a right to tell you who you should date or marry. I'm sorry."

"I am, too," said Ricky.

Brett kept brushing but he did slow down.

"If you love Emily and are going to marry her, then she will be my sister-in-law and I will accept her into our family."

"The Carter family will do the same," said Ricky.

He stopped brushing the horse and turned to face the two boys.

"I'm sorry I lost my temper and called you liars," said Brett, "maybe you are right Ricky, and maybe Emily was different in high school. If you saw where she lives and what her parents are like, that poor girl never stood a chance. She's not like that now."

"Is there anything we can do to help you with the wedding plans? We would like to help," said Ricky.

"You know what we could do?" said Tim. "Have the wedding and reception right here. If you guys get married when it is a little warmer, we could do it in the backyard." He was talking excitedly now. He wanted to help his brother and salve over the fight they just had.

"Yeah," said Ricky, "I bet Uncle Charles would give us a steer haunch to barbecue and the Carter ladies could bring food. You know Uncle Charles has tents they use for the county fair. We could put some of those up. How would that be Brett? We could have a real shindig."

Brett was staring at them. "Thanks guys, I don't want to be mad at either of you. Please accept Emily."

"We will; I mean we are. If you love her, that is good enough for us, huh Ricky?"

"I like your ideas," said Brett, "I'll see Emily tonight. I'll run them by her. Thank you. Do you think Charles would do that?"

"I bet he would. He's done it before for family."

—⁓—

The night that Brett went and picked up Emily after he had talked to Tim and Ricky and told her about the wedding plans, she pretended to be as ecstatic as he was. She didn't care what he did for wedding plans. Her family wasn't going to do anything. She just wanted to be married.

She told him she had picked out her wedding dress but it was a little more expensive than what she had originally planned. He asked her how much. "Oh Honey, I know it's a lot but I love it so and wait until you see me in it. It's seventy-five dollars."

Brett couldn't believe anyone would pay seventy-five dollars for a dress but he knew how much she wanted it so he gave her the money. The dress was really only fifty dollars and she pocketed the rest. How gullible can one man be? He bought her that cheap engagement ring. Oh well, when he was a doctor, she'd soon replace that and buy many more.

XX

The Wedding

The month of May was picked for the wedding. It was decided that it would be a small wedding but of course after all the Carters were invited, it became larger than originally planned. On Emily's side there were her parents and brother, a couple aunts and uncles and a couple cousins.

Brett also wanted to invite his Grandmother and Joshua. This caused some confusion as when Brett introduced Emily to his Grandmother, she asked if she was his father or his mother's mother. Brett promptly answered his mother's. She then told Marguerite how charming she thought her mother was.

Marguerite looked at Peter and said, "My mother? My mother's been gone a long time."

"I think Brett probably said Gladys was his mother's mother," said Peter.

They then realized that mystery Brett had not told his bride that he was adopted and that he had other parents. When it dawned on them what had happened, Marguerite just smiled and said, "Well, Gladys is a nice person. I guess she could be my mother."

Teasing, Peter said, "If she had you when she was twelve years old." Marguerite promptly hit him.

Marguerite and the rest of the Carter women decorated the outside of the backyard. They had strung lighted lanterns, balloons and tied flowers to posts. They made an archway and covered that with flowers where the bride and groom were to stand for the ceremony.

Charles did bring the steer haunch and he, Peter, Hughy and Tim all took turns turning it over the spit. Peter and Marguerite decided that they would hire the rest of the meal through a catering service. They also hired waiters to serve the guests. They rented tables and chairs for under the tents. It was all a very beautiful and simple affair.

When the Jacksons arrived, Marguerite greeted them. She and Peter had suggested several times to Brett that they meet the Jacksons in advance but Brett couldn't seem to get it arranged. The Osterhauses had even suggested going out to dinner but that never happened either. So when they came, Marguerite introduced herself and took Emily and her mother to Brett's room so she could change her clothes and get ready. Brett got ready in Tim's room.

Then Marguerite took Rufus and John Jackson outside and introduced them to Peter. They shook hands and Peter told them that he was glad to finally meet them. Marguerite took the Jackson men around and introduced them to all the Carter brothers and sisters, and to Grandma and Joshua.

The Jacksons didn't dress as if they were going to their daughter's wedding but they were clean. The men had plain button shirts and pants, no suits. Amy Jackson had on a nice dress but not usually what the bride's mother would wear. Brett had told the Osterhauses the condition the house was in and how the Jacksons enjoyed their booze.

The minister arrived and was shown to the flower archway. Tim, as best man, Ricky and Hughy all stood beside Brett on the left side of the minister. Brett asked that they all be at his side, he joked that in case he tried to run away he especially wanted Hughy there. These were the boys that Brett was the closest to. Emily had a cousin as her maid of honor. She probably had run out of girlfriends long ago after ogling all their boyfriends.

Marguerite and Peter had seen that there would be a piano and player to play the bride's march. They couldn't get an organ but they did manage to get a small piano. Brett and his entourage came out and stood next to the minister. Brett and the men in the wedding party plus Peter all wore black tuxedos with white shirts that Peter had arranged for from a rental company. When the music started to play, everyone rose and Rufus Jackson walked his daughter down the aisle. Emily was beautiful. Her blonde hair was wrapped in a bun and her mother had woven flowers in it. The white taffeta dress was stunning on her shapely figure. Brett could hardly believe his eyes. His bride was the most beautiful girl he had ever seen.

They exchanged their vows, the minister pronounced them man and wife and they ran down the aisle to tons of rice being thrown.

The reception was perfect. The beef was cooked and fit for any king and queen. The food was great and Peter had made arrangements to purchase a very fine wine.

Tim and Ricky had decorated the buggy with crepe paper and flowers. They put a sign on the back "Just Married." They gave Brett and his wife a weekend's stay in the Boston Mariner, a classy hotel, for a wedding gift.

The couple opened their gifts at the reception. Each gift that Emily opened she would say, "Oh Bretty Baby look at this. Oh, isn't it grand. Thank you so much," in that whiny voice of hers.

Ricky whispered in Tim's ear, "Bretty Baby?"

Tim elbowed him and then he whispered "I think I'm getting sick. Let's go get some wine."

"If the Jacksons left any," Ricky said. They picked up Hughy and Andy and the boys all went over for wine.

As expected, the three Jacksons were standing near the wine table guzzling the wine. They weren't even watching their daughter open the wedding gifts.

After the gift opening and people started dancing and partaking in the refreshments, Ricky said to Tim, "Watch this."

"Don't do it Ricky, he'll kill you."

Ricky smiled.

"You better take Hughy with you," Tim added.

Ricky walked up behind Brett and whispered in his ear in his very annoying sing-song voice, "Hey, Bretty Baby." Brett swung his fist around high purposely missing Ricky. He never planned on hitting Ricky and they both laughed and shoved each other back and forth.

Peter was sitting at a table sipping wine and watching the party. Brett was so happy and so full of himself. He wished he could be happy for him. He hoped with all his heart this marriage would work out but he was filled with a sense of dread. Marguerite was sitting next to him and she was beautiful tonight. She again had picked a peach–colored dress which really went so well with her skin tone. Peter turned and gazed into his wife's eyes. He wished both of his boys could find a wife like his. He put his arm around her and pulled her gently into him. She looked at him and smiled.

"Stop worrying," she said, and patted his arm and then put her hand in his. How well she could read him.

The couple left around eleven o'clock and the party started breaking up after that. The Carters promised to come back Sunday morning and help with clean-up.

Brett and Emily drove to the hotel. A groom took their horse and buggy and they checked in. When they got to the room, they found that Hughy had paid for a bottle of champagne for them. They drank the champagne and laughed and rolled on the bed. Brett wanted this night to never end so he took it very slow.

They undressed to their under things and crawled into bed exploring each other and removing the last of their garments a piece at a time. Brett was disappointed that she was not a virgin but he resolved that in his mind; it didn't really matter he was still in love with her. He was much more awkward than she and she actually led him through the whole sexual experience. He was so naïve that he didn't even realize how experienced she was. He had talked to Peter about intimacy with his wife. Peter was glad to give him advice on how to be gentle and bring her to fruition before actually having intimate relations with her. "Let the juices flow for both of you," was Peter's advice.

The next day they took the buggy out and rode all over town and then out into the countryside. They took a picnic lunch and found a beautiful park to have lunch. They stopped by a small lake and there were rocks and trees all around. Brett set up a blanket and they got out the picnic basket. They drank wine and ate pieces of chicken along with crackers and cheese.

While lying on the blanket, Brett started kissing and hugging Emily, tenderly running his hands over her, in her hair and pulling her face to his, kissing her. The air was warming into summer and there was a gentle breeze coming off the water in the lake and gently gusted over the two of them as they lie on the blanket. He just wanted to hold her and tell her again how much he loved her. She went further though and started stroking Brett on the outside of his pants, teasing him. He became aroused and was uncomfortable with this since they were out in the open in a public place.

"Wouldn't it be fun to have sex out here in the park?" said Emily.

Brett was appalled, "Oh Emily, out here in the open?"

"Oh come on," she said, "what's the harm? It just adds to the excitement of it."

"What if someone catches us?" Brett lamented.

He wasn't going to get naked in a public place and take that chance. He was so adamant about it that Emily gave up and they got in the buggy and went back to the hotel. He could tell she was angry with him for not going along with her corny idea but once they got back to the hotel, she forgot her anger and they hopped back in bed like the newlyweds they were. After their love making, they washed and dressed and went to a nice restaurant for dinner. They then came back to the hotel, Brett bought another bottle of wine and they got naked, drank wine and enjoyed each other some more before falling to sleep.

—␣␣—

However, when they came from their weekend after the wedding and moved in together in their apartment, Brett soon saw another side to his bride. The first few months of their marriage Brett was so in love that he would do anything for Emily. He soon realized, however, that his soft loving sensitive need for intimacy with his wife was not what Emily wanted. She wanted sex and wanted it rough and painful. It started bothering Brett the way she was acting and he lie awake after their love making and thought about how demanding she seemed to be about sex and how it seemed to be the only thing she wanted – no foreplay or sweet talk. Maybe she was a lot more experienced than he had thought. When Ricky first told him about Emily, he didn't want to believe it. He thought maybe Ricky had her mixed up with some other girl. Surely as sweet as she was with him, there was some mistake.

Brett was a young virile man, very much in love and easily aroused. When they went to bed, however, Emily would bite him on the neck and chest and leave bruises. She also sometimes left scratches across his back or down the back of his neck. This upset him and although he tried to talk to her about it, it seemed like she wasn't listening.

He was working long hours in the hospital in his residency and Emily was doing he had no idea what. When he came home the house was never clean, it looked like her parents' house. She never made any attempt at cooking. Brett cooked when he got home and she many times went out at night leaving him alone, saying that a girl had to have some fun. When he offered to take her out dancing or any place she wanted to go, she would turn him down saying it was more fun going out with girlfriends. Brett started wondering if she was really going out with girlfriends.

One day when Brett had the day off from the hospital and so was not near as tired as he sometimes was, he encouraged Emily to help him clean the house and together they worked on the apartment all day. He fixed a nice dinner and was very encouraged that things were looking up.

After dinner, one thing led to another and they ended in the bedroom. They were rolling around on the bed, touching and kissing and teasing each other both of them laughing and wrestling on the bed as couples sometimes do. He said to her, "Honey, I can't wait until we have a baby." He loved kids. He helped his father at the orphanage. He doted over all the smaller Carter kids at the picnics and he and some of the other older kids played many different games with them.

"A baby!? A baby!? Oh God, no brats Brett. Oh, that's funny, no Brett brats, Brett." She was laughing hysterically, and kept repeating, "No Brett brats," like it was the funniest joke she had ever heard. "I'm not losing my shape for a baby. Get that out of your head. I never agreed to that." She then said her "No Brett brat" joke again and started laughing hysterically.

Brett was hurt and very disappointed. He got up out of bed and slipped into his robe and went into the living room flopping down in the big overstuffed chair.

"Oh now Brett I suppose you are mad. Well get over it. I never agreed to a kid. If that was important to you, you should have said something before this."

He didn't think her "Brett Brat" comment was funny at all. What was he to do? He had taken it for granted that they would have children. He realized that they should have had more discussions before he jumped into this marriage. He remembered Peter trying to convince him to wait a little longer and get to know each other better. He had told Brett that he and Marguerite dated all through his college years before they were married. By then they had talked about everything and each knew where the other stood on all kinds of issues. What an idiot he was!

Several nights later after dinner, she again insisted on sex. He wanted to please her and he was making an effort to give her the sex she wanted but he was so tired. It had been an extremely busy day at the hospital and he had put in five solid days of working a ten to twelve-hour shift. They were in bed and she was running her hands over his naked body trying to get him aroused. He rolled up onto his side and started stroking her but he was so exhausted he kept falling asleep and his hand would drift off to his side. She got angry and slapped his face hard, "Brett, wake up. What is wrong with you?" He tried again but her anger and the fatigue he was suffering from caused him not to be able to get an erection.

She angrily got out of bed, got dressed and left the apartment. Brett rolled over but now even though he was tired, he couldn't sleep. He finally dozed off and woke up when she came into the apartment throwing things around. She got undressed and crawled into bed, turned her back on him and went instantly to sleep. He smelled the strong alcohol on her breath.

—⁂—

The summer months were busy with family outings with the Carters. Many times Emily wouldn't go and Brett went alone or he opted out also. If they went, it was up to Brett to make food for the picnic because Emily never would. On Sundays when Brett did not have to work at the hospital, they would go to the family home for dinner and sometimes cook-outs. Brett couldn't get Emily to go to church on Sunday so he stopped going but they did go to the house to visit his family and for dinner after they returned from church. Brett still helped Marguerite prepare the meal. Marguerite noticed that he was different. He was much quieter and she saw bruises on his neck and knew what kind of marks they were from. She was surprised that Brett would tolerate that since he was a doctor at the hospital. Those kinds of marks could be embarrassing. She sometimes pushed him a little to talk but he would only say a few things and then quickly change the subject. Usually after they ate dinner, Emily would want to go home. Sometimes Brett would start a game of checkers or chess with Tim or Peter and she would interrupt and tell Brett she really wanted to leave. In order for her not to make a scene, he would dutifully rise and take her home. He would borrow a horse and buggy and bring it back the following day and walk back home or Tim would drive him home.

Between some of the visible marks he had, the sleepless nights worrying about what Emily was doing and her behavior at his parents' home, he started making excuses to his family for not coming on Sundays. Sometimes he would just stop in unexpectedly to see them. He missed them and they of course missed him, too. Emily never said but all three of them knew not to stop at the apartment. Once or twice Tim stopped by and it was obvious Emily did not appreciate him coming to their home. He too, stopped going to the apartment but did meet Brett occasionally for lunch. It seemed that that was the only way he got to see his brother.

—m—

There were times when everything went right and Brett would then have hope that their marriage would get better and could be saved. One day Brett had a day off from the hospital and slept longer in the morning and felt rested. He again cleaned the apartment and then he convinced Emily to go out for dinner and they actually were having a good time. They each had a glass of wine at dinner but didn't over do the drinking. They came home and when it was time to go to bed, Emily again made a play for Brett.

Brett felt energized from the good night's sleep he had had the night before and the good time they had had throughout the day and at dinner. They lay together naked in the bed and after several kisses, Brett was getting very excited and he rose up and hovered over her. Just as he was about to make love to her, she latched onto his neck with her mouth leaving a bruise and then grabbed him digging her fingers into his buttocks. When he pulled back from her fingers, she raked him leaving scratches with her sharp nails across his back and butt. He lost his temper along with his erection and jumped back away from her. This time she was really angry. As he was leaping off the bed away from her, she angrily lashed out at him with her sharp nails and raked him all the way across his belly scratching him with her deadly long nails.

He jumped back and screamed at her, "EMILY I'M TIRED OF ALL THIS SCRATCHING AND BITING." Then he dropped it down a notch, "That's not the way sex should be." He lowered his voice and got control, "It should be loving and gentle, Honey," he said. "Can't we talk about this?"

"Oh, poor Bretty Baby can't take a little rough sex. That makes it fun. You just want to cuddle and kiss? I should have known when you wouldn't do it before we were married you'd be like this. I don't understand you. Aren't you man enough to do a little rough stuff?"

They both calmed down. She had turned her back to him. He sat on the bed and rubbed her back. "Please don't be angry with me, Emily. I love you. I want to do what you want but can't you try and be a little gentler? I don't like going to the hospital and have people see all these marks on me. The scratching and biting puts me off." He tried to explain.

She turned toward him and he took her into his arms and they started into loving each other but again she started biting him on his chest and leaving a bruise and although he was trying hard, he couldn't get an erection. His abdomen where she had scratched so deep was stinging and it seemed that his heart was willing but his mind was cautious. The conflict in his body was keeping him from being able to do anything. She became very angry at him and that made matters worse and when he tried again, she had him in such a state that he was as limp as a little boy. She was furious and she screamed at him, "YOU CALL YOURSELF A MAN? YOU CAN'T EVEN SATISFY YOUR WIFE."

He jumped out of bed, dressed and ran out of the apartment, down the stairs and out into the dark night. She was screaming after him, "THAT'S IT RUN HOME TO MOMMY. THAT'S YOUR STYLE."

It was a little less than three miles to his house and he ran almost all the way, stopping only occasionally to catch his breath. He felt degraded and rejected. He felt worse than when he was at the shooting house and his father used to slap him in the face for missing shots. He had missed some shots all right – some big ones. What should he do?

—⚍—

Tim looked out the kitchen window and into the barn. "There's a light on in the barn."

Peter said, "Suppose we better go out there."

"Let me," said Tim, "he may be more comfortable talking to me."

"All right but when you get out there if it's Brett, pick up the lantern and hold it up to the window."

"And if not."

"Get your body out of there." They both laughed. What burglar would go in someone's barn and light a lantern?

Tim walked out to the barn. He opened the door and raised the lantern as his father asked. Brett was sitting on a bale of hay, his elbows resting on his knees, head in his hands and looking down. Tim sat down next to him and pulled out a piece of hay and put it in his mouth and started chewing it. "Never could understand why farmers do this. Hay has no flavor."

"Does to horses," Brett said and he picked a piece of hay out of the bale and threw it on the floor.

"What's up Little Brother? Want to talk?"

"I may have made a big mistake, Tim. "

"There's no mistake that can't be fixed."

"Not sure this one can."

"Want to talk about it?"

"Tim, I can't seem to do anything right. I'm so tired and so tired of this relationship going this way. Marriage is nothing like I thought it would be." He looked at the floor, "I can't seem to give her what she wants – nowhere. I don't make enough money; I'm no good in bed." He shook his head miserably.

"Well Brett, you are kind of burning the candle at both ends. Look how much you are working at the hospital. How are things when you have days off?"

"She just wants more. I have to come home and cook and the house is never clean. We are always struggling to pay bills. She keeps spending money. She wants everything and she wants it now. I can't keep up with her."

Tim let him talk, chewing on the piece of hay and listening thoughtfully, then he said, "Want to run away?"

"Don't really know what to do."

"I've got an idea," said Tim.

He got up and brought Morgan out of his stall. He was the biggest of the horses. He put a bridle on him and turned to Brett, "Come on".

He led the gelding outside and jumped up on a bench outside the barn and then over onto his back without a saddle. He slid forward to give Brett room and reached down to take his arm. Brett also got up on the bench, took hold of Morgan's mane and with Tim's help pulling him up by his arm, leaped up onto the horse behind Tim.

"Hang on," said Tim.

Peter in the house watched his sons through the window. Marguerite walked up and stood beside him. "There's trouble brewing, huh?" she said.

"I believe so and I don't know what we can do."

"Just be there when he needs us. Give him a soft place to land."

Tim trotted the horse down the driveway, the two boys bouncing to Morgan's trot and Brett started laughing. It felt good. The road wasn't busy this time of the night so Tim cantered the horse down the road. When they reached the training area where people brought horses to train and exercise, he stopped Morgan, threw his leg over the front of the horse and slid off. "Here," he handed the reins to Brett. "Go for it."

There was a mile track around the perimeter of the field. The moon was full and lit up the track almost like daylight. Brett looked at his brother and turned the horse onto the track. He let the horse canter to start and then he leaned forward on the horse's neck. He put his head against Morgan's neck and urged him on with his voice. Morgan loved to run and Brett let him go all out. He placed his hands in front of the animal's shoulders so he could feel the power in those legs as they drummed up and down like pistons in a freight train. He heard the thudding of the hoof beats as he ran; Morgan snorted and pulled at the bit. Brett let him out another notch. Brett was swaying back and forth with the rhythm of the horse and it felt so good. It was a cool night; he had run out of the apartment without his hat and the breeze tousled his hair and blew into his face and the smells, oh those smells. There was the pungent odor of the horse, the woodsy smell of the trees and surrounding foliage and the clean smell of the night air. Brett drank it in and it felt better than any drunk he could have gotten from alcohol.

Tim smiled. His brother so needed that. His father had really been right. He was so glad he followed his advice and made things right with Brett. This was not going to solve all his problems but at least it gave him a break. Brett flew around the mile track and then half again. He pulled up the horse gently and cantered back to Tim.

He stopped Morgan and rubbed his neck. "I think he liked that as much as I did," he said to Tim. "He's tired of pulling that buggy all the time with his brother."

Tim laughed. "My brother says, 'There is something about the outside of a horse that is good for the inside of a man'."

"I'll walk him and cool him off," said Brett. Tim sat back down on the bench. He would wait until Brett was done with whatever he wanted to do with Morgan. He watched as Brett rode the horse at a walk around the track, stroking his neck and talking to him all the time. What kind of a conversation do you have with a horse, Tim thought? How else could he help Brett? He wished he knew. He couldn't believe even Emily could be so cruel and to such a sweet guy. She really didn't know what she had.

Brett came around the mile track and stopped in front of Tim. He slid off Morgan and handed Tim the reins. "I can walk from here."

"I can take you home."

"No, I'd like to walk and cool myself out."

Tim took the reins and slapped Brett on the back, squeezing his arm as his hand dropped to his side. "Be careful, Little Brother. You know that if you need me for anything, I'm on call."

Brett nodded and walked off. Tim stood there holding the reins of the horse and watching his brother walk away to an unfriendly apartment, his shoulders slumped. Tim cringed and then jumped up on the bench and onto Morgan's back.

When Brett got home, he took his boots off and went to sleep in the chair. He didn't want to awaken Emily for two reasons. He still loved her and he didn't want to bother her but he didn't want the fight to continue either. Even though he felt that his mother was the correct one in her fights with Mike about leaving, he now understood how his father felt sleeping in a chair all the time. The ultimate rejection!

He was sound asleep when he thought he heard someone at the door. Was someone trying to break in? Then he heard the key in the lock. Here he thought Emily was in bed and she was out somewhere. When she came in he could smell strong alcohol from where he was sitting.

He kept pretending he was sleeping while she stumbled around the apartment knocking into things and knocking things off the tables and finally she made it into bed.

XXI

The Break-Up

The next day, Brett didn't go to work at the hospital. Emily was still in bed at eleven o'clock in the morning when he left the apartment. He went to his father's office. He was going to try and catch him for lunch hour when he thought he didn't have any appointments. He walked in and greeted Nancy.

"Hi Nancy, is my father busy?" he asked.

"Hi there Handsome, how's married life? I think he is finishing up with a patient now."

"Oh, fine," he said. Oh if only she knew. Well, I guess she did know, she was married but probably not the way he was.

Peter walked out with his patient and was surprised to see Brett. "Hi Son, want to go to lunch?"

"Can I talk to you?"

"Sure. At lunch or in my office?"

"Office."

"All right, come on back."

He took Brett into his office and signaled him to a chair not right in front of his desk like he did his patients but off to the side. Instead of going around and sitting at his desk, he pulled a chair around so he could sit close to Brett facing him. "What's up?"

"I've got a problem and if I don't get it resolved, I'm afraid Emily will leave me."

"If I can help I certainly will," he could see that it was painful for Brett to talk. He was looking at his boots, his hat in his hand. Peter could never remember Brett being so uncomfortable. He always would look a person right in the eye even if he was scared and now he was clearly avoiding eye contact with Peter. "Take your time, Brett," Peter said gently. Peter was so good at coaxing information from Brett. He had a soft tone of voice and a quiet manner that calmed people and made them want to confide in him.

Brett ran his hand through his hair. "Dad, I'm having . . . having a hard time . . ." and then he blurted, "performing sex. Emily is very mad at me. She says I'm not a man."

Peter looked at his son and took in a breath. He never expected him to say something like this. For a father to see his kid hurting like this was so hard. Then Peter noticed how Brett looked. He looked like he had been in a fight. He had bruises on his neck and one up by his ear. Peter could also see scratches on him. What the rest of him looked like Peter could only guess. There were dark circles around his eyes he was sure from lack of sleep and he looked worn and tired.

"Do you mean that you can't get an erection or you can't maintain it? What seems to be the problem, Son?" he said as gently as possible. He saw that Brett was really upset.

He was still looking at the floor and nodded his head. He would still not look at Peter.

"How many hours have you been working at the hospital, Brett?"

"Usually around fifty to sixty hours a week."

"And what does Emily expect of you when you get home?"

Brett finally looked up, "Dad, she demands sex. Full blown, rough, no holds barred."

"Brett, sex is more mental than physical. Men aren't like women. If we are under stress, tired, depressed, we can't perform. I can examine you but from the sounds of it, you just need some rest and Emily needs to take it a little easier."

Brett said, "Dad, what should I do?"

"Would you like to bring Emily in and I'll counsel the two of you?"

"She'll never do that," and he looked back at the floor.

"Well, try talking to her and explain how you feel. Explain to her that you need more time preparing for sex and she needs to be a little gentler. Explain to her that she need not be in such a hurry. It's more fun taking your time. It might be such a thing, Son, she has been mishandled and thinks this is the way sex should be."

"There's no shot you can give me or medication?" Brett was a doctor now, he knew better but he was grasping at straws.

"Not if there is nothing wrong. Can you take a couple days off work? It's Wednesday. If you could take Thursday and Friday off and possibly the weekend, maybe just a good rest might do it. The two of you spend time together. Not just performing sex but doing other things, a concert, a play, dinner and a dance. Here," he took out his wallet and took out a twenty-dollar bill, "let me treat." He handed it to Brett. He took it but tentatively.

"Maybe she is overreacting because she doesn't get enough time with you. Maybe she is just over excited to see you and be with you." Peter knew he didn't believe that but he too was grasping at straws and trying to do everything not to be angry at Emily and help Brett. "What does Emily do when this happens?"

"She's not understanding, let's just put it that way."

Peter saw that Brett couldn't talk about it anymore. He was shutting down. He stood up to leave.

"Thanks, Dad."

After Brett left, Peter sat behind his desk with his hands clasped together in front of him leaning his chin on his hands for a time deep in thought, very troubled for his son and very worried about Brett's flash temper. He had really grown to love this kid and he hoped he could stay out of trouble. He had come such a long way, trusting people and handling himself around strangers. Peter had been so proud of the changes he had made. He had such a bright future he didn't need this.

Nancy walked into his office, the door was open. "Something wrong?" she asked.

He shook his head out of his daze. It all was wrong he thought. Here he was trying to counsel men on how to be gentle and giving to their wives and his poor son was getting abused. He never thought about it being the other way around.

That night in bed, Peter lie on his back and stared up at the ceiling, sleep was impossible.

His intuitive wife rolled up on her side toward him, leaning her head on her elbow and said, "It's Brett, isn't it?"

Peter swallowed hard and nodded and he couldn't help tears gathering at the corners of his eyes. Marguerite had not seen him cry since Joseph had died. "He came to see me today."

"Tell me," said Marguerite gently, placing her hand on his chest.

"I can't."

"We've never kept secrets from each other before. Peter, men think women are so soft that they have to hide things from them. We aren't. We might be the soft place to land but we can handle anything a man can. Share it with me and at least you'll feel better. When we took Brett on, we decided he would be OUR son."

"I don't know what to do for him. Emily is much worse than any of us suspected." Peter told her everything his voice choking up at times. It seemed to hit him harder because he was a man and could feel the pain Brett was going through.

"You should see him Marg. He has bruises and scratches on his neck and that is just what I could see." As Marguerite predicted it was so good to get it off his chest. She pulled him into her and he fell asleep in her arms. So even if she couldn't help Brett right then, she did help Peter.

Brett didn't take any time off work. He just kept on working because work was the highlight of his week now. It was the one thing that he did that he felt confident about.

A few days later, he got called into the administrator's office. When his residency was finished how would he like a job in the hospital? He was ecstatic and said, "Yes" right away.

He raced home to tell Emily. "That's nice," she said.

"Let's celebrate. Dad gave me some money to take you out, kind of a gift. How about we go out to dinner and if you want to go dancing or have a few drinks we can do that."

"Oh, I don't really feel like going anywhere. I'd have to get cleaned up and I'm comfortable." There was no place she could go that men wouldn't know what she had been doing. She couldn't take Brett to a bar.

Brett was disappointed. He went to the kitchen to see what he could fix for dinner. The old feeling he had with his first father of never being able to get approval for anything he did came back to him.

The months went by and soon it was May again and their first anniversary. Brett took Emily to dinner at a fine restaurant. At about the same time his residency was winding down and he was preparing to take his exams to become a doctor. He and Tim went together and both took their exams; all that was left was to get the results.

In the next several weeks, he did his best to try and please Emily both in and out of bed. There were times when it was all good and he had hopes that there was a chance for them to resolve their issues and have a happy marriage. It didn't last however, and Emily was back at biting his neck and digging her nails into him. When this happened his body reacted and he couldn't give her the sex she craved. He sometimes started making excuses and avoiding intimacy with her entirely rather than trying and failing. Eventually, she demanded less and less of him and he felt like a beaten dog and wanted to slink away.

One afternoon the Emergency Room where he was working was having a slow day. The head physician asked Brett if he would like to go home early. He said Brett looked tired. He had been working really hard and deserved a break. Brett jumped at the opportunity to spend some time with Emily. He had been thinking a lot about their relationship and what he could do to try and save it. He bought some flowers from a vendor by the hospital and stopped and picked up some Chinese food at the restaurant down the street from their apartment to surprise Emily.

He came into the apartment and was going to yell something corny like, "I'm home, Dear" but he felt something just wasn't right. He looked around and there in front of the couch was a pair of men's boots. He stopped dead in his tracks. On the couch was a man's shirt he didn't recognize and Emily's blouse. He heard a man's voice and then he heard Emily's voice. He heard the old bed squeak and the two of them laughing.

He was instantly furious, he couldn't ever remember being so angry. He went to the desk, opened the drawer and took out both guns. He loaded both, strapped on the holster with one gun and put the other one in his belt. He walked up to the bedroom door, drew the gun in his belt and kicked the door. It flew open and there they were both naked and in THEIR marital bed. Brett was numb – it was like he wasn't even there – like he was on the outside looking in. He stood there for a moment shocked at what he saw even though he expected it.

The two of them looked up, saw the man with the black eyes glowing red and then they saw the gun, and Emily immediately started screaming. The look in those eyes from this man she had so abused now made her afraid for her life.

The man she was with only hesitated a second. He instantly lost his sex drive! He jumped out of the bed yelling, "Hey . . . hey Mister, I didn't know – I didn't know she was married."

Brett was standing at the foot of the bed. He was ignoring the man and looking straight at Emily. His head was swirling, his brain not even functioning.

"Brett, don't kill me," Emily screamed. "Don't kill me. I'm sorry Honey; I'll never do it again."

He started shooting. She was screaming and holding her hands to her ears. She tried to sink into the mattress. The man was now out of the bed and running for the door trying to put his pants on as he ran. He had one leg in the pants and was hopping along trying to get the other leg in. Brett shot five evenly placed shots into the wall above the headboard of the bed. Then Brett turned and shot one in the floor right behind the man and he ran like a scared rabbit holding onto his pants and forgetting about trying to get the second leg into them.

Brett suddenly realized that he was in trouble. He ran out of the apartment and out into the hall. His neighbor was standing there, "What's going on? Who was that man?" said the man. "I heard shots, I'll get the police." Brett ran down the stairs and out into the street, tucking the gun under his belt.

He ran as fast as he could toward his parents' home. He then thought better of it. He didn't want to bring the police down on his family.

—m—

The knocker on the door of the Osterhaus house was banging. It was close to midnight. Peter put his robe on and went downstairs. Tim wasn't home; he was staying in town for an early meeting regarding the lab. Marguerite put her robe on and stood at the top of the stairs knowing something was wrong. Who would be pounding on their door at this hour? Peter opened the door, the Sheriff was there.

"Good evening Dr. Osterhaus. Sorry to disturb you. Brett here?" he asked rather calmly.

Dread filled Peter. "Come in. No Sheriff, he's not here. What's wrong?"

"Well he shot up his apartment, tried to kill his wife."

Peter thought he was going to be sick; Marguerite let out a sob.

"How badly has she been shot?" He was afraid the Sheriff was going to say she was dead.

"Oh he didn't shoot her at all, just scared her good." Thank God, Peter started breathing again. "But I have to take him in."

Peter said, "Please, I'm begging you Sheriff. Let me bring him in. I don't want him hurt. I give you my word, I'll bring him in. He's not here but I think I know where he is." He knew Brett. If the police surrounded him, Peter could just see him in a shoot-out. When he got scared, there was no telling what he would do and he had those guns.

The Sheriff thought for a moment. He didn't like hurting people either and he liked Brett ever since he bought the big gray horse he was training. He also knew Peter's reputation and knew Peter through all the work he did in Boston. He was not the kind of man who gave his word and didn't keep it. "All right, I'll give you until this morning. But you have to bring him in by then."

"Thank you, Sheriff."

Peter ran upstairs, threw on any clothes he could find, kissed Marguerite on the cheek, told her not to worry and ran out of the house. He threw the harness on the first horse and hooked it up to the buggy. He slapped the reins on the horse's back and yelled at it to move and raced down the road to John's livery stable. It was only two miles down the road. When he got there, he tied up Virgil to the hitching rack and cautiously went into the barn. He found a lantern near the door. He set it on a bale of hay and lit it.

"Brett," he called softly, "it's me Son, Dad. I'm alone, no police. Will you come out and we'll talk." Nothing. "Please Brett, we don't have long. It will kill your mother if you get hurt. Please come and talk to me."

He looked around. Brett was slowly coming down the ladder from the hay loft. He walked over to his father with his head down. Peter motioned him to sit down on a bale of hay and he sat down next to him.

"You can't run away, Brett. You have to face up to what you did. We have tried to instill in you boys that you have to take responsibility for your actions. Do you want to tell me what happened?"

Brett shook his head, "No, in the morning I'm going to catch the first train for the West and I'll be gone."

Peter was heart sick. "I know you haven't been with us long but hasn't anything we have tried to teach you sunk in? If you run now Son, where will your career go? All that hard work to become a doctor, you'll be throwing it all away. Not only that but you are going to be looking over your shoulder for the rest of your life. Do you really want that pressure? Let's go to the Sheriff's office. I'll go with you. I'll get you an attorney. If the Sheriff didn't lie to me, you haven't shot anyone, is that right?"

"No, I didn't shoot anyone but I wanted to."

"Let me have your guns, please. I'll take them to our house for you. Let's go to the Sheriff. Your mother and I will be there for you all the way, Son."

Brett raised his head and looked at Peter, "Why? Why Dad, why don't you give up on me? Can't you see I'm turning out just like my father?"

"Maybe we don't believe that. If you run away now, just think what that will do to Tim. He worships you. Don't mess up your future by running away. Let us help you. Remember Son the talk we had when we took you in. No matter what you do we are still a family. You accepted that when we all agreed to the adoption. Please do the right thing for all of us. Trust me we will see you through this no matter what it takes.

"We are running out of time and I'm asking you to do this for your mother, Tim and me. If you love us, please go with me to the Sheriff's office."

Brett reached down and took off the gun belt. He craftily flipped open the barrel on the gun and emptied all the bullets out and put them in the gun belt, slid the gun back into the holster, wrapped the belt around the holster and handed it to Peter. Then he took the gun out of his pants and checked it. He popped the empty shells out of it, closed the barrel and handed that to Peter. They got in the buggy and Peter drove him to the Sheriff's office.

—≈—

Peter called Mark Wagner at home at six o'clock in the morning. Mark explained that in their law firm there were several attorneys and they all handled different types of matters. This meant that each one was a specialist in his field which gave the client the best possible representation.

Dan Shinny was the criminal attorney. He was a brilliant attorney and loved his job. Peter was in their office at eight o'clock before the doors were even open. Mark introduced him to Dan. Dan said he would go right over to the courthouse as soon as it opened, find out what Brett was being charged with and then go to the jail to see him. He told Peter that he would probably be arraigned that day in court and bail set but he wasn't sure of a time yet.

The courthouse opened at nine o'clock and Dan was there right at that time. He found out that Brett had been charged with attempted murder of Emily Ballin. He had randomly fired a gun several times in their small apartment in the bedroom where she was sleeping after they had a disagreement. How could anyone fire a gun in a small apartment bedroom randomly and not shoot her? Really, attempted murder? Seems like it would have been murder or not. It didn't make sense. Dan got the legal paperwork regarding the indictment and went over to the jail.

He went into the Sheriff's office and greeted Fred.

"Hi Dan, you here on the Ballin case?" Fred Tompkins asked.

"Yeah, looks like I get to represent this criminal. Is he real dangerous?"

The Sheriff laughed, "Oh yeah!"

He took Dan back to Brett's cell. The boy was sitting on the bed, his elbows on his knees and his head in his hands. When the Sheriff unlocked the cell, Brett looked up; he hadn't slept a wink all night. Dan saw a kid that looked like one of the slum kids he represented. He was wearing hospital garb with short sleeves and Dan could see bruises and scratches on his face and neck. There were deep furrows in his brow and big black circles around sad dark eyes; he probably was a very handsome boy but he looked like he had been beaten. Dan had been told that he had come in voluntarily – what was with all the cuts and bruises? He hadn't seen such a look of hopelessness in a man for a long time.

"Hi Brett, I'm Dan Shinny. I work with Mark Wagner. Your father sent me to see you." He held out his hand and Brett took it. Even his handshake was weak.

"Want to tell me what happened last night?"

At first Brett just looked at him as if he wasn't sure if he could trust him but then he decided he had nothing to lose. His father had paid this man, he at least better tell him his story. "I came home early from the hospital . . . ," he started telling him, but then he looked down thinking of how he had come through the door of the apartment and heard Emily with that man in their bedroom. He shook his head as if to clear it, ran his hand through his hair and went on, "there were men's boots in front of the couch . . . a man's shirt and my wife's blouse on the couch." He paused again. "I heard them in the bedroom . . . her and him laughing."

Immediately Dan said, "Whoa, wait a minute. There were two of them. You mean she was in bed with a man?"

Brett nodded and gave Dan a sideways glance, "Yes, of course, that's why I got out the guns. I at first thought I was going to shoot them both . . . but when I got into that bedroom, I knew I couldn't take anyone's life."

"And you say their clothes were in the living room?"

He nodded, "A pair of boots, his shirt and her shirt."

"Hang on, Brett." He stood up and walked to the front of the cell, "Hey Fred, can you come here please?"

"What is it Dan?"

"When your people investigated the apartment, were there boots and articles of clothing in the living room and on the couch?"

"Don't know but if there were, it was probably thought that they belonged to the residents."

"Is anyone in that apartment now or been in it since the shooting?"

"No, Mrs. Ballin was too shook up. She went to her parents' home. We locked it up and sealed it off as a crime scene."

"Have your people go to that apartment and get the boots and two shirts that are on the couch and mark them as evidence. Will you do that?"

"Sure, the boots and clothing are not yours, Brett?"

"No, I have my boots on," said Brett, "I only have one pair."

After the Sheriff walked out of the cell area, Dan started again, "Tell me then what happened."

He told Dan about the man bailing out of bed and trying to get his pants on and how he had fired five shots above the bed and one into the floor by the man.

"Can anyone verify that this man was there?"

"Sure," said Brett, "my neighbor. He came over after he heard the shots. He went and got the police. He saw the man coming out of our apartment."

"Brett," said Dan, "this changes everything. Didn't you tell anyone about this?"

"No one asked me."

"The neighbor, he lives in the next apartment?"

"Yes, his name is Evans or Everett, something like that."

"Let me tell you what is going to happen next. You will be taken for the bail hearing and to declare your innocence or guilt at one o'clock. Then your parents can post bail and we can get you out of here. I'll meet you in Court. I'm going to pin down our witness. Brett, things are looking up. Don't you worry, Boy," and he slapped him on his shoulder.

At a little past noon, the Sheriff took Brett over to the Courthouse in hand cuffs. His family was there, Peter, Marguerite and Tim but no Dan. He looked at his family and ducked his head. He especially could not look at his mother. They called his case and he stood up and the Sheriff walked with him and told him where to stand behind the podium. The judge was asking him where his attorney was when Dan came through the door.

"How do you plead?"

"Not guilty, Your Honor," said Dan, racing to the podium.

"Does the State have a recommendation for bail?"

"Your Honor, this Defendant nearly killed his wife."

"Come on Runner, a child couldn't miss at point blank range. He had no intention of killing his wife," said Dan. Gregory Runner was the prosecuting attorney.

"Let's set bail at $2,000," said the Judge, "after all no one was hurt."

"It's not necessary to have bail," said Brett, "I don't have any money. I'll stay in jail."

Peter stood up. "Your Honor, I'm prepared to pay his bail," he said.

"NO, I DON'T WANT IT. I'M STAYING IN JAIL," Brett was shouting now.

"Dr. Osterhaus? What is your standing in this case?" asked the Judge. He recognized Peter from council meetings and also knew how Peter had done a lot of charity work in the city.

"He's my son."

Brett sunk and ran his hands through his hair, why did he do that?

"Oh, I didn't recognize the name."

"My wife and I adopted him but nonetheless he is still our son."

"You are willing to vouch for him? That he won't run and will appear in Court?"

"Of course," said Peter.

"Then I will release him into your custody."

"Thank you, Your Honor," said Peter.

"Trial will be scheduled for two weeks from today. Court is adjourned."

The Sheriff turned to Brett and took off the handcuffs. Dan walked over to him. His family was walking up also. "Brett, I feel real good about this case. Don't you worry. I'm sure I can at least get the charges reduced." He turned to Peter, "Peter," he said and shook his hand, "Tim" and shook Tim's hand and nodded to Marguerite, "Mrs. Osterhaus," and walked away.

"Come on let's go home," Peter said to his family.

"You should not have done that." Brett was angry. He wasn't shouting because of where they were and he didn't want a scene, but his tone was angry. "Now everyone is going to know that I am Peter Osterhaus's son."

"Are you ashamed of that?" asked Peter.

"You know I'm not and you know perfectly well what I am saying."

Tim put his hand on Brett's shoulder and steered him toward the door. "For richer or poorer, in sickness and in health, until death do us part," he said as he guided his brother out the door.

Peter put his arm around Marguerite and they followed the boys. Peter shook his head. Children sure put a different spin on life.

XXI

The Trial

Everyone came to the trial, Peter, Marguerite, Tim, Ricky and Hughy all lined up in one whole row in the Courtroom right behind the Defense's table. Gregory Runner, the Prosecutor, and his assistant took their places at the prosecution's table. Brett and Dan came in and took their places at the table. Brett looked at his family and they all smiled at him. He ducked his head, his dark eyes glistening. Why did they come? He had told them not to come. If he had to go to prison, he didn't think he could stand to look at his mother and father as they took him away.

Brett looked great. He was wearing a gray pin-striped suit that Marguerite bought for him to try and cheer him up. He had a white shirt, black tie and he bought some new black dress boots. With his black hair, dark complexion and dark eyes he looked like an Adonis. He had had two weeks to heal from the bruises and scratches and most were gone or faded so that they were hardly visible. The gaunt appearance and black hallowed look in his face had disappeared. He was sleeping fairly well although sometimes he would wake up and look for Emily in his bed. Then he would remember what had happened and couldn't get back to sleep. He tried to make believe it never happened but reality would sink in and he became tense and agitated. That's when he would withdraw from the family since he didn't want to take anything out on them; they had been understanding enough.

—⁂—

During the last two weeks from his arrest to the trial he spent a lot of time alone and every time he thought about what had happened, he got chills and almost sick remembering Emily in bed with that man – seeing both of them naked.

Sometimes in the early morning hours they would find him out on the back porch watching the dawn come in. The porch had an overhung roof so that it wasn't exposed to the weather and one day when there was a hard rain coming down, Brett went out and sat in the chair on the porch watching, listening and smelling the rain. Rain made him feel pensive and he sat and reflected on his life and some of the stupid mistakes he made. He especially regretted what he had done to bring on this trial. Not especially for Emily or for himself but for what he had put his family through especially Peter. How would he ever make it up to these people for all they had done for him and yet he kept messing things up? Why did they continue to love and support him?

—∿—

The State was first to present its case and Runner called Emily Ballin to the stand. After Emily took her oath and answered the usual preliminary questions for the court reporter, she turned, sat down in the witness chair and suddenly saw Brett. She did a double-take. He was so handsome and she knew what had attracted her to him in the beginning. Even though he was glaring at her, she had a pang of regret at how she had treated him. That, however, she kept to herself.

Dan had warned Brett not to look at Emily in any angry way. Dan was fully aware of his dangerous eyes and he told him, "Keep your face impassive. Remember, the jury is judging you every minute you are in the courtroom."

So when Brett at first looked at her, he suddenly realized that he didn't feel anything toward her. He knew he didn't hate her but yet he felt like he couldn't love her either – he just kept seeing her naked in that bed with that man and it made him nauseous. Now when he looked at her he felt cold and numb but he did as Dan warned and once he looked at her, he then looked down at the table trying to keep his eyes calm and his face impassive showing no emotion. He had a notebook, he was keeping notes about the trial and he wrote in the book although sometimes what he wrote made no sense – it was just something to do to occupy his mind.

—⁂—

Right behind and a little to the left of Brett sat Marguerite. A person could not look at Brett without noticing Marguerite. She was that close behind Brett and Emily did notice her mother-in-law and she almost shuddered from the look on Marguerite's face.

Peter saw how Emily looked first at Brett and then he noticed the change in her expression and realized she was looking at Marguerite. He suddenly realized what was going on between these two women. Men got angry and went to fisticuffs – woman against woman was death-defying. His eyes widened and he raised his eyebrows; he leaned over and whispered in his wife's ear, "All right Momma Bear. Are you protecting one of your cubs?"

Marguerite didn't look at her husband. She continued to look at Emily and smiled but it wasn't a pleasant smile and her eyes said everything she was feeling. As a matter of fact, Peter had never seen such an evil look on his gentle wife's face before. He was glad he was not the recipient of that look. Marguerite looked at Emily and her eyes said it all. See Emily, see what you could have had and missed out on. You could have had it all and so much more!

—⁂—

As soon as Emily sat down in the witness chair, she immediately started crying holding her handkerchief up to her face and dabbing at her eyes. Tim looked at Ricky and both boys whispered that they thought they might be sick. Peter hushed them but inwardly smiled.

She too had dressed in her best dress, her blonde hair tied up on top of her head and had hardly any make-up on instead of her garish make-up – the better to look like the poor little down-trodden housewife and no make-up accentuated her red eyes from crying.

"Now, Mrs. Ballin, will you tell us in your own words what happened the afternoon of July 21st please."

"I was very tired after cleaning house all day and so decided to lie down for a nap. Brett gets furious if the house isn't clean. I live in fear of this man; he nags me constantly about the house and cooking, everything, and has slapped me on occasion. He's just dreadful."

It was too much for Brett. He jumped up and shouted, "I NEVER HIT YOU."

"Mr. Shinny, get your client under control," said the Judge.

"Yes, Your Honor, if I could have a minute." Dan turned to Brett, "Brett, sit down," Dan commanded. "Please let me handle this. The judge will find us in contempt of court if you keep interrupting and it makes you look like someone who can't control himself. We sure don't need that right now," he whispered so Brett only heard him.

Brett nodded, "But I never hit . . ."

"I know, but this is my job. You'll get your chance. Please be quiet and just listen."

"Please continue Mrs. Ballin," said Runner.

"Well, I fell asleep and lost track of time. I planned on getting up and fixing supper but I was just so tired and Brett came home early and I was still lying down. Brett came in the apartment and then he came into the bedroom and started yelling at me. He was saying why was I still in bed and where was his dinner? All that stuff. Then he went and got a gun out of his desk and came back into the bedroom. I was trying to get up and find out what he wanted me to do but he was so angry. I've never seen him that angry and he just started shooting up the room. I slunk back into the bed and tried to get real tight to the mattress so he wouldn't shoot me." She let out a big sob, "I was so afraid he was going to kill me," and she literally broke down on the stand sobbing.

Then it was Dan's turn. He stood up, approached the witness stand and he asked, concern in his voice, "Mrs. Ballin, are you all right? Do you need a minute? How about a glass of water?" Dan walked back to the defendant's table; Brett looked up glaring at him. He smiled at Brett. It was a Relax-I-know-what-I-am-doing smile and he poured a glass of water, turned back to the witness stand and handed it to her. Brett ran his hand through his hair. Whose side was he on but he stopped glaring and looked back down at the table scribbling in his notebook?

Dan waited a moment while Emily took a sip of the water, composed herself and then she straightened up, stopped sobbing but still dabbing at the alligator tears in her eyes and nodding to Dan, she said, "Thank you."

He said, "So you say that when Brett came home that day, he started yelling at you for no reason?"

"Yes, he was upset that I took a nap but I was tired from working all day on the house."

"And he asked you where his dinner was?"

"Yes, he expects dinner on the table when he walks through the door."

"So if I called Wong Lo from The China Garden Restaurant to the stand and he states that Brett bought Chinese food from his restaurant that afternoon, he would be lying?"

"Well, maybe he did . . . I'm not sure now . . . maybe that was another day."

"Mrs. Ballin, were you alone in bed that afternoon?"

"Well of course, Brett was out doing something. I don't know what."

"Would he have been working that day at the hospital? I have his sign-in sheet here from the hospital if that helps you. He signed in at eight o'clock AM and signed out at three o'clock PM. What time did he get home?"

"Oh, well maybe he was working. I can't keep track of him. He's in and out."

"What time did you say he got home?"

"I don't know. I was sleeping."

"To refresh your memory, the police report says that as close as they can figure the incident took place approximately between 4:00 and 4:30 PM. Would that be accurate?"

"I suppose if that is what the police said, sounds right."

"Now, you did say you were alone?"

"Yes, of course."

"Whose boots and shirt were in the living room?"

"I don't know. Maybe they were Brett's?"

"Are you asking me? I don't live there. Tell the Court, were they or were they not Brett's?"

"You're confusing me. They had to be Brett's," she started sobbing again and took a deep breath for emphasis. The jury was all male and she was playing to them to the hilt.

"Just to make sure we all understand, Mrs. Ballin, you are saying that you cleaned the apartment all day so the apartment was clean, you were alone taking a nap and Brett brought home supper. Is that right?"

She nodded, "Yes, I guess that's right," she answered in a low tone of voice.

"So, Mrs. Ballin, what was Brett yelling about? Seems to me everything was perfect and then irrationally he started shooting up the bedroom – why would he do something like that?"

"I don't know, he does those things," she sucked in a breath and went back to dabbing her eyes with her handkerchief.

"He does those things? He has shot off his guns in the apartment before this time and you never told anyone?"

"Well . . . no, he never did that before . . . but he does get angry about stuff."

"And when he is angry, what has he done in the past?"

"He yells – you heard him yell at me in this room."

"He yelled today because you said he hits you. He was defending himself. Now you are saying he only yells. Does he just yell when he's angry or does he strike you?"

Even Emily couldn't say out and out that Brett had hit her. She looked down at her handkerchief. "I guess he mostly yells," she said quietly.

"I have no further questions of this witness but I reserve the right to recall her."

The next witness was the Sheriff. He went through the investigating reports and what was found as evidence in the apartment.

When it was Dan's turn, he asked about the boots. The Sheriff testified that they had been found in the living room and so were the shirt and the lady's blouse.

Dan turned to Brett, "Brett, please stand up." Brett did.

"How tall would you say my client is? Just a guess from your experience of identifying witnesses."

"Oh probably about five feet nine inches."

"Would you say these boots would fit someone five feet nine inches tall?" Dan said holding up the boots. The boots were huge.

"Objection, your Honor. The Sheriff is not in a position to answer that question."

"Sustained."

Dan turned to Brett again. "Would you take off your jacket please Brett?" Brett did as he was asked and took off his suit coat and laid it on a chair.

Dan walked over to him and handed him the man's shirt. "Just put this on over your shirt," he said. Brett did and it was obvious that it was way too big. The sleeves came down over his hands. "I'd like it noted as a matter of record that this shirt could in no way be the Defendant's," said Dan, "the sleeves are hanging over the Defendant's hands and the shoulders are hanging down on his arms it is so large."

"Now Sheriff Tompkins about the bullets in the wall, I have your investigator's report here. It says that this was an outside wall. Is that right?"

"Yes."

"So there was no danger of the bullets going through two layers of wood with insulation in the middle, would you say?"

"That is probably true."

"And indeed when your investigators checked, none of the bullets went through the outside wall, is that correct?"

"Yes, that is what is on the report."

"Your investigator measured from the floor to the bullet holes, says here six feet five and a half inches. Every bullet was in a straight line all the way across the top of the bed and only varies approximately an inch in height either way for all five shots. Would you verify that please?"

"If that is what my investigator put in his report, then I would say it is true."

"Mrs. Ballin is five feet six inches tall so even if she jumped up while Dr. Ballin was firing, it was impossible for her to jump high enough to get hit by one of the bullets. Would you concur?"

"Objection, how would the Sheriff know that?"

"Because he does criminal investigations. I'm simply asking for his opinion from his experience."

"Overruled. I'll allow some lead way here."

"It sounds like that would be accurate, yes," said the Sheriff.

"So-o-o, if the investigator's report states that the bullets were evenly placed across the top of the bed at six feet five inches high with only a one inch variance in height, would you say that was a random wild shooting?"

"Objection."

"Don't have to answer that question, Sheriff. The answer is obvious to everyone. No further questions." Dan took the shirt from Brett and put it back in the evidence bag.

Next was the Defense's turn and Dan called Brett right off. They went through the preliminaries, name, address etc. Then Dan said, "Tell us what happened the afternoon of July 21st, Brett."

Brett took a deep breath and then told his side of the event not looking at his family. He did look directly at the jury and those confident eyes of his said he was not lying. Peter, Marguerite, Tim and the cousins never knew that there was a man in the apartment and he had found him in bed with Emily. When they heard that from Brett, they all exchanged looks. Peter put his hand to his head, closed his eyes and shook his head. Marguerite took his hand. No wonder Brett had refused to talk about any of it in the interim time between his arrest and the trial. Brett never actually told anyone except Dan. He was too embarrassed and couldn't talk about such matters to his mother.

—⁂—

In the two weeks he was home between the arrest and the trial, he stayed relatively quiet. He was actually quite depressed and had the whole family worried about him. Brett wouldn't ride the horses because he didn't want his father to think he might run away and truthfully the thought had crossed his mind so he felt it best to not throw a leg over a horse. One of the biggest reasons he didn't run away was the fact that Peter had sworn to the Court that Brett wouldn't. He could never do that to his parents, but he fought the urge to run constantly.

During this time he mostly read and took walks. He played a lot of checkers and chess with anyone who would play and Tim was always there for him when he wasn't working. Hughy came to the house quite often and they played chess whenever possible knowing that Brett needed a diversion. Some of the other cousins came over mostly Ricky, Hughy and Andy and the boys played some baseball. Most of the time, however, Brett stayed laid-back and wouldn't discuss the trial at all nor what happened in the apartment not even with Tim.

Several times Tim tried to talk to him about what happened but he wouldn't push Brett too far. When Brett would go out on the porch, Tim would leave him alone for a while but then he would go out, give Brett a cup of coffee or sometimes bring home a bucket of beer and hand Brett a glass of beer and ask if he minded if Tim sat with him. Brett always said that was fine. One day while they were sitting on the porch, he outright asked Brett what had happened.

Brett was staring out into space. The horses were loose in the corral and he was watching them. Brett wouldn't look at Tim, "I can't talk about it Tim. I was stupid for what I did. I'd give anything to take it all back. My temper gets me in so much trouble." He turned and looked at Tim and smiled, "Sure wish I was more like you. I guess you still haven't rubbed off on me, huh?"

Tim saw the pain in his face and he didn't bring it up again. He figured Brett would tell him what he wanted him to know. Now when they were here in the courtroom and Tim heard what had happened, he felt really bad for him. He knew it would be a while before Brett would recover from this and he vowed silently to be patient with him and help him all he could. Please, if there is a God, please don't let him get sent to prison, he prayed. He doesn't deserve that.

—⚋—

"Your Honor," said Dan, "I'd like to do a little demonstration if I may."

"If it helps the case, go ahead."

"I need the help of your bailiff." The bailiff was also a deputy sheriff. The judge nodded and the bailiff came forward.

Dan walked back to his table and took a gun out of his briefcase. He showed it to the bailiff. "Deputy, do you see that the firing pin is missing from this gun?"

"Yes."

"A gun cannot be fired without a firing pin, is that right?"

"Yes, that's right."

"And the gun is not loaded, is that right?"

The bailiff took the gun, flipped it open and spun the barrel, "Right," he said, closed the gun and handed it back to Dan.

Dan whipped around, yelled Brett's name and threw the gun at him.

Brett caught it in mid-air and flipped it around so that he was holding it by the handle and carefully pointed it at the floor. Dan walked up to Brett and said, "Let me have the gun."

Brett neatly flipped the gun around and gave it to Dan butt first. What was this about?

"Does this man look like he can't handle a gun?" he said to the jury. "I have no further questions."

Dan walked over, sat down and placed the gun on his briefcase.

It was the prosecutor's turn at Brett. Dan had warned Brett before Court. "You cannot get angry at anything he says. It doesn't matter what it is. If you feel you are getting angry, take a minute to calm down. Take a few deep breaths before you answer. This is crucial. If at any time, you act out of control, and believe me he is going to try and get you to do just that, it's only going to show that you could have really lost it in that apartment. I'm portraying you as calm, cool and collected. Please play the part."

"That's a game," said Brett.

"You got it Son and everything you've worked so hard for is on the line right now. Believe me, you don't want to go to prison."

"Dr. Ballin, you say you came home and found your wife in bed with another man," stated Gregory Runner. "What was this man's name?"

"I don't know. I didn't know him."

"What did he look like?"

"From what I recall, he was a tall man, quite a bit taller than I am also very stocky. He had dark brown hair. I was mostly concentrating on Emily, I don't remember too much about him. Oh yes, he was naked and after he jumped out of bed, he was hopping around trying to get his pants on, does that help?"

A snicker went through the Courtroom.

"So it goes without saying that the Defense cannot provide this OTHER MAN."

Brett said nothing. There wasn't a question. He took Dan's warning to heart. He was not going to lose his temper. He looked directly at the Prosecutor and when he turned his head he looked directly at the jury. Not once did he look at the floor or act submissive. On the other hand, nor did he act angry. He kept his face calm and impassive as Dan had instructed him to do.

"Dr. Ballin, you can't produce a man because there was no man, isn't that right?"

"NO," said Brett loudly, and then saw a warning look from Dan and he lowered his voice, "that is not true. I did see a man and he was in bed with Emily. I fired a shot in the floor when he was trying to leave."

"So are you admitting that you tried to kill him also besides your wife?"

Brett was onto him now and he had regained his composure. "I never tried to kill anyone. I was just trying to scare them. I am a pretty good shot and we were in close quarters. Believe me, Mr. Runner, if I wanted to I could have killed them both. That was NOT my intention."

The Prosecutor walked a couple steps toward Brett and suddenly leaned toward him and said, "Had you been having problems functioning in your bed with your wife?"

Tim leaped up, "HOW CAN YOU ASK A QUESTION LIKE THAT?"

Ricky grabbed his arm and pulled him back down, Peter glared at him but his face was red with anger also. Marguerite felt so bad for Brett. Ricky and Hughy looked at each other and shook their heads. They would like to get that Prosecutor alone in a dark alley. The Judge banged his gavel and admonished Tim, pointing his gavel at him, "One more outburst like that and you will be removed from this Courtroom."

While some men would shrink with embarrassment in this line of questioning, whenever Brett was hammered on, he always went the opposite way. He looked straight at Runner, his face did turn red but he stayed in control. He said and not angrily but clearly, calmly and deadly, "How do you mean?"

"You know, couldn't satisfy her?"

"No, I don't know what you mean. Maybe you could ask her. Seems like she was getting satisfaction somewhere."

Runner thought he could get Brett angry and he would lose his temper with this line of questioning. When it didn't work, Runner was starting to get angry – taunting Brett he tried again, "Didn't the fact that you were not able to give your wife the intimacy she desired the reason that you had fought that morning before you left for work? There was no man in bed with your wife."

And when Brett still didn't react but simply leaned back to get away from the Prosecutor who kept leaning closer to him, Runner got even closer and more into Brett's face and he was menacing, his anger escalated and he was even louder and pushed further toward Brett, "You wanted to kill her didn't you? You thought about it all day at the hospital and when you had the chance to go home early, you got your guns and decided that you would kill her. Then when you realized that it would be too obvious that it was you who had killed her, you backed out of it like the coward you are and only shot above her head. You couldn't keep up with her desires and you were so afraid she would expose you. ISN'T THAT THE WAY IT WAS, DR. BALLIN?" As he was interrogating Brett, he was pushing into his face. Brett was backed up against the chair and had pulled his face back so his neck and head were over the back of the chair and Runner was an inch from his face. His prey instinct kicked in, it was too much. The mountain lion waits for his chance to jump the prey and he suddenly took both of his hands and slammed them into Runner's chest. The man flew backwards and fell into the defendant's table. Brett jumped to his feet. Tim jumped to his feet jerking his arm away from Ricky and ready to defend his brother no longer caring where he was.

Sheriff Fred Thompson and the bailiff charged toward Brett, who remained in the witness box but was standing, his face clouded over and his dark eyes glaring at Runner. The two lawmen stood between him and the Prosecutor. Peter rose from his chair and walked around Marguerite to his son blocking him.

Dan leaped to his feet, "OBJECTION! OBJECTION!" he shouted. "YOUR HONOR, the Prosecutor pushed my client into this. He asked him three questions all at the same time without giving him any chance to respond and his line of questioning has nothing to do with this case. He badgered him and actually assaulted him getting way too close and into his face."

The Judge was banging his gavel and calling for order. He pointed his gavel at Tim, "SIT DOWN, YOUNG MAN." He turned to Brett, "Dr. Ballin, sit down," he commanded.

Tim and Brett both sank into their chairs and Peter backed up and sat down next to Marguerite.

"MR. RUNNER," said the Judge. Gregory Runner was rising from having been knocked against the table and falling backward almost onto it. He smoothed out his jacket and faced the Judge. "You have gone too far," continued the Judge. "I am finding you in contempt of court and invoking a one hundred dollar fine against you as sanctions for what you did."

Marguerite reached over and patted Tim on the arm and then she took his hand and brought it into her lap. She gave him the mother-smile, the one that says "Behave".

"Now," said the Judge still looking at Runner, "confine yourself to one question at a time, keep your distance from the witnesses and I also would like to know where you are going with this line of questioning?"

Dan's objection and the judge's admonition actually gave Brett a chance to think about an answer. Brett pulled himself back together. He had heard what Dan had told him when they talked before the trial; his whole future was on the line here. If he wanted to be a doctor which right now he wanted more than anything in the world, he would have to maintain his composure. He sucked in his breath and then he turned to the Prosecutor and said, "Which question would you like me to answer?"

"Yes, Mr. Runner," said the Judge. "Mr. Shinny's objection is sustained. I think you better rephrase your question."

"I apologize to the Court, Your Honor. I was trying to bring out the point of why the defendant attempted to kill his wife."

"Then get on with it and move on to something else."

Runner turned back to Brett, "You and your wife had had many fights prior to this incident and as a matter of fact you had fought that morning. Tell the Court what those fights were about, Dr. Ballin?" This time, however, he stood back from the witness stand.

Then Brett turned his head toward Runner, took a breath and Runner saw no fear or submission in those dark eyes and Brett said quietly and with a lot of venom in his voice, "I'm sorry but I don't see the relevance of these questions," he said quietly, his full attention on Runner. "We had a disagreement that morning but what difference does it make what it was about? It has nothing to do with this case." Brett stared right down into Runner's soul and Runner felt very uncomfortable but he had no way of showing the jury how deadly those black eyes were and the anger in them. Brett was now staring totally at Runner but had the good sense not to speak angrily.

He took a breath and nervously licked his lips; he looked at the jury but then glanced back at the Prosecuting Attorney, "I was able to get off work early that day. I felt bad that we had not been getting along lately. I even stopped and bought her flowers and bought our supper. When I got home she is in bed with another man. Tell me, Mr. Runner, what would you have done?" He maintained a calm cool voice with absolutely no anger almost too cool and ominous and he stared at the Prosecutor until Gregory Runner felt like he was on the witness stand on trial.

Brett had never told Dan about the sex issues in his marriage. Truthfully, he never expected it to come up. He was naïve enough to believe that the trial would simply be about him shooting up the wall.

"I have no further questions for this witness," Runner finished.

When Brett returned to the Defendant's table and sat down, Dan put his hand on Brett's arm, "We're about to stick the knife into old Runner and let some air out. Your revenge is coming, Son, enjoy it."

Dan rose and said, "I call Everett Higgins to the stand."

After swearing in and the name and address was told, Dan asked, "Where exactly is 801 – 21st Street, Apartment 3-B in relationship to the Ballins' apartment?"

"Right next door," said Higgins.

"In your own words describe what happened the afternoon of July 21st when this incident took place."

Higgins told his story. "I was reading in our sitting room when I heard shots. I told my wife to stay in the apartment and I peeked out into the hallway and looked around. First I saw this man come flying out of the Ballins' apartment with one leg in his pants and trying to get his other leg in his pants. Then I saw Dr. Ballin come out of the apartment. I don't know the Ballins very well, they kept to themselves. I knew he was a doctor and worked long hours. I had no reason to fear him so I asked what had happened. Then I noticed he had a gun and was sliding it into his belt. He didn't say anything, looked confused and started running down the hall. I went into their apartment to see if anyone needed help. Mrs. Ballin was in the bedroom lying in bed with the blanket pulled up to her face and she was crying, sobbing actually. I asked her if she was hurt and she shook her head 'no". So I ran downstairs to get the sheriff."

"So you saw another man besides Dr. Ballin coming out of the apartment?" asked Dan.

"Yes, it was quite comical actually. He had one leg in his pants and was hopping along trying to put his other leg in his pants. He was buck naked except for that one leg in the pants, no underwear at all," and he chuckled.

"He finally got his other leg in his pants and he took off like a scared rabbit. His pants were the only clothing he had on – he was even barefoot," and he laughed.

"Mr. Higgins, was that the first time you saw anyone coming out of the Ballin apartment besides Brett or Emily Ballin?"

"Oh heavens no. There were other times when I saw a man come out of there usually during the day when Dr. Ballin is working. When this incident took place, I told my wife 'I would not have shot over her head.'"

Tim looked at Ricky, gave him a thumbs-up and mouthed the word, "YES!"

"Thank you Mr. Higgins. Your witness."

"No questions," Runner was hung and he knew it.

"Closing arguments, gentlemen," said the Judge.

Gregory Runner for the State was first. "It is plain to see that Emily Ballin is a small delicate woman. She has been badgered and traumatized by her husband the entire first year of their marriage. On July 21st she had worked all day cleaning the apartment, trying to make a nice home for her husband, Brett, trying her best to keep him happy so he would stop being angry with her. After doing all that, she was tired and decided to take a nap.

"The next thing she knew her husband came into the apartment, picked up the argument where they had left off that morning and THEN WITH NO WARNING TOOK HIS GUNS OUT OF THE DESK DRAWER AND STARTED SHOOTING UP THEIR BEDROOM.

"It is possible that the bullets could have gone through the wall in these apartments. Brett Ballin could have killed someone in another apartment besides killing his wife.

"Brett Ballin may be a good shot and may be able to handle a gun but when a person loses all lack of control, he also could have killed someone with his act.

"If for some reason someone finds that he is no longer compatible with a spouse, the legal thing to do is file for divorce – not shoot up their home. If for no other reason than to show others that this behavior cannot be tolerated, you must find Brett Ballin guilty of attempted murder."

The Judge turned to Dan, "Mr. Shinny," he said.

Dan slowly rose from his chair, buttoned his jacket and walked around the table to the jury. Twelve men because men could only serve on juries at that time, women did not have the vote.

"Brett Ballin is only twenty-two years old. He has accomplished major educational feats. He has graduated college and medical school with top honors – first in his class actually both times. He was completing his residency program and destined to become a very good doctor. He was working long hours, fifty to sixty hours a week. Boston General Hospital had offered him a position on their staff when his residency was completed.

"He loved Emily Ballin and was struggling to keep her happy financially as well as socially. Emily Ballin had no reason not to work and help the newly married couple get a start. Many women have done so but she chose not to. Instead she chose to spend her days sleeping in bed and her nights partying at bars.

"On July 21st, Brett had the opportunity to get off his shift at the hospital early. He had been very concerned about his relationship with his wife. They had had an argument that morning prior to him going to work. On that afternoon, Emily Ballin said that he came in, started an argument, got out his gun and shot up the apartment. If he were inclined to kill his wife, why wouldn't he have done it that morning in the heat of an argument? He stopped on his way home from the hospital and bought flowers for her; he also bought Chinese food. Does that sound like a man who was thinking of going home and killing his wife?

"He came into the apartment excited, wanted to surprise her with flowers and dinner, wanted to try and mend the relationship but what did he find? Men's clothing in his living room, his wife's blouse on the couch, he heard laughter from a man and his wife in HIS BEDROOM, IN THEIR BED. So what did Brett Ballin do? He was very upset. He got out his guns and he kicked in the door to the bedroom. There they were naked in bed, THEIR BED." Dan turned and faced the jury, "Ask yourself, what would you have done? Would you have had the restraint to not kill them both? An eight year old child would be capable of killing them at that close range. Brett Ballin still did not wish his wife dead. He wanted to scare her was all; he wanted to show her how much she had hurt him. He didn't even shoot the man who was with his wife.

"Gentlemen, I have a very good relationship with my wife, but I am not sure I could have had the restraint that Brett had that night especially when I was twenty-two years old and especially under the stressful conditions he was enduring. You heard the Sheriff testify, the bullets were not random. They were placed in a straight line across the top of the bed, high enough so that no one no matter what they did could have gotten hurt. You saw Brett catch the gun and how he handled it. That was not staged. I never told Brett I was going to do that. This is a man who knew exactly what he was doing. There was no random shooting. There was no attempted murder here. How could there be? If he wanted to kill his wife, he could have easily done it – an eight year old child would have been able to kill someone at point-blank range with a Colt 45 pistol.

"I'm asking that you return a verdict of not guilty in this case. This is clearly NOT attempted murder. Attempted murder is when someone tries to kill someone and fails. Brett Ballin made no attempt at trying to kill Emily Ballin."

The jury came back in after a couple hours of deliberation. They had a verdict.

The Judge read the verdict, told the Defendant to rise and asked the foreman of the jury to read the verdict.

The foreman stood up and said, "On the charge of attempted murder, we find the Defendant, Brett Ballin, not guilty."

Peter, Marguerite and the boys all breathed a sigh of relief.

The foreman went on, "on the charge of firing a weapon in the city limits, we find the Defendant, Brett Ballin, guilty."

The family breathed another sigh of relief, a misdemeanor, which would not affect his becoming a licensed doctor at all.

The judge said he was ready to pronounce sentencing immediately.

Brett and Dan were already standing after the verdict.

"Young man, firing a gun in the city limits may be a misdemeanor but in this case I am not treating it as such. What you did was endanger the lives of at least two people. If that wall had not been an outside wall, you could have killed someone in the next apartment as thin as those walls are. For that reason I am going to give you the stiffest punishment I can impose."

Marguerite was shaking. Peter on one side and Tim on the other, both had their arms around her.

"I see here that you are a doctor. I also have had your transcripts pulled from Boston University and Boston General." He stopped for a moment, "they are very impressive. You will be a good doctor but it still does not excuse what you did. For that reason I'm going to sentence you to six months" (Oh

God, thought Marguerite, my poor Brett is going to prison. He'll never be the same again.) "medical duty at the Scott Hopkins Center."

Marguerite nearly collapsed in relief. Tim looked over at Peter in shock.

The Scott Hopkins Center is where they take people who had no money for medical care. They took in street people and indigent people all kinds of people with all kinds of conditions. The police brought in people who were found shot or stabbed on the streets and either had no identification or had no means of paying for medical care. Brett loved helping people especially the poor. He had even thought about applying to the Scott Hopkins Center before Boston General offered him a job which when Brett was arrested, they told him they had no position for him. The only reason he didn't was the difference in the pay scale and he felt he owed it to Emily to make as much money as he was able.

The Judge went on, "You are living in a plush home with many advantages. It is time that you saw how other people live. I am sure your talents can be put to good use at the Scott Hopkins Center and that would do more good for our city than sending you to prison. Dr. Ballin, do you have anything you would like to say?"

Tim had his head down, his hand was over his mouth and he was making snuffling noises. Ricky whispered, "Tim, are you crying?!"

He shook his head and whispered, "Laughing. That judge just threw the fox into the hen house."

"Yes, Your Honor. I was wrong for what I did. I will never do anything like that again. I am really not a violent man. I apologize to Emily for putting her through this. I will accept my punishment and thank the Court for allowing me to keep my medical license."

Accept his punishment, Tim thought. You phony, you will love your punishment.

"I see no reason to give you a punishment that would preclude you from practicing medicine. You did not hurt anyone and as your attorney has pointed out, you easily could have. I think you will make a fine doctor and the Lord knows we really need good doctors. I hope you have learned something here and I certainly hope I don't see you back in this Courtroom again."

Brett merely nodded, "Yes, Sir."

"Court is adjourned."

XXIII

The Divorce

On the following Monday after the trial, Brett reported to the Scott Hopkins Center to start his six months of medical service as punishment for shooting up his apartment. His hours were to be from eight o'clock in the morning until five o'clock in the afternoon Monday through Friday. As predicted, Brett loved working there. He treated every kind of case known to mankind. Because these people had no money for medical care and were without any kind of financial help, they many times waited too long to have treatment. This meant that the doctors had to work hard to heal them and in some cases save their lives for conditions that if treated early would not have been anywhere near as serious.

The gunshot wounds and knife wounds were easy for Brett. More challenging were the illnesses that came in, infections and skin conditions many made worse due to unsanitary conditions in which these people lived. Hardest of all for Brett were the children. He just wanted to scrub off the filth and take them all home with him.

Brett learned a lot but he also taught all of the staff including his supervisor a lot of what he had just learned in medical school and with his voracious appetite for reading every medical journal that came into his possession. Tim brought home a lot of different ones from the laboratory. Every journal or magazine in existence was sent to the University Lab. Brett also read all the latest books and tried whatever was not detrimental to the patient. He was a great innovator and if he thought he could make things better, he would point it out to Dr. Donald Dunbar, his supervisor. Some supervisors would have resented his interference but not Dr. Dunbar. He realized that with his budget, he never would have been able to afford a doctor of Brett's caliber and he was going to take advantage of it for as long as possible.

Brett did one other thing for the Hopkins Center, he talked Tim into negotiating with the Laboratory to give the Hopkins Center equipment and supplies they no longer used or needed. Many times in the laboratory they used experimental equipment and moved on to something different. The retired equipment was just put into storage or discarded. It was still much better than anything they had at the Hopkins Center and still useable.

Brett never treated the staff like he was any better than they were mainly because he never felt that way. Even when he was a child and the most intelligent kid and probably person in the town, it wasn't he who rejected the other children it was they who rejected him. He encouraged all the workers and when someone was tired and grouchy or discouraged which happened a lot working under the conditions they worked under, he did his best to cheer them up but was never inpatient or lost his temper with them. It didn't take long before he was working much longer hours than the required hours. He usually showed up at seven o'clock in the morning and didn't leave before 5:30 or 6:00 o'clock in the evening. He also sometimes came in on Saturdays.

Peter and Marguerite did their best, however, to keep him from working on Sundays and keeping that for the family and he complied with their request. After all, he was not making any money at all for the first six months because this was his sentence. With the hours he was working there was no time for him to get another job. They were totally supporting him and even giving him money occasionally.

He hated that he had to freeload and it made his punishment that much harder for him. He would find money on his nightstand and knew it came from Tim.

One day he found a twenty dollar bill on his nightstand. This was not the first time and he felt guilty taking their money. He picked it up and holding it out in his hand he confronted Tim when they were all in the sitting room. "I found this in my bedroom," Brett said. "It must be yours because I have no money."

"Not mine," said Tim, "I don't know anything about it."

Peter and Marguerite were also sitting in the big sitting room and Brett turned to his father, "DAD?"

"I know nothing," said Peter throwing up his hands and going back to smoking his pipe and reading his paper.

"Wasn't me," said Marguerite. "I don't have any money. Your father has it all," and she went back to her knitting.

"Well the good fairy didn't drop it off – now whose money is it?"

"Must be yours since it is none of ours," said Tim. "Ever think there might be a good fairy?"

This happened more than once and Brett finally gave up confronting them. He would shake his head and count it as one more thing he owed to this family.

He did get a nice dividend check from Caldwell and that helped get him through the six-month period of no income. He wrote down any money any of the family gave him planning on paying them all back. It was hard though because no one would say who gave him the money.

After dinner one night during family talk time, Peter brought out a file folder with paperwork in it. A process server had knocked on their door that day and served Marguerite with subpoenas for all three of them to appear before an arbitrator having to do with Brett and Emily's divorce.

"Why you?" asked Brett.

"Oh," said Peter, "it has to do with the money I gave you when you were married to help you out."

"I've been meaning to ask you about that. You said at the time that that was part of the money that Josh gave you from my grandfather's estate. That couldn't be could it Dad? That money had to be gone. Did it even get me into Medical School?"

"Well, with what you had from your father and the smaller amounts Josh and your Grandmother gave you that we tucked away, it got you through the first year of Medical School. I knew you wouldn't take money unless you thought it was your money," Peter said.

"Well, I'm going to pay it all back just as soon as I start making money again."

"Not necessary," said Peter, "you're going to get it in the end anyway. We are just giving you your inheritance a little early that's all."

"I'm not getting an inheritance. It is all Tim's. He's your son."

"Uh huh, you agreed," said Tim.

"I agreed to what?" said Brett, his voice rising to a higher pitch.

"When we adopted you, you agreed to share everything. That includes any inheritance."

"Well, I spent mine already," said Brett.

"Uh huh, I had sixteen years on you. You only caught up. Now we are even."

"TIM . . ." Brett shouted but was interrupted by Peter.

"All right, Boys, don't fight over your inheritance especially in front of us. We aren't ready to check out yet. Maybe we'll just spend it all," said Peter and he laughed and so did Marguerite.

"Good idea," said Brett. "When do we have to go to this arbitration hearing?" he spat out "arbitration hearing".

"Wednesday, day after tomorrow. You better get the day off. We have to be there at ten o'clock in the morning."

Brett woke up early on Wednesday. He went out and brushed the horses, fed them and put their harnesses on so he would only have to put on their bridles and hook them to the two-seater carriage when they were ready to go.

When he went into the house, Marguerite was fixing breakfast. "Mom," he said, "I can't eat anything. My stomach is in knots."

"Oh Brett, don't take this so serious. It is probably just a formality, everything has been settled. Your father has paperwork on the school account."

"Just having to look at her will give me a stomach ache and a headache." He went back to his room to get dressed.

Peter and Tim came in and ate breakfast. After Tim ate, he went to Brett's room and knocked on the door. Brett said to come in. He was looking in the mirror and trying to tie his string tie. His hand was shaking and every time he got the loop to a certain point, he lost it. He was getting frustrated and he jerked the tie off his neck.

"Here," said Tim taking the tie from him, "turn around." Brett faced Tim and held his head up so Tim could raise the collar on his shirt and put it around his neck and tie it. Then Tim straightened his collar and slapped his brother on both arms and said good luck. He left for the lab hoping everything would go well.

Brett went out and hooked up Virgil and Morgan to the two-seater carriage. He drove up to the door and took Marguerite's hand and helped her into the back of the carriage and Peter stepped up into the carriage next to his wife. Brett told them they could sit in the back and he would drive. When they did he smiled coyly and said they could cuddle. Peter knew he was nervous.

As Brett drove them to the courthouse, Peter said, "Brett."

"Yes Dad?"

"Do you remember what Dan told you about the trial and not losing your temper?"

"Yes Dad."

"Well, same goes for this hearing. You lose your temper and you are going to show that you can't control yourself."

"You mean I can't jump over the table and choke her?"

"No Son."

Mark Wagner met them at the courthouse and they headed for the hearing room.

"Dan didn't come?" asked Brett.

"Should he have?" asked Mark.

"He might be needed," retorted Brett.

"Better not be, Buddy. You hold your temper."

They went inside. The Jacksons, Rufus, Amy and Emily were sitting with their attorney, Jack Jensen, on one side of the table.

The Osterhaus family and Mark trooped in and sat opposite them. The arbitrator, Gerald McIntyre, sat at the head of the table.

"Let's start with the lawsuit naming the parents," said Mr. McIntyre. "I don't understand why Rufus and Amy Jackson are suing Peter and Marguerite Osterhaus. I see no reason for it."

"The Jacksons were forced to put their daughter in therapy after Dr. Ballin nearly shot and killed her."

Brett stiffened. He was quiet but he was seething.

"Really?" said Mark. "If they chose to do that, that is fine but Emily Jackson and Brett Ballin are not minors. The Jacksons have no claim on the Osterhauses for that."

"Emily was only twenty years old when they were married. The age of majority in Massachusetts is twenty-one," said Jensen.

"When the shooting took place," said Mark, "Emily was twenty-one and Brett was twenty-two."

"Well," said Jensen, "then there is the matter of the money left to Dr. Ballin by his grandfather. Peter Osterhaus has that money and it was never declared in the divorce settlement. I understand it was a substantial amount."

"The money given to Peter Osterhaus by the Simmons family was used for Brett's schooling. The account which held the money was closed before Brett even met Emily. Dr. Osterhaus has proof from the bank as to when that account was closed.

"He told Brett that it was from that account because he knew Brett would not take the money unless he thought it was his. Dr. Osterhaus was just trying to help the couple out when they needed money for rent and food. How much money did the Jacksons give Brett and Emily?"

"Is there proof as to when that account was closed?" asked the Arbitrator.

"Yes, Mr. McIntyre," said Peter, "I have it right here, a statement from the bank giving the date of the last withdrawal and that the account was closed at that time."

Peter handed the Arbitrator a paper from the bank. "I might add also," said Peter "that this money was given to Brett when he was just starting college, way before he ever even knew Emily so how is it a marital asset?"

"Well from this notice from the Bank, it could not be a marital asset since the account was used before the parties were married. I see no reason for the parents of both parties to be involved in this case. I'm dismissing all four parents."

"Does that mean we ain't gettin' no money? That ain't fair," said Rufus.

"The parents may leave the hearing," said McIntyre.

"I want my parents to stay," said Brett. "I have nothing to hide from them."

The Jacksons got up and left grumbling the whole way how the court system was so unfair. They put all this money into their daughter and weren't going to get a thing when in fact they fabricated the whole thing and had never paid a dime to have any therapy for Emily.

"I don't see what else there is to settle," said Mark. "Brett has consented to allowing Emily to have everything in the apartment. He does have some personal belongings left there but it is mostly clothes. Neither Brett nor Emily has any money. Brett is serving his sentence with Scott Hopkins and makes nothing at all. He's being supported by his family."

"That's his fault," said Emily. "He deserved more than that. He tried to kill me."

Brett still held his temper. He was starting to feel proud of himself.

"There is one more matter to settle," said Jack Jensen. "The matter of the guns."

Brett's head popped up. He felt the heat rising in his face.

"My client is in fear of her life as long as he has those guns. She would like them turned over to her."

Brett flew out of his chair before anyone could stop him. He stood up, leaned over the table and yelled at her, "EMILY HOW COULD YOU DO THIS? YOU KNOW WHAT THOSE GUNS MEAN TO ME. YOU ARE JUST DOING THIS SO JOHNNY CAN GET THOSE GUNS. He's wanted them since he first saw them."

Mark grabbed his arm and told him to sit down but he just jerked his arm away from Mark and turned to the arbitrator. "She can't have them, Mr. McIntyre. Those were my father's guns and they are all I have to remember him by. You can't give them to her, PLEASE." He was totally out of control and yelling.

Peter was sitting on the other side of Brett and he said, "Brett, please sit and settle down." Peter was talking very quietly. He put his hand on Brett's arm. He had always found that speaking quietly and calmly to Brett brought him back under control. "Mr. McIntyre, I have a solution which should work for both parties," said Peter. Brett sank into his chair and turned his head away so he wouldn't have to look at Emily.

"Let's hear it, Dr. Osterhaus."

"I have a safe in my medical office and only I and the Sheriff have the combination. I could lock up the guns in the safe and Brett would not have access to them. You can see how much they mean to him. I'm asking you not to take them away from him. They are the only thing he has that belonged to his father. Brett is our adopted son and he was raised by his natural father, Michael Ballin, until his death when Brett was only fifteen years old," he said in way of explanation of why they were talking about Brett's father.

"I think that is a good solution," said McIntyre. "I'll put that in the form of a court order."

"I'll take them to my office the first thing in the morning and put them in the safe."

"Gentlemen and ladies," he said nodding to Emily and Marguerite, "that should conclude everything. Please go in peace and do not have any contact with each other. I'll put forth all the judgment entries dissolving this marriage and a separate entry that the guns be locked in Dr. Osterhaus's safe in his medical office."

Brett was so angry, he was seething. Once they got outside the courthouse, Peter turned to Brett. "Can you live with that ruling?"

"Yes, I don't have a problem with you taking them. It's just how sneaky Emily and her brother planned that. I would just hate to see Johnny get those guns."

The next morning Peter was up earlier than usual. Marguerite heard him get up. He shaved, washed and was dressed when she was climbing out of bed.

"Why are you up so early?" she asked.

"I want to get those guns and get out of here before Brett gets up. I feel funny about taking his property but I couldn't think of anything to do to keep the guns for him. "

"I think it was a brilliant move. Everyone knew what she was doing."

"I'll get something to eat later, Dear." He kissed her and left.

Marguerite dressed and went downstairs to fix breakfast for her boys. Brett was coming out of his room and Tim was coming down the stairs almost at the same time. They went into the kitchen.

"Where's Dad?" asked Tim.

"Oh, he thought it would be a good idea to start early and get the guns locked up."

"When did he leave?" asked Brett.

"About a half hour ago."

"You know, Mom," said Brett, "I think I'll leave early, too. I really have some patients in dire need of care at Hopkins." He kissed her on the cheek and left.

"Don't fix me anything either," said Tim and he ran out after Brett.

When he got in the barn, he said to Brett, "You have a feeling about Dad taking those guns, don't you?"

"I'm going to Dad's office," said Brett.

"Let's go," said Tim.

They ran the two geldings almost all the way to their father's office. They tied them up next to the buggy and went inside the building and up to the second floor. As they rounded the corner toward their father's office, they could see his door standing open. Brett took off down the hall and Tim was right behind.

Brett got their first and yelled, "Oh God, Tim, come quick."

Tim ran into the waiting room. Peter was lying face down on the floor, a pool of blood congealing around his head. Brett carefully rolled him over and cradled his head in his lap. Tim got a towel and pressed it against the wound to stop the flow of blood. Brett held the towel and pulled back each of his eyelids.

"Looks like a concussion? What do you think?"

Tim had his wrist and was feeling for a pulse. "There is a pulse, not real weak but not real strong either. We got to get him to the hospital."

Tim went and got some bandages and he and Brett wrapped them around his head and Brett raised him partway up and slid out from under him laying his head gently on the floor.

"Let's get some blankets to wrap him in. He's going into shock."

Tim went and got two blankets and the boys wrapped them around him and were getting ready to carry him out when Nancy came in.

"Oh no, what happened?" she exclaimed.

"Stop your husband. We can use help."

Nancy ran out and yelled for Jim just as he was pulling into the street. He turned the buggy around and came back.

"It's Peter, he's hurt," Nancy said. "Go help Brett and Tim."

Jim jumped out of the buggy and the three of them got Peter in Tim's buggy.

"Take him to the hospital, Tim," yelled Brett, "I'll go get Mom and meet you there."

He turned to Nancy and Jim. "Nancy, you have keys to the office?"

"Yes, of course."

"Then please lock up and get the Sheriff. Would you please give him a message for me? It may not make sense to you but I think he'll know what I mean. Tell him 'they have my guns and he should come to the hospital for me to explain'. Can you do that, Nancy?"

"Sure Brett, you go take care of your family."

She and Jim knew Brett's story. What a wild boy he had been and how Peter and Marguerite had taken him in and adopted him. They really liked Brett and knew that he was really loyal to the Osterhauses.

Brett mounted Morgan and took the reins on Virgil and rode home as fast as he dared. He tied up the horses and ran into the house yelling for his mother. She came into the kitchen and screamed when she saw Brett covered in Peter's blood.

"What did you do? Brett, are you in trouble?"

Brett forgot he had his Dad's blood all over his shirt because he had held his head when he first found him. "No Mom, listen," he took hold of her shoulders. "Dad's been hurt. Tim has him at the hospital. Get ready. I'll change my shirt and hitch a horse to the other buggy and take you to the hospital."

XXIV

The Vigil

On the way to the hospital, Brett filled Marguerite in on what he knew up to that point.

"Brett," she said in tears, "you would tell me if your father wasn't alive, wouldn't you? You wouldn't keep that from me?"

"Oh Mom, of course, but don't you think I would be in much worse shape if I thought Dad wasn't even going to make it? He had a good pulse. I'm guessing a brain concussion. He was hit on the head."

"Why?" she asked.

"For those damndable guns," spit out Brett.

He got them to the hospital in record time, helped his mother out of the buggy, took her arm and they went inside. He approached the receptionist and she told them where Peter was. They followed her directions and found Tim pacing the hall outside his door. He turned toward them relieved that at least he wasn't alone anymore.

"The doctors are in there with him now," he said.

"Do you know anything?" asked Brett.

"No not yet."

Marguerite sat on the bench outside the room but both Tim and Brett paced. It was almost comical the way one went one way and the other went the other way passing each other as they paced the hallway.

Finally, Marguerite said, "Will you two PLEASE sit down?" They came over and sat on each side of her Tim leaning his head against the wall and Brett sitting with his head in his hands. Tim lasted about five minutes when he got up and started pacing again. Brett reached over and took his mother's hand and stayed next to her.

Finally two doctors came out. All three flocked to them. "Well, it's just too soon to say for sure but we think he has a brain concussion and we don't think it is real serious. He may be unconscious for a while but we think he will recover. We did have to stitch that wound, it was fairly deep but it didn't look like the skull was damaged. There is nothing more we can do right now but to pray. I will tell all of you, he has our prayers. We respect and look up to Peter. He is a friend, a good doctor and one fine man."

The second doctor turned to Marguerite. "Mrs. Osterhaus, we think he stands a very good chance of full recovery."

"Thank you, Doctors," she said and both boys echoed the same sentiment.

They all trooped into the room where Peter lie on the bed so still. His face was almost as white as the bandage around his head. They all gathered around him. They gathered chairs and all sat nearby. The hospital chaplain came in and they all bowed their heads and asked God to please let them have Peter a little longer. The chaplain was very nice and took Marguerite's hand and wished them all well.

Marguerite sat the closest and held his hand. Brett sat next to her and Tim paced. Finally, Tim said he was going to go get them all some coffee and he left. Tim came back and passed around the coffee.

"Brett," Marguerite said, "you think Johnny Jackson is responsible for this don't you?"

Tim turned and looked at Brett. He had heard what had taken place yesterday in the hearing. "Yes I do," said Brett.

"Will you promise me that you won't go after him? All I can think about is you getting shot with your own gun."

"No Mom, the only plans I have are to stay right here with Dad. Johnny is not a threat to us anymore. He got what he wanted. I just want to make sure that the Sheriff knows that those guns are no longer in any of our hands so if he commits some crime, I won't be blamed."

"Then I have no reason to worry?"

"No Mom."

Later in the day Sheriff Tompkins came to Peter's hospital room. Brett excused himself and walked out into the hallway. He told the Sheriff what had happened in the hearing the day before. "When Emily and I were married, I kept my guns in a bureau drawer in the dining room of our apartment. They weren't locked up. Johnny came over one day and Emily got the guns out, much to my objection and showed them to Johnny. He offered me five hundred dollars for them. Emily was furious when I said I wouldn't take it. We needed the money, that was for sure, but those guns are all I have of my father's, my natural father, and I wasn't going to give them up for anything."

"Describe them for me Brett," said Fred Tompkins and he took out a pad and pencil and wrote down the description of the guns as Brett told him. "Johnny has been in and out of trouble since he was a boy," said the Sheriff. "I'll do my best to get the guns back for you, Brett, but I can't say it will happen. Lord only knows where he has gone and what he is doing."

Brett nodded. "I appreciate it, Sheriff. Right now though I just want to be with my father."

"Take care of him," said Fred, "your mother said the doctors thought he would be all right?"

"Yes, he's what matters the most. If prayer works, he has a lot of that going on for him."

Fred smiled and clamped Brett on the shoulder and turned and left. Brett went back into his father's hospital room.

Tim walked over to his mother and said, "Mom, would you like to go home and get some rest? I can take you and bring you back in the morning. I really don't think Dad is going to wake up tonight, do you Brett?"

"No I don't either. He's sleeping pretty deep."

She nodded, got up and kissed Peter and left with Tim.

Brett stayed right at his bedside. The nurses came in and reached all around him until he did get up and let them do their job. When they left, he took his father's vital signs himself. He had taken a stethoscope and a thermometer from the closet. After all, he had done his residency here so he knew where things were kept. He checked his father's heart and lungs, temperature and pulse after each time the nurses did. He would get a basin of water and wipe his face and around his head where the bandage was. He changed the bandage and in the morning he bathed him and changed his hospital gown. The nurses hardly had to do anything, Brett did it all. He sat there all night holding his father's hand.

In the morning, Tim brought Marguerite back. "Have you been in the same spot all night?" he asked.

Brett just nodded but he did yield to Marguerite. Then he would move down so she could sit close to Peter and hold his hand. About three o'clock in the afternoon, Tim talked Brett into going down to the cafeteria with him and getting something to eat. He told him it would be good for Marguerite to have some private time with Peter.

When they got to the cafeteria, ordered two sandwiches, carried their food back to the table and sat down Tim asked Brett, "Did you mean what you said to Mom? You are not going to sneak out and try and get the guns back from Johnny Jackson?"

"I didn't think I looked crazy," said Brett, "he's got the guns. I'm not stupid enough to go bare-handed against a man with two loaded guns. You know, Tim, I thought those guns meant so much to me. I fought to keep them for how long? I fought with you and our parents about the guns; I fought with Emily about the guns. I thought I couldn't live without my father's guns. It all hit me when I saw our father lying in that pool of blood. The only thing important to me is Dad not those stupid guns. Guns can be replaced. I don't care if I ever see them again. They have some kind of hex on them."

Tim looked at him and he could tell he was being truthful. After they ate, they went back to the room taking back a sandwich and coffee for Marguerite. She drank the coffee but she didn't eat the sandwich.

Tim asked Brett if he would take their mother back home so she could get some rest there. To Tim's astonishment, Brett said "No". He said, "I'm sorry, Tim but I'm staying right here next to our father. It's my fault he got hurt and I'm staying right here until he wakes up no matter how long it takes."

Tim overlooked the Brett's-fault comment because he was too tired to argue with him. He worried about their mother though and he said he would take her home so she could get some rest. On his way home, however, he started thinking about what Brett had said. He had had it with his brother and he was going to have it out with him. Suddenly he wasn't tired any more. He helped his mother into the house but he left the horse hitched to the buggy. When he felt his mother was in bed and resting, he went back out and went back to the hospital. Brett had continued his vigil at his father's bedside and was surprised to see Tim walk in. Tim closed the door after him.

"Brett, we need to talk," Tim started. "You know Mom, Dad and I have done about everything we can to convince you that we accept you for who you are. We expected changes and we got them but I just keep getting the feeling that we have accepted you, but you won't accept us."

Brett opened his mouth to say something but Tim held up his hand cutting him off. "No, just listen, don't talk. You are not your father. You have broken that chain of violence in your family from your grandfather, Elijah, and your father, Mike, both sides of your family. You haven't killed anyone even when others have been unjustifiably cruel to you. You are a doctor, a healer not a killer.

"I didn't care when you wanted to keep your last name after you were adopted. What's in a name? I don't care if you want to call yourself 'Ann Marie' you are an Osterhaus, a part of our family. It's time that you accepted that. It means that you are no longer alone and don't have to tackle the world alone. You are not responsible for every bad act that has taken place back to and including the crucifixion of Christ. You are not responsible for our father being injured. If he dies . . ."

Brett jumped in, "Tim, don't say that."

Tim continued but in a lower gentler voice because it hurt him to say it also, "If he dies, it will be Johnny Jackson who killed him not you. One more time I'm going to say this: I love you; Mom and Dad love you. You are a part of our family and we are one unit. It's not each of us against the world. It's all of us sharing in the world. Now you chew on that Little Brother, while you sit here with OUR father. And in the morning when I bring Mother to see Dad, you are going home and taking a proper bath and shave and go to bed for a few hours and let us take over this one-man vigil," and Tim walked out the door.

"TIM," Brett called after him, "TIM DON'T . . . ."

Brett was stunned. Tim had never been this angry at him in the whole time he knew him. He started thinking about what Tim had said. He started seeing what he meant. He didn't realize it. He had been alone for so long, really all his life. Lila and Mike had cared for him and in their own way they had loved him but there was no demonstration of the love like the Osterhauses had given him. He never got the feeling that there was someone there that wanted to know about him personally, about his likes and dislikes. They were too busy with their own lives. He had always been "the take-charge kid" even in his work. He had never let anyone else take charge of him. He thought about it so hard and was so tired that he laid his head down on the bed next to his father and fell asleep.

He was awakened by a hand stroking his hair. There was a soft hoarse voice which said "Brett?" He sat up. Peter's eyes were open and he had stroked his son's head while he slept beside him.

"Dad, you're awake! What can I get you? Do you want some water?" He noticed how hoarse he was. Brett had tried to hold ice for his father but he was too unconscious to do anything with it so Brett would wet his lips and the inside of his mouth but couldn't really get him anything to drink. Peter nodded and Brett got a mug of water, helped him sit up and held it for him so he could drink.

"Easy Dad, not too fast, you'll choke." After his father had some water, Brett went and got the nurse and told him Peter was awake. She said she would see what doctors were there.

Soon one of the doctors came in that Brett recognized from when they had first arrived. He checked Peter all over and said he felt he was going to be fine. He was happy to say that he needed rest and some tender loving care which he was sure Marguerite could provide, but he should fully recover. He told Peter that he should take things easy for a while and not be real anxious to go back to the office but that he could do whatever he felt like doing. He should probably stay in the hospital one more day but if things stayed the same or got better, he could go home day after tomorrow. He told him what medication he could take for the headaches that would probably plague him for a while. He shook both men's hands and left.

Brett asked if he were hungry and when he nodded, he went and got him some soup. He was still weak and shaky so Brett fed him the soup and was cleaning up with the towel and wiping his face when Tim and Marguerite came in. "Look at who rejoined us," Brett said proudly.

Marguerite started crying and Tim was overjoyed. He kissed his father and let his mother fawn all over her first and only love.

Brett turned to Tim, who looked a little uncomfortable and sheepish after laying into his brother the way he had the night before.

Brett said, "Come on, let's give them some privacy," and walked out the door. Tim followed.

In the hallway, Tim said, "Brett, I'm sorry. I was too hard on you last night. I was tired and all this with Dad and . . ."

"No Tim," Brett cut him off, "you were right. I do have to accept the fact that I am a part of this family and we need to be there for each other. It's not all about me. I need a reminder sometimes that I am no longer alone. Give me another chance?"

Tim smiled a little choked up, wrapped an arm around Brett's shoulders and pulled him close and said, "We are not going to give up on you, Little Brother."

"One thing though, I'm not real fond of the name 'Anne Marie', could I keep 'Brett'?" They both laughed. Brett continued, "Come on, coffee and breakfast are on me." Then Brett did a sideways glance at Tim, "Oh, can I borrow some money?"

XXV

Suzi

Peter was in the hospital a couple more days, than the family brought him home for Marguerite to nurse back to health. The brothers went back to work.

—m—

One evening a couple weeks later, there was a knock on the door. Tim went to the door and it was Sheriff Tompkins. "Hi Tim, is Brett, here?" he asked.

The hair on the back of Tim's neck stood up; how could he get in trouble now he's been too busy and they knew where he had been all the time. But he said, "Yes Sheriff, in the sitting room." He took the Sheriff to the sitting room where Peter and Brett were playing chess and Marguerite was knitting.

"Doctor, Mrs. Osterhaus, Brett," the Sheriff nodded to each. "Brett, Johnny Jackson is dead."

"Oh Lord," said Marguerite.

"I didn't . . ." said Brett.

"No, No, my deputy shot him. He was holding up the general store. He shot my deputy in the arm, just a flesh wound, he'll be fine but he fired back and shot Johnny in the chest. He died at Boston General."

Brett shook his head sadly.

"Here," said the Sheriff, and he handed him a paper bag.

Brett opened it and there were his guns and the holster. Brett just stared at them.

"Well, I need to be going. I'm glad you got your guns back, Brett. It's kind of sad that the Jacksons just don't seem to be able to get their lives together."

Tim showed him out. Brett sunk into a chair and took the guns out of the bag. He checked to see if they were loaded but they weren't and there weren't any bullets in the belt of the holster. They certainly didn't look like they did when Brett had them. They weren't shiny anymore; they were dirty. Brett had always cleaned them and kept them clean even though they weren't hardly used. He just stared at them in his lap.

"You don't look like you are very happy about getting them back," said Peter.

"I never expected to see them again. I don't know if I want them."

"They meant so much to you, Brett. What's wrong?" asked Marguerite.

"They are hexed. All the people they killed with Mike; then they got Dad injured, now poor Johnny, that didn't need to happen. He and Emily just never stood a chance coming out of that family. Their parents, always drunk, never showing any sign of affection toward their children. No wonder they were so messed up."

"You are feeling sorry for Emily?" said Tim astonished, "after all she did to you?"

"She didn't know any better. And what will happen to her now? No one will ever love her the way I did. I kept hoping I could make the difference. I wonder if I shouldn't give the guns back to the sheriff or have Joshua melt them down in the plant."

"Whoa there, Brett," said Peter, "I think you better think about that. You know those guns don't have a life of their own. They can't do anything without someone using them. They are tools just like a hammer or a saw. All tools can be dangerous in the wrong hands. Why don't you clean them up, lock them back up in the drawer and if you ever want them, they'll be there."

Brett was still staring down at the guns but he nodded.

—ɯ—

The weeks went by and one Sunday after church, Marguerite and Brett were in the kitchen fixing dinner. Brett was peeling potatoes. Peter still was not completely healed but was getting around fairly well. He hadn't returned to the office yet but was thinking about it.

Tim had taken the team to the barn, was stripping them of the harnesses and was going to turn them out into the corral. Suddenly, he came running into the house, "Brett, something is wrong with Suzi."

Brett dropped the potato he was peeling and ran to the barn. Suzi was down in the tie stall thrashing around trying to roll kicking the side of the stall. At first Brett thought she was cast in the stall; something horses do if they lie down and get too close to the wall. Their feet get up on the side of the wall and they can't figure out how to get up. If not helped they will give up and die because a horse cannot stay down for long periods of time. Suzi was doing too much thrashing though to be cast. Brett picked up a buggy whip and slapped her a couple times across the rump.

Tim was horrified that Brett would do that, "Brett, don't do that," and he started to run into the stall to help Suzi. Brett grabbed his arm and with all the force he could muster because his brother was bigger and heavier than he was, he hurled him back almost knocking him off his feet.

"Are you crazy? You can't go in there, she'll crush you."

"Brett, it's Suzi."

"She's panicked, Tim, she doesn't know you or me." He cracked her a couple more times with the buggy whip and she got to her feet. Brett dropped the whip, went in Virgil's stall and climbed over the side into the front of Suzi's stall up by her head. He undid her tie rope and backed her out of the stall. He could see she had bloated, her stomach was distended. "Go get me a stethoscope," he said to Tim. Tim started running for the house and Brett led her out into the yard.

He started walking with her until Tim came back. He stopped her and placed the stethoscope on her belly and brought it back by her loin. He was listening for bowel sounds with the stethoscope. "Tim, you better take one of the geldings and go get Dr. Masters." Jack Masters was the veterinarian.

Tim left and Brett started walking the mare. He kept her moving even if he had to give her hind legs a couple cracks with the buggy whip. He would walk her for short periods – ten to fifteen minutes and then let her rest for five minutes never allowing her to lie down even though that is what she wanted to do.

Tim returned with Dr. Masters and he went up to Brett and the mare. "What do you think, Brett?" He knew Brett from the barns he had trained horses at.

"Not good," said Brett.

After Dr. Masters listened to her stomach with his stethoscope, he shook his head. "Well, let's drench her and see if that does any good."

Brett nodded.

Brett held her while Dr. Masters ran a tube through her nose and into her stomach pouring mineral oil down a funnel he had placed in the tube.

"About all we can do," said Dr. Masters. Brett nodded and started walking her again.

Peter and Tim were standing by the corral. Dr. Masters walked up to them.

"Peter, Tim," he said acknowledging them.

"Jack," said Peter, "what's going on?"

"Well the mare has bloated and I think she is in torsion. When they bloat or take in so much gas and if they can't get rid of it, they are so uncomfortable that they lie down and roll. You have to get them up fast or the thrashing they do causes an intestine to twist which cuts off the digestive system. I drenched her with mineral oil and we walk them to try and get a bowel movement and get them to settle down. He's walking her for ten to fifteen minutes and then letting her rest. If we can get a bowel movement then we know all the plumbing is working and there is no torsion but if not, then we are in trouble."

"So then what?" asked Peter.

"There is nothing more we can do. When the bowel twists, it cuts off everything, part of the bowel dies and peritonitis sets in. It is a horrible way to die, very painful and takes hours. We can't operate on a horse in this condition. It's too complicated of a surgery and not successful so the best thing is to euthanize them."

Brett had stopped and placed his stethoscope along her belly again.

"He's listening for bowel sounds. If we have good bowel sounds, we know things are working. When he checked her earlier, she didn't have. What do you think, Brett?" called Dr. Masters.

"Not much bowel sound."

"Want to call it quits?"

"I can't yet, Doc, I have to give her a chance."

"All right, if you need me, send Tim."

Brett went back to walking the mare.

"He has a hard time giving up especially I get the idea he really likes this horse. He's done some marvelous things at the barns but if you want the truth I don't think he's going to succeed here."

Brett had stopped Suzi to let her rest. He was rubbing her neck and Peter walked up to him. "Brett, if you and Jack think we should put her down, let's just do it while he is here."

"I can't yet Dad, it's too premature. I have to give her more time. I couldn't live with myself if I thought she might recover and I didn't give her a chance."

Peter said to Dr. Masters, "I think he should have been a veterinarian and not a doctor."

"Well, he'd be a good one but he probably likes horses too much to keep putting them down."

Peter paid Dr. Masters and he left.

Marguerite called them into dinner. No one ate much and the table was quiet. Tim made Brett a ham sandwich and poured him a cup of coffee. He took it out to him and walked the mare while he ate it. Brett kept yelling at him, "Don't let her slow down. Keep her moving."

As soon as he finished eating, he went back to walking the mare and giving her periodic rests. Each time he stopped to rest her, he checked her stomach area with his stethoscope for bowel sounds but sadly he noticed that the little sounds he originally had were now decreasing. Tim got a chair off the porch and sat out by where Brett was walking Suzi. He kept asking if Brett wanted to take a break but he would have none of it.

An hour went by from the time Dr. Masters had left. Brett stopped her again and listened with his stethoscope, hardly any bowel sounds and when he moved his stethoscope to her heart he found that her heart was racing and she was making a chuffing sound. He walked up to her head put his face next to her mouth and despite all her pain, she nuzzled his cheek. A horse in pain can be a dangerous animal but Brett just had a way with horses that they always understood he was their friend and would do his best to help them.

Peter and Marguerite were standing in the doorway of the house. "Did you see that?" said Marguerite.

Peter shook his head, "With my own eyes."

Tim couldn't believe it – just a horse huh? Not to his brother.

Then the inevitable happened as Brett knew it would, she started to go down. Brett put his hand on her withers and when Tim saw what he wanted to do, he jumped up to help him and the two men eased her to the ground so she didn't fall hard. She was still making the chuffing noise somewhere between snorting and panting.

Brett knelt down beside her and started stroking her neck. He looked up at Tim who was now standing and looking at Brett, he said, "The key to Dad's desk is in my nightstand. Get it and bring me my gun with some shells."

"Oh, Brett, let me get Dr. Masters," Tim said in a shaky voice. He knew how hard this would be for Brett.

"She's not going to suffer anymore. It will take an hour to get Dr. Masters and come back. PLEASE TIM, DO WHAT I ASK," he said emphatically.

Tim ran into the house passed his parents and into Brett's room and got the key. Peter followed him and said, "What's going on?" Tim was unlocking his desk.

"He wants his gun." Tim was shaky. He wasn't into horses the way Brett was but he did like their horses.

"What about Dr. Masters?"

"He said it would take too long. He doesn't want her to suffer any longer."

"It's my horse, I should do it," Peter said.

Marguerite was standing behind them listening to the conversation and feeling so bad for her menfolk. She saw how upset they all were and she knew Brett would really be upset about having to shoot the mare, his Suzi.

Peter and Tim went out to where Brett was kneeling on the ground, stroking the mare's neck and face and talking to her in soft tones, "It's all right, Girl. Your suffering will be over soon. I'm sorry I couldn't help you."

Peter took the gun and bullets from Tim. He realized he didn't even know how to load a gun. He walked over to Brett and put his hand on his shoulder. "If you load this, I'll do it. You love her so much, you shouldn't have to do this."

"NO, it's because I love her so much that it needs to be me," he said, no nonsense in his tone. "She trusts me. She should die in the hands of a friend. It will be less stressful for her. Besides you have never even shot a gun. If you don't know what you are doing, you might not do it the first time. Her suffering needs to end."

"Then we'll stay here with you," said Peter. He didn't want to argue with Brett and prolong what needed to be done.

Brett loaded the gun and held it up in the air working the barrel to check where the bullets were in the chamber. He placed his left hand on her neck and stroked her and talked to her; he put the gun into her ear and pulled the trigger twice.

Peter, Tim and Marguerite, who was standing at the back door, all flinched with each shot, but Brett merely stroked the mare's neck, waited a few minutes and then placed his stethoscope down by her heart. He unloaded the gun and motioned for Tim to take the gun and remaining bullets.

Tim took it and walked back by Peter's side. Peter said, "You know, Son, I neglected some of your training. I always thought I was good to my horses. I gave them the best food, good veterinary care, a corral for their days off, never over worked them, taught you to take care of them after you rode. But I never got to know them, never thought much about a horse having a personality. I guess we had to learn that from your brother. Come on let him say good-bye." They went into the house and left Brett stroking the mare.

Brett stayed with Suzi for a short time and then got up and went into the house. He poured himself a cup of coffee and went into the sitting room. He stopped in the doorway and leaned against the door jamb sipping his coffee. "I'll stop tomorrow on the way to the Center and tell the knacker to pick up the carcass."

"What do they do with dead horses?" asked Tim.

"Grind them up and use them for fertilizer," he said sipping his coffee.

"Oh my," said Marguerite, "you would let them do that to Suzi?"

"That's not Suzi," said Brett, "Suzi is gone. That's only the envelope she came to earth in and now that she is done with it, it doesn't matter what happens to it."

"Interesting way to look at it," said Peter, "what are you thinking we are?"

"Same thing. Our bodies are not important if we can't use them. It's our soul that's important."

"But animals don't have souls," said Tim.

"That's your opinion. The animals I love live on in my soul and when I die, they will all go where I go."

"So you wouldn't care if you were ground up?" asked Tim.

"TIM," shouted Marguerite.

But Brett only smiled. "No, why would I care? I'm not there, I'm gone. I hope to be in a better place if I stop threatening old men and young girls."

Everyone couldn't help but laugh at that.

"It's going to be hard on Tim," said Marguerite.

"Harder than us," replied Peter.

—⁕—

It was only a couple months later that Brett made his announcement. Winter was nearly over, spring approaching. His first mother had always said Mike had the wanderlust and she could tell when it was coming on and he wondered if he might have inherited that from Mike. Brett waited until everyone had eaten and even retired to the sitting room. He started the conversation, "I have something I want to say."

Everyone was quiet as if they knew what was coming and they did know. "I want to move back out West. Boston is crowded; my job is the same thing day in and day out. I'm so tired of being cooped up eight to ten hours a day in a smelly confined place looking at filthy people, terrible diseases that could have been prevented with some sanitary conditions or at least not be as bad as they are and the children break my heart. The only good thing that has ever happened in Boston is you and your family." He suddenly realized how quiet it had gotten and he looked around. "Mom, please don't cry."

"I'm trying not to Brett. I don't want to hold you back. We want you to be happy, Son."

"I wish you would all move with me."

"Brett, we knew a long time ago, that this day would probably come," said Peter.

Tim just sat in the old rocker and violently rocked back and forth choking with emotion.

"I gave my notice to Scott Hopkins today. I have given them a month. I want to leave the end of March right in the spring of the year."

"What will you do with Partner?" asked Peter.

"He can stay. Tim can ride him. He needs a lot of work, Tim, but I think he is safe for you. I can show you some things to work on with him then he will just need miles and miles, a lot of wet saddle blankets," he said smiling. He turned toward his brother who was still rocking and not saying a word.

He too knew it was coming but he had prayed so hard that Brett would change his mind. Suddenly, Tim got up with a look of horror on his face, hitting the rocker so hard it tipped over backward and he left the room. He charged upstairs to his room. Brett looked at his parents and threw up his hands.

"What do I do?" his voice was cracking.

"Let him get used to the idea for a little while," said Peter.

Tim didn't come back downstairs and wouldn't answer his door when Brett went and knocked on it and tried to talk to him. Brett finally came back downstairs and went into his room. He wished they would go with him but he realized that just as he was having a hard time living in Boston, they would all have a hard time living out West. None of them even knew how to handle a gun and it was dangerous out West without a gun. The culture was so different between the East and West, it would be near impossible for them to adjust. Then there was their occupations, their home, Peter's work with the charities and City Council. As hard as he tried, he realized that there was just no way for it to work.

He finally fell to sleep but he woke up several times with all kinds of dreams running through his head. He dreamt of his first parents and traveling with his father – Arthur and Little Red. Then he would switch gears and dream about Emily still wondering if he should have given her more of a chance. Finally, he went back to sleep and he dreamt that Tim was yelling at him not to go. He woke suddenly and jumped up. He slipped into his pants and went out on the back porch and sat in the cool night air and looked at the stars until it was time for him to get dressed and go to the Center.

XXVI

The Partner

The months at Scott Hopkins passed quickly since Brett was so busy. In the mail he received an order from the Court stating that his six months service to Scott Hopkins had been fulfilled. The judge had a personal note congratulating him on the fine evaluation he had gotten from his supervisor, Dr. Donald Dunbar.

When he reported for work the next day, the Administrator called him into his office. He stated that since he had just received the termination of his sentence from the court he noticed that he had actually worked an extra month. He asked if it was all right with Brett if he gave him a check for one hundred dollars for the extra month. Brett was totally willing for that it had been so long since he had money. Then the Administrator begged him to come on as a doctor at the same rate per month. Brett decided that he would stay. He felt that he was making a difference if not with the people at least with the Center and he finally was drawing a salary. At about the same time, he got a check from Caldwell Munitions as a dividend for his stock. He felt rich.

It was after dinner and when they were all gathered around the table that he announced he wanted permission to buy another horse. Everyone wondered why he had been coming home later than usual even later than when he worked extra hours at Scott Hopkins. This horse, he said would be his horse but the family was welcome to use it once he had it trained. He had found a horse he wanted. The horse was a three-year-old tri-color paint. He was currently a stallion but that would be fixed before Brett brought him home. He had some training problems but Brett felt that it wasn't anything he couldn't train. He liked the fact that the horse was young and Brett really liked his conformation.

Peter said he would pay for the horse since it would be for the family but Brett said no. He had wanted a horse for a long time but realized they didn't have room for four horses so this gave him the chance. Everyone agreed that he could buy him.

As soon as day broke on Saturday, he and Tim started out with the two geldings to pick up the pinto. Brett wanted to go early before the roads became busy with the freight wagons and folks traveling to work and errands. This was a young horse and had not had too many hours in training. Brett planned on leading him from their horses but still wanted to avoid as much noise and flow of wagons, buggies and the like as possible. He instructed Tim that when they were ready to return, they would put the paint between the two geldings so he would pick up on how Virgil and Morgan handled all the congestion they might confront on the road. It would also trap him so he couldn't bolt or do something that would get him or someone else injured.

Peter and Marguerite were sitting on the back porch when the two brothers rode in, Brett leading the painted colt. "Wow," said Peter, "I see why he likes him. He's beautiful." He and Marguerite started walking toward them.

Brett dismounted and handed his horse's reins to Tim and took a shorter hold on the lead rope of the colt. He started stroking his neck and talking to him. Peter walked up to Brett and looked the colt over. He reached up and scratched behind his ears.

"What do you think, Dad?"

"He's a beauty."

He was a big colt. Most paints were small since they came from Indian ponies but although this colt's mother was an Indian pony, his father was a thoroughbred race horse. He stood about fifteen hands (a hand is four inches). He had his father's large intelligent eye, broad skull, short well-shaped ears, long neck that went into sloping laid-back shoulders, a strong back and proper turn of stifle, a good slope to his pasterns and straight hocks from behind. He had his mother's strong hard hooves, beautiful color and one blue eye called "a watch eye". He was black and white with bright gold spots interspersed with the black spots. He was a very intelligent animal and had figured out a few things he should never have figured out. Brett bought him fairly cheap because the owner could no longer keep him tied up. He broke everything he tried to tie him with.

After everyone looked the colt over, Brett turned him loose in the corral. He strutted around, snorted and blew and bucked a little. Everyone was leaning on the fence. "He looks like he might be a handful," said Tim. "What are you going to call him?"

"Yes, what gunfighter are you going to name him after?" Peter asked laughing.

"Come on, I was just a kid. I'm going to call him 'Partner' because I hope that is what he will be."

Everyone agreed that was a good name for the colt.

Brett started working less hours at Scott Hopkins and spending more time training Partner. He worked him in the morning for about a half hour and then for as long as he dared in the evening.

A couple weeks later on a Saturday morning, Peter was sitting at the kitchen table eating breakfast. Out in the barnyard he heard a horse nickering in panic and he could even hear the horse's hooves pounding on the ground. He was getting ready to look out and see what was going on when Tim came into the kitchen. He had just gotten out of bed and dressed and was wiping the sleep from his eyes, running his hands through his hair. "What's wrong with that horse? Why is he carrying on like that?" he said. He went to the door. "That's Brett's horse."

Peter got up and they both looked out the back door. Partner was tied to a heavy post. There was a rope around his neck in a noose and it went down through his halter and was tied to the post. All of a sudden the colt backed up and almost sat down pulling back against the rope. When it closed around his neck, he started fighting and screaming, shaking his head back and forth and pulling with all his strength against the rope. He would then lunge forward and bang his chest against the post and then lean backward again and sit down on the rope, screaming all the time. The rope was choking him when he backed and lay back against it and that made him angrier and he fought harder shaking his head and squealing in rage, pawing with a front hoof and throwing himself as much as the rope would allow back and forth.

"He's choking," said Tim, "where is Brett?" Tim ran out the back door and then he saw Brett standing in the doorway to the barn casually drinking a cup of coffee. Tim looked at him and couldn't believe it. "Your horse . . ."

"Stay away from him, Tim," said Brett, "You're going to get hurt."

Tim stopped and looked at Brett. He pointed at the horse, "Brett," Tim said in a panicky voice, "he's choking." Peter was watching from the back door, curious also at how Brett didn't seem to care and was just standing there watching the colt.

"He's got a choice," said Brett, "all he has to do is stop fighting and stand up."

Tim walked up to Brett and now Peter was coming out of the house. "Brett," Peter said, "don't you think that is kind of cruel?"

"Look, you two," said Brett, "do you see how he is fighting that rope. Do you want to ride that horse to town and tie him up with a thin leather rein? How long do you think he'd stay tied? He has to learn. The idiot that owned him let him learn that he can break lead ropes and snaps by pulling back and sitting down. He thinks now he can break anything. He is worthless if we can't tie him."

Just then the horse stopped fighting and walked forward toward the post. He was sweaty from fighting and breathing hard. Brett handed his mug of coffee to Tim and walked up to him. He talked softly and stroked his neck, loosened the rope around his neck and gave him a piece of apple. Just as suddenly, Partner lunged back against the rope, Brett jumped back and let him fight some more. Brett walked back over to Tim and Peter and took another drink of coffee. "We are not dealing with a forty pound dog here, that horse weighs about nine hundred pounds, he could kill you," Brett continued.

"It looks so cruel," said Tim. "Can't you think of something else to do?"

"I'm open to suggestions."

"Can't you figure out something, you're the horse trainer?"

"That's right," said Brett smiling at them. He finished his coffee and set down the cup. This time the horse didn't fight as long. As soon as he quit, Brett would approach him, loosen the rope and give him a piece of apple as he stroked his neck and talked to him. "Good boy. You don't need to fight."

It seemed as though he was giving in but Brett knew it would take many sessions for the horse to learn that no matter what he did, he would not be able to break loose. He had succeeded in breaking the ropes he had been tied with too many times for him to give in easily. Brett went in the barn and got some brushes and a towel. He rubbed the horse down with the towel since he was sweaty then started brushing him. The horse lunged back one more time; Brett stepped back out of his way. The horse jumped forward and quit fighting instantly. Again, Brett rewarded the horse, stroked and talked to him. When he finally stood quietly for several minutes and it was obvious that he was giving in, Brett untied him and took him into the corral and turned him loose with the other horses. Morgan thought him a pesky kid and when Partner ran up to get a mouthful of hay, Morgan put his ears back and bit him. It was just a bite warning and made no mark. Brett laughed, "Respect you elders," he shouted.

—⟋⟋—

The following Saturday evening, Tim and Ricky talked Brett into going out to a new bar and grill which attracted a lot of younger people mostly single people meeting, eating, drinking and dancing. There were also slot machines and poker. Brett absolutely refused to date any of the girls Tim tried to fix him up with. He wanted no part of any women since Emily. Tim promised him if he would go with them, they wouldn't push him but would let him do as he pleased. Brett had been working so hard at the Center that Tim wanted to get him out of the house and have a little fun.

The three boys ate dinner and played around with the slots for some time and were having a good time. They were sitting at their table and having some beers. Tim and Ricky asked girls to dance. A couple asked about Brett but Tim just told them his brother was shy. Tim and Ricky went out on the floor with a couple girls and were doing a line dance with a whole group. Brett had just gone back to the table after playing some of the slots. He had thought about playing poker and seeing if he remembered what his father had taught him but he didn't want to lose any money. He really didn't have that much to spare.

He was smiling and watching his two companions, when a woman's voice said, "Brett? It is you, Hi."

His skin crawled and he suddenly felt shaky. He took a deep breath and thought he could cover it up. "Hi Emily," he said.

"Brett, you're looking good. Where are you working now?" Her voice was soft and kind and not the whiny "Bretty-Baby" voice she used to use. She seemed very different, very subdued. She didn't wear any of the wild make-up and was tastefully dressed. Her blonde hair was styled beautifully conforming to the styles of the day.

"Still at Scott Hopkins. I like it. I was really sorry to hear about Johnny, Emily, really I am. I know you two were close."

"I know you are Brett. That's the kind of person you are. I have remarried to a very nice man. He's coming over now. I'll introduce you."

A tall handsome dark-haired man walked up. He smiled at Emily. Brett stood up and Emily said, "This is my husband, Craig Owens. Craig, this is Brett Ballin, an old friend."

Craig smiled and Brett offered his hand, "Nice to meet you, Craig." He didn't seem in the least bit threatening so perhaps he wasn't worried about "old friends" of Emily's.

"Nice meeting you, Brett." He turned to his wife, "Hon, the guys got a poker game going, all right if I play for a while?"

"Sure," she said.

"Maybe Brett will dance with you," he said.

Well, thought Brett, that was about as non-threatening as you could get. Guess he wasn't worried about her.

"Could I sit down for a minute, Brett?"

"Sure," he said, sitting back down.

"I just wanted to tell you that . . ." she stammered, "I'm so sorry for all that happened between us. You were so kind to me and I was a bitch. After our divorce and then when Johnny was killed, I moved out of my house. I never see my parents anymore. I moved in with a girlfriend. I think I came to realize that so much that had happened to me was my fault or maybe the way I was brought up. Don't know but then I met Craig and we got married. You're a good person Brett. I hope you find happiness with another lady as I have with Craig." She reached over and took his hand. "Even though you may hate me, I'll never forget that you were the first man who treated me like a lady." She stood up still holding onto his hand.

"I don't hate you, Emily. I resolved that feeling a long time ago. I'm happy for you. Craig seems like a nice guy."

Tim and Ricky were out on the dance floor when Ricky stopped and excused himself. He elbowed Tim and Tim excused himself also. "The blonde," said Ricky nodding toward their table.

"Emily?!"

Ricky nodded.

"Ricky! What do we do?"

"He's a big boy. I guess he'll have to handle it."

Right then Emily walked around the table and kissed Brett on the cheek and walked away.

Brett sunk back down into the chair.

When the boys saw Emily walk away, they started toward the table and Brett. Ricky hung back a little knowing that Tim and Brett were so close that he would let Tim talk to him first, but he did see the look on Brett's face as his eyes followed Emily across the room.

Tim sat down in a chair right next to Brett. "Are you all right?"

"I think so."

Tim looked at him. Brett's eyes followed Emily across the room as she went up and stood behind her husband. It could have been him. Maybe he should have hung in there a little longer; maybe their relationship was his fault as much as hers; maybe, maybe, maybe.

Tim said in a whisper, "Brett, you're still in love with her!"

Brett took a long swallow of his beer as he stood up, "Probably always will be."

He put some money on the table and said, "I have to go," and walked out. Tim and Ricky followed. Tim thought why in the name of God had he brought him here? They hadn't been out in so long and brilliant Tim had to come to this place.

—m—

The training of Partner became the highlight of Brett's day. He threw himself into his work at Scott Hopkins and training Partner. Again he had to forget Emily. He was restless and thinking more and more about going back out West.

Through the years with his family and the Carter family, everyone knowing how much he loved the West, they had given him many books about Western life including picture books, Indian culture and anything pertaining to Western culture and life. He had a bookcase in his room and it was full of material on the West. He went to the library and got books that weren't in his collection.

He subscribed to the <u>Kansas City Herald</u>. It took forever to get to him and by the time it did, the news was very old but he still read it cover to cover. He even checked out dime novels that were in the library or picked them up occasionally at the store. These were fiction novels written usually by newspaper reporters and authors about gun fighters and others in the West. They were filled with untruths and tall tales sold for a dime, thus their name "dime novels".

One Sunday when everyone was relaxing in the sitting room, Peter and Tim playing chess and Marguerite knitting, Brett was reading one of the dime novels. He started laughing.

"What's funny?" asked Tim.

"These novels," said Brett. "This is nothing how the West really is. These authors make these gun fighters out to be heroes. They are far from it. They are nothing but hired killers. They goad a man into a fight, get him to draw his gun first and then they kill him. Half the time the men they push into fighting aren't even professional gun fighters and are easy to beat on the draw."

Tim was interested, "Did you ever see your father shoot someone?"

"Tim," said Marguerite, "you shouldn't be asking Brett that." She was afraid it would open up old wounds, knowing how Brett's father had died and Brett had witnessed it.

"It's all right, Mom. Time heals all wounds." And having a wonderful family also helps, he thought. "To answer you Tim, no I never saw my father kill anyone. I did see him shoot a young man once. Want to hear about it?"

Tim stopped playing chess and turned his chair toward Brett. Peter was interested also and he looked up from the chess board.

"Well I have to give Mike credit. There are plenty of young men, sixteen, seventeen-year-olds, even a little older that try their hand at a gun fighter. They think that if they can kill a big-name gunfighter they will have this tough reputation and they will be known as big gun fighters and be famous and then everyone would fear them because they won a fight with Joe Gunslinger.

"When one would go after Mike, he would say, 'I'm not playing this game, Kid. No one is paying me to shoot you. Get someone to pay and I'll gladly shoot you.' Sometimes when that didn't work, Mike would draw and put a shot in front of the kid or hit him in the toe of his boot. Mike was lightning fast and most of the time these kids were not that fast – they just thought they were. If he could draw his gun before they could even pull leather, he wouldn't shoot them, he would just do something to scare them and make them realize they weren't as good as they thought.

"Anyway, this one day we were in a saloon and some young buck came up and decided he was going to fight Mike and he was determined. Mike tried everything but the kid kept goading him. Some of these kids were quite fast and if a gun fighter wasn't careful or didn't take them too seriously, the kid could draw and shoot before the gunman was ready and could easily kill the gunman. There was a danger to trying not to enter into a gunfight. Anyone with a gun can kill you. Anyway, Mike was watching him and the kid was getting more and more insistent. I didn't know what to do. I knew we were getting ready to leave town so I told Mike to come on and let's get the horses. He seemed like he was going to do that too but just as he tried to step to the side and avoid the boy, the boy started drawing his gun. Well, Mike sidestepped, drew his gun lightning fast as usual and shot the boy right in his gun hand.

"The kid started screaming in pain, blood dripping all over the floor. Mike pushed me out the door and said, 'He'll never be able to shoot fast with that hand again.' I think it was his way of getting the kid out of the gunslinger business. It wasn't long after that that we went to Mineral Springs and he turned me loose to go to Boston," his last remarks made his voice fade away thinking about what had happened to Mike right before he left for Boston.

"Ironic," said Brett. "He was never beaten in a gun battle. No one ever outdrew him but a spineless coward shot him in the back. Hmmm." Brett's black eyes turned sad.

The room went silent.

—m—

One night in bed, Peter pulled Marguerite close to him and held her tight in his arms. "You know your wild cat is about to bolt, don't you?"

"I know. What should we do?"

"Give him our blessing. We can't hold him, Dear. We knew it was coming. That horse probably gave us an additional year."

Marguerite snickered, "He wants to be sure it is safe for us all."

"We have to let him go Marg. We probably have had him longer than I thought we would anyway."

XXVII

"Go West Young Man"

The month went by fast. Brett and Tim spent a lot of time together with Partner. Brett wanted to feel comfortable that at least Tim could handle him and not get hurt. He told everyone that he needed a lot of work on the buggy. Never should they let Marguerite drive him. If he started pulling some of his shenanigans, she wouldn't be strong enough to hold him.

On a Saturday, Brett got the brilliant idea of hooking Partner up with Morgan as a team. Morgan was big and strong and he dominated the younger colt. Tim went with Brett and they took them out on the two-seater carriage. Every time Partner had one of his little boy temper tantrums, pulling at the bit, stamping and pulling away from the singletree, Brett would stop the team and Morgan would pretty much hold him there until Partner settled down.

Brett had to laugh because Morgan would reach over and bite Partner on the neck as if to say, "Smarten up, Boy" when Brett clicked to him to start up again. The winter thaw was starting and the sun was warm on a day that Brett and Tim took the team out for a work-out. The boys had packed a picnic lunch and Tim forgot that Brett was going away. They laughed and joked and had the best time.

Every time Partner would try and lunge in the harness or dance around, the stoic Morgan would just hold his own at the youngster's antics. Then he would turn and bite Partner as they moved on. Brett even got to the point where he was able to trot the team back home.

After that, Brett and Tim would take them out a couple times a week. Partner was learning some patience and settling in the harness. Partner wasn't pulling anymore when tied either. He had come a long way under the patient but firm hands of Brett.

One Sunday, Brett decided to drive the family to church using Morgan and Partner. It would be a good test for the colt because church only lasted an hour, a little more with greetings and farewells and it would be good for the colt to stand that long tied. With Morgan at his side, Brett felt sure there would not be a problem but he and Tim did sit in the back of the church and watch them out the window.

Partner was a perfect gentleman. Morgan was not only his disciplinarian but also his security blanket to fall back on. Morgan showed Partner that standing tied was how a horse had to behave. Brett couldn't help but brag about him all the way home. Everyone was complimentary about what a good horse he had become.

Every time something came up, however, about Brett leaving, Tim would leave the room. When Brett tried to talk to him about it, Tim would hold up his hand and then shoo him away with a wave of his hand and walk away. "Brett," he would say sharply, "I don't want to talk about it." This bothered Brett very much. Finally Peter stepped in.

One night, Brett was working late at Scott Hopkins. He was trying to be sure they understood everything he had taught them before he left. Dr. Dunbar, who was not happy at all that Brett was leaving, asked him to give lectures on some of the procedures they weren't yet familiar with and to review some of the procedures that Brett had taught them earlier.

Tim had gone to bed and Peter went upstairs and knocked on his door. "Come in", said Tim.

"What's wrong, Son? You're not yourself lately, Brett leaving?"

Tim turned his back to his father. Peter put his hand on his back and rubbed it. "Tim, we are all going to miss Brett, and I know it will probably be the hardest on you since you two are buddies but we knew this day would one day come. We can't hold him here. He loves the West. Boston has been pretty hard on him. There are a lot of bad memories here for him. You have to let him know that you are all right with this. You don't want him to be miserable and feel guilty. You can always go and visit him."

"What am I supposed to do now, Dad? Pretend I am happy for him?"

"Basically, yes, it goes back to what I have told you before. If you love him, you have to let him go and you can't make him feel guilty. That's not fair to him. Think about it."

The next day at breakfast, Tim looked over at Brett. "Will you write?"

"A journal," said Brett and smiled.

"All right, Bro, you win. Just keep in touch or I'll have to come down there."

"Now that's incentive not to keep in touch," said Brett.

The day Brett was to leave came and the family was up and about early. Brett's train left at nine o'clock in the morning. Brett hooked up Morgan and Virgil to the two-seater. He was traveling light. He had his saddlebags which he had filled with medical supplies. He didn't know what he would run into and being a doctor, he wanted to be prepared. Tim had bought him a new duffle bag saying "a man can't go anywhere without a duffle," and everyone laughed. He filled that with his father's guns and a couple changes of clothes along with some of the money he had been saving. He said he would come back and get the rest of his stuff when he was settled somewhere with a home of his own since he didn't know what he was going to face when he got there and where he would end up settling.

He asked if it were all right to leave some of his personal items like the pictures of his original family including the one that set on his dresser of Lila, Mike and himself as a little kid, the Charles Russell painting and the iron horse his father had brought his mother from one of his trips. Peter and Marguerite said that was fine and joked with him saying that it meant that at least he would have to come back one more time. He took with him, however, a picture of Peter, Marguerite, Tim and himself at their Medical School graduation.

He also put Tim on his bank account and left some of the money he had been saving all year in the bank. Then if he needed money, Tim could wire it. He made arrangements for his stock dividends to go into that account also.

They all drove to the train station, Tim driving and Brett in the front with him, Peter and Marguerite in the back seat. Brett got out his belongings and kissed his mother, hugged his father and brother and mounted the steps into the train. He didn't want to stand around on the station platform. He thought he might just forget about leaving. His stomach was in knots. He found a window seat right in line with where they were standing. He sat staring at them out the window and they stared back. The train was crowded and there was constant chatter and noise from all the passengers. A child was crying and his mother was trying to comfort him but Brett didn't hear any of it.

"Young man, HEY YOUNG MAN," Brett felt a poke on his arm and suddenly realized someone was talking to him. He turned his head and a man was standing there. He was taller than Brett and probably about eight years older. He was stocky and very tan even though it was just turning spring, had dark brown hair and blue-green eyes. He probably had an outside job. He was in working condition and had rancher clothes on shirt, pants, leather vest, cowboy boots and a Stetson hat. "Is this seat taken?"

"Oh, no, help yourself."

The man sat down and looked around Brett through the window at the Osterhauses standing on the station platform in a row with sad faces. "Your family?"

"Yes."

"Mother, Father and brother, that's it? No other brothers or sisters?"

"No."

"First time away from home?"

"Yep."

"Your mother is crying."

"I didn't need to hear that," said Brett, tears starting to form in his eyes even though he was fighting hard to hold them back.

"Going out West to make your fame and fortune, huh?"

"Something like that."

"Go West young man," he said laughing.

Brett heard the conductor yell, "Last call. All aboard." Brett thought about bolting off the train but he didn't.

The train started up and the man said, "My name is Ben Camaron." He held out his hand to Brett and he noticed the man's hand was hard and calloused. He didn't look Brett directly in his face so the boy wouldn't be embarrassed about the tears welling up in his eyes.

Brett took his hand and said, "Brett Ballin," and he kept his eyes averted downward because he was embarrassed about his tears, although crying is a good thing, it's a great release but then women know that better than men.

TO THE READER: I hope you enjoyed reading The Coyote Kid *as much as I enjoyed writing it. If you would like more adventures of Brett after he travels out West, you might want to read* The Medicine Man. *THANK YOU!*

D C ANDERSON